"Who wants to hurt you?"

Aiden waited expectantly for the woman to answer, but instead she merely shivered in his arms.

Eventually she sighed and relaxed, her slender body shifting against his and making his chest tighten—but pleasantly. The moment threatened to become intimate as a sexual charge started to build between them. He knew better than to indulge himself like this. He'd sworn off women. Turned over a new leaf…and apparently been lying to himself like a big dog about the fact that he'd actually changed.

"I'm a filmmaker," she announced as if that answered everything. "I was collecting footage for a documentary on the commercial deep-sea-fishing industry."

He frowned. "Are you sure it was fishermen who ran you down?"

"I'm not sure of anything except that my boat is gone, and I'm really glad you came along when you did and saved my life."

So was he.

D0188784

Books by Cindy Dees

CINDY DEES

started flying airplanes while sitting in her dad's lap at the age of three and got a pilot's license before she got a driver's license. At age fifteen, she dropped out of high school and left the horse farm in Michigan, where she grew up, to attend the University of Michigan. After earning a degree in Russian and East European studies, she joined the U.S. Air Force and became the youngest female pilot in its history. She flew supersonic jets, VIP airlift and the C-5 Galaxy, the world's largest airplane. During her military career, she traveled to forty countries on five continents, was detained by the KGB and East German secret police, got shot at, flew in the first Gulf War and amassed a lifetime's worth of war stories.

Her hobbies include medieval reenacting, professional Middle Eastern dancing and Japanese gardening.

This RITA® Award-winning author's first book was published in 2002 and since then she has published more than twenty-five bestselling and award-winning novels. She loves to hear from readers and can be contacted at www.cindydees.com.

CINDY DEES

Breathless Encounter

HARLEQUIN®
entertain, enrich, inspire™

If you purchased this book without a cover you should be aware that this book is stolen property. It was reported as "unsold and destroyed" to the publisher, and neither the author nor the publisher has received any payment for this "stripped book."

Recycling programs
for this product may
not exist in your area.

ISBN-13: 978-0-373-27786-5

BREATHLESS ENCOUNTER
Copyright © 2012 by Cindy Dees

THE DARK SIDE OF NIGHT
Copyright © 2008 by Cindy Dees

All rights reserved. Except for use in any review, the reproduction or utilization of this work in whole or in part in any form by any electronic, mechanical or other means, now known or hereafter invented, including xerography, photocopying and recording, or in any information storage or retrieval system, is forbidden without the written permission of the publisher, Harlequin Enterprises Limited, 225 Duncan Mill Road, Don Mills, Ontario M3B 3K9, Canada.

This is a work of fiction. Names, characters, places and incidents are either the product of the author's imagination or are used fictitiously, and any resemblance to actual persons, living or dead, business establishments, events or locales is entirely coincidental.

This edition published by arrangement with Harlequin Books S.A.

For questions and comments about the quality of this book please contact us at CustomerService@Harlequin.com.

® and TM are trademarks of Harlequin Enterprises Limited or its corporate affiliates. Trademarks indicated with ® are registered in the United States Patent and Trademark Office, the Canadian Trade Marks Office and in other countries.

www.Harlequin.com

Printed in U.S.A.

CONTENTS

Dear Reader,

When my mother and mother-in-law were diagnosed with cancer within a few weeks of each other, it sparked a flurry of research about possible treatments. Along the way, I read a whole bunch about advances in modern medicine. I'm delighted to say that, five years later, both moms are cancer-free.

I continue to be fascinated by the latest ongoing medical research. As a writer, I can't help asking myself what some of these technologies might mean for our future. Many of the ideas currently under development are highly controversial, perhaps partly because the misapplication of them could be truly terrible for mankind.

Of course, that got me thinking. While governments might restrict their own researchers from delving into some extreme experiments, a private company would be under no such restrictions. What do body-altering technologies mean for the individual field operative who volunteers for them? How do they change the person? Can such an altered person live any semblance of a normal life? How does a regular person attempt to love a quasi-superhero? Is it possible? Dangerous?

And voilà, the Code X project was born. Please join me on the breathless roller coaster that is loving a superhero. Who knows? Maybe you've already got one of your own, or maybe yours is waiting for you when and where you least expect it….

Happy reading!

Warmly,

Cindy Dees

Breathless Encounter

I was thrilled to dedicate a book to my mother and mother-in-law during their simultaneous fights against cancer, and it's my great joy to dedicate this one to them in honor of their double win against the beast. For all of you who have fought the good fight yourself, or who have watched a loved one go through it, win or lose, my heart is with you. You know the true meaning of courage.

Chapter 1

Ankle deep in salt water, Sunny Jordan stared in dismay at the silent diesel engine in her boat. It was dead, and all her plans were dead in the water with it. An urge to cry washed over her. Her documentary film was dead, her goal of exposing the more egregious operators in the commercial fishing industry was dead. She didn't dare think about the porpoises and sharks and sea turtles that would die without her exposé to rouse the public to save them.

She yanked the hand starter on the bilge pump. At least it coughed to life, and sluggishly began to suck in water and spit it overboard. The *New Dawn* had a slow leak somewhere, but she'd been unable to locate it so far.

Wearily, she closed the engine cover and slogged over to the ladder. She climbed through the cramped cabin that contained all her worldly possessions and up on deck to stare at the horizon. A slow, three-hundred-sixty-degree check revealed nothing but water and more water stretching away to infinity along the earth's faint curve. No wonder ancient sailors thought it was possible to sail off the edge of the world.

Not the smallest bump of land or even another boat marred the smooth line of the horizon. She was marooned in the middle of nowhere—literally. If she had half a brain she'd be worrying about her own life and not the helpless little fishies below. But no one had ever accused her of being overly bright when it came to matters of self-preservation.

She ducked inside and turned up the volume on the UHF radio. Static crackle filled the tiny space. She checked her position near the junction of the Arabian Sea and the Indian Ocean, not too far south of the Yemeni archipelago of Suqutra. She jotted down the location coordinates off her GPS before picking up the microphone.

"This is the *New Dawn* requesting assistance. My engine has failed and I need a tow. I am currently located at eleven degrees, twenty-five minutes, thirty-six seconds north latitude and fifty-four degrees, four minutes, seven seconds east longitude."

She repeated the message twice more. Now she simply had to wait. Despite its desolate appearance, this stretch of water was crisscrossed by plentiful shipping lanes and fishing grounds. And it was the rule of the sea that any ship who heard a distress call must respond to it. Nobody might own these international waters, and nations might fight like dogs over them, but sailors stuck together.

The sun set in a brilliant splash of crimson and faded into the violet hues of twilight without anyone responding to her periodic radio calls. As the utter blackness of night at sea fell around her, she sighed and settled down to wait out a long, uncomfortable night. She needed to preserve her battery for radio calls and had turned off all unnecessary equipment, which meant no air conditioner or even an electric fan for her tonight.

She must have dozed off because the stars had wheeled around in the sky overhead and the night was balmy when she blinked her eyes open. The *New Dawn* bobbed on light swells, pulling against the sea anchor she'd deployed to keep from drifting too far from her reported position.

A faint rumbling caught her attention. She looked about eagerly for the running lights of her rescuer and gasped as a massive black shape loomed off her port side. The sharp point of a ship's prow was bearing directly down upon her. Fast.

Yikes. That ship was *really* bearing down on her fast! Her sleepy mind exploded to full consciousness as the deadly danger of her situation registered.

"Hey! I'm here!" she shouted, waving her arms frantically over her head. As if anyone would hear her over the roar of the much bigger vessel's engines. A white V of water sliced away from the black blade of the prow. The ship displayed no lights whatsoever as it raced at her like an attacking shark closing in for the kill.

Panicked, she scrambled backward, stumbling and falling over her waterproof camera bag. She hit the deck hard and her head smacked the cabin wall painfully. She flung herself toward the railing, every survival instinct screaming at her to get out of the way before that ship sliced the *New Dawn* in half. Clutching her camera bag in one fist as she rolled, she plunged over the side and into the icy water.

The Pacific Ocean closed in over her head, entombing her in a dark so cold and heavy, she felt as if she'd been buried alive.

Panic gave way to shock as every muscle in her body clenched at the frigid grip of the sea. She kicked hard for the surface, but it was as if she attempted to swim through concrete. No matter how hard she tried, she couldn't seem to get anywhere. Assuming she was even headed in the right direction. She tried to feel which way the bubbles racing past her skin were headed, but who knew if she'd gotten it right. For all she knew she was kicking down toward Davy Jones's locker with all her strength.

And then a new threat registered—a deep throbbing noise that pounded through her body rhythmically, growing in volume and intensity with every beat. Oh, God. The larger ship's propellers. She kicked like a madwoman, praying her random swimming would carry her clear of the rotating blades before they made bloody chum out of her.

The water grew violently turbulent, tossing her head over heels in a chaotic swirl that left her so dizzy she wanted to throw up. Probably not a good idea with the single breath in her lungs already running painfully low on oxygen. Little sparkles of light erupted behind her eyelids.

The ocean calmed around her as abruptly as it had gone mad. She was farther than ever from knowing which way the surface and air might be. Perhaps her best bet was to quit fighting and let her natural buoyancy and lungful of air lift her to the surface. But would it be in time before she passed out?

In a few seconds she wouldn't be able to hold her breath anymore and she would inhale a single, lethal lungful of salt water. And then in twelve to fifteen seconds, as the last oxygen in her brain was used, she'd lose consciousness. Without the buoyancy of air in her lungs, she would slip down into the depths of the sea, lost in its cold embrace forever. Vague curiosity about whether or not there was life after death passed through her mind. *Guess I'll know one way or the other pretty soon.*

Who'd have imagined she would end up like this? It seemed like such a waste to die so young. She was only twenty-seven. She'd assumed she had so much more time. So much more to experience. Her parents' faces flashed through her mind. Her sister's face—Chloe was going to be furious at her for dying.

Sunny reached deep and fought one last time. It was simply not in her nature to give up. She'd go down trying to save herself. But her kicks were feeble now, and to no avail. As she used up the last of her strength and oxygen, the darkness claimed her.

Aiden McKay scanned the ocean through binoculars from the bridge of the *Sea Nymph,* one-hundred-forty feet of pure yachting luxury on loan to him from billionaire Leland Winston.

"Do you see her?" he asked the *Nymph*'s captain, Steig Carlson.

"Negative. We are exactly at the last coordinates the girl transmitted, though."

Aiden frowned. The sexy female voice had been making periodic calls throughout the day asking for assistance with her marooned vessel. He'd been annoyed at having to break off his mission to respond to the call, but it wasn't as if he had any choice. He was one of the good guys, after all.

"Large vessel off to port," Steig announced. "Must have responded to the *New Dawn*'s distress call, too."

Aiden snorted. Every vessel within a hundred miles had probably set course at full speed toward that girl's sensuous voice coming across their radios. Sailors were nothing if not a lonely bunch.

He swung his binoculars around to port. It was a dark night, but he made out the bulk of a good-size ship. "That vessel's moving fast," he commented, frowning. Looked to be pushing twenty-five knots or more. Why would a ship searching for a small boat be tearing along like a bat out of hell? Wouldn't they be trawling slowly like the *Sea Nymph,* searching the waters quadrant by careful quadrant?

He swung his binoculars to the next quadrant of his search, in front of the speeding boat, and lurched. He thought he'd caught a glimpse of—

He swore as the *Nymph* rolled and he momentarily lost his target. He scanned left and right with the binoculars and caught sight of it again. A small vessel bobbing like a helpless cork in the swells directly in front of the racing ship.

"Sweet Mother of God," he breathed. "Those bastards are going to ram her."

Steig swore beside him. "They're going to smash her boat into matchsticks at that speed." He reached for the throttles and threw the sleek yacht's twin diesel engines to full power.

Aiden shouted into the radios, "Unknown rider, alter course! You are about to collide with a small craft. I say again, alter course immediately!" But the black hulk in front of him either didn't hear or didn't care. Or worse, it knew good and well that it was about to sink the disabled cabin cruiser that could only be the *New Dawn*.

Aiden watched in helpless horror as the blacked-out ship slammed broadside into the smaller boat. With a terrible grinding noise audible even from here, the big ship's prow crashed through the *New Dawn*'s hull. The little boat lifted up in the air like a toy in a bathtub and then all of a sudden disappeared underneath the larger ship, dragged below the water like flotsam in the ship's path.

The girl with the sexy voice was on that boat!

He kicked off his deck shoes frantically and reached for the swim goggles that were always in his pocket.

"Don't do it," Steig bit out. "The water will be full of debris and it's too dark to find her."

"This is what I do. Who I am."

"But, sir—"

He was already shirtless, so he merely tore off his pants and dived directly off the bridge of the yacht to the sea below.

"Aiden!" someone shouted behind him as his body knifed through the air and into the welcome embrace of the sea that was his true home. He swam with powerful strokes toward the last position of the *New Dawn*.

The silence and pressure closed around him, and with them came the peace he always found in the ocean. A jagged piece of white-painted timber came into view.

He surfaced near where the boat went down and shouted, "Hello! Where are you?"

No response. The *Sea Nymph*'s spotlights came on, illuminating the wreckage in harsh light. He made a quick visual search of the debris field. No sign of any human clinging to a piece of the *New Dawn*. He took a big breath and dived under the surface. His ears popped as he reached a depth of fifteen feet or so, but the rest of his body absorbed the crushing weight of the water with something resembling relief.

No sign of the girl. He swam in a wide circle that encompassed most of the debris field. She had to be here somewhere. He kept a time count in a corner of his mind. Two minutes. Three. He widened his search area, worry setting in. If he didn't find her soon, it wasn't going to be a search and rescue anymore. It would be a corpse recovery.

He kicked harder. Spotted a flash of white waving softly in the current like a piece of fabric. He pulled powerfully toward it. A shirt. A pale face flashed in the scant light from overhead.

The girl. Unconscious and drifting down toward the depths. Angling deeper, he came up underneath her, catching her slender body in his arms and kicking mightily toward the light above. Four minutes.

He swore mentally. If she'd been down here four minutes, she could be very close to brain death. He stopped kicking to plaster his mouth against hers tightly. Angling her head down so he was directly below her, he blew into her mouth enough to clear the water out. Then, he exhaled hard into the air pocket he'd created, forcing air into her lungs. Underwater mouth-to-mouth wasn't exactly the ideal way to prevent drowning, but he couldn't just hold her in his arms and let her die!

He closed her mouth with one hand, while his free arm went around her once more. He resumed kicking hard toward the surface and air.

After sacrificing his own oxygen reserves to the girl, he actually began to feel the burn of it in his muscles. Thankfully, his body was extraordinarily efficient at processing oxygen. Although he was getting close to his limit, he had enough gas left in the tank to save the girl.

They burst up out of the depths, and he took a long, gasping breath. He looked around frantically for something big and flat and buoyant, and spotted a portion of the destroyed boat's hull not far away. Pinching her nose shut, he breathed another lungful of air into the girl's mouth. Then he dragged her over to the hull and quickly up onto the makeshift raft. He clambered onto his knees beside her and commenced CPR.

"Come on," he growled. "Don't you die on me."

He'd been compressing her chest for about thirty seconds when, without warning, she threw up a bunch of seawater. He rolled her over onto her side fast. She coughed and more water came out of her mouth. She drew in a rasping breath and coughed some more.

At least she was alive.

Steig had obviously seen him surface with the girl because the *Sea Nymph* was making painstakingly slow progress through the debris field toward them. Several of the crewmen were leaning down over the prow with long poles in the water, shoving debris aside as the yacht crawled forward. When the yacht pulled alongside, the crew lowered a backboard to him on a pair of ropes, and Aiden horsed it underneath the unconscious girl.

He was huffing hard by the time he got her strapped onto it. He swore. *Not now.* But he should have known. He'd just spent a long time underwater and then surfaced and exerted himself hard. That wasn't how his gift worked. Now he got to pay the price of it. As the crew hoisted the girl upward, his chest tightened until it felt like a massive anvil was parked on top of him. He lay down on the makeshift raft.

Inhale slowly. Exhale fully. Relax. Don't freak out. His nebulizer was just a few yards away aboard the *Sea Nymph.* He'd be fine in a few minutes. But in the meantime, he got to endure the mother of all asthma attacks.

He vaguely heard voices shouting from above.

"Aiden's down!"

"…send a man to him…"

"…help him up the ladder…"

"…don't think he'll make it…"

And then all was darkness and silence around him.

He dreamed of a mermaid with warm brown hair streaked honey-blond. Her tanned skin was dewy and flawless, her eyes a golden-green hazel that matched the sensuous warmth of her voice. Her lips were bee-stung and rosy, her body slender but juicy enough to promise sinful delights. Her aquatic lower half was covered in golden-green scales that glittered exactly the color of her eyes.

She hovered easily in the water before him, her elegant tail fin waving just enough to hold her position. She reached for him with a dazzling smile, her slender arms beckoning him into her eternal embrace. She was the sea. And he loved it—her—more than earthbound life itself. He swam forward, surrendering himself to her.

Her arms closed around him with surprising strength, and she turned, kicking with controlled violence, shooting them downward toward the inky depths of the abyss. His lungs felt strangely tight, and the clock in his head ticked past six minutes. Seven. Eight was about his normal limit.

Nine minutes. Ten.

If she didn't turn around pretty soon, his beautiful mermaid was going to kill him!

He struggled in her embrace trying to tear free. But she was too strong. Completely disinterested in his silent pleas to let him go. Down, down she went with him. The pressure was too much. Every cell in his body screamed for relief. For air. He thrashed violently. He had to break free or die!

"Wake up, Aiden. For God's sake, quit flailing around! We just got your breathing settled back down."

Disoriented, he opened his eyes. Bright lights blinded him and he squinted against the painful glare. Something plastic descended to cover his mouth and nose, and he sucked in the aerosolized bronchodilator medication desperately.

The pressure in his lungs eased. His panic receded. Exhausted mentally and physically, he sagged back against the pillows. Memory returned. "The girl?" he rasped.

The ship's medical corpsman answered, "Alive. You

got to her in time. Gemma doesn't think she suffered any brain damage, but we won't know until she wakes up. Gem's got her sedated and on antibiotics."

Aiden relaxed. Dr. Gemma Jones was the best. He took belated note of his surroundings and recognized one of the yacht's cabins. As he recalled, it was outfitted with two twin beds. He turned his head on the pillow and spied the occupant of the other bed. He lurched.

His mermaid.

Except she was pale against the white sheets, her glorious hair dry and spread out across the pillow like honey-streaked silk. Her eyes—if they were the golden-hazel of his dream—were closed, her breathing light and slow.

He took the nebulizer off his face and sat up, swinging his legs carefully over the side of the bed. He felt as if he'd gone a few rounds in a boxing ring against the Champ…and lost.

He stood long enough to shift his weight to the edge of the girl's bed. He couldn't resist running his fingers through the soft strands of her hair. "Who are you?" he murmured. "What were you doing out on the open sea by yourself?"

Her eyelids fluttered slightly.

"Can you hear me?" he said more urgently. "Can you open your eyes?"

Her eyelids fluttered again and then opened. They *were* his mermaid's eyes. Except right now they were confused. Frightened.

He spoke gently. "You're safe. You're aboard the *Sea Nymph*. I rescued you when your boat sank."

The girl frowned. "Water," she croaked. "Dark. Cold. Dying."

His recent nightmare of nearly drowning vivid in his mind, he didn't have to ask what she meant. "I dived for you and pulled you out," he explained.

Her gaze filled with tears and her hand slid across the sheet to touch his. He jolted at the touch of human flesh against his. It had been so long. So very long...

She whispered hoarsely, "Thank you."

"Sleep now. You need rest."

"Be here? When I..."

As her eyes drifted closed he answered low, his voice rough, "I'll be here when you wake up."

Sunny drifted in a white world that was safe and warm and blessedly bright. And always her rescuer was there with her. Anytime she opened her eyes, his was the only face she saw before she drifted, comforted, back into her cocoon. But eventually the demands of her body began to intrude. Thirst. Hunger. An ache in her chest and raw soreness in her throat.

She opened her eyes. The small, mahogany-paneled room was familiar as if she'd seen it before, but she had no memory of it. She turned her head and spied another bed. With a person in it. More specifically, a man. The one who'd saved her from a watery death, apparently. A bronze and godlike hunk of a man with muscular arms and a sculpted chest above the white blanket. Wavy blond hair with the electric shine of a frequent swimmer fell back from a strong face. He wasn't exactly beautiful—his face was more about character and strength—but it was a compelling face nonetheless.

She lifted her own blanket and looked down. Whose tank top and shorts was she wearing? At least she was decent. Startled at how wobbly she was, she climbed out of bed. How did she get here? She cast back for details, but it was foggy.

And then a piece came back to her. Something big and black bearing down on her. The shock of cold. And then darkness. Abruptly, she remembered the terror. Suddenly, she was in the water again, panicked, unsure of up or down, knowing that her time was running out and that she desperately wanted to live. She stumbled toward the door, bumping into the sleeping man's bed, but not caring in her panic. She had to get out of here! Outside. Into the open air. Sunlight.

The man's eyes opened. He asked sharply, "What's wrong?"

"Have to get out," she gasped. "Claustrophobic…"

He jumped out of bed quickly. Holy cow, he was tall. Even more imposing upright than he'd been in bed. He put a hand on her back and whisked her toward the door. A dim, narrow hallway beyond was no comfort, but the man moved down it swiftly, his big hand propelling her forward.

Up a short flight of steps, and then they were outside. Blessed sky, big and open and blue and bright, opened up above her. She breathed deeply as her pounding heart slowly returned to normal. She became aware of her surroundings and got her first good look at the vessel she was on. Good grief. This yacht was huge.

"Who are you?" she asked her rescuer. "Whose yacht is this?"

"I'm Aiden McKay. And the *Sea Nymph* belongs to

a friend of mine. I'm borrowing it for a little deep-sea fishing expedition."

"What are you fishing for…Moby Dick?"

He smiled briefly, and his face transformed from striking to mesmerizing. Wow. "Apparently, I'm fishing for mermaids." He paused and then blurted, "What's your name?"

"Sunny. Sunny Jordan."

He nodded awkwardly. "How is it that ship ran over your boat last night? Was it an accident?"

She stumbled as last night's terror rolled over her and she managed to practically fall into him. She didn't plan it, honest. But all of a sudden, she was plastered against his chest as his surprised arms came up to catch her. He froze and went statue stiff. It was like cuddling up to the Rock of Gibraltar.

"Are you going to, umm, faint?" he mumbled.

"I never faint," she retorted indignantly. But her whole indignation vibe was ruined by the quaver in her voice and trembling of her knees.

His arms tightened fractionally as if to say he had her now and she was safe. She snuggled deeper into his rigid, but somehow comforting, embrace.

A sobbing breath escaped her.

"Who was on that ship?" he persisted. "Did you get a good look at it?"

She glanced up at him and he was staring fixedly over her head at a distant point on the horizon. He looked acutely uncomfortable. And yet, his arms stayed wrapped around her.

"The ship was all black. And so big. It came at me so fast…." She shuddered.

He repeated more urgently, "Was it an accident?"

The answer scared her almost more than being run down in the first place. Almost more than nearly drowning. She whispered hoarsely, "I don't think so."

He drew back to stare down at her. "Who are you? Why would someone try to kill you?"

Chapter 2

Aiden waited expectantly for the woman to answer, but instead she merely shivered in his arms. "Who wants to hurt you?" he insisted.

Eventually, she sighed and relaxed, her slender body shifting against his and making his chest tighten—but pleasantly. Far too belatedly, dismay flowed through him. He knew better than to indulge himself like this. He'd sworn off women. Changed his ways. Turned over a new leaf…and apparently been lying to himself like a big dog that he'd actually changed.

"I'm a filmmaker," she announced as if that answered everything. "I was collecting footage for a documentary on the commercial deep-sea fishing industry."

An uncomplimentary portrayal, no doubt. But uncomplimentary enough to kill her over? He frowned. He didn't recall seeing the giant cranes used for deploying

and hoisting fishing nets protruding from the silhouette of the vessel that had sunk her boat. "Are you sure
it was fishermen who ran you down?"

"I'm not sure of anything except my boat is gone,
and I'm really glad you came along when you did and
saved my life."

So was he.

The moment threatened to become intimate as a sexual charge started to build between them. He was desperate to lean into it, to lose himself in the feeling he
knew so well. But he wasn't that guy anymore. He didn't
party his way into the bed of every hot chick he laid
eyes on. He had a purpose now. Focus. At long last, he
had some self-respect. Still. This particular hot chick
felt pretty fantastic in his arms—

A voice intruded from behind him. "I see my patients are up and about."

He stepped back hastily from the girl. Whether he
was more chagrined at the interruption or abjectly relieved by it, he couldn't say. "Hey, Doc," he mumbled.

"Aiden. How's your breathing?"

"Fine." An awkward silence descended. It had been a
long time since he'd had need for social niceties, but he
roused his rusty skills to mutter, "Sunny, this is Doctor
Gemma Jones. Gem, meet Sunny."

The two women nodded at one another. "How're you
feeling today?" Gemma asked Sunny.

"Okay, I guess. My throat feels awful."

"It'll clear up in a few days." The doctor added, "If
you've got a little time later, I'd like to run some simple
neurological tests on you."

Sunny answered, "Give me a shout-out whenever you want to do it."

"How about now, then?" Gemma responded briskly.

Aiden scowled at the interruption of their time together. He was making good progress—

He cut off that train of thought sharply. He did not *progress* with seducing women anymore, dammit.

Gemma announced, "I'll get my bag and be back in a few minutes."

The doctor's departure was apparently the cue for the ship's captain to make an appearance. Aiden sighed. It was a plot to keep him from having any time alone with Sunny. Or more likely, they'd come to enjoy watching him squirm. It wasn't often these days he interacted with women for this long. "Sunny, this is Captain Steig Carlson."

"As in the ship's captain?" she asked, eyeing the big blond Swede a little too appreciatively for Aiden's taste.

Steig smiled and held out his hand to her. "That's right, Miss Jordan."

"Call me Sunny."

"Only if you'll call me Steig."

Aiden managed not to roll his eyes, but it was a close thing. "So, Steig. I assume you tracked the ship that wiped out Sunny's boat?"

"We followed it until it rounded an island and we lost radar contact. By the time we passed the headland, it had blended in with the other traffic in the shipping lanes. I can tell you one thing, though. It was fast. We had to push the throttles wide open just to maintain the gap between us."

The *Sea Nymph* could run at thirty knots if she

had to. And the other ship had been able to match that speed? Modern whaling ships could move that fast, but not too many other fishing vessels could do it. "Any idea who she was?" he asked.

Steig shook his head regretfully. "We never got visual on her again after we picked you and Sunny out of the water."

"Did it look like a fishing boat to you?" Aiden asked.

"No. Wrong rigging for fishing. It looked more like—" the Swede frowned "—I'm not sure what. Research vessel, maybe."

Aiden and Steig traded grim looks. They were both thinking the same thing. A surveillance ship of some kind. Why would some foreign government have it in for a lone, independent filmmaker? They both looked over at the woman leaning on the rail, eyes closed, face turned up to the sunshine. Who was she? And what in the hell had she really been doing out here?

Aiden asked in sudden recollection, "Sunny, what was in that bag you were clutching when I dragged you up to the surface?"

She frowned, then her eyes lit up. "Did my camera bag make it aboard with me?"

Aiden had no idea. He'd passed out shortly after resuscitating her. Steig answered, however. "Yes, it did."

"Where is it?" she asked eagerly.

The captain was prevented from answering by the arrival of Doctor Jones to test Sunny's brain function. Gemma shooed Aiden and Steig away with a promise to return their shiny new toy to them later.

As Sunny threw a startled glance in his direction,

Aiden scowled at Gemma. The doctor had the social skills of an amoeba sometimes.

A sailor called for Steig to return to the bridge, and Aiden made his way belowdecks. It was a simple matter—track down the cabin where Sunny's clothes, laundered and pressed, had been hung in a closet. Sure enough, her bag sat on the floor beneath the hangers. Steig's crew was nothing if not efficient.

He should leave the bag alone. Let the poor girl have her privacy. The new Aiden didn't pull stunts like this. And yet, he pulled the waterproof sack out of her closet. He needed to know if the reason she'd nearly been killed was something she'd recorded, right?

Armed with that thin logic, he dumped the contents of the bag onto her bed. A few dog-eared family photos. Cell phone. Wallet. A flash drive. An impressive array of high-tech camera gear, including memory cards for her digital movie camera. Dozens of them.

He loaded a random card into her camera and pushed the play button. The footage had been taken underwater. A school of dolphins was circling, playing with the cameraperson—presumably Sunny. Shafts of sunlight streamed down into the sea and various fish darted in and out of the light. It made him want to take off his clothes and dive overboard right now. But then, his longing for the water was never far from him.

He popped the memory card out and put in another one. The footage jolted him. It was of live sharks thrashing on the deck of a fishing vessel as their fins were sawed off. They were rolled into the ocean still alive, mutilated and bloody, to die. The waste of it was sickening. If they were going to kill a shark, couldn't they at least harvest the entire animal for its meat?

He fast-forwarded to another set of footage, fuzzy images of ships at a distance. But the quality of the film was poor. It had been shot through rain and the visibility wasn't great.

Without warning, the door opened behind him. "This will be your—" A steward broke off in surprise. "Oh! I'm sorry, sir…"

"That's okay," Aiden replied, hastily stuffing the camera back into the bag.

But he wasn't fast enough. Sunny had spotted what he'd been doing. "Hey! That's my camera. What are you doing with it? I didn't give you permission to mess with my stuff."

He winced. She was, of course, entirely right. He explained hastily, "Somebody tried to kill you. I'm trying to find out why."

The steward backed out discreetly and closed the door as Sunny retorted angrily, "That's none of your business."

She was magnificent in her indignation. Her eyes sparked golden fire and her entire body vibrated with passion. Lord, to bed all that exploding energy—

Not. Happening. Chagrined on several levels, he made a lame attempt to justify himself. "If you're going to be aboard this ship, anything that might bring danger to it is my business. I wanted to know what threat we're dealing with."

"If I'm such a danger, put me ashore. Sail for the nearest port and I'll disembark. Or if you really want to get rid of me and my personal baggage, have a helicopter come get me. I saw a snazzy landing pad for one up on deck."

His voice rose in frustration. "I'm not trying to get rid of you. I'm trying to protect you!"

"It looks to me like you're trying to invade my privacy…and doing a pretty good job of it. I don't need your protection."

Was she completely without a clue as to how much danger she might be in? He snapped, "Right. That's why your boat was run over and I pulled you from the water more dead than alive. Because you're doing such a bang-up job of taking care of yourself."

She snatched the bag out of his hands and clutched it to her chest in much the same way she had done underwater the night before. What was on those other memory cards she seemed so desperate to protect?

"If I'm not mistaken," she said stiffly, "this is my room. That being the case, please leave."

She was throwing him out? After he'd saved her life? Exasperation slammed into him. He was only trying to help, dammit. He surged to his feet and headed for the door. A citrus scent wafted to him as he passed by her. It was tart and sweet on his tongue and begged to be tasted more fully, and it only succeeded in making him madder.

He paused in the doorway and spoke, his voice sounding stiff even to him. "I'm sorry if I offended you. But since my help is obviously not welcome, I'll leave you alone. I'll have Steig arrange to put you ashore as soon as possible."

* * *

Sunny stared at the door in dismay as it closed behind Aiden. She didn't mean to make him get all angry and distant like that; she'd just been mad that he'd been rifling through her bag. Its contents were all she had left in the entire world. Literally. Everything she owned had been on the *New Dawn* and was now lying on the bottom of the ocean. She didn't need some stranger—even if he was glorious to look at—pawing through what little remained of her life.

She was probably overreacting. And it didn't help that she was already on edge. Spending more than thirty seconds in the company of Gemma Jones was enough to make any woman feel inferior and a little tense. The doctor was so intelligent it was hard to have a conversation with her; her mind worked so quickly that she leaped from subject to subject almost too fast to follow.

Not to mention, Sunny was a little jealous of the easy relationship Gemma seemed to have with Aiden. Which was silly because she herself barely knew him. But something funny happened to her stomach whenever he smiled at her. And after he'd saved her life, she'd thought they had some sort of special connection. Maybe in her semiconscious state she'd just imagined it.

Disappointment coursed through her. For a little while there, she hadn't felt alone in the world. And it had been nice. But then he had to go and intrude in her life. What was left of it. Still, she *did* owe him her life, and she *had* snapped at him.

She left her cabin in search of Aiden to apologize, but he was nowhere to be found. At least nowhere the crew wanted to tell her about. He'd probably given them orders to keep her away from him. Maybe Steig could intervene on her behalf.

It was hard to believe a person could get lost on a yacht, but this one was huge. And plush. She'd never seen anything as luxurious in all her years of sailing. Eventually, she found her way to the bridge. She stepped into the high-tech space and stopped to stare.

A sailor in a crisp white uniform spotted her. "Can I help you, miss?"

"Is Captain Carlson available?"

The guy glanced at a closed door at the far end of the bridge. "If you'll follow me?"

Steig stood up when she walked into his compact and very tidy office. "Is anything wrong, Miss Jordan?"

"I thought we agreed you'd call me Sunny."

He smiled and ducked his head.

"I need your help. I think I made Aiden mad, and I want to make it up to him."

Steig looked frankly shocked. "Aiden? Mad? Do tell."

She explained quickly. "I snapped at him when I caught him going through my things, but I'd like to apologize. Make it up to him. I thought maybe dinner with him—" Why did Steig look so stunned? "Is something wrong?" she asked quickly.

"Not at all. Continue."

"If I invite him to eat with me he might say no. But I thought if you were to ask him, maybe he wouldn't refuse. It doesn't have to be anything fancy. Something simple like a picnic, peanut-butter sandwiches on deck, would be fine. I just need to talk to him before he throws me off the ship."

"Throws you off?" Steig exclaimed. "Just how angry did you make him?"

"I kicked him out of my cabin," she confessed. "He yelled at me first, though."

"Did he, now?" Steig was beginning to look amused. "He actually yelled? I definitely think I can help you. But my chef would not be caught dead serving peanut-butter sandwiches to a guest. I'll take care of the arrangements. Say, seven o'clock tonight in the salon?"

"Uhh, okay."

"Gemma will be delighted to help you with some clothes. Be sure to mention to her that Aiden yelled at you." He waved her out of his office with one hand while an unholy smile spread across his face. "I've got some calls to make."

What had she done? Had she just set up Aiden to be the butt of some horrible practical joke that would only make him more angry at her? She visited Gemma, who reacted just as strangely as Steig to the fact that Aiden had yelled at her. The doctor pronounced it excellent news and immediately agreed to set up Sunny with a nice dress for dinner.

What on earth? Why were they all so thrilled she'd made him mad?

The arrangements for her grand apology in place, Sunny made her way back to her cabin. She managed to take a fretful nap but woke to the memory of a giant black shark bearing down on her with the intent to kill. She jolted awake in a cold sweat.

Why would anyone try to kill her? Had she really made a bunch of fishermen that angry? It wasn't as if deep-sea fishing practices were any big secret. Plenty of other documentaries had been filmed detailing their more outrageous behavior.

Someone knocked on her door, and Sunny opened it to reveal a steward holding a sexy little black dress on a hanger. He also held out a clear plastic bag that contained panty hose, high-heeled shoes that looked a little big for her but would probably work in a pinch, a curling iron, hair spray and makeup. Lots of lovely makeup. God bless Gemma Jones.

Sunny might happily sail all over the world for months on end and never see a tube of lipstick, but when she got a chance to doll herself up, she enjoyed doing it as much as the next girl. Sighing in delight, she took the offerings from the steward and retreated into her tiny bathroom to play.

At ten minutes till seven, another knock sounded on her door. After a quick spritz of some heavenly perfume, whose name she would have to get from Gemma, she opened the door. Steig, wearing a white dress uniform, looked smashing.

"I'm here to escort you to dinner, Miss Jordan."

"Sunny."

"It's Miss Jordan tonight. And may I say, you look lovely." He held out his forearm to her. Smiling shyly, she laid her hand on it and let him lead her up two decks and down a passageway to a massive living room. At the far end of it she spied a linen-covered table sporting red roses, tall candles and cut crystal.

"You're not pulling some kind of joke on Aiden, are you?"

"Not at all. Why would you think that?"

"This isn't exactly peanut-butter sandwiches on deck."

"Please don't disappoint the chef. He spent all afternoon working on making this meal perfect. He doesn't often get a chance to go all out. The crew's a bunch of crusty old sailors who don't appreciate his finer gastronomic efforts."

"You shouldn't have gone to all this trouble," she murmured.

"My pleasure. Aiden needs someone in his life who...inspires emotion."

Now, what did that mean? Before she could ask, Steig made a formal little bow and announced, "I'll leave you now. Bon appétit."

"Uhh, thank you."

The salon felt huge and hollow as silence settled around her. A subliminal rumble of engines was the only sound in the background. But then, out of hidden speakers around the room, quiet chamber music started. She was so not a violins-and-haute-cuisine kind of girl. But hey. If the captain thought this would work on Aiden, she could roll with it.

Promptly at seven, she heard movement behind her. She turned a little too quickly and stumbled in her heels, which were a tad loose. Strong hands caught her shoulders to steady her.

"What's this all about?" Aiden demanded sharply.

She stared down at his Italian leather loafers in utter humiliation. So. The joke wasn't on him, after all. It was on her.

"I'm sorry," she mumbled. "I asked Steig to help me

apologize to you. I told him a picnic and peanut-butter sandwiches would be fine, but he insisted on all of this."

"Ahh." He released her shoulders and took a step back.

She waited for the explosion, but none came. When she couldn't take the suspense anymore, she risked a peek up at him. It was like looking at a painted portrait. It looked like Aiden, but nothing of the real man was there in his eyes. He looked…dead. Had she alienated him that badly?

"Gemma lent you a dress?" he asked neutrally.

She plucked at the clingy black fabric. "Yes."

He nodded noncommittally. "The flowers and music?"

"Steig's idea."

"Hmm."

Finally, she burst out, "Say something, will you? Yell at me and tell me how mad you are or what an ungrateful bitch I am."

He replied politely, "You look lovely."

She stared in equal parts confusion and frustration as he moved away from her and over to a leather-and-brass wet bar. "Drink?" he asked mildly.

"Sure," she replied in utter confusion. What was up with him? He was treating her like a rather inconvenient bug.

He concocted something that involved a shaker and lime wedges and poured it into a pair of glasses filled with ice. He carried the drinks over to the picture window where she stood and handed one to her.

"To your health," he commented wryly.

"Why are you being like this?" she demanded.

"Like what?"

"So…polite. Aren't you furious with me for throwing you out of my room?"

"I *was* going through your things without your permission. You probably should have slapped me."

"I don't slap. I have a wicked right hook, but no slapping."

"Check. Beware the right hook." A pause, and then his voice thawed slightly. "Anything else I should know about you?"

"You're really not mad at me?" she asked in disbelief. Her family had been full of passion. Lots of arguments and shouting, but also lots of laughter and love. His cool, unflappable demeanor was totally foreign to her.

"I'll admit, I was…annoyed…earlier. But you were right. I'm just not used to anyone calling me out for my bad behavior. You surprised me. That's all."

"Oh." She paused for a moment, then asked, "How come no one calls you out? Are you that rich?"

That made him smile. "I already told you this yacht doesn't belong to me. I'm just borrowing it from a friend to use as bait."

She glanced around in surprise. "This is bait? For what? A rich wife?"

His smile widened. "Hardly. I'm fishing for pirates."

"Excuse me?"

"Pirates. This is exactly the sort of yacht they love to steal. They board the vessel, kill everyone and take the ship. After a few exterior modifications and a new name to disguise her, she'd go for millions on the black market."

"Isn't trying to attract pirates dangerous?"

"That's why the *Nymph*'s entire crew is ex-military

and heavily armed. Any pirates who mess with this boat are in for a nasty surprise."

"Still. It sounds dangerous."

"No more so than running around solo in a tiny cabin cruiser filming commercial-fishing outfits doing their worst."

"Touché." She raised her glass to him.

"Any new thoughts on who might have tried to kill you?"

She shook her head. "I wonder if I accidentally filmed something I shouldn't have. Maybe something that has nothing at all to do with fishing."

"That was my thought, too. That's the only reason I was looking at your film, by the way. I was trying to spot whatever got you in hot water."

"The way I remember it, the water was freaking cold."

He winced at the mention of her near drowning. "Next time, don't go swimming in the ocean alone."

She shuddered at the idea of submerging herself in water of any kind ever again. Even the idea of submerging herself in a bathtub terrified her. Her hands and knees started to shake at the thought, in fact, and suddenly she felt more than a little nauseous. She swayed dangerously.

Aiden moved fast to her side and lifted her drink out of her nerveless, icy fingers. "You just went ghostly white. Are you all right?"

"Can we talk about something besides swimming?"

A look of dawning understanding lit his face. "Scared you, did it?"

"Wouldn't coming within a whisker of drowning freak you out, too?"

"I wouldn't know. I'm a pretty good swimmer. Haven't ever come near drowning."

"Lucky," she muttered.

He shrugged and a shadow passed through his eyes. "That's one word for it."

"What word would you use to describe your swimming ability?"

He pursed his lips. "Spectacular."

"Modest much?" she retorted.

He chuckled, thawing another few millimeters. Maybe the guy was a recluse of some kind. Or just shy. She got the feeling engaging in this much sustained conversation was unusual for him. He kept pausing as if searching for the right words.

"I'll take you out swimming with me sometime. You'll see what I'm talking about."

"Not me. I'm done with fishing exposés and underwater anything, thank you very much."

"It's a little soon to declare yourself finished, isn't it? Give yourself time to get over the shock of your accident."

She shook her head resolutely. No way was she getting back in the water. The sea had taken her parents, and it had nearly taken her. She wasn't dumb—she knew when it was time to quit and walk away. She opened her mouth to say just that but was interrupted by a male voice behind her.

"Dinner is ready, Miss Jordan. Mr. McKay."

Aiden rolled his eyes. "A simple 'chow's on' would have been sufficient, Jens."

The steward cleared his throat. "With all due respect, you haven't seen the meal Chef prepared. *Chow* is emphatically not the right word for it."

Aiden sighed. Then, awkwardly, he held out his arm to her. She took it, eyeing the steward with new respect as Aiden guided her to the table. The sailor was burly beneath his white monkey suit and moved with the assurance of a soldier. How could she have missed that before? She must've been too besotted with Aiden to notice any other males on board.

She did notice, though, when Aiden gestured the steward aside and pulled out her chair for her himself. She glanced up at him in thanks and her breath caught at the way he was looking at her. As if she was the main course for dinner. Her stomach tumbled and she suddenly felt a little lightheaded. She was grateful to sink into her seat while she regained her bearings. Talk about a lady killer! The man was dangerous. He could knock her off her feet with a single glance. And she dared not even think about what his arms felt like around her.

As course after course of incredible continental cuisine came forth from the kitchen, she surreptitiously studied her companion. Aiden carried himself like a man used to wealth. Power. Having people do what he said. She didn't care what he said. The man was definitely rich, or at least very powerful.

Not that she'd ever measured people by the thickness of their wallets. It was just interesting that he'd gone to such lengths to make sure she knew he didn't own the *Sea Nymph*. If he was trying to lessen her intimidation factor at his suave sophistication, it didn't work. It felt as if she was having supper with a movie star. He was perfectly polite, but there was a certain cool distance to him that was completely impenetrable. Of course, it was entirely her fault it was there, so it wasn't as if she could hold his reserve against him. But it still got to her. Furthermore, it goaded her to try to break through it and find the warm, engaging man she'd glimpsed when she first met him.

"What's your story?" she finally asked him.

"The men in my family all served a stint in the navy. My father was stationed at Pearl Harbor. I spent my youth in Hawaii. A rough gig, I know. But someone had to do it. When my father retired, my family moved back east. But I stayed in California to go to college at Stanford. I played hard, but I managed to get a degree in nanoengineering. That means I design and build tiny little robots. During my obligatory tour in the navy, I partied my way through every major port in the Pacific theater. Then Jeff Winston offered me a job in his grandfather's company. And here I am."

She considered the detachment with which he'd recited his life story. Beneath the lightness of the rendition, it all sounded very snooty and blue-blooded. No mention of friends, lovers, emotional connections to his family. Nor did he strike her as the party animal he'd described himself to be. She cast about for a neutral question. "How did you become a spectacular swimmer?"

Odd. He looked away evasively, but he did answer. "I've always lived near water. I suppose it came naturally. What about you? What's your story?"

Trying to distract her. Weird. She supposed she owed him an answer, though, since he'd told her about himself. But she didn't usually like to talk about her past.

She answered reluctantly. "My parents were environmental activists. And yes, they were raging hippies. We even lived in San Francisco when we weren't bebopping all over the world. I have a little sister, Chloe. She's the ultimate anti-hippie, however. Don't get me wrong. She's awesome. But we have absolutely nothing in common. Most people who meet us don't even think we're related. At any rate, my family went to wherever the next big environmental crisis was brewing and tried to stir up public concern about it."

"Where are your parents now?"

"Dead." She was able to say it without opening the door to all the old grief and loss and anger, but she desperately hoped he'd get the hint and leave the subject alone.

He didn't. "How?" At least he seemed to have sensed that he'd touched a nerve and was keeping this conversation brief and to the point.

"They went down at sea. No one knows how."

"Where?"

"Not far from here, in fact. A couple hundred kilometers south of our current position." She'd finally worked up the nerve to sail through the area a few days ago. It had been eerie, knowing she was following the last known coordinates her parents had reported before they disappeared.

For all she knew, she'd sailed right over their watery graves. She hoped she had, at any rate. She'd waited nearly a decade to say a proper goodbye to them. Although, she wasn't at all sure that downing most of a bottle of cheap wine and going on a drunk crying jag had been much of a farewell. Yet another screwup in her life to live with.

She noticed that Aiden was staring at her. "What?"

"No wonder you freaked out at nearly drowning. It had to bring back thoughts of how your parents must have died. I'm sorry."

Thank God she hadn't thought about it when she'd been fighting for her own life against the sea. It would have done her in. Even now, thinking that was how her parents had spent their final moments was enough to choke her up. She laid down her fork with excessive care and stared unseeing at the china pattern wavering beyond her tears.

Hands reached down for her. Pulled her to her feet. A warm chest materialized against her cheek and awkward arms surrounded her.

A chagrined voice murmured in her hair, "I've gone and done it again, haven't I? I've upset you." A sigh. "I'm sorry."

Why so many tears came, she had no idea. It wasn't as if she hadn't shed plenty over the years for her parents. They'd died ten years ago, for crying out loud. And yet, the wound felt as raw and unbearable as ever. Maybe it was being out here so close to where they'd died that brought out the old feelings of loss and abandonment.

She cried hard enough on Aiden's chest that her borrowed mascara had no doubt ruined his shirt. She must look as bedraggled as a wet dog. "I'm so sorry. I don't know what came over me. I never cry this much."

"You had a pretty bad scare."

"But I'm not normally a wimp."

"I already gathered that. Any woman who'd come out here alone and take on big international fishing companies has too much courage for her own good."

She swiped at her face. "I must look like a bad clown."

He handed her a discreetly monogrammed handkerchief. "I think I like you better without makeup."

She smiled gratefully. "You're a gentleman for saying so, but it's not necessary with me."

"Why not? Don't you deserve to be treated with respect? Like a lady?"

That made her laugh. "A lady? Me?" She was a hippie environmentalist wannabe following somewhat pathetically and entirely unsuccessfully in her family's footsteps.

He looked her up and down in a way that stole her breath away. "Yes, you, a lady."

"Brain's a little waterlogged from all that swimming, huh?"

One corner of his mouth twitched up wryly. "I've been told that before."

"By whom?"

"Gemma says so frequently."

"Why is she out here helping you guys nab pirates? She doesn't strike me as the type."

"She's a scientist," Aiden answered cryptically.

She got the distinct feeling he didn't want to say any more on the subject. "What's she studying?" Sunny persisted.

"Aquatic stuff."

Wow. That was descriptive. Was there some big secret around the doctor's research? Maybe he was worried she'd film Gemma's work or something. She was trying to figure out a delicate way to ask him if that was his concern when a male voice intruded sharply over a loudspeaker.

"Incoming pirate vessel. All hands on deck. Prepare for combat."

Chapter 3

Sunny started as the man across from her transformed from an urbane, sophisticated host who wore this yacht with the same ease he wore his suit into…she wasn't quite sure what. His face went hard, his eyes glittering with violent satisfaction.

"Go to your cabin," he ordered her tersely. "Lock yourself in and don't come out until Steig or I come for you."

"What's going on?" she demanded.

He shoved away from the table, already unbuttoning his shirt. What the heck? He ripped the fabric off shoulders that made her gulp as he kicked off his shoes and reached for his fly. Was he going to *strip* in front of her? Here? Now? Confused, she sat unmoving and stared at him. He peeled down his trousers, revealing powerful thighs. Thankfully, he was wearing some sort of compression briefs like a biker might wear.

"What are you waiting for?" he bit out. "Get out of here!"

"Where are you going?"

He reached into the pocket of his discarded pants and came up with, of all things, a pair of goggles like swimmers would wear. "I'm going fishing." He moved across the room to a desk and opened a drawer. He pulled out a round disk about the size and shape of a smoke detector and stuck it inside the waistband of his shorts. Its circular outline poked out on his hip.

"What on earth are you talking about?" she demanded.

"Go." He turned and raced for the door. He dashed out onto the walkway around the salon as he snapped the rubber strap of the goggles around his head. She heard someone shout—it sounded as if they were telling Aiden to wait for something—and then he jumped. Or dived, to be more precise. He soared out into space in a graceful swan dive reminiscent of a cliff diver. Or a complete nut job.

She didn't hear the splash as he hit the water, for more shouting erupted. And then gunshots. A massive, noisy fusillade of them that sent her diving for the floor in panic. An overwhelming urge to run for her life made her tremble from head to foot. But where to go? No power on earth was convincing her to follow Aiden's example and jump into the ocean. *Cabin. Hide. Lock the door.*

She jumped up on legs that felt too weak to hold her weight and too fast to belong to her. She bolted for the salon door, but skidded to a stop as gunfire exploded down the passageway. A man in white sprinted into view then ducked down a side passage. A second man, this one dark-skinned and dressed in green fatigues, barged around the corner and into view.

For the first time in her life, she froze. Her entire body refused to move. Not a single muscle would respond to her command to take cover. She just stared at the man's ginormous gun and the wild look in his eyes. His weapon came up in front of him. The barrel swung toward her. An evil grin spread across his face. He took aim.

And then the entire right side of his body exploded in a fountain of blood and flesh as a barrage of automatic-weapon fire raked him from head to toe. The sweep of nausea through her gut, her stomach retching against the combination of rich food and incomprehensible gore, finally unfroze her.

Stumbling, she turned and ran back into the salon looking around frantically. She had to hide. But it wasn't as if ships were rife with unused nooks and crannies that would conceal an adult. More gunfire erupted somewhere close and she dived for the oak bar, careening around its bulk and ducking down. She curled up in a little ball, hugging her knees like she hadn't since she was a child. She rocked back and forth, more or less incoherent with fear.

Where was Aiden? Was he all right? What had he meant by *going fishing?* She prayed urgently that the *Sea Nymph's* crew would win the fight. That they would be safe. That no one would die. But from the amount of gunfire out there, wholesale slaughter sounded more likely.

Did pirates still take female prisoners? Make them clean their cabins and warm their beds? Or force her to walk the plank? The very idea of plunging off a board into the ocean made her quake with terror.

Footsteps pounded nearby. It sounded as if someone was running down the hall in this direction. She swore under her breath and prayed they'd go away. But someone entered the room moving stealthily.

She had to find something to defend herself with. A weapon. She was not getting kidnapped by pirates, and that was all there was to it. She glanced around for something likely. Unopened bottles of liquor were stored on a shelf under the bar. She grabbed two with long necks. Then, tucking herself as far under the bar as she could, she cocked her arm back and waited grimly for the bastards to come.

Aiden sliced through the water cleanly, exhilarated that his plan was finally coming to fruition. He had faith Steig and his crew would have no trouble fighting off the pirates. Most of them in this part of the world were abjectly poor Somali with little to no education, ancient weapons and barely seaworthy boats.

But because of their small vessels and familiarity with the local coast, the pirates were slippery and hard to track. Various navies of the world had failed to find and eradicate their highly mobile and secret bases of operation. And that's why he was out here. Several private shipping companies, fed up with government failures, had hired Winston Security to kick a little pirate ass.

He swam deep enough that he wouldn't be readily visible from the surface but not so deep that he couldn't see his target. There. Just ahead. The curving hull of a wooden boat. If the ramshackle underside was any indication of its overall condition, it was in grave danger of sinking momentarily. But then he spied the twin propellers—state-of-the-art and brand-spanking-new. He'd lay odds the engines turning those babies were in similar shape. The bastards knew where to put their ill-gotten money.

He knifed upward directly underneath the pirate boat. With one hand on the hull to steady himself, he pulled out the tracking device and pondered where to put it. A powerful magnet would hold it in place, but he had to find something metal to attach it to. He eased back toward the propellers, which were idling at the moment.

It would be dangerous, but if he could get his arm past the blades and stick this thing inside the hull, the odds of it being discovered anytime soon were nil. He approached the props cautiously. He happened to love his fingers—his entire arm, in fact. As long as the boat didn't move while he did this, he should be fine.

He reached past the nearest prop carefully. There were only about six inches to spare between the turning blades and his biceps. He felt around with his fingertips and found a flat metal plate that was probably part of the engine mount. He slapped the tracker down onto the plate and then gave it a good tug. It didn't budge.

He eased his arm out of the narrow opening. If he were above water, he'd breathe a big sigh of relief. Now that it was done, he had to admit it had probably been a stupid maneuver to attempt. But all was well that ended well.

A massive explosion of turbulence slammed into him as the engines on the pirate vessel were abruptly jammed into gear.

Crap! He pulled back against the suction of the props with all his might but couldn't resist the force of hundreds of horsepower drawing him in. He got an arm against the hull a foot above the props, and then a foot on the other side of the twin blades. He gave a mighty shove and flung himself to the side.

Clear.

He swam down and away from the vessel as fast as he could go. Damn, that had been close. He searched in the gloom behind him for the white bulk of the *Sea Nymph,* but visibility was too poor to see it from here. He probably ought to head back to her before Steig got any bright ideas about giving chase to the pirates and accidentally left him behind. He hadn't had time to tell the captain he'd gone overboard in the moments before the attack. Until Steig went looking for Sunny and she told the captain he'd jumped, he was on his own.

He estimated he had another two minutes worth of air. He swam for the *Nymph,* angling deep to avoid any stray bullets. Sure enough, as he drew close to the yacht, occasional white tracks zinged into the water where bullets penetrated the sea.

He surfaced on the far side of the yacht from the pirate boat. The smooth white curve of the *Nymph*'s hull loomed over him as he breathed deeply. How to get back on board? The ship would be in full security lockdown, which meant the swimming deck would be retracted and locked that way. Unless the crew deployed a ladder or rope down to him, he was pretty much out of luck. He could shout, but over the cacophony of the gunfight still in full swing, no one would hear him. Besides, he didn't need to draw the attention of any armed pirates.

And then something alarming dawned on him. All the gunfire he was hearing was automatic. Since when did the local pirates carry heavy artillery like that? They usually used crappy World War II surplus M-1s and their ilk. A few pirates on any given crew would have modern weapons that could lay down a lot of lead fast, but it sounded as if they all were carrying AK-47's or better up there.

What was happening? Was Sunny okay? Had she done like he'd told her and gone to her cabin to hide? Somehow, he doubted she would follow his orders. A bit of a…nonconformist streak clung to her. Darned hippie.

He swam around to the rear of the ship, tested the slit where the swim deck was stowed and was able to wedge his fingers in it. He pulled himself partially out of the water and reached up for a ring that a waterskiing line would normally be routed through. He hauled himself out of the water and got his toes in the slit. It was painstaking work finding finger and toe holds, and he had a few tense moments when he nearly lost his grip. But finally, he managed to pull himself onto the lower aft deck, where he lay panting for a moment.

No time to rest and recuperate, though. He had to join the fight. The crew would no doubt mount a pitched defense of the bridge and the engine room. He could hook up with Steig's guys in the engine compartment, assuming they didn't shoot him as he approached.

He pressed to his feet and moved cautiously toward the passage that would take him belowdecks. Nothing like strolling into a war zone armed with a Speedo and an attitude. This might possibly be dumber than sticking his arm past that propeller. Why was it he'd volunteered to become a superhero, anyway?

Quiet footsteps slid across the carpet, drawing near. Sunny tensed, waiting in an agony of impatience. And then a leg came into view. Clothed in ragged denim and terminating in scratched and unpolished combat boots. No way would any member of Steig Carlson's crew get away with a crappy shoe shine like that. She swung the bottle with all her might, smashing it into the guy's knee. The bottle shattered and glass and booze sprayed everywhere. The pirate collapsed, shouting, his weapon discharging wildly at the ceiling.

She pounced out from behind the bar, shifting her spare bottle to her right hand. She brought it down over the guy's head fast and hard. It, too, smashed into smithereens with a satisfying thud.

The pirate lay still and unmoving, drenched in vodka. God bless those heavy Russian bottles. She didn't stick around to see if she'd killed the guy. Not when she heard shouting and running feet headed her way.

She looked around the salon in panic and on a hunch raced for the built-in sofa under a picture window. A yank at the seat cushion and, sure enough, it lifted to reveal a storage compartment. She shoved aside a pile of blankets, climbed inside and was encased in stuffy blackness. Feet and voices came into the salon. But they were muffled enough that she couldn't tell if they belonged to good guys or bad guys.

Frankly, she didn't care. She wanted no part of this fight whatsoever. She just wanted to curl up and jam her fists over her ears until it all went away.

Aiden ducked back around the corner just in time to avoid a barrage of bullets flying out of the engine room. "Hold your fire!" he shouted. "It's me. Aiden McKay."

"Cease fire!" someone bellowed.

He poked his head around the corner cautiously, prepared to yank back again fast. But this time no rain of bullets peppered the wall above his head. He moved forward into the engine room quickly. Someone pressed an assault rifle into his hand and he slung the shoulder strap over his head.

"Is that your formal combat attire?" someone asked drily.

He grimaced and started to make a snappy retort, but incoming gunfire silenced him. Apparently, he was just in time for a breakout from the engine room because the chief engineer, coincidentally a senior Special Forces man, hand signaled for them to move out.

For once, Steig's obsession with good order and discipline paid off. They'd practiced this drill a dozen times and every crew member knew exactly what to do. Aiden counted his position in line. Number five. Which meant his field of fire would be to the extreme left and high. He pointed his weapon in that direction as they burst into the first stateroom to clear it. Cabin by cabin they cleared the deck, leaving men behind to

ensure this deck stayed cleared and no pirates snuck in
behind them to hide.

"How's the fight going?" he asked the chief engineer during a break in the action while they waited on
instructions from Steig on the bridge as to where to go
next. Coordination was vital in a fight like this with
multiple skirmishes in separate locations.

"Rough. Bastards are numerous and well armed."

"Do we have any prisoners?"

"They're fighting to the death."

Since when did pirates do that? Aiden frowned. The
plan had been to capture a few of the pirates and lean
on them for information. The more they knew about the
pirates' organization, tactics and logistics, the easier it
would be to take them down. But if the pirates were
dying rather than surrendering, that could be a problem.

Steig's voice crackled over the radio, ordering their
team to secure the mid-decks while his men cleared the
topside. Aiden was just spinning into a tiny bathroom
and clearing the empty shower when a shout went up
outside. He poked his head out cautiously.

The chief engineer was grinning. "They just bugged
out. Pirate vessel's retreating at a high rate of speed."

"Tell Steig I got the tracker set on that boat. We
don't have to follow right away. Let them get out of visual range."

Roving teams of crewmen started clearing the yacht
room by room. There was no way they were allowing a
single pirate to stow away aboard the *Nymph* and sabotage it later. The six bodies of the dead pirates would
be given a funeral at sea later, when the ship was fully
secured.

The crew debriefing after the attack would be very interesting, indeed. Who in the hell had those men been, and who had trained and armed them? He'd lay odds they were no ordinary pirates. Or worse, they were a sign of times to come when pirates got a substantial upgrade in gear and training.

Aiden hurried toward Sunny's cabin to give her the all clear. She must be scared out of her mind. He reached her door and knocked on it gently. "Sunny? It's Aiden. You can come out now. We're safe and the pirates are gone."

Nothing. He waited for a few seconds and knocked a little louder. Still nothing. Panic blossomed in his gut along with a sick certainty that she hadn't obeyed his order to come down here and lock herself in.

He checked the door handle. Unlocked. Swearing forcefully, he barged into her room. Empty. He was going to kill her when he found her. Assuming the pirates hadn't found her first and—

Oh, God. Snatched her.

He raced out of the cabin, shouting for Steig. He tore onto the bridge, panting. Thankfully, every hand that reached for a sidearm recognized him in time not to blow his head off. "Sunny's not in her cabin," he announced. "Has anyone seen her?"

"I assumed she was with Gemma in the panic room," Steig answered grimly. "When was the last time you saw her?"

"In the salon."

One of the sailors piped up. "We found a pirate in the salon. Dead from a head wound. Looked like blunt trauma."

Christ. His worst nightmare come true. A civilian, a woman he was responsible for, hell, a woman he was interested in and attracted to, made a victim because she'd been too close to him. This was exactly why he never got close to other people! Guys in the superhero business couldn't afford any personal attachments.

Had the pirates seized her to use as a hostage? To ensure a safe getaway? What would they do to her after they were clear of the *Nymph?* With every new question, his gut twisted a little tighter. This was his fault. He'd gone back to his old ways, been wining and dining the hot chick instead of doing his job and watching out for pirates. When would he learn? Women and work—at least his work—did not mix. Ever.

Sick with worry, he listened as Steig gave terse orders over the ship's public address system. All hands were to stop what they were doing and search for Sunny.

"How come we didn't find her when we were hunting for pirate stowaways?" Aiden demanded.

"We're not finished clearing the ship yet," Steig replied. "Maybe she'll still turn up." But the Swede didn't sound convinced.

"What's left to be searched?" Aiden demanded.

"The upper decks."

"I'm on it. Starting in the salon. I'll see if I can find some hint there of what happened to her."

He barreled into the same room where they'd been having a romantic dinner only an hour ago. It was impossible to miss the pool of blood, broken glass and the overwhelming smell of lemon vodka. Clearly, there'd been a fight by the bar. She'd put up a hell of a struggle if the damage was any indication. He spied bullet holes in the ceiling and his heart dropped to his feet. But then he registered that it looked like an uninterrupted trail of holes, as if the fusillade of bullets hadn't hit anyone in its track across the room.

He worked his way outward from the bar, methodically searching for clues. It was nearly impossible to go slowly, to be thorough. But he dared not miss anything important in his panic. He'd almost finished searching the room when he got to the banquet-style sofa under one of the big windows. He lifted it and leaped back with a shout of surprise. The lid banged shut on whoever was hiding inside.

He grabbed for the pistol at his hip, yanking it clear just as the sofa seat raised up again.

"Jeez, Aiden, did you have to slam the seat down on me like that? You almost broke my nose."

He jerked his weapon up and away from Sunny and holstered it, sagging in relief. "You scared the living hell out of me, woman."

"Are the pirates gone?"

"Yes. The ship's being cleared as we speak. What happened in here?" He glanced over at the stains by the bar.

"I, umm, clobbered a pirate."

"You killed him."

"Really? I just hit him as hard as I could."

"With what?"

"A bottle. Vodka, I think."

"Effective." He might be speaking calmly, but his heart was pounding a mile a minute. His legs shockingly shaky, he walked to the intercom and pressed the button. "I found Sunny, Steig. She was hiding in the salon. She's all right."

A tinny "thank God" came back over the speaker.

He turned back to her. "Would you care to explain why you didn't do as I told you and go to your cabin?"

"I tried to. Really. But a pirate was in the hall and then someone shot him and I backed in here. Then I heard someone coming and hid behind the bar and he had bad boots and I knew he was a pirate and I hit him with my bottle and I didn't know what to do and..."

He pressed his fingers gently over her mouth to stop her babbling, which was becoming more hysterical by the second. "It's over. You're safe. The pirates are gone."

And that was all it took. For the third time that day, she sobbed in his arms. They were starting to make a habit of this. At least this time he wasn't wearing a shirt for her to ruin with her running makeup. He had to admit it wasn't all bad having a soft, sexy, sweet-smelling female nestled in his arms as if he was a conquering hero who could defend her from the entire world.

"I was so scared," she whispered. "And I was so worried about you—" She broke off and took a step back to glare up at him. "What in the world were you doing, jumping overboard like that? You could've been killed!" She smacked him across the upper arm with enough force to sting.

"Oww! I was doing my job, thank you very much. I planted a radio tracking device on the pirate vessel so we can track it."

"You did what?" Her voice rose in growing outrage

and she whacked him a second time. "Don't you ever do anything that dangerous again, Aiden McKay!"

She opened her mouth to berate him some more, but being an efficient man, he took the most expedient route to silencing her and kissed her.

And all of that fiery fury sparking and crackling on her skin was suddenly turned on him. Except in an instant it transformed to fiery passion that burned him alive. Suddenly, her body was pressed against his, her arms twined around his neck, her fingers tangled in his hair the same way their tongues tangled together.

He should stop this. Right now. Panic erupted in his head, but somehow it got all tangled up with his panic from earlier, and then his relief that she was alive and unharmed overwhelmed everything else in his head.

How his arms got around her, how he dragged her up against him even tighter, how his thigh rode between hers, he had no idea. The moves came back to him more naturally than he could believe. It was so easy to slip his fingers under her shoulder straps. To slip them off her shoulders. To taste the smooth flesh exposed there.

Man, it had been so long. Craving for this most basic human contact rolled through him like a tidal wave, drowning the tiny voice in his head warning him not to go here, that this would end in disaster, that people would get hurt.

Who was he kidding? This was who he was. He'd been a ladies' man his entire life, and no empty promise to himself that he was done with women was going to change that. A lifetime's worth of habits wasn't going to change on some whim that he should turn over a new leaf.

He backed her up against the wall, and hands were everywhere. Hers, his. Clothes fell away from warm satin skin. His mouth was on her flesh, her mouth on his. It was a mad, chaotic rush of long-denied craving breaking free, until it dawned on him abruptly that they were naked and on the floor and about to consummate their very young relationship.

At long last, the voice inside his head shouted at him loudly enough to be heard. It screamed at him to stop this madness. He froze. It was impossible to ignore the press of her breasts against his chest or the sleek softness of her belly against his, but he tried. "Uhh, Sunny. This is happening pretty fast. We should cool it. I don't want to rush you."

"Rush, dammit!" she panted.

The little voice in his brain swore violently. She was supposed to call a halt to this. Then he'd have an excuse to back away from the abyss. To keep his flimsy promises to himself. She wasn't supposed to cling to him as if she couldn't get enough of him or have that sexy little catch in her breath.

Holding her was like hugging a volcano. She burned him alive. All the carefully constructed ice in his soul just melted away before the force of her sex appeal. He tried in desperation, "It's not gentlemanly to take advantage of you after you've had such a scare—"

"Distract me."

Apparently, that hadn't been the right argument to use with her. She tugged his head close and kissed him until his toes curled and all thoughts of behaving himself evaporated in the white heat of her passion. In fact, all thought evaporated. What remained was blinding lust pounding through him until he thought he'd explode.

He jolted when her hand grasped him, guiding him into the core of the volcano. *No! Oh, no. Oh, yes.* Sensations he hadn't allowed himself to feel in years burst across his brain in a fiery inferno. How had he ever turned his back on this? What in the hell had he been thinking? The pleasure was so intense as to be almost painful.

And Sunny…she was warm and soft and wild, pulling him inside her being with an abandon that was nothing short of miraculous. In short, she was everything he wished for in a woman and more.

He tried to hold back. He really did. But she surged impatiently beneath him, her legs wrapping around his hips and urging him onward. And then she laughed. Not in amusement, but in pure, unadulterated joy. He was completely seduced by her carefree exultation. She threw herself into making love with as much passion as she did everything else. But then, why should that surprise him?

Even he couldn't ignore the magic between them. The way their bodies fit together perfectly. The delicious slide of flesh on sweaty flesh. The way the incoherent sounds she was making drove him out of his mind. The way her fingernails raked across his back in sharp, pleasant counterpoint to the massive pleasure she gave him.

Something broke within him. That wall of restraint, of distance from the human race, that he'd built so carefully over the past two years crashed down around him in a spectacular implosion. He reached desperately for its tattered remnants, but it was gone. Just…gone. What else was he to do? He gave himself over to Sunny completely.

They found a rhythm quickly and drove each other closer and closer to oblivion. It might be raw lust spurred on by sheer relief at being alive, but it was powerful stuff. She stripped away all his civilization, all his polished manners, all his polite detachment. He rode the wave building between them, losing himself in it, letting it carry him away from himself completely. It was a glorious journey, made sweeter by the vague knowledge that there would be a high price to pay for this moment of weakness.

Sunny's breath caught and her eyes glazed over.

She gasped. Paused. Gasped again, and then let out a long, shuddering moan that sent him right over the edge. He relished every moment of their epic climax, memorizing it, hoarding it for all the long, lonely nights to come.

They collapsed together, spent.

His mind was one-hundred-percent, completely, totally blown. In all the wild years, all the wild partying, all the wild women, he'd never experienced anything that came even remotely close to *that*. To *her*.

He was able to savor the moment for a few more seconds before reality reared its ugly head and began to jaw at him. He braced himself for an onslaught of guilt he fully deserved.

Even in the worst of his wild days, at his most drunk and most debauched, he'd never, ever had wild monkey sex with women who expected anything more than that from him. He'd always made the rules of engagement

crystal clear well before said monkey sex commenced—
a little fun, a lot of pleasure, no commitments, no second dates. And yet, tonight, he'd blown off his most sacred tenet without a moment's thought.

He also didn't jump nice girls like Sunny on a living room floor where someone might walk in on them at any second. "I'm sorry," he muttered. "That was thoughtless and selfish of me."

"You mean having fantastic sex?" she asked, sounding confused.

"No. I mean doing it here. Now. Like this. It was all wrong."

"What's wrong with this?" She still sounded confused. "I thought it was darned near perfect."

"Yes, but...on the floor? In the salon? When you're all upset and frightened?" He shook his head. "It was my mistake. I take the blame."

She pushed on his shoulders and he rolled away from her. Sitting up, he reached for her nearest clothes and passed them to her in silence. She snatched them out of his hands and yanked them on.

Her anger he understood. It made much more sense than that sleepy, delirious smile she'd been sporting a minute ago. He'd be furious, too, if he'd been in her position.

"You're a jerk," she declared.

"You're right. I'm sorry." He wasn't about to pick a fight with her when he was so clearly in the wrong.

She stood and marched over to the door in magnificent fury while he continued to sit on the floor, one arm propped on his upraised knee. She opened the door, pausing to look over her shoulder. "The hell of it is you don't even know what I'm talking about!"

He frowned. "What are you talking about?"

"God, you're a colossal jerk." And on that note, her nose went up in the air and she stormed out of the salon to destinations unknown.

He was worse than a colossal jerk. He was a fraud. He'd spent years telling himself how noble and pure he'd become. How he was a superhero in more than just his ability to swim like a fish. That he'd embraced the nobler ideals of selflessness and service to mankind. And it was all a crock. The first beautiful, passionate woman that came along, he fell on her like a horny beast and had his way with her. It didn't make one bit of difference that she'd been willing and seemed to enjoy herself. Even if she didn't know it, he'd betrayed her as badly as he'd betrayed himself.

What in the hell was *she* talking about, then? Why was she so mad? Did she know who he was? Did she know of his sleazy reputation with women? Surely not.

Regardless of what she knew or didn't know, he shouldn't have taken advantage of her emotional distress and overwrought state to seduce her. It had been wrong on every possible level, and he felt like as big a jerk as she claimed he was. But for some reason, he got the impression she was talking about something else entirely. Clearly, he was missing something. But *what?*

Chapter 4

Sunny's eyes burned as she emerged onto the deck the next morning in glaring sunshine. The big cry she had last night probably hadn't helped her eyes feel any less salty and grit filled. Why Aiden's insensitivity should upset her like that, she couldn't fathom.

She'd been around enough men in her day to know they could act like completely clueless louts without having the slightest intention to do so nor any idea that they were doing it. But to apologize after having just given her the best sexual experience of her life? To call it a *mistake* to her face? That went beyond clueless to royal jerkdom.

Of course, she'd been a willing participant in said mistake, too. It wasn't all his fault. She knew it was stupid to go for the gusto with a man she hardly knew and who clearly came from a completely different world from hers. She stacked up her stupidity to her overall stress at everything she'd been through the past few days. Okay, the past few years. It was hard making her way alone in the world, particularly in her chosen career of documentary filmmaking. She lacked both funds and experience, and without one it was impossible to gain the other.

"Sleep well?" Steig asked cheerfully from behind her.

"Uhh, yes. Thank you," she mumbled. "Where's Aiden?"

"Swimming."

She glanced out at the crowded port in front of her. "In all of that?" A jumble of ships, varying from decrepit, two-man fishing boats to giant container ships clogged what she recognized as the Port of Djibouti.

Irritation flitted across Steig's Nordic features. "Yes. In all of that. He insists upon guarding the *Nymph*."

"From whom?" she asked curiously.

"Pirates. They've been known to seize ships and steal cargo right here in the harbor. They are…what's the word in English?…brazen."

"That's the word," she answered, searching the choppy water for any sign of Aiden. "How long has he been out there?"

"Several hours."

"Hours? Isn't he getting tired?"

Steig laughed. "Not him."

She frowned. Ocean swimming was hard work even in the best of conditions, and these turbulent waters were far from ideal. "I don't see his bubble trail."

"He's not using scuba gear," Steig replied.

"Didn't Dr. Jones say something about him holding his breath a long time?"

"Did she, now?" was the sailor's noncommittal answer.

She turned to press the man for a real answer to her question, but the Swede was saved by the sight of Aiden's lithe body knifing up out of the water in a shockingly dolphinlike move. "Oh! There he is," she exclaimed.

She moved over to the rail to wave to him, but he'd already dived again. She waited for him to surface again. Two minutes passed. Three. He might be able to hold his breath a long time, but she was getting nervous. As she counted off another thirty seconds in her head, panic erupted.

"Steig!" she called out. "He's been under too long. Something's wrong!"

"He's fine," the sailor answered casually.

She scanned the water again. She must have missed him surfacing. Maybe he'd gone around to the other side of the *Sea Nymph*. It really was an unsafe water practice not to have a swim buddy. Not that she had any intention of getting in the water with him.

He popped up, treading water easily this time.

"Aiden!" she shouted, waving her arms at him.

He looked her square in the eye and dived, disappearing infuriatingly from sight. Moments later, she heard the splashing of someone climbing aboard the swim deck extended at water level behind the yacht. She hurried aft.

"What on earth were you doing out there?" she demanded. "You could've been hurt or killed!"

"I was keeping you from getting hurt or killed," he replied stiffly.

Damn. He was back to being the polite, distant man who would never dream of making passionate love to her again on the floor. "You shouldn't have been out there alone."

He shrugged. "I'm a good swimmer. And I like swimming alone."

"Why?" To her, the wonder of the ocean had always been something to be shared. It was why she'd filmed it. So other people could share her love of the sea with her.

"It's peaceful," he answered. "I like the silence."

She knew the feeling. There was a certain magic to the sea. A ballet in its constant movement. And sometimes, when the noise of the world became too much, she felt drawn to the primal wordlessness of it all.

"Still," she admonished. "You should buddy swim, particularly if you're expecting trouble. I hear this port's far from safe."

That earned Steig an annoyed glance at the far end of the deck. "We are trouble free this morning."

"Have you brought the *Nymph* to Djibouti to make repairs?"

He nodded.

"Then I guess this is as good a time as any for me to disembark," she announced quietly. "I'll go pack my things."

If she'd secretly been hoping for him to stop her, to invite her to tarry aboard the *Nymph,* to repeat last night's encounter, she was sadly disappointed. He turned away, toweling himself off, and didn't even watch her go.

Tears welled up in her eyes as she made her way to her cabin. Of course, packing took approximately thirty seconds. And it only took that long because Gemma had insisted that Sunny keep the cosmetics and toiletries the doctor had so kindly shared with her. She slung her sea bag over her shoulder and headed topside. No sign of Aiden.

Steig made docking the big yacht look like child's play. Sunny eyed the pier cautiously. The mostly men ashore were a mishmash of nationalities and cultures. Westerners in jeans and T-shirts, Muslims in traditional robes and Somali in loose, togalike wraps jostled on the pier.

She watched two of the *Nymph*'s crew tie off the vessel and deploy a gangplank to shore. Still no sign of Aiden. Wow. He was a bigger jerk than she'd realized. Wasn't even going to say goodbye after their one-night stand, was he? Dismay and hurt tussled in her chest for supremacy.

She made her way to the gangplank, and Steig materialized from somewhere belowdecks. "Miss Jordan, it has been a pleasure having you aboard."

"Thank you for saving my life. And please pass my thanks to Aiden, too."

"I will. Do you know where you're going?"

"No. I'll find somewhere to stay until I can get my bearings."

"May I recommend lodgings for you?"

She winced. She highly doubted she could afford any place he would recommend, given the luxury he and his guests were accustomed to. "Of course," she said politely.

He pulled out a business card and a pen and scribbled something on the back of it. "An American security firm operates this place. You'll be safe there. And I dare say if you flash a little leg they'll put you up for free."

Frowning, she took the card he thrust into her hand.

"Don't walk there. Take a cab. Djibouti City can be a lawless place. The civil war was not that long ago. And it's a conservative Muslim town. A Western woman like you needs to be especially careful."

He shook her hand vigorously, and then there was nothing to do but leave. She'd delayed as long as she could without looking stupid. But Aiden had never shown up. What. A. Jerk. What on earth had she been thinking to make love with him? Yet again, her impulsive nature had led her down exactly the wrong path. She *had* to learn to do the opposite of what her instincts urged her to do.

In a horrendous funk, she disembarked and let the throng swallow her. She was predictably jostled and groped a few times but made her way to a city street without any truly serious trouble. She flagged down a cab that was more rust than steel. The driver spoke no English, but he nodded and smiled when she showed him the address on Steig's card. The jalopy jerked into the flow of humans, carts, trucks and buses. The dust was chokingly thick and the heat stifling. But thankfully, the cab ride was not long.

The vehicle pulled to a stop, and she handed over the fare in U.S. dollars. She probably should have haggled the price down a few dimes, but she was too depressed by Aiden's rejection to bother. And she was so close to broke that a few cents didn't really matter at this point.

She climbed out of the cab and looked around in surprise. She'd assumed Steig had sent her to a hotel. But no such building was anywhere in sight. In fact, all that loomed before her was a tall hurricane fence topped by rolls of barbed wire and a gate. Across the street was a seawall and water beyond. What the heck?

A guard shack that looked like a miniature fort stood beside the tall gate. A maze of cement barriers blocked direct entry through it. Nobody loitered by the fence, and on the other side, a man wearing jeans and a casual shirt sported an enormous rifle of some kind.

This was clearly an industrial area. How in the heck was she supposed to get to a hotel from here? For lack of any other options, she made her way to the guard shack and prayed someone there spoke English, or at least knew the word *phone.*

A Caucasian guard stared at her as she approached the shack. "Do you speak English?" she asked.

"I'm from N'Awlins, but she be English we speak in dat dere Big Easy," the guy drawled, grinning, in a thick Cajun accent.

"Thank God. I think there's been some sort of mistake. A friend suggested I come here to find lodgings."

"Aiden McKay?"

She blinked, startled. "Actually, a friend of his." Aiden had arranged this for her? What did it mean? Was he signaling that he cared about her a little, after all? Or was it just his man's way of offering an oblique apology?

"McKay called a little while ago. Told us to be on the lookout for you. Come on in. I'll need to see some ID first and get you a visitor's badge."

"What is this place?"

"Private security business. We leased this base when the French Foreign Legion moved out of it. We provide guards for ships in the region. Do a little pirate hunting, too."

"Ahh. So that's how you know Aiden. Did he tell you about the attack yesterday?"

The man's friendly gaze went granite hard and just as transparent, which was to say, not at all. He said stiffly, "I can't talk about operational information, ma'am."

"Sorry. So you run a hotel in here, too?"

"Not exactly. But there's a ton of barracks space, and we occasionally share as a favor to a friend."

"Aiden's a friend?"

"Hell, yeah."

Huh. Interesting. She followed the guard inside the shack, coughed up what ID she had and was escorted by another man—a mercenary, apparently—to a two-story building that looked like government-built housing in a bad section of an American city.

The room he showed her to was spartan but clean and reasonably comfortable. Okay, she had a temporary roof over her head. Now what?

Not even a hint of an answer to that one came to her. Every time she closed her eyes and tried to think about her future, the memory of Aiden's arms around her, his mouth on hers, his body claiming hers, came to mind and pushed all other thoughts aside. She silently screamed at him to get out of her head. But it didn't do a lick of good.

Aiden felt like screaming at someone for no good reason. The impulse was startling and unpleasant.

"What do you mean you don't know if she went to the American base? I told you to send her there."

"I gave her the address, Aiden," Steig answered, "but she's a grown woman. She can go where she wants."

He needed to know she was safe, dammit. This town was a cesspool of bottom feeders that would love to snap up a tender, tasty morsel like Sunny Jordan. Aiden paced restlessly. "Call them. Find out if she went there."

Frowning, Steig dialed. Aiden listened to the Swede's end of the conversation impatiently. "…that's right. Sunny Jordan…Brown hair. Hazel eyes. Attractive… yes. Great legs, that's her…Thanks."

Steig ended the call. "She's there."

Aiden felt like throwing up in his relief.

"So. What are you going to do about her?"

Aiden looked up at his old friend's question. "What do you mean?"

"You're not just going to let her walk away, are you?" Steig demanded.

"What am I supposed to do? Like you said, she's a grown woman. She can make her own decisions. And she left the *Nymph.*"

"Did you ask her to stay?"

Hell, hadn't that been what making love to her last night without laying down the rules of engagement had been? He turned away from Steig and stared out at the pier full of questionable characters. He winced at the idea of Sunny out there somewhere all by herself fending off slimeballs and criminals. But she'd *left.* Walked off the *Nymph* this morning and never looked back. He knew. He'd been watching her.

Logic said he was well rid of her. She had a knack

for breaking down his defenses. Made him feel things that distracted him from his primary mission. Made him break his promises to himself.

Like it or not, he was different from other men. From other humans. He didn't have the luxury of allowing himself a normal life. He held himself apart from the people around him for good reason. His work was incredibly dangerous, not to mention the rest of them didn't understand what it was like to have his special ability. With it came special responsibility to use it for good. And that left him with no time for a personal life.

No, he was better off without Sunny Jordan.

"There you are, Aiden. Ready for your physical?"

Gemma. He'd forgotten that she wanted to check his breathing on dry land after his swim this morning. "Coming." He sighed. He followed her down to her research lab belowdecks.

As she hooked him up to electrodes and passed him a respirometer, she asked, "How are you feeling physically?"

"Okay."

"Psychologically?"

He shrugged. She knew him too well, dammit, and pounced. "What's going on? Are you feeling more of a sense of withdrawal from humanity?"

The hell of it was he'd signed a contract when he entered her research project to share all pertinent information with her for research purposes. "Actually, exactly the opposite, Doc."

"Ahh. We're talking about Sunny, I gather. You like her?"

"Doesn't matter. She doesn't like me."

Gemma snorted. "Men can be so dumb."

He stared, dumbfounded. Since when had supergeek Gemma become such an expert on relationships?

The doctor declared, "She cried all night last night. I heard it through the wall. Kept me awake for hours. She's crazy about you."

"But she was crying…"

Another snort. "Dumber than dirt," Gemma pronounced him.

"I don't understand."

"Obviously. She's waiting for you to make a move. She set up that big, elaborate date with you to signal that she's interested in you."

"She said it was an apology."

"Aiden, think about it. You used to date women all the time. She put on makeup and high heels and a sexy dress for you. Even I know she was sending you a message."

A message he'd received loud and clear. Like a proper Neanderthal, he'd thrown her to the floor and made passionate love to her in response, in fact. *And she'd walked away this morning and never looked back.*

But there was that whole business about her calling him a jerk last night. She'd been right, of course. He hadn't treated her with the courtesy and consideration she deserved. Although he'd gotten the feeling at the time that he was missing something when she'd declared his jerkness. As if she thought he was a jerk for an entirely different reason than he did.

He frowned. "So, what do you think I should do now, Doc?"

"Find her. Talk to her. Tell her how you feel."

How he felt? Hell, he hadn't the slightest idea how he *felt*. He spent most of his life trying not to feel anything. It made keeping his distance from humanity so much easier.

Gemma interrupted his train of thought by announcing, "I spoke to Leland Winston a little while ago. He wanted me to remind you of your conference call with him this afternoon."

Aiden scowled. Leland would no doubt want a detailed report of last night's attack on his yacht and the extent of the damages to the *Nymph*. And knowing Leland, he'd want to go over the plan in detail to find and capture the pirates now that the tracker was in place. Ugh. The call could take most of the afternoon.

And then Aiden was scheduled to dine with the Djiboutian Minister of Trade this evening. Damn. What he really wanted to do was go check on Sunny. What he *needed* to do was stay far, far away from her.

"Here. Breathe into this," Gemma ordered, holding out the respirometer again to measure his lung capacity.

Scowling, he shoved the respirometer in his mouth.

Chapter 5

Sunny took a deep breath and approached a man who looked like some sort of harbormaster. It had taken her nearly three days to find this guy and get permission to speak to him. He took one derisive look up and down her Western-garbed frame and sneered.

"Excuse me, sir," she murmured deferentially. "I'm looking for a ship. I was told you know everything and everyone who sails in this harbor."

"And I'm very busy. I have an entire harbor full of ships," he snapped. "Pick one."

"This one is special. It's about the size of a commercial whale fisher but not rigged for fishing, all black, narrow prow, twin propellers. Fast."

She was sure she caught a flash of recognition in the man's dark gaze. "What's its name and how's it flagged?"

"I didn't see a name and she displayed no flag."

"Every ship is required to have a name and a flag."

"Well, this one didn't."

"Then I can't help you."

More like he wouldn't help her. He knew something. At least she had a little more information than before. The ship had been here before, probably to refuel. And where a ship berthed once, it was likely to berth again.

If she hung out down here for a few days—or weeks—and kept an eye on the traffic, maybe she could spot the ship that had sunk her boat. Once she knew its name and registry, she could demand compensation from the vessel's owners. It wasn't a great plan, but it was better than no plan at all.

And Lord knew, it was better than spending the past two nights crying into her pillow and trying to forget her encounter with Aiden. That plan hadn't worked at all.

She found a perch on a seawall out of the cranky harbormaster's way but overlooking the harbor. The port was a busy place and she lost herself in its rhythms as she watched and waited for the black ship to show itself. It took a few hours, but she managed to achieve a mindless state where, as long as she didn't think about anything specific, she also didn't think constantly of Aiden. But the exercise left her feeling empty.

Late that afternoon, she was half dozing under an umbrella she'd bought off a kid for a dollar to ward off the sun when a strong hand grabbed her arm, startling her badly. She let out a little scream of surprise and whipped around, prepared to wield the umbrella like a sword to defend herself.

"What the hell are you doing out here all by yourself, Sunny?"

Aiden. And just like that, everything she'd been doing her darnedest to purge from her system came flooding back. Her fingers and toes tingled, and she suddenly felt alive again. He glared at her furiously. So much for Mr. Distant, apparently.

"You're the only person who's assaulted me and scared me half to death since I set foot onshore," she snapped. Her heart was racing and her stomach fluttering madly. It was just the scare he'd given her. Nothing more. "You could've been some bad guy out to mug me or worse."

"Exactly," he ground out. "What were you thinking sitting here like this ignoring everything going on around you, just asking for trouble?"

She frowned. "I'm watching the harbor."

"Why?" he asked incredulously.

"I'm looking for the ship that hit me so I can demand repayment for the loss of my boat."

"Are you crazy? That ship's crew will slit your throat long before they'll cough up a cent to you."

Her gut said he was right. But her stubborn side wasn't about to admit that to him.

"Look, Sunny. This place is beyond dangerous. You need to get out of here. Go somewhere safe."

"Like where?"

"Hell, I don't know. Go home."

She didn't *have* a home. But beyond that, the words hurt. Yet again, he was trying to get rid of her. What had she done to make this man dislike her so much? He'd liked her well enough when they'd been making love....

Maybe that was it. Maybe he resented her for seducing him. Although the way she remembered it… "You kissed me first, you know," she blurted.

"Excuse me?"

"You started it. I didn't seduce you. You seduced me." Although truth be told, she'd darn well been a willing participant once he got the ball rolling. But that wasn't the point at the moment.

He looked around uncomfortably. "Do we have to talk about that here?"

"What's wrong with here? Do you see somebody within earshot who's going to tell all your friends that you hooked up with some penniless chick you fished out of the ocean?"

"Penniless—" he spluttered. "Like I care about that?"

"Then *what* is your *problem* with me?" She was really getting sick of his cryptic comments that made no sense at all.

"I—" He broke off. "Not here."

Ooooh. He was so frustrating! "You don't own me. I can do whatever I want, and what I *want* is to sit here until I find the boat that ran me over. In the meantime, I *want* you to go away."

He looked stricken. It was there in his eyes for just a second, and then that stiff, polite look he defaulted to came over him. But a second was long enough. Remorse coursed through her. She didn't really want him to go away. She couldn't think about anything but him when he was gone, and when he was with her, she couldn't look at anything or anyone else. He completely filled her senses.

He turned on his heel and took a step.

"Wait," she cried.

He turned around to face her but didn't take the step back toward her.

"Why did you come looking for me?" she asked.

"To—" a long pause "—apologize." She knew as sure as he was standing there that wasn't what he'd been about to say. He mumbled awkwardly, "You know. For not seeing you off when you left. I had business to attend to," he added lamely.

"Oh." He could deflate her faster than anyone she'd ever met. "Thanks," she mumbled.

He nodded once, a small, uncomfortable jerk of his head, and turned again to walk away. This time she didn't call him back.

She spent the next hour until sunset staring at the harbor through a watery curtain of tears. That damned black ship could've sailed right past her and she wouldn't have seen it.

Even she wasn't suicidal enough to hang around the harbor after dark. She hurried back toward the American mercenary base as twilight fell over the city. Of course, she'd failed to take into account the Maghrib, or sunset prayer, of the Muslims who comprised most of the local population. She ended up ducking into a rug shop to wait out the nasal call to prayer that reverberated from the city's minarets and the subsequent prayer period.

When she was able to resume walking back toward the compound, dark was falling fast. It didn't help that she took a wrong turn somewhere. She knew the general direction she had to travel, but this neighborhood was rougher than she remembered.

Long stretches of dark shadows swallowed what sidewalks there were. She detoured into an alley to get around a stack of barrels taller than she was, and that was when the men jumped her. There were three of them. Little more than teenagers but still dangerous looking.

One of them yelled at her in what sounded like Arabic.

"I'm sorry. I don't understand you," she tried in English. Not that she really had to understand the guy to know he wanted her valuables. She sidled back toward the street.

"Gimme moh-nee, lady," the kid snarled in terrible English.

"Oh! You want some money," she replied in exaggerated comprehension. A few more steps and she'd be back in sight of the street. Not that anyone would necessarily help her. But maybe someone would call an ambulance for her if this went badly.

She fumbled in her pockets. Another step.

"Stop!" the kid yelled at her. "No move." A wicked-looking knife appeared in his hand. She froze. The other two youths flanked her from behind, closing in on her menacingly. She didn't look back at them, but she had no doubt they were armed, as well.

And then, without warning, a flurry of movement exploded behind her. Something big and fast-moving slammed into one of the teens. Two bodies went down, rolling in the dirt. The second teen in the rear jumped into the fray. Whoever her rescuer was, he had his hands full with holding the knife of the first attacker away from his throat while fending off the fists of the second one.

The teen who'd been yelling at her rushed past her toward the fight. She took advantage of his distraction to kick him in the privates as hard as she could as he passed her. He went down shouting and swearing in multiple languages.

She turned to run but then caught a flash of blond hair in the tangle of struggling bodies. *Aiden.* She raced to the fight and kicked one of the teens in the back, right over a kidney, with all her might. He writhed away from the fight, moaning and swearing as he clutched at his back.

Down to an even fight, Aiden was able to force the knife away from his face and fling the kid off him. He leaped to his feet and grabbed her by the arm. He bit out a single terse instruction. "Run."

They fled side by side. Aiden seemed to know where he was going and guided her by the elbow as they sprinted away from the scene of the attack. Shouts followed them but faded into the distance soon enough. They ran for several more blocks, and then Aiden waved her to a walk.

Panting, she was grateful to slow down and catch her breath. A wheezing noise made her look over at Aiden in alarm. "Are you hurt?" she demanded. "Did that guy cut you?"

"No. Asthma," he gasped.

"Do you have an inhaler?" she asked urgently. He looked ghastly. In the light spilling out of a restaurant, he looked almost gray.

He fumbled in his jacket pocket until she reached

forward to help. She found the slim metal canister and plastic mouthpiece and held them to his mouth quickly.

"Long, slow breath in," she told him. Her sister'd had asthma as a kid, but never this bad. Aiden sounded and looked on the verge of passing out. "Hold the medicine in your lungs as long as you can."

He did as she instructed, exhaling explosively after just a few seconds. Not good.

"We'll give that a minute to open your airways a little, and then we'll do another puff."

She glanced over his shoulder worriedly, on the lookout for their attackers. She thought she saw some movement a few blocks back that looked suspicious. "Can you move at all?" she whispered. "Someone's coming."

He straightened and assumed a defensive stance immediately. She saw the effort it cost him and heard him fighting to control his breathing, to slow it and keep it even. But it wasn't working. He was inhaling too fast and shallow. He'd never make it through another fight. They had to hide.

She looked around fast. "This way." She guided him into the restaurant, which was dim and mostly empty. He stumbled a little but righted himself beside her. As long as he could walk, they'd be okay. But there was no way she could bodily drag him anywhere.

She stopped in the narrow hallway that led to the kitchen and made him take another long pull on his inhaler. Thankfully, this one seemed to have more effect. A little color came back into his face and his breathing slowed slightly. He only looked half-dead now.

In a few moments, he muttered, "We've got to keep

moving. They're big on vengeance in this town. Those kids will call in their friends and family to hunt us."

She nodded and followed him back outside. A trio of men was moving toward them. She looked around frantically, trying to get her bearings. They actually weren't far from the piers. "Is the *Nymph* still docked?" she asked as he steered her away from the advancing men.

"Yes."

Thank God. It was their best bet for safety.

The next hour was a nightmare. Aiden's condition deteriorated until he was barely conscious. They couldn't move fast or he immediately went into severe respiratory distress. Which meant they had to sneak most of the way to the docks. And she was no ninja-stealth expert.

But eventually, she peered across the street and spotted the sleek outline of the *Sea Nymph*. And a more beautiful sight she'd never seen. "Almost there," she encouraged Aiden.

He nodded wearily. She felt him gather himself to move one last time. She had to give him credit for determination and self-discipline. In spite of her fear of overdosing him, she'd had to give him two more puffs of his inhaler to keep him conscious. But he'd fought for all his worth to stay with her.

"Put your arm across my shoulders," she instructed. Their height difference made the position reasonably comfortable, but as his weight rested more and more upon her, she became vividly aware of just what a large man he was. His lean swimmer's physique and perfect proportions tricked the eye into not noticing the volume of muscle he carried.

"A few more steps," she grunted.

And then they were there. A guard on the deck of the *Nymph* spotted them and immediately spoke into his collar. In a few seconds, a pair of sailors were quickly extending the gangplank to them. The men rushed forward and took Aiden out of her grasp and half carried him aboard.

All of a sudden she was alone on the dock, unsure of what to do. No one had given her permission to board the *Nymph*. But she didn't relish making her way across the city to her room by herself after the scary attack.

A struggle broke out on the *Nymph* as Aiden wrestled free of the men supporting him. "What are you waiting for?" he threw at her. "Come aboard so the ship can be secured." And on that note, he passed out. The sailors caught his body as it collapsed toward the deck.

Not a ringingly warm invitation, but she wasn't about to turn it down. Her worry for him overrode all of her stubborn and argumentative urges. She hurried aboard the *Nymph* and followed the crewmen as they carried him down to the infirmary. Gemma slapped a nebulizer over Aiden's face with terse observations that he was a fool and that he would be fine. Sunny could definitely agree with the doctor on the first score.

The crew, consummate professionals that they were, treated her as politely as ever. She sensed no judgment or derision as they showed her to her old room and, yet again, supplied her with pajamas and a toothbrush. She had to quit coming aboard this ship with nothing but the clothes on her back. But she had to admit its luxurious embrace made her feel safe like she hadn't felt since she'd left the vessel.

She spent another restless night, but this one wasn't punctuated by tears. Only worry for Aiden's health. The next morning found her on the sundeck under a striped umbrella sipping hot, black coffee and nibbling at a croissant. Steig joined her.

"How's Aiden?" she asked immediately.

"About usual after one of his bad attacks. Gemma dosed him up on medications and he slept through the night. He woke this morning without any ill after-effects."

"Does he have asthma attacks often?" she asked curiously. "Maybe he should change medications if his episodes aren't under better control."

Steig grinned widely. "I'll mention it to Doctor Jones."

"Not that I'm criticizing her," Sunny added hastily. "I'm sure she knows what she's doing."

"There are none better," Steig agreed, still smiling.

Sunny got the feeling she was missing something here. What was the big joke about Aiden's health problems? Asthma had the potential to be a dangerous and even deadly disease.

But before she could question the Swede further, a shadow fell across the table. Without a word, Steig stood and melted away into the recesses of the ship. She supposed she didn't have to turn around and see who was standing behind her.

She murmured into her coffee mug, "Good morning, Aiden. How are you feeling?"

He sat down across from her at the small table and answered formally, "Fine, thank you."

Frustration soared through her. "Oh, could you just

drop the whole mysterious-and-inscrutable thing already?"

"Excuse me?" He looked shocked.

She crossed her arms and glared at him. "It's not polite to act like that."

"I'm always polite," he flared up.

She grinned cheekily. "Better."

He reached for a croissant, scowling.

"I was talking to Steig about your breathing issues."

Aiden looked up quickly. "Oh?" he asked noncommittally.

"How is it you can hold your breath forever underwater, but as soon as you're on dry land you have this terrible, uncontrollable asthma?"

"What makes you think it's uncontrollable? I'm fine today."

"Yeah, well, you weren't last night. I thought you might die before I got you back here to Gemma."

He gave her a long, searching look. "Thank you for bringing me back," he said soberly. "I guess that makes us even. I saved your life, and now you've saved mine."

He looked away from her, gazing out at the open ocean beyond the harbor. His withdrawal was a tangible thing, and it cut like a knife.

"So that's it?" she asked. "We're all square now, so you can shut me out and walk away?"

His gaze snapped back to her. "As I recall, you're the one who walked away from me."

"Excuse me?"

"You left the *Nymph*."

"It's not my boat. I can't just move in and make myself at home."

"It's a yacht," he corrected absently.

"Yacht, schmact. Don't change the subject."

"Djibouti City is too dangerous a place for a woman alone, particularly one as attractive as you."

He thought she was attractive? Warmth filled her. But then reality came crashing back. "I lost nearly everything I owned when the *New Dawn* sank. And what little I do still have is across town in some mercenary compound. Where do you expect me to go, and how exactly do you expect me to get there, Aiden? I've got to start somewhere. And this town is where I happen to have landed. I'm stuck here until I marshal some funds."

"If it's money you need, I'll write you a check."

Humiliation washed over her. She didn't want his money. She didn't want to need anyone's help. She had always taken care of herself, and she would find a way out of this mess like she always did. Although this was a bigger mess than most. Okay, this was the mother of all messes.

"What do I have to say to get you to stay on the *Nymph* until you figure things out?" he asked.

"You might try asking."

"Stay." He added belatedly, "Please?"

"Why should I?"

"Because I want you to, dammit!" he exploded.

"But *why?*"

He opened his mouth but no words came out. He tried again, but still nothing. Finally, he surged up out of his chair and came around the table in two powerful strides. He reached down for her and dragged her to her feet. Or more precisely, dragged her up against him. His mouth swooped down and crushed hers in a kiss that left her gasping for air.

The kiss intensified. Deepened. And all those sparks that had been there between them before ignited in a shower of heat and fury. Everywhere he touched her, she burned. He broke the kiss, breathing hard, and she tugged his head back down for more. God bless Gemma Jones for whatever drugs she'd given him to help his breathing because he kissed her so thoroughly this time before he came up for air that her knees went weak.

Finally, he lifted his mouth from hers far enough to mutter, "Say you'll stay."

"If I don't?"

"I'll have to tear your clothes off and make love to you until you do."

"Then I definitely refuse to stay."

He laughed against her mouth.

She started to insist on clothes-tearing and hot, sweaty sex immediately, but then she heard movement behind her. Drat. They had company. Aiden stepped away from her hastily. Why was he in such an all-fired hurry to pretend as if he hadn't been sucking her lungs out? Was he ashamed of her? The thought burned like acid in her gut. Lord knew, she wasn't nearly classy enough to fit into his world. But still, the notion that she was an embarrassment to him hurt.

A sailor announced, "Captain wanted me to tell you that, whenever you're ready, the *Nymph* can get under way."

Aiden nodded briskly. "I think we've collected everything we need from this town. Let's go."

The resulting flurry of activity distracted her long

enough that the harbor was retreating in the distance before she remembered her personal things. There wasn't much, but it was all she had left. A handful of photographs—the last remnants of her parents. Her camera. And her film. If she was lucky, she'd find a way to cobble together a documentary from the footage she already had and salvage something from this disastrous trip.

"My stuff—" she started in rising panic.

"In your closet," Aiden interrupted.

"But how?"

"I had the crew fetch your things."

She frowned. "When did you give the order? You passed out before they got you to the infirmary last night, and they told me when I woke up this morning that you weren't awake, yet."

"Yesterday afternoon."

She turned to face him squarely. "Yesterday?" she asked ominously. "Care to explain how *that* happened?

"After I saw you at the docks, I realized I couldn't deal with worrying about you constantly. You were coming back to the *Nymph* with me last night one way or another."

"What if I'd refused?"

The corner of his mouth turned up in a smile so sexy it curled her toes. But then it faded, replaced by a look of…she wasn't sure what. Chagrin. Self-loathing. He answered reluctantly, "You wouldn't have refused me."

"But what if I had?" she insisted.

"Then I'd have thrown you over my shoulder and carried you here."

"You'd have kidnapped me?"

He answered grimly, "If that's what it took."

There wasn't anything even remotely playful in his words. It was almost as if he hated the fact that he would have kidnapped her but would have had no other choice. Well, then. She turned to stare out at the ocean's deep, deep blue. Maybe he wasn't quite as detached and disinterested as he tried to be, after all. But what did it all mean?

Aiden was appalled to realize he would, indeed, have kidnapped Sunny if necessary. Truth be told, he hadn't thought that far ahead when he'd given the order for her personal possessions to be fetched.

He felt as if he'd been split in two and the separate halves of him were at war with one another. His head could not believe he'd safely gotten rid of Sunny and had turned around and dragged her right back aboard the ship. What was he thinking? He *knew* better.

His heart exulted in the fact that she was here again. He craved the way she made him feel; not just the sex, but how she made him laugh and yell and really experience every emotion. He hadn't felt this alive in years. Even in the height of his wild days, he couldn't remember the last woman who'd made him feel like this.

Yes, his sense of duty replied, but what of his work? What of his vow to grow up and quit acting like a spoiled kid? His vow to use his special skills to protect mankind and work for justice and truth?

His heart's answer was blunt. *What. Ever.* He had a right to a little happiness along the way, didn't he? Why couldn't he do his job and have a personal life? Other people did it all the time. Even people in dangerous jobs serving the public good like soldiers, policemen and firemen. How was he so different?

The one thing both sides of him agreed on unequivocally was they knew what they'd *like* to do with her. But it was a far cry from what he *should* do with her.

Deeply conflicted, he spent the afternoon on the bridge where the crew was trying to acquire the signal from the tracking device he'd planted on the pirate vessel. The radio's limited size meant it also had a limited range. They would have to sail within about a hundred miles of it to pick up the signal. Assuming the pirates hadn't already found it and disabled it.

The *Nymph* had been repaired and ready to go for the past two days, but he hadn't been able to bring himself to give the order to leave Djibouti. Not while Sunny was there alone and in danger. Even if he'd been too stubborn to approach her directly and tell her how he felt about her, he still felt responsible for her safety.

The hell of it was Steig and Gemma seemed to have entered into some sort of conspiracy to force him to face up to his feelings for Sunny. It wasn't that they nagged him about her. It was nothing as open as that. But Steig had put up no protest when he'd fielded a lame excuse about the crew needing to have a little shore leave before they went back out and confronted the pirates. And Gemma merely nodded when he suggested that he was worried about having a major asthma attack if he didn't spend a few days resting in port.

Aiden sighed and looked around the bridge. Was he the only person aware of how badly he was letting a woman interfere in an important mission? This was exactly why he'd sworn off women in general when he'd agreed to take Gemma's experimental drugs and work in Jeff's special unit.

It might be supremely rude of him to avoid Sunny by taking supper in his room, but he seriously needed to put some distance, both physical and emotional, between himself and her. He was supposed to be a man alone in the world, but here he was fretting about a girl. Aiden paced the master suite restlessly until his breathing started to tighten up and he was finally forced to lie down.

It was deep into the wee hours of the night when he woke up. He extended his senses outward into the room seeking what had disturbed his rest. There. A dark figure stood in the shadows by the door. His adrenaline surged in response to the threat, but the intruder did not move. His hand slid under his pillow and grasped the wickedly sharp bowie knife hidden there.

"Who are you?" he demanded, coiling himself to leap out of bed and fight for his life.

"It's me."

Sunny. He'd know that honey-sweet whisper anywhere. The last time he'd heard it she'd been whispering her most secret desires in his ear while she did shockingly erotic things to his body, mind and soul.

"I didn't mean to wake you up, Aiden. I'm sorry."

"What are you doing here?"

"I was listening to you breathe."

The candid innocence of her confession arrested him. As did the note of arousal in her voice. Listening to him breathe turned her on? All of a sudden, the pleasure she took in his most basic life function turned him on a little, too.

She added shyly, "I couldn't sleep. I was worried about you."

"I'm fine," he mumbled roughly to cover up how shaken he was.

"Why didn't you eat dinner with the rest of us?"

He should lie. Make some excuse like needing to rest or having work to do. But for some reason, when he opened his mouth, the truth came out. "After our last dinner together, I didn't want to chance the same outcome."

"A pirate attack?" she asked, sounding confused.

"No. What came after the attack."

"Oh," she said in a small, disappointed voice. "I thought—" She backed toward the door. "Never mind. I'll go now."

How was it he always seemed to say exactly the wrong thing around her? He surged up out of the bed to stop her. She cringed away from him and he realized belatedly he was brandishing a foot-long knife at her. It fell to the floor, its turning blade catching the faint moonlight seeping in around the curtains.

"Stay." When was he going to get over his habit of giving orders like that? Berating himself, he added more gently, "Please."

She paused in her headlong flight. "Are you sure?"

"Yes. I am. I'm glad you came."

She perched on the edge of the bed while he paced. "Aiden, you confuse me worse than just about anyone I've ever met. I don't know how to read you. One minute you're pushing me away for all you're worth, and the next, it's almost like you're…seducing me. Trying to draw me in."

If she was half as confused as he was, then she had good reason for saying that. He sighed and shoved a distracted hand through his hair. "You're not wrong."

"What's confusing you?" she asked.

He undoubtedly owed her more of an explanation than he'd offered her so far. He sighed. "I'm not...I wasn't...a good person for most of my life. I was wild and irresponsible. I partied and slept around with pretty much anything female and willing."

"You were a typical college coed, in other words?"

He smiled a little. "I was worse than most. I really was an ass. I'd like to say I was rebelling against something, but the truth is I wasn't. I just didn't want to step up to the family name and uphold the McKay tradition of public service."

"What does this have to do with you and me?" Sunny asked.

"When Jeff Winston approached me a few years ago and invited me to—" Crud. He'd almost let his secret slip. She was so damned easy to talk to. Too easy. He took a deep breath and continued more carefully. "When he invited me to work for him, I knew it was my last chance to get my act together. I promised myself I'd change my ways. Become a better person."

Her voice took on a subtle note of tension. "So you're telling me I'm a mistake? A fallback to your old ways? I'm...convenient?"

"That's exactly my problem!" he exclaimed.

She stood up, indignation painted on her shadowed features, and headed for the door. He lunged forward to grab her arm and stop her so she could hear him out. "Let me finish, Sunny. Please."

She turned to face him but did not look happy.

"At first I was worried that I had slipped back into my old habits with you. To be perfectly honest, I haven't been with a woman in two years."

Her indignant look gave way to one of surprise. He'd been pretty damned surprised to find himself naked and in her arms, too.

He continued, "And then you came along. In one day, there we were on the floor of the salon together. And I panicked. I'd gone and done it again, in spite of my vow to myself not to be that guy anymore. I ought to stay the hell away from you, but I *can't*. It's like ice cream's my favorite food in the entire world, and you're a perfect banana split with all my favorite flavors and toppings, complete with whipped cream and a cherry on top."

"So it's my fault I tempted you?"

"No! It's my fault for giving in."

"Gee whiz, Aiden. I'm so sorry I had to go and nearly drown and inconvenience your life so badly."

"That's not it at all, Sunny. I'm confused. And believe me, for all those years I was such a ladies' man, I was never confused. I knew exactly what I wanted."

"But you don't know now?"

"No. I don't. But I do know I should back off until I figure it out."

"And when will that be?"

"You want an exact date?" he asked, startled.

"That would be helpful."

If only. He'd give anything to have a chance at a real relationship with her. But she deserved better than him. More of a man than him. Someone who could give all of himself, all of his humanity, to her. "You're so beautiful," he murmured.

"You're kind of pretty yourself," she retorted.

He held his arms out to her and she flew into his embrace. It was a mistake as surely as he was standing there. But he could no more hold himself apart from her than he could hold back the flood of emotions she provoked in him. Nor could he hold back the raging need he had to lose himself in her and find himself again.

But holding her wasn't enough. He needed naked flesh, warm and silken. He slipped off her oversize T-shirt, briefly annoyed to recognize it as belonging to Steig. He wanted her to wear his shirts, dammit. The unfamiliar flash of jealousy hitched at the sight of her bra, a sexy little scrap of black lace that fired his imagination.

Her palms smoothed across his chest and he caught himself holding his breath. Not a good idea on land. He didn't want to pass out in the next few minutes. He exhaled carefully. And then she was leaning forward to kiss in the path of her fingers. She bent her legs, her mouth sliding down his torso. She reached his belly button and his stomach muscles contracted hard as she continued lower. As bold in love as she was at everything she did, she grasped his male parts and murmured in wordless approval as his flesh leaped to attention in her hand.

He lifted her easily in his arms, striding toward the bed with her. He lowered her to the mattress, following her down with his mouth already seeking hers. But she surprised him, sitting up and pushing his shoulders, rolling him over onto his back. Bemused, he gave in to

the pressure. She threw a leg across his hips and strad-
dled him, staring down at him warmly. Ahh, his wild
mermaid was back.

The smile faded from her face and her eyes grew
dark, smoky, as she gazed at him. "You are a temptation, Aiden McKay."

"Look who's talking," he muttered back. "I have no
place for you in my world, and yet, here you are. And
I don't want you to be anywhere else."

"Where is this thing between us headed?" she asked
reflectively.

"I have no idea. But shall we find out together?" He
sat up, holding her in place on his lap. She really was a
tiny little thing. But her personality was so big it was
easy to forget. She fit him, though. She was soft where
he was hard, curved where he was angular, welcoming
where he was demanding.

"I can't get enough of you," he murmured.

"I'm right here. All of me for the taking. I'm yours
if you want me."

He groaned, torn apart by her offer. He'd kill to take
her up on it. He'd give up—

His lustful thoughts screeched to a halt. Would he
give up everything for her? He didn't even know if he
could at this point. If he stopped the injections tomorrow, would his body eventually revert to normal or not?
It was one of the unanswered questions of Gemma's research. But beyond that, could he walk away from his
duty, his social responsibilities? To leave behind the
terrible isolation of his life…to feel the things she was
offering him…to *love*…

Sunny squirmed impatiently in his lap, her hand

going between them to grasp his raging erection. She guided him inside her and was suddenly moving on him and with him, ripping away all thought or reason from him. And all that was left was the feel of her internal muscles gripping him as strongly as she held his heart.

She was heat and lust and life, and she overwhelmed him completely.

With a groan he surged up into her, taking over the rhythm of their lovemaking with a vengeance. He flung himself into the abyss, and it was glorious. The endless fall into his own damnation was the sweetest thing he'd ever experienced. And his own personal angel took him there.

After the first time, he stunned himself by hardening again inside her. And whereas the last time it had been a frantic rush of hard-driving lust and wild surrender, this time was the opposite, all languorous kisses and long caresses. They found an easy rhythm as smooth and endless as the ocean's waves.

Ahh, yes. Hell was sweet, indeed. He gorged himself shamelessly upon its false delight, for surely its price would be a bitter thing. But that was a meal for tomorrow. Tonight, he would savor her, come what may.

Sunny woke up alone in Aiden's bed. The light streaming around the curtains announced it to be morning. She felt a little sore and in need of a soak in a hot bath, but oh, so very well loved. Last night had been…

There were no words for it. Incredible. Magical. Life changing. When Aiden had finally cut loose and come out from behind his shell, he'd absolutely blown her away. The man behind the mask was one of a kind.

Eager to see him again, to just look at him and be in his presence, she opted for a quick shower and raided his drawers for a clean T-shirt. She headed out to find him.

Of course, a crew member was in the passageway as she emerged from Aiden's room. He glanced away quickly but not before she caught the grin lurking at the corners of his mouth. She had no illusions: the entire crew no doubt already knew she'd spent the night in the boss's cabin. There was no help for it. Yachts were tiny places that kept no secrets. Her euphoria this morning was such, though, that she brushed off the momentary embarrassment.

"Have you seen Aiden this morning?" she asked the steward.

"Last I saw, he was eating up on deck."

She headed up to the sundeck to find him, but the space was empty when she got there. She strolled around the walkways and didn't spot his tall, perfect form. Impatient, she headed up to the bridge and spotted Steig on the catwalk, looking out to sea through a pair of binoculars.

"Good morning, Miss Sunny. Sleep well?"

To his credit, there was no sleazy innuendo in the question. In fact, if anything, she thought she caught a note of approval in the Swede's voice. "I slept fantastic," she replied jauntily. "Do you know where Aiden is?"

"Out there." He gestured with his chin to the open ocean.

"I suppose he's swimming alone again, isn't he?" she demanded.

"Yes, ma'am."

"Don't ma'am me. I'm just the refugee you were kind enough to take in."

"You're Aiden's special guest…ma'am."

She didn't quite know what to say to that. She gazed out at the ocean's lazy waves trying to spot her lover. No sign of him. "How long has he been under?" she asked.

Steig, staring out at the ocean again, answered absently, "Six minutes, give or take."

"Six—" She broke off in horror. "Free diving with no oxygen for *six* minutes?"

Steig looked startled and a sheet of dull red chagrin spread across his cheeks.

"Exactly how long *can* he stay underwater?" she asked ominously.

"Maybe you should talk to Dr. Jones about it. Or Aiden himself."

Her suspicion blossomed into full-blown certainty that something strange was going on around here. Nobody could hold their breath for six minutes and counting. At least not anybody normal. A world-champion free diver might pull it off on a single dive after careful pre-breathing and preparation, but not dive after casual dive like Aiden did. Steig wasn't even showing the slightest sign of concern as the seconds ticked away.

"What the hell is going on with him?" Sunny demanded.

"Really. You need to talk to him about it." Steig made a production of peering through the binoculars and turning his attention back to the water.

"Oh, I definitely will."

How was it that she could make passionate, mind-boggling love with Aiden and feel as if she'd connected with him at the deepest and most fundamental level, and *still* not know him at all? What in the world was he hiding from her? What were they all hiding from her?

Chapter 6

Aiden was by turns terrified, exhilarated and appalled. He cycled through the sensations almost too rapidly to process. He swam with a vengeance, doing his darnedest to wash away the storm of emotions. But it didn't work. No matter how he deep he dived, how long he pushed himself to stay under, how much he exhausted himself, the roiling in his gut refused to go away.

The usual comfort of the sea eluded him. Even the plentiful fish in this region seemed determined to avoid him today. The water remained silent and empty around him, and no answers were forthcoming as to what to do about the woman who'd invaded his soul.

He swam for hours. The sun traversed the zenith of the sky and was starting down toward the western horizon when he finally gave up seeking a peace that refused to come.

Heading back to the white oasis of the *Sea Nymph,* he hoisted himself out of the water on tired arms. He picked up the towel someone had laid out for him and wiped the salt water off his skin. And as he did so, he spotted Sunny's slender curves on the bridge deck.

The defensive set of her shoulders, the way her arms were clasped around her middle spoke volumes. Alarm coursed through him. He probably shouldn't have slipped out while she slept this morning. But he'd needed distance from her, some perspective. A chance to remember his purpose in life, to reconnect to his faltering sense of duty.

He jogged up the ladder that was the fastest route to the bridge deck. He noted the furtive way Steig vacated the deck as he approached. What had the Swede been talking to Sunny about?

"Good swim?" she asked as he drew near and kissed her on the cheek.

He shrugged. "Tiring."

"How tiring?"

"I beg your pardon?"

"How do you do it? No normal man can hold his breath as long as you can." Suspicion vibrated in every syllable.

Ahh. He cursed mentally. He should've known she'd spend the afternoon watching him swim—and how could she not realize something was up? No help for it now. His only option was damage control. He answered lightly, "I told you. I'm a spectacular swimmer."

"What you can do is Guinness World Records stuff and then some. It's superhuman. How do you do it?"

"Practice?"

"How stupid do you think I am, Aiden?"

He sighed. "I've never thought you were anything other than highly intelligent and perceptive."

"Then please don't insult me. I'd like an answer to my question."

"I can't give it to you." It was no big stretch to know what her next question would be.

She obliged by delivering a terse, "Why not?"

"I just…can't."

"Does this have something to do with why a research scientist like Dr. Jones is aboard the *Nymph?*"

Nope, Sunny was not slow on the uptake. She'd gotten to that bit of logic all too fast for his comfort. How long before she made other, more damaging connections? "If I asked you to just leave it alone, would you?"

"Would you if you were in my position?"

"No."

"Well, there you have it."

"It's classified. I can't talk about it," he tried desperately.

She stared at him thoughtfully. "Which means Gemma is involved. Which means she's doing some sort of research that involves you. How did you describe her work? Aquatic stuff?"

Crap. Sunny had a good memory, too.

She continued her uncomfortable line of reasoning. "So, you either are a natural freak she's studying, or she's done something to enhance your ability to hold your breath."

Since there was no explicit question in her remark, he did not make any response.

"And, since I've never heard of anybody, ever, who

could hold their breath the way you can, I'm betting that Gemma did something to you. Care to tell me what it was?"

"Absolutely not," he blurted, vividly aware all of a sudden that a filmmaker who specialized in exposés was grilling him.

"This yacht is very small. Nothing can stay secret aboard a boat for long. You know it, and I know it. So why don't you just cut to the chase and tell me what's going on?"

Sadly, she was right. "Once you know, there's no going back. You have to live with it forever."

She shrugged. "That's how all knowledge works. It changes you."

Easy for her to say. She had no idea how much knowing his secrets would change her life. And he couldn't explain it to her without revealing too much. "Curiosity is not always a good thing, Sunny. This is one time you need to walk away and not ask any questions."

"And yet, I'm not. This involves *you,* Aiden. I want to know."

It was his fault. Had he not made love to her— twice—she wouldn't be in such an all-fired tizzy to know every last detail about him. He'd brought this on himself. In his selfishness and loneliness, he'd dragged her into his life. He was a fool. He'd known from the day he met her that she was insatiably curious and doggedly determined in pursuing answers. He'd *known better.*

The bottom line was, the project was not his to reveal. It was Gemma's work and the work of his boss, Jeff Winston, the first recipient of the stem-cell transplants that had artificially enhanced his body. In Jeff's case, it had been his bones, and hence his strength, that had been boosted.

Apparently, he'd waited too long to respond to Sunny. She declared, "Fine. If you won't tell me, I'll just ask Gemma."

He snorted. "Good luck with her."

Sunny smiled mysteriously. "She rather likes me. And us girls have to stick together. She happens to think you haven't been treating me very well, and she also thinks you need someone like me to shake you out of your shell. She said so last night when you didn't show up for dinner. In fact, the two of us spent the evening together getting chummy."

Oh, God.

She turned away from him, presumably to go track down Gemma. He huffed in frustration. "Sunny, stop."

She turned around to stare at him expectantly.

"If you have to hear it, you may as well hear it from me."

An expectant expression entered her snapping hazel eyes.

"This conversation will go best if there's alcohol involved." He added under his breath, "Lots of alcohol." Louder, he added, "I'll meet you in the salon in five minutes. There's something I have to get first."

Five minutes stretched into ten as Sunny waited to hear what the big secret was. Aiden had been so serious about it all. He'd scared her more than she liked to admit. A lot more. Fear that something was terribly wrong with his health nagged at her.

Finally, he joined her, and she noted that he'd taken

time to dress in a white shirt and slacks that made him look every inch the old-money blueblood he apparently was. And he had a stack of papers in his hand. But it was the grim set of his jaw and the sober expression in his eyes that really captured her attention.

"Sit down," he said shortly.

She moved over to the poker table in the corner where he held a chair for her.

He put the papers and pen down in front of her and said tersely, "I need you to read these documents and sign them."

"What are they?" she asked curiously.

"They're self-explanatory."

Not feeling real talkative, huh? She glanced down at the papers. A nondisclosure agreement? She scanned the legal documents quickly. They made clear in no uncertain terms that lawyers for Winston Enterprises would sue her into the Stone Age if she ever talked about anything she learned aboard the *Sea Nymph*, and that said lawyers would just be getting warmed up. The papers promised to destroy the rest of her life if she broke the terms of this document.

Becoming more alarmed with each signature, she signed page after page of legal papers. Finally, she'd worked her way through the whole stack. She pushed them across the table to Aiden. "Okay. Talk," she said.

"Jeff Winston is an old friend of mine. We went to college together. And he approached me two years ago with an unusual proposition, which I accepted. A doctor whose research he'd been funding needed human subjects for a highly secret medical experiment, and he wanted me to be one of those people."

"Gemma Jones?" she interrupted.

"Correct. This is Gemma's project. She is not only a physician, but also an internationally renowned geneticist. And she discovered what she believed to be a way to use stem cells to super activate certain genes."

"What does that mean?"

"She can use stem-cell therapies to accentuate or change certain features of individuals."

A chill skittered down Sunny's spine. She saw where this was going, but she couldn't quite bring herself to believe it. "Like what?" she asked cautiously.

"In Jeff's case, Gemma was able to enhance his bone density and deactivate certain amino acids that limit muscle strength. The end result is that he can develop and skeletally support more muscle than a regular person can."

"He's superstrong, then?"

"Yes."

She had to force the words out, but she had to know. "And you? What about you, Aiden?"

"My cells have greatly increased their capacity to absorb and use oxygen, particularly when under high ambient pressure."

"Translation into plain English for us nonscience geeks?"

"I can hold my breath underwater for a really long time."

"How long?"

"Longest so far is nine minutes and twenty seconds. Gemma believes I'll be able to go longer than that as more of my body tissues make the shift and the changes in my cells become permanent."

Her filmmaker's instincts kicked in and questions crowded into her mind one on top of another. "How many people are participating in this project? Do they all have different abilities? Can anyone enhance something about themselves, or only specific people? Does the government know about this? My God, what are the side effects? And what about the other human test subjects—"

Aiden raised a hand to stop the deluge. "I'm not at liberty to talk about anyone else. And frankly, the less you know, the better."

"Why? Because I have a movie camera?"

"Because you champion causes. Because you live to publicize that which you think other people should be aware of. And yes, because you have a camera."

"I signed all your documents."

"I think you'll agree that this project has the potential to be…explosive…if the public finds out about it. The temptation to talk might be more than you could resist."

"Why did you tell me about Jeff Winston, then?"

"The government already knows about him."

"And they haven't shut down Winston Industries and thrown Gemma in jail till the end of time for pursuing this research?"

"Are you kidding?" He snorted. "Uncle Sam is our biggest fan. They're pushing us to do more and faster."

Shocked, she just stared.

"Think about it, Sunny. Scientists all around the world are messing with stem cells right now. Someone else is bound to stumble across the same information Gemma did. But that someone may not be the slightest bit friendly to the United States. What if, say, China could create an army of millions of enhanced soldiers? Where would that leave the United States?"

"Ohmigod," she breathed.

"Our edge as a nation is all about having better technology than the other guy. We have no choice but to keep up in this field of science, too. Problem is, the U.S. government has so tied the hands of American scientists in the field of stem-cell research and genetic engineering that we're rapidly falling behind the rest of the world."

"Some people would argue that the restrictions are to prevent us from playing God."

"Those people may be right. But the reality is that Uncle Sam is delighted to have Winston Industries take it upon itself to do this research. It relieves the Feds of moral responsibility for the work but keeps them on the leading edge of military technology development."

"But you're mutilating your body!" she exclaimed as the implications of what he'd told her began to sink in.

"Do I look mutilated?" he asked in amusement.

"Is this why you have those terrible asthma attacks?" she challenged.

"The downside of my gift. My cells work best under high pressure. Helps keep the oxygen from dissolving into solution. In air, like this—" he waved a hand around him "—my cells aren't so efficient anymore. As long as I don't exert myself on dry land, I'm fine, though."

"It's barbaric," she declared.

"It's a miracle," he countered.

"How can you say that? You've distorted your body into something unnatural!"

"I've enhanced it into something more than it was before."

"But why?" she cried.

"Because somebody has to do it. Better me than some psychopath who'd lose his head and turn into a criminal or try to get rich off of it."

She just shook her head, too appalled to speak at the moment.

He continued, "My special abilities allow me to help other people. We stop terrorists and catch criminals and save innocent people. Like you. Without my skills, you'd have died. I was able to spend long enough underwater to find you before you drowned."

How was she supposed to argue against that? "Don't get me wrong, Aiden. I'm glad I'm alive. But I can't condone what you've done to yourself."

"I'm not asking you to condone it. Just accept it."

"What are the long-term side effects?"

He sighed. "Cataloging those is a work in progress. The treatments appear to gradually change gene structure. Gemma's trying to determine if the changes are permanent or if they'll get passed on to our children."

"Ohmigosh. She can breed superhumans? Once word of this gets out, the entire human race will be irrevocably changed!"

"Hence that stack of nondisclosure documents you just signed." He added gently, "And trust me. The federal government will have something to say if you try to reveal this project. I suspect they won't stop at lawyers, however. They'll send in a black-ops team to silence you permanently."

Her eyes widened. What had she stumbled into?

"Welcome to the future, Sunny."

But whose future? Mankind's maybe. But what about hers and Aiden's? Had any chance for the two of them just evaporated in a stack of legal documents and bizarre science experiments?

Chapter 7

Aiden stared out the salon's picture window while Sunny stared at nothing behind him. Who'd have guessed that telling her the truth would have driven her away from him so much more effectively than lying to her?

His heart was slowly cracking in two inside his chest, and there wasn't a damned thing he could do about it. She'd insisted on knowing everything. Of course, he should never have put her in a position to be able to ask the questions. Any chance they'd had for a relationship was history now, anyway.

Abruptly, a distinctive whumping noise came from the rear of the boat, along with a brief, bright flare of light.

"What was that?" Sunny asked sharply.

"The chaff blower," he grunted as he took off running across the salon. No surprise, Sunny was right on his heels as he raced for the bridge.

"Chaff as in distract a bomb from hitting us?" she panted.

An explosion and flash of light rocked the *Nymph*. He grabbed the door frame to steady himself and then resumed running. "The ship's sensors must have picked up something incoming and blown the chaff pods automatically." Something like a missile or a rocket-launched grenade. Who in the hell would fire something that high-tech at a civilian yacht?

"Pirates?" she asked as they raced up the stairs and burst into the bridge.

"No idea," he bit out. Since when did pirates have missiles? And why would pirates armed in such a manner come after the *Nymph?* With that kind of armament, pirates could take over a supertanker and steal millions of dollars' worth of oil. Why bother with a single yacht? Sure, it was a nice yacht and worth a lot, but its value was a drop in the bucket compared to a big ship.

Steig was rapid-firing orders to his crew, who were all working with grim efficiency over their various consoles. Aiden didn't interrupt. These guys were the best at what they did. The most important thing he could contribute was to stay the hell out of their way.

Finally, Steig looked across the room at him grimly and announced, "Three pirate ships at roughly our twelve-, four- and eight-o'clock positions. Our antimissile countermeasures automatically deployed. A total of three heat-seeking projectiles, one from each hostile ship, have been diverted successfully by chaff. It has been three minutes since the rocket salvo fired. My guess is they don't plan to fire any more missiles at us."

"Were the shots an attempt to sink us or merely scare us?" Aiden asked.

"I don't know. Maybe a test of our defenses."

Steig ordered men to the gun turrets, which had been retrofitted onto the yacht for this voyage. They were disguised as radar domes and held fifty-millimeter cannons with an accurate range of close to a mile. If any of those pirate boats came near, they were in for a nasty surprise.

Everyone stared at the radar screen and the three red blips that held their positions exactly three miles from the *Nymph*. For the next several minutes, the standoff continued with no one yielding their position. And then, as quickly as the pirate ships had appeared, they moved off and sailed away. One headed for shore, one passed behind a landmass and disappeared from sight, and the other blended into the traffic of a shipping lane some ten miles south of the *Nymph*.

Aiden let out a long breath of relief.

For his part, Steig demanded, "What the hell was that all about? I've never heard of pirates behaving that way. And those bastards never operate with such close coordination and discipline."

Sunny piped up from behind him. "Then maybe those weren't pirates."

As soon as he heard the words, Aiden knew them to be exactly right. No pirate acted like that. Therefore, those hadn't been pirates firing at them.

"Who, then?" Steig voiced for them all.

Who, indeed? Aiden studied Sunny as he spoke

slowly. "We sailed around out here for three weeks with nary a nibble from pirates toward this yacht. Then you came aboard, and we were attacked immediately. Within one day of leaving port with you aboard, we were jumped again."

The shocked expression that came over Sunny's face looked genuine. Of course she could just be a fine actress. "Are you saying those guys are after *me?* That makes no sense at all. It seems a whole lot more plausible to me that they're after *you*."

A nauseating chill rippled through him. Was she right? Had someone found out about Gemma's research? About his extraordinary skills? Was this all an elaborate attempt to destroy him and set back, or even end, Gemma's research?

Everyone on the bridge was staring back and forth between him and Sunny.

"She knows?" Steig bit out.

Aiden nodded tersely. He winced as eyebrows shot up all around. And then the knowing looks came. He sighed. Nope, no secrets on a boat.

"She does have a point," Steig said slowly. "Did you talk to anyone during those three days you were in Djibouti City tracking Sunny?"

That occasioned a predictably sharp look from her. He winced again. He hadn't exactly confessed to her that he'd followed her morning, noon and night to make sure she didn't get in trouble or hurt. And he wasn't about to confess it now.

"I didn't talk to anyone," he retorted. "I know full well that my life rides on Gemma's work staying secret."

Steig sighed. "I know. I had to ask, though."

Sunny piped up. "Could there have been a leak at the other end of this operation? Didn't you say your boss was involved? Maybe he leaked something."

"No way. His life is on the line the same way mine is."

"Yes, but other people work around him and with him," she argued. "Surely some of them know about this project. The more people who know, the more likely it is that someone let something slip. Didn't you say the government knows about Jeff's enhancements?"

Aiden glanced down at the radar screen, which was blessedly blank at the moment. Was it possible? Had he been marked for death?

He didn't mind the idea of dying for a good cause. But the idea of being hunted like a dog and cut down in cold blood—that did *not* warm the cockles of his heart.

He said heavily, "I'll call Jeff Winston as soon as it's a decent hour in Colorado and see if he has any indications that there might be a leak. If someone's trying to kill him, then we'll know it's probably me those ships were after. If not, I think we have to entertain the possibility that they're after you."

The bridge felt as if its walls were closing in on him. Its dim red lighting was claustrophobic all of a sudden. He had to get out of there.

Sunny tried to say something to him as he stumbled past, but he pressed on by her. He needed to think. Try to figure out who was trying to kill him. How they would come after him. Hell, he had to figure out how to stay alive when they did come.

The last thing he needed to do was drag Sunny into the middle of this. She was in enough danger just being aboard this ship with him. And to think, he'd brought her to the *Nymph* to keep her safe. Chalk up yet another failure for him where she was concerned.

Although she half-expected it, Sunny was disappointed when Aiden didn't show up for breakfast the next morning. The chef had laid out a light continental buffet of fruits and pastries in the salon that the crew was strolling in to graze on. She tarried in the salon for almost an hour in hopes of seeing him, but no dice.

She'd perched on the same sofa she'd hidden beneath before, her bare feet tucked beneath her on the cushions, a mug of coffee cradled in her hands as she stared out to sea. It was so vast and aloof this morning. So much like the man who shunned mankind and found his true home out there.

"Mind if I sit with you?"

Sunny glanced up at Gemma, surprised. She hadn't pegged the doctor as the chatty sort. "Sure."

"How're you doing, Sunny?"

"What do you mean?"

That elicited a chuckle. "Don't try to evade me. Better patients than you have tried and failed."

That made Sunny's gaze snap to the doctor. "Do tell."

"Look. It's no secret on this vessel that you and Aiden have…a thing. That can't be easy for you."

Curiouser and curiouser. Why was Gemma poking into her relationship with Aiden? "Why do you say it can't be easy?" Sunny asked.

"I know him, remember? He's the king of throwing up walls and pushing people away."

"Yeah, I noticed," Sunny couldn't help grumbling. "Why is that?"

"Maybe you should ask him."

"Have you? Do you know the answer?"

Gemma shrugged. "I have asked, but he's never answered me. My guess is it has something to do with guilt."

"Over what?"

"He was quite the heartless womanizer in his youth. Right up until Jeff Winston called him and recruited him for my research project. Now that he's grown a conscience and a sense of responsibility, I think he regrets some of the things he's done."

"And he's taking that guilt out on me?" Sunny blurted.

"That's up to you to find out and deal with, now, isn't it?"

"I'm not sure I want to deal with anything where Aiden's concerned. He's made his intention not to pursue a relationship with me pretty clear."

"Has he? My impression is that he wants very badly to pursue a relationship with you. Take it from me, I've never seen him react to another woman the way he reacts to you. You bring him out of his shell like no one else."

Sunny leaned back, sipping at her coffee to disguise her surprise. Really? That was interesting.

"I'll tell you something else, Sunny. I'm worried about Aiden. He's been pulling back more and more from meaningful interaction or even simple contact with other human beings ever since he started working with me. On top of his self-imposed guilt issues, he seems to be struggling to deal with his differences from other people."

"How different is he? Is there more to what you've done to him than him holding his breath a long time and having asthma on land?"

Gemma looked startled that Sunny knew the details of his condition. "No, that's most of it. His brain functions at a slightly higher rate than before, no doubt due to his higher blood-oxygen levels."

"Is it true that his children may inherit his ability?"

"It's possible they would inherit something but not necessarily the same ability as the enhanced parent. The DNA of sex cells would probably react like any other cells in his body to the stem-cell therapy he's been getting, but I have no way of predicting exactly *how* they would interact. How the offspring's DNA would change is anyone's guess. I've got lab studies running on it now. The first results in my primate testing should be available in a few months."

Sunny shuddered at the idea of an entire race of little mutant children. It just wasn't natural. If this technology got loose in the world, how long would it be until the human race was no longer human?

Gemma leaned forward and spoke with quiet intensity. "I see from the horror on your face that the possible ramifications of breeding specifically to get mutations has occurred to you. That is exactly why we have to control this technology. To know it and know how to stop it before someone less ethical than me or Jeff Winston or Aiden gets their hands on it."

"It's like inventing a nuclear bomb, Doctor. Once it's invented, it can't be un-invented."

"So you would have had the United States not develop the nuclear bomb and instead wait for Germany to come up with it and nuke us? Estimates at that time put the German program only a year or two behind ours."

Sunny shivered. Gemma was right, of course, but still. The whole thing was creepy. It was a really scary technology to be messing around with. "Just promise me you'll keep a close eye on Aiden, Doctor. Don't let him lose himself in his enhancements."

"Gee, and I was going to make you promise the exact same thing to me."

Sunny stared. "Me? You think I can save him from himself?"

"I think maybe you're his last, best hope."

And on that note, Gemma stood up and walked out of the salon without looking back. Man, the people on this yacht made great exits. Sunny shook herself.

Aiden's last hope? Was he that far gone? Had their lovemaking been that gigantic an anomaly for him, then? Huh. Who'd have guessed? She was by turns complimented and terrified. Their relationship was tenuous at best. She wasn't at all sure she was strong enough to hold on to him if she had to drag him back from the abyss all by herself. If she lost her emotional grip on him, he'd be lost for good. The responsibility for another life resting heavily on her shoulders, she headed for the back of the yacht and the swim deck.

The *Sea Nymph*'s engines were idling at the moment and a sea anchor was deployed against the currents, which could mean only one thing. Aiden had gone swimming.

Was he insane? There were people out there trying

to kill him. And he wanted to go out alone and put himself in harm's way? What was he thinking? Unless, of course, he was thinking about sacrificing himself to save the rest of them. He'd been willing to use this boat as bait to catch pirates; why not use himself as bait to draw out the people trying to kill him? Offer himself up as a sacrificial lamb in return for the safety of the *Sea Nymph* and everyone aboard her.

The more she thought about it, the more convinced she was she had his misguided motives pegged. And the madder she got. She was going to kill him…assuming the bad guys didn't get him first. It was a warm morning already and well on its way to becoming a blistering-hot day. She climbed down onto the floating swim deck resting on the water's surface.

Knowing it could be a while before he made his way back to the yacht, she kicked off her sandals and sat down to dangle her feet in the water. The sea felt cool and welcoming against her skin. In a few hours, when the sun was beating down overhead, this water would be heavenly to slip into and cool off in. Sudden memories of darkness and cold and terror slammed into her. She no longer swam in the ocean. It had tried to kill her.

Although, in defense of the Indian Ocean, an anonymous ship had actually tried to kill her. The sea had just been there to catch her and finish off the job. It hadn't really been any malicious action on the ocean's part that nearly killed her. Man had taken care of that.

It dawned on her that she was thinking of the ocean as a living being, and she snorted at herself. She supposed it came from sailing around for months on end all alone. People got a little weird during periods of extended isolation like that. The ocean either became your enemy or your friend. Although, anyone who heard her thinking that way would probably label her crazy. Except maybe Aiden. He would understand. He had the same sort of relationship with the ocean.

She kicked her feet a little, splashing droplets of the cool water on herself. That felt nice. She kicked a little harder. Bent down to scoop up a little water and dribble it down the back of her neck. As the day heated up, she dipped her arms deep into the water and even splashed a few handfuls of water on her face. She might not want to immerse herself in the thing, but the ocean felt good on her skin.

Aiden headed back toward the *Sea Nymph,* disappointed that no bad guys had come looking for him. At least the swim itself had felt good. He'd burned off some of the terrible tension gripping him and stretched out his muscles. Not to mention a long swim had reset his respiration to a happy place. Ideally, he would swim at least once a day to keep his body working at peak efficiency.

As he approached the *Nymph* from below, he spotted a pair of feet splashing in the water. The slender, shapely calves attached to those feet announced that either Gemma or Sunny was waiting for him. And Gemma wasn't the sort to sit around for more than about thirty seconds. He mentally sighed.

He had no idea what to do about Sunny. He wanted her with every fiber of his being. But as sure as the sky was blue and water was wet, he wasn't good for her. He'd already put her in terrible danger by insisting on keeping her close to him.

Steig had the right of it. He should have dumped her in Djibouti at that American security firm's compound. She would have been surrounded by people with the skill and will to keep her safe and who would have seen to it she got home safely. But he just couldn't let go of her. He needed her at some deep, fundamental level he didn't understand.

He was a selfish bastard. And she would die if he didn't get over it. As hard as it was, he had to break off any budding relationship he might have with her and send her far, far away from him. It went against every fiber in his being to let her out of his sight where he couldn't protect her himself. But it would be best for her.

Reluctantly, he swam for the platform.

Sunny let out a little scream when he abruptly surfaced beside her, bursting out of the water and popping out onto the teak decking. "Aiden!"

He flopped down beside her, letting the sun warm his body as it adapted to being back in atmospheric conditions. Okay, he enjoyed showing off for her. So sue him. Dammit, he was with her for two seconds and all his resolve to stay away from her evaporated. He *had* to be strong. If he cared about her at all, he'd keep his distance.

"You're using yourself as bait to protect the rest of us, aren't you?" she accused.

Wow. He wasn't that transparent, was he? "Nah. I just went for my daily swim. Gotta do it to keep my breathing on an even keel."

"Couldn't you just submerge yourself in a bathtub for a while instead of heading out into the deep to invite bad guys to kill you?"

"Not enough pressure in a bathtub. I need to be six or eight feet underwater to get any benefit from the swimming. And ideally, I'll go deeper than that for a while. Gemma says my body processes oxygen most efficiently between fifty and a hundred feet underwater."

"A hundred? Good grief, how deep can you go?"

"World-class free divers go up to 265 or so meters down. Of course, they have to use weights and fins to get there and back on a single breath."

"And I suppose you can do better, can't you?" she asked in resignation.

"Oh, yeah."

"What's the world record for breath-holding underwater?" she asked curiously.

"Around eleven and a half minutes. But the difference between those folks and me is I'm fully functional for that long. They have to sit still and let their bodies mostly shut down."

"The thought of being underwater that long makes me ill."

He reached up to squeeze her shoulder sympathetically. "You had a bad scare. It takes time to get over it. And this is a good start."

"What is?"

"You're sitting by the water, kicking around in it, getting wet."

"I got hot waiting for you."

His mouth quirked as a blush climbed her neck. He didn't compound her embarrassment by commenting on her verbal slip.

"What are the odds I could get you to slip into the water?" She tensed beneath his hand and he added hastily, "I'm not talking about actually swimming. Just floating next to the deck. You can even hang on to it the whole time. I'll be right beside you."

"I don't think so...."

"Sunny, the longer you refuse to face your fear, the more it will grow in your mind until it becomes something insurmountable. I'm not suggesting you throw on scuba gear and head for the ocean's depths. I'm just suggesting you start taking baby steps toward overcoming your fear."

"But why? Plenty of people live perfectly productive and normal lives without ever coming within a hundred miles of an ocean."

"But they're not you. If I'm not mistaken, a large portion of your life has centered around water. Do you really want to give up that part of yourself for good?"

"Quit being so reasonable," she complained.

He sat up beside her. Slipped back into the water. "C'mon. You don't even have to leave the deck," he coaxed. "Just scoot forward until your legs are all the way in the water."

She slid a few inches closer to the edge of the deck. Her expression was apprehensive. He treaded water easily in front of her until her frown relaxed. "Roll on your stomach, sweetheart. Lay on the deck and let your hips slide into the water."

He moved in close and put an arm on either side of her, gripping the dock until he created a human safety net around her. The position had the fringe benefit of giving him a great view of her juicy tush. No doubt about it, Sunny had a great figure. Slowly, she rolled to her stomach and eased deeper into the water.

Of her own free will, she slid nearly to her waist into the sea. And then, very slowly, she eased fully into the water. She maintained a death grip on the edge of the deck, though, and he stayed right behind her, their bodies nearly touching.

"Are you okay?" he murmured.

"Getting there," she gritted out.

They floated together in silence for several minutes. He'd give anything to know what she was thinking about, but she didn't share. Eventually, she pulled herself toward the deck.

"Had enough?" he asked.

She nodded jerkily. He submerged below her, grabbed her by the waist and gave a mighty kick upward, launching her up onto the deck easily. He surfaced and hoisted himself up beside her.

They lay there in silence so companionable it hurt. How could someone who felt so right to him be so damned wrong for him?

"Same time tomorrow?" he murmured.

"For what?"

"Another swimming lesson." She tensed beside him, and he added, "I won't make you do anything you don't want to, Sunny."

She relaxed fractionally.

"You have to admit I don't make a half-bad personal lifeguard."

That made her smile. "I suppose not."

Her smile tore his heart into little pieces. Dammit, he couldn't do this anymore. He couldn't stay all breezy and casual when what he really wanted to do was throw her down and make love to her until she confessed she couldn't live without him any more than he could her.

He popped to his feet and jerked a towel around his waist. "Tomorrow, then."

Sunny stared at Aiden's retreating back. What had she done to make him so grouchy? They'd been talking and happy, and then all of a sudden, he just scowled and took off.

His abrupt rejection was almost too painful for her to stand. She retreated to her room to shower off the salt water and lick her emotional wounds, but she found no relief in her tiny stateroom. She longed to be with Aiden every moment she was apart from him, and she dreaded his departure every moment she was with him.

She had to find something to do to distract herself. She was too tense to read, and she'd never been the type to browse magazines. The yacht had a good collection of movies, and she headed for the rec room where those were stored. Too bad she couldn't work on her own movie—

Why not? This ship supposedly had the very latest in computer technology. She headed for the bridge and the ship's communication officer. The guy was a sweetie and hooked her up with a computer and monitor tucked away in a corner of the bridge so she could start editing her raw film footage. She plugged her camera into the front of the computer and loaded up the first memory card.

She was engrossed in cataloging a graphic scene of dolphins struggling to free themselves from fishing nets to surface and breathe when a male voice behind her exclaimed, "What the hell is that?"

She looked up at the sailor, surprised. "Dolphins drowning.".

"God, that's awful."

"Welcome to the commercial fishing industry. You ought to see what Japanese sailors do to the dolphins they catch. This is nothing."

"People like that ought to be rounded up and shot," the man declared.

"That's why I'm making this film. To get the public angry enough to take action."

The guy pulled up a chair beside hers. "What else have you got?"

"I think the next sequence isn't quite so unpleasant. What's your name? Mine's Sunny."

"Everybody on the *Nymph* knows who you are. And I'm Grisham."

"That your first name or last?" she asked.

"It's just Grisham."

She sensed a story but didn't push for more. He didn't look like the type to share his life story at the drop of a hat.

An underwater film sequence came up of thousands of small fish darting around the camera. The silver flashes created a mesmerizing dance as they dashed one direction and another in perfect synchronization.

"Did you film this?" Grisham asked.

She nodded, remembering how happy she'd been that afternoon. How at peace in the sea. The contrast to today's earlier dip in the ocean was shocking. She murmured, "I was documenting the food chain. These herring are plankton eaters and in turn are eaten by midsize predatory fish."

"Nice," the sailor commented. "I'd keep some of that for your final film."

Assuming she ever got the funding to compile the darned thing. She still had no voice-overs, no interviews and a ton of statistical research left to do. It would take thousands of dollars to make a finished film happen. And at the moment, she had little more than the clothes on her back to her name. Were it not for Aiden's generosity, she'd be basically broke and homeless.

Being so dependent on another person made her extremely nervous. And it didn't help that she'd slept with the guy. The whole thing smelled like some sort of tawdry trade of sex for room and board. She didn't think for a second that was what it was, but the appearance of it made her wince. Still. It was yet another reason she should never have jumped in the sack with Aiden McKay…no matter how hot he was.

Aiden was right. They never should have hooked up with each other. But how she was going to keep her hands off him going forward, she wasn't quite sure. She had self-discipline, but resisting the pull between them was going to be a Herculean task. Hopefully, he had lost all interest in her after she insisted on knowing the truth about him, and there would be no sparks between them going forward. He'd been polite but definitely distant this morning.

She felt a presence behind her and knew instantly that it was Aiden. Her skin tingled and her entire body felt energized. She couldn't resist glancing over at him and caught him scowling at her. Their gazes met for just an instant. But it was enough. Her pulse leaped and her insides went liquid and needy. Dammit. She was in huge trouble.

"What's this?" Aiden demanded.

What was his problem? But then Grisham slid his chair several inches away from hers, and it hit her. Aiden didn't like the sailor cozying up beside her watching her film footage. Well, that was just tough. If Aiden wasn't going to keep her for himself, then he didn't have any say in who else she got chummy with. She smiled brightly at Grisham.

"Ready for another nasty sequence? In the next bit, I used a telephoto lens to capture a Japanese fleet that was shark fishing. Or shark finning, to be more accurate."

Grisham made a face. "I've heard about it. I'll pass on watching it." He got up and moved away from her monitor. Although whether it was the horrifying film or Aiden that drove him away, she wasn't quite sure.

She watched film footage well into the evening. The chef sent up a plate for her, and it was closing in on midnight when the footage she'd shot in the rainstorm came up on the screen. Her eyes were gritty, and the gray fog enveloping a distant fishing boat didn't make the footage any easier to make out. This footage was a bust. It was of far too low quality to salvage anything for a film. She yawned and pressed the button to fast-forward past the footage.

But from behind her, Steig, who was pulling a bridge shift, barked, "Wait!"

She looked up, startled.

"What was that on your screen?"

Surprised, she answered, "That was just a bunch of rain and some fuzzy fishing boats in the distance. I think they were whalers. I tried to shoot them because I was surprised to see them so far north in such warm waters."

"Go back. Let me see them again." The Swede bent down over her shoulder to peer at her monitor.

"What's so interesting?" she asked.

He answered absently, "That's not a fishing boat."

She stared at the fuzzy image anew. Now that he mentioned it, the rigging extending out from the sides of the vessel didn't hold the lines and nets that went with deep-sea fishing. They looked more like…antennae?

"Can we enhance this image?" he asked.

"I have no idea. This is your computer equipment. A good film studio could probably enhance the pixilation and get a clearer image."

"Or a good photo intelligence analysis program," he replied.

"Don't government agencies use those?" she asked.

"Yes. Or well-equipped yachts out hunting for pirates." He grinned. "Let me call up Grisham and see what he can do with those images. He's our resident computer wizard."

In short order, her earlier film-watching buddy was hunched over his computer, typing rapidly. "It'll take a couple of hours to run the program, but I can push the pixilation."

"Do it," Steig ordered. "If you want to go catch a nap, Sunny, now would be a good time. You must be getting tired after all those hours working on your film."

He was not wrong. She headed wearily for her cabin,

but her steps faltered as she passed by Aiden's room. What she wouldn't give to crawl into his bed and into his arms for a cuddle. With a sigh, she continued on to her own room and her lonely bed. Would they ever get past their respective hang-ups and find a way to be together?

Chapter 8

"Wake up, Sunny!"

She jerked awake, disoriented. She'd been dreaming about eating chocolate with her third-grade crush, Tommy Spencer. "Huh? What? Are pirates attacking?" she mumbled.

It was Aiden, not Tommy, looming over her bed. And he looked more gorgeous than any man had a right to. He said impatiently, "You need to come up to the bridge."

"Why?" She all but fell out of bed and stumbled to her feet, vividly aware that she must look like Frankenstein's bride right about now.

"We identified that ship you filmed. And it's not a whaler."

She grabbed her jeans and the last of the T-shirts the

crew had donated to her and retreated to the bathroom to change. "What is it?" she called out.

"It's a surveillance ship."

"What's that?"

"Just what it sounds like. A spy vessel for a government."

"What government?"

"We don't know. It's unmarked."

She yanked a hairbrush through her tangled locks and threw on mascara fast. Since when had she become such a cosmetics junkie? Irritated with herself, she asked, "What's it spying on?"

"That's what we're hoping you can tell us."

She burst out of her bathroom, staring at him in dismay. "How am I supposed to know?"

Aiden merely stared at her grimly.

She stepped fully into the bedroom. "You don't seriously think I'm a spy of some kind, do you?"

His jaw rippled.

"Aiden! That's crazy. I'm no more a spy than—" She broke off. She'd been about to say, *than he was.* But given his superhero skills and all his talk about serving mankind and being one of the good guys, it was entirely possible he worked clandestinely for the U.S. government. "Than a fish in the ocean," she finished lamely.

He turned silently and led the way to the bridge. She followed in trepidation. Did they all think she was a spy now, sent to infiltrate their yacht and…do what? Collect their names and send them to the bad guys? Suss out the capabilities of the *Sea Nymph* and pass them to her employers?

Or maybe they thought this was about Gemma's secret research. But if they thought foreign governments would go after the doctor's work, the next obvious question was, what else hadn't Aiden told her about Gemma's work that could scare an entire country?

She stepped onto the bridge. A cluster of men crowded around a computer screen, studying it intently.

Steig glanced up at her. "Come have a look at this. Can you identify it?"

She looked at the screen and gasped. The black narrow-prowed ship bristled with antennae and satellite dishes loosely draped with cargo netting. "That looks like the ship that ran down my boat!"

"It's an intelligence-gathering and surveillance ship," Aiden supplied. "We think it's Russian but are waiting for final confirmation on that. Where did you film this?"

Sunny frowned. "I didn't write down GPS coordinates to go with each memory card. I just shot my film."

"I need you to figure it out," Aiden said soberly.

"Well, it was raining. When was the last time it rained out here?"

There was a brief pause while Grisham accessed the ship's weather logs on a computer. Apparently, the *Sea Nymph* recorded such things as a matter of course. And didn't she just feel like a completely inadequate sailor now?

Grisham called out, "Ten days ago, if we're talking the Gulf of Aden."

Sunny thought back. "I was farther south than the gulf, closer to the Horn of Africa."

"Then that would put this filming...fifteen days ago," the computer technician replied.

It had rained the day before she sailed over her parents' last-known coordinates. And that had, indeed, been about two weeks ago. "This was filmed in the vicinity of where my parents went down at sea. I had the exact coordinates of their last-position report written down. Unfortunately, my logbook went down with the *New Dawn,* so I don't have any way to get the location for you."

Sober silence met her comment. Aiden asked quietly, "What was the name of your parents' ship?"

"The *Sunshine Girl.*" The name stuck in her throat. Her parents had named their boat after her. Through a haze of tears she saw Aiden nod at Grisham, who typed again on his computer. She beat the tears back, but it wasn't a pretty fight, and she sniffed louder than she would have liked to.

She hated crying in front of these tough, disciplined soldier types. It made her feel weak and incompetent. Although, she was operating on practically no sleep, Aiden was making her crazy and people were trying to kill them. She supposed she was authorized to be a tiny bit weepy.

"I've got the coordinates from the Somalian Coast Guard search-and-rescue order," Grisham announced.

Aiden asked her with blessedly impersonal briskness, "What direction did you have to sail from filming this footage to get to your parents' grave?"

She thought back. She'd been upset enough at approaching her parents' resting spot that those few days pretty much blurred together in her mind. "North. I had to sail north to get there."

Stieg nodded. "That would have put her toward

Somalia for sure. In this area. How far did you have to sail to get to your parents' coordinates?"

"I don't know. Twelve hours or so under sail once I cast anchor."

Grisham called out, "I'll pull up the prevailing-wind reports for that day and calculate how far her boat sailed. What did the *New Dawn* weigh and what was its draft?"

She provided the technical details on her boat, a little stunned at how efficiently these guys were zeroing in on the location of that fuzzy film footage.

"I have a preliminary location," Grisham announced.

"Relay it to me," Steig ordered, bending over a navigation chart spread out across the map table in the middle of the room. In moments, a course had been calculated and laid in to the *Sea Nymph*'s autopilot.

"Can I go now?" she asked no one in particular.

"Yes," Aiden answered. "Thanks for your help."

"Uhh, sure." God, he sounded so formal. Back to being his most distant and aloof self. Except now she knew it for the complete act that it was. And somehow that made it just that much harder to swallow. She turned and left the bridge quickly lest she burst into tears for real this time.

When she woke up the next morning, the first thought to go through her mind was *I'm going swimming with Aiden today.* Although one part of her looked forward to spending the time alone with him, the rest of her dreaded it. And it wasn't just about her fear of the ocean. Which Aiden would show up today? The kind, gentle, compassionate man who'd coaxed her into the water yesterday or the unapproachable recluse who wanted nothing to do with the female half of the human race?

When the engines cut off and the *Sea Nymph* drifted to a stop a little before noon, she made her way to the swim deck astern. Aiden was waiting for her, looking too good to be legal. He had a classic swimmer's physique—broad shoulders tapering to narrow hips, and slab upon slab of ripped muscle. Memory of what that body felt like moving against hers made her insides tremble.

"I wasn't sure you'd come," he said with a smile.

Oh, God. Pleasant Aiden had shown up. This man night actually get her into the water and help her overcome her fear.

"How come you're the only guy on the whole crew who swims when the boat stops? Don't any of the other crew members swim for exercise?"

"Yes, in fact, most of them swim quite well. Today I asked them to give you some privacy so you wouldn't feel self-conscious."

She blinked, startled by his consideration. "That's incredibly thoughtful of you."

"You say that like I'm not usually thoughtful at all," he replied wryly.

Her first impulse was to say the polite thing, to disagree and assure him he was just fine. But then her frustration kicked in. That and the knowledge that, if they were ever going to have any kind of decent relationship at all, they had to be honest with each other. And now was as good a time as any to start.

"It's not that you're not thoughtful," she said slowly.

"It's that you…disconnect…with the people around you."

He stopped in the act of kicking off his flip-flops to stare at her.

She continued self-consciously, "You hold yourself apart from the people around you. Women in particular. As if we're not quite good enough for you. Or we don't quite measure up to your standards."

"That's not true at all," he replied strongly.

"Ask Gemma. I've talked with her about it. Or rather she has talked to me about it. She didn't want me to take your aloofness personally."

"Are you saying I've hurt your feelings? What have I said or done to upset you?"

"It's not so much that you say or do mean things. It's just that—" she searched for the right words, but it was hard with him staring at her like that "—you give me emotional whiplash. I never know which version of you I'm going to get from day to day or minute to minute. One second you're the kindest, warmest, most passionate guy ever. And the next, you don't surround yourself with a brick wall, you become a brick wall. You're cold and hard and completely impervious to anyone or anything around you. The other man inside you just… disappears. It's scary."

"I scare you?"

In for a penny, in for a pound. She answered honestly, "Yes. Sometimes you do. I'm scared for you and who you will become if you continue down this path."

He was silent at that. He dived into the water and disappeared under the surface. God only knew how long he'd sit down there sulking. With a sigh, Sunny sat down on the edge of the swim deck. She dangled her feet in the water and splashed water over herself again. She contemplated slipping into the water and hanging on to edge of the deck by herself, but she wasn't quite ready for that alone.

About five minutes later, Aiden surfaced in front of her without warning. He resumed the conversation as if no time had passed. "What path is it you think I'm traveling down?"

"You're isolating yourself. Cutting yourself off from mankind—or at least from all women. You're heading for a life of being completely and totally alone. With no one to love you. And in my world, that's a tragedy."

"In my world, it's my only choice."

"No, it's not!" she cried.

"Look. You know who I am. *What* I am. I can't have any kind of normal life."

"News flash, Aiden. Nobody's normal. Everybody has their own personal challenges and problems to overcome. My family was weirder than most, and I craved normal for years. When my folks died, I went looking for normal with a vengeance. And I found out eventually that it doesn't exist."

He countered, "I'm tied to the ocean for the rest of my life, and I'm useless on dry land."

"So, you live on or near a beach. And you hire someone else to mow your lawn and do manual labor around the house."

"You make it sound so simple."

"It is simple."

"What about fighting crime?"

"What about it? Lots of men have jobs where they

travel to do their work. You'll run off to do your missions, and then you'll come home when you're done. And you won't be Mr. Super Crime Fighter forever."

He shook his head. "But I'm not—" his voice dropped so low she almost didn't catch his next words "—entirely human."

Alarm jolted her. "You look pretty human to me, and with no intent to be crass, I've seen most of you."

"My exterior hasn't changed much. I'm different inside."

"Just how extensive are the changes to your body?"

"They're mostly at the cellular level. My cells absorb and hold nearly three times as much oxygen as normal cells. The veins in my arms and legs constrict faster and more strongly in response to pressure than normal people's. That keeps blood in my core and brain so I remain conscious longer. My lung tissues fill with plasma at four times the normal rate under pressure so they don't collapse when I dive deep."

"I get it. You're ideally suited for swimming and diving. That doesn't make you inhuman."

"It does make me a freak."

"To quote Albert Einstein, 'Everybody is a genius. But if you judge a fish by its ability to climb a tree, it will live its whole life believing that it is stupid.' Aiden, you happen to be a fish who found his way to water. That doesn't make you a freak. It merely makes you someone who discovered that which they are brilliant at."

He stared at her a long time, absently and effortlessly treading water in front of her. Finally, he said briskly,

"So are you going to sit there all day, or are you coming swimming with me?"

Changing subjects, huh? Well, maybe she'd given him some food for thought, after all. "Can we start small and take baby steps to work up to swimming?" she asked hesitantly.

He grinned. "Tomorrow, I'm bringing you a pair of those blow-up floats they put on kids' upper arms."

"Water wingies?"

"Yes. And a pink polka-dot bikini with ruffles on the butt."

"You wouldn't."

He grinned. "Oh, I definitely would. You'd be adorable."

She stuck out her tongue at him, grateful that he'd made her laugh, and slid off the deck. She maintained a death grip on the teak lip of the thing, though, as the cold embrace of the ocean closed in around her.

And all of a sudden, warm, strong arms were around her, too, Aiden's tanned hands gripping the deck on either side of hers. She leaned back against him, craving the reassurance of his body.

"Rest your head back against my shoulder and close your eyes," he murmured. "Relax. Let your body move with the water. Float on the current like a piece of seaweed."

She tried it but suspected she was more like a rigid hunk of driftwood than anything so fluid as seaweed.

"You're the mermaid I've been dreaming about every night since I found you," he replied low.

If only.

"Shift your hands to my wrists," he suggested softly.

The bones beneath his skin were strong and reassuring, the muscles of his forearm flexing beneath her fingers in a sexy display. His chest spooned against her back, warmer than the water, a bulwark against harm. Gradually, the easy movement of the water lulled her, soothed her. The tension left her body. They floated like that until she almost felt sleepy. It dawned on her that she felt safe.

"I think we're making progress," she announced. She opened her eyes to smile up at him and wild disorientation slammed into her. The *Sea Nymph* was at least a hundred feet away from them. And nothing but dark, deep, fathomless water surrounded them.

"Oh, God!" She went board stiff as panic smashed into her. She kicked her legs and flailed her arms reflexively, which meant she let go of Aiden's wrists and promptly slipped through the circle of his arms.

Her head went under the water. She was drowning! The ocean closed in over her and she couldn't breathe. Couldn't move. She wouldn't make it up to the surface. She was going to *die*.

Strong arms went around her thrashing body. The viselike grip terrified her all the more and she fought harder against the sucking pull of the sea. She fought toward the surface, but she couldn't move. Her arms were pinned to her sides and her legs tangled with something that wouldn't let her kick properly.

And as quickly as she'd gone under, her face burst out of the water.

"Quit fighting so I can hold you up!" a male voice grunted in her ear.

The words penetrated her panic, but their meaning

didn't fully register. She gasped for air. No matter how much or how fast she breathed, it wasn't enough. It would never be enough.

"You're hyperventilating, Sunny. Hold your breath and count to ten before you exhale or I'm going to have to put my hand over your mouth and nose for you."

Horror at the notion of someone forcibly stopping her breathing reached her mind. *One. Two. Three. Four.* She couldn't make it to ten. She exhaled hard and tried again. This time she made it to six. It took her a few more tries, but she finally got to ten.

When she finally calmed enough to take a look around her, the *Sea Nymph* was almost within arm's reach. She lunged for the swim deck and grabbed on for dear life.

"I'm sorry, Sunny. I didn't mean to scare you that bad. When you've calmed down a little, I want you to remember how good it felt to float in the water with me. Just focus on that feeling and try to hang on to that."

"I'm really tempted to turn around and punch you in the nose," she snapped.

"Fair enough," he said evenly. "But I promise, I did it for your own good. When your terror subsides, you'll see that."

"What in the hell were you thinking?" she demanded. "You said I'd take baby steps. That was a giant leap for mankind!"

He chuckled beside her. "Gemma said you needed a shock to force you to face your fear. That you should experience it again but with a positive outcome this time. It's called 'desensitization.'"

"Remind me to punch her in the nose when I see her," she grumbled.

"I will. Just promise I get to be there to see it."

She managed to turn her head far enough to scowl at him. It took her a few minutes to untense enough to even consider climbing out onto the swim deck. Aiden didn't seem inclined to boost her aboard today, and she was too embarrassed to ask. Eventually, she mastered her body enough to push herself up onto the deck. She flopped onto her stomach and then hoisted herself the rest of the way out. As Aiden popped out beside her, turning midair to land in a seated position on the deck, she sighed.

"I feel like a beached whale beside you. You're so obnoxiously graceful around water."

"Yeah, but I suck at climbing trees," he murmured.

She ventured a small smile at him. "You make a lovely fish, though."

"Thanks."

She wasn't quite sure what he was thanking her for. She got the impression it was for more than just the compliment. "Anytime."

"I'll hold you to that."

Startled, her gaze snapped to his. Well, okay, then. Maybe they'd had a breakthrough, after all.

"Forgive me for scaring you half to death?" he asked.

Now that she was safely seated aboard the swim deck with the bulk of the *Sea Nymph* at her back, her panic seemed far away. A little silly, even. Her head had gone underwater for maybe five seconds. It wasn't as if she'd ever been in the slightest danger of drowning. Not with

Aiden less than a foot away from her. "I guess so. Although I forgive you with great reluctance."

"Why's that?"

"Because you'll be tempted to try a stunt like that with me again if you get away with it this time."

"I don't think I'll be able to sneak up on you twice. You'll be on guard next time."

"Darn tootin' I will, mister. And next time I *am* going to punch you in the nose."

"Duly noted. Can I interest you in a bit of lunch? Swimming always makes me hungry."

"Well, jeez, I should think so. The way you swim you must burn off thousands of calories at a time."

He grinned. "I've been known to eat ten thousand calories a day to maintain my weight."

She raised a warning hand. "Stop. Don't say another word. Being able to eat that much and not gain weight is grounds for murder on behalf of women everywhere."

He laughed and reached a hand down to help her to her feet. He followed her up the ladder to the aft deck, and if she wasn't mistaken, his hand passed lightly over her behind as he joined her on the deck.

All in all, she had to admit their swim date had gone very well. Except for the part where she was momentarily sure she was going to die a horrible death by drowning. As residual panic bubbled up inside her, she tried Aiden's suggestion and instead focused on the blissful relaxation of floating on the ocean swells cradled in his arms. To her chagrin, it worked. Her racing pulse calmed and her breathing settled.

Most of the crew was eating when she entered the salon. It was a jovial affair, although she'd have preferred to continue her intimate conversation with Aiden in private. As she was eyeing the chocolate cake slathered in frosting and wondering if she'd burned enough calories swimming to justify a piece of it, Steig's voice came over the loudspeakers.

"Aiden, Grisham, to the bridge. We've picked up the signal from the tracking device we planted on the pirate vessel."

The salon emptied in about two seconds, leaving her alone with the temptation of that luscious cake. Oh, what the heck. She cut herself a big slice and settled in to savor every last crumb of it.

Chapter 9

Aiden watched each sweep of the radar screen intently. They mustn't lose that signal at the very edge of the screen. Whoever was trying to kill him could very well be at the other end of it. If there was a leak in Gemma's project, it had to be plugged. His life and the lives of his colleagues depended on it.

"The target's moving fast," Grisham announced from the seat in front of him.

"Don't lose it, Steig," Aiden urged. "We've got to find these guys and silence them."

"I'm fully aware of what's at stake here," Steig replied grimly. He directed his crew to shift course slightly to take advantage of a prevailing current to give them a little more of a push. Aiden couldn't fault the guy's seamanship. Steig was coaxing every last knot of speed out of the big yacht.

Slowly, slowly, they closed the gap between themselves and the red blip on the radar. The sun went down and night fell around them, and still they pursued the pirate vessel.

Steig spoke up from the captain's seat. "Aiden, have you considered the possibility that this is a trap? That we're being led exactly where these guys want us to go?"

He frowned. It was possible. And they'd been sailing away from the spot where Sunny had filmed that spy ship at a high rate of speed for hours now. If the intent was to draw them away from something the bad guys didn't want them to see, it was working.

"We should start painting the Somali coast soon," Grisham murmured from in front of the radar screen.

"Are we that close?" Aiden retorted, surprised.

Sure enough, as he spoke the words, the solid line of a coastline tickled the edge of the radar screen. Over the next few minutes it advanced across the screen as their target pulled closer and closer to shore.

"There!" Aiden exclaimed. "They've gone into some sort of cove or anchorage."

The tension on the bridge exploded into anticipation. Finally. They had the pirates trapped. The bastards could only go to land now, and this crew was as capable of pursuing and capturing the pirates on land as they were at sea. Maybe more so.

Steig gave orders to deploy two rigid inflatable boats and man them with armed teams.

"I'm going with you," Aiden announced as his name was left off the list of men to go.

"I don't think that's a good idea—" Steig started.

"How else do you expect to disable their boats without them realizing we've done it? You need me. I can prevent the pirates or their boats from escaping by water."

"But you can't help us on land."

"Then I'll stay in or near the water. You'll need somebody to stick around and guard the boats, anyway," Aiden reasoned.

Steig huffed. "You make a good point. But I don't like it. You're not a Special Forces guy."

"No, but I am a trained superhero."

"In water, maybe," Steig grumbled.

Aiden recognized that tone. Steig was going to capitulate and let him go and was grumpy because they both knew it. "Thanks, buddy. I'll stay out of the way and stick to what I'm good at. I promise."

Steig scowled and turned his attention to launching the RIBs.

Aiden hurried to the armory, where Steig's men were donning black sea-land suits and loading and checking weapons. He donned one of the black suits, as well. It was waterproof when submerged, but once it dried, it breathed like regular fabric, allowing the wearer to sweat normally. Its dark color would camouflage him nicely. He put black grease on his face and hands and smeared the stuff in his hair until it was black and plastered to his head.

"You look like a mobster, dude," the team leader, a bag man named Clyde, joked.

"I feel like one."

"Just remember, you're not there to kick ass. That's

our job. You disable their boat if you can and guard ours. That's it."

"Yeah, yeah," Aiden groused good-naturedly.

In a matter of minutes, they were speeding across the ocean, banging along the tops of the swells at well over fifty knots. There were six men on each vessel, and they stayed in contact with Steig via earbud/microphone combinations. As they neared the coast, the boats slowed, settling into the water more like regular boats as they eased forward. Small electric motors were deployed to make a stealthy approach to the pirate's cove. And then the men in the lead boat signaled Aiden's that they had visual on the pirate vessel.

Steig murmured, "Aiden, is that our pirates? You got the best look at their boat the last time."

Aiden was passed a pair of low-light binoculars and, in a few moments, replied under his breath, "Yup. That's them." He'd recognize that piece of crap hull and gleaming propeller shafts anywhere. The boat was moored in a small cove, maybe fifty feet offshore, with a white strip of beach beyond it."

Clyde murmured, "We won't be able to get much closer undetected. I'm going to dump out Aiden and let him do his thing. Once he's taken out their engines, we'll put ashore a few hundred yards down the coast and make our way back here by land.

"Sounds good," Steig agreed.

Someone passed Aiden a black nylon backpack holding various underwater explosives and hand tools—a saboteur's tool kit. He donned the pack and two of the men on his boat lowered him noiselessly into the water. It was shallow here and nearly bathtub warm. He gave his body a few seconds to acclimate, took a deep breath and headed for his target.

He swam only about six feet down. Much deeper than that and it got too dark to see where he was going. The hull of the pirate boat came into sight, a pale bulge in the surface of the water. He eased up toward it slowly. Anticollision radar systems would detect anything metallic or fast-moving approaching the vessel. He touched the hull, which was rough and in need of a good scraping.

Steadying himself, he moved toward the twin props, which were still and silent at the moment. Vividly aware of how they'd cranked up the last time he stuck his arm inside the engine compartment, he approached carefully.

From under the water, he couldn't see much. He reached around the corner and into the engine compartment, feeling for the metal plate where he'd attached the tracking radio. There was the plate. His elbow touched the hull. The radio should be right…there.

But it wasn't.

Frowning, he extended his arm more fully into the space. Ahh. There it was. He frowned. He was sure he'd only stuck his arm in the compartment to the elbow the last time. It was why he'd been able to yank his arm out fast enough and with enough clearance that it hadn't been sliced off by the accelerating propeller.

It could mean only one thing. The tracker had been found, removed and replaced. Which meant this was a *trap*.

He had to warn Clyde and the others! He eased his arm back out of the engine compartment. He gathered himself to push away hard from the boat, to surface as soon as possible and make a radio call. But he stopped himself just in time. *Motion detectors, dammit.* If this was a trap, the pirates were bound to be watching for divers.

He drifted away from the boat with the tide, letting each wave carry him a few more feet away from the boat. He started to ease up toward the surface when a tiny orange light caught his attention. Someone was smoking on the deck of the pirate boat, probably leaning over the rail as he did so.

He had a few more minutes' worth of air in his lungs, although the way adrenaline was pounding through his veins, he'd probably burn through it pretty fast. He opted to turn and swim for the bottom, gliding along the sandy seabed and out toward open water. It was maddening having to stay under until he rounded the headland, but he had no choice. He had to warn Clyde and Steig.

He surfaced and immediately breathed into his radio, "It's a trap."

Steig's reply was immediate. "Teams One and Two, freeze. Be advised this is a trap. I repeat, it is a trap. Retreat immediately and with utmost caution."

And that was when the sound of gunfire rang out across the water.

"Talk to me, Steig," Aiden murmured. "What's going on?"

"We're under attack!" Clyde bit out. "Surrounded. Team Two is pinned down. They're spraying us with automatic fire from at least three positions."

"Team Two, report!"

"It's a firestorm. Two men hit. We're completely pinned down. Give us some covering fire, Team One, or we're not getting out of here!"

Aiden listened in agony to the garbled radio chatter. There wasn't a damned thing he could do to help those men. But he could make sure they had a way out of there once they hit the shore. He swam strongly for the RIBs, which were hidden somewhere along this coastline. Nobody was messing with them on his watch.

Aboard the *Sea Nymph,* Sunny paced in her room. There was obviously something big going on, but darned if anyone would tell her what. She'd waylaid two different sailors as they hurried down the passageway outside her door, and both men had apologized with the barest of courtesy and hustled away without telling her a thing. Both of them had been wearing high-tech wet suits as if they planned on going diving tonight.

She tried to approach the bridge and a sailor she'd never seen before told her in no uncertain terms to return to her room and stay there until further notice. Were they under attack? It didn't sound like it. The *Nymph* was perfectly silent at the moment. Even the engines, which had been turning at what sounded like full power for most of the day, were cut off.

Frustrated, she tried to watch a movie on her television but couldn't concentrate and gave up on it. Where was Aiden? Was he all right? Her gut told her that if there was danger to be had tonight, he'd be in the thick of it.

She had to be near him. She left her cabin, padded down the passage to Aiden's stateroom, let herself into the darkened room and crawled into his bed. She hugged his pillow apprehensively, inhaling the scent of him. But even that failed to comfort her. Something was wrong. She could feel it.

She lay for a long time staring at the flickering play of reflected moonlight on his ceiling. As time passed and there was only silence and dancing shadows, her eyes drifted closed.

Sunny roused vaguely when a dark shape slipped into the room. It was male and wearing one of those black wet suits she'd seen some of the crew in earlier.

"Aiden?" she murmured.

The tall shape approached the bed silently. She started to hold out her arms to him, to welcome him into his bed, when his arm shot out fast. Something cold and wet covered her mouth. She struggled for a few moments, but then black fog descended over her, and she slipped away.

The *Nymph*'s teams were getting low on ammunition. Five men were injured, two seriously. There had to be something he could do to help. Frantic, Aiden hoisted himself into the first boat and searched around for something, anything to help the trapped men. He found a lockbox with a pair of pistols inside. It wasn't much, but it was better than nothing. He stepped across the gap between the RIBs and searched the second boat quickly. This one yielded a semiautomatic assault rifle and two clips of ammunition. Now he was in business.

He grabbed the weapons and ammunition and waded ashore. He didn't need to ask for directions. All he had to do was follow the sounds of shooting. Aiden peered through the foliage using the low-light binoculars from the RIB. Jeez. It was a mess out there. He was looking over the shoulders of a trio of pirates toward a pitifully small berm of dirt that must be all the cover Clyde and his men had. The dirt was being pulverized by a machine gun as he watched. Too much more of that, and the berm would be chewed away to nothing. And then Clyde and all his brave men would die.

He shouldered his assault rifle, clicked it to full automatic and let rip at the pirates in front of him. They went down in eruptions of blood and gore from their torsos. He raced forward and turned the machine gun on the muzzle flashes from a second pirate-gun emplacement. He held the trigger down in a withering barrage of lead.

Shots winged in over his head, and he couldn't tell if they were from Clyde's guys or another pirate-gun position he hadn't spotted.

Without warning, a flurry of gunfire came from behind the berm and a half-dozen black-clad men rose up in a charge toward him, firing their weapons to their sides and rear as they sprinted toward him.

He aimed his machine gun past them. All of a sudden, it quit firing. Whether it was out of ammo or had jammed, he couldn't tell. He whipped out his pistols and fired them into the brush behind Clyde and his men, too.

Clyde reached him first. "Let's go," he shouted over the deafening gunfire.

Aiden rose up and turned to run for the boats, and it was as if someone had tightened an iron band around his chest and then shrunk it to about half its original diameter. Crud! They already had too many men down.

The two badly injured men each hung between their comrades' shoulders, limp.

Aiden took the deepest breath he could muster and held it. His body would react as if it were in the oxygen deprivation of the sea for this one breath, but after that breath ran out, it would be game over.

He ran like a man possessed, crashing through the dense underbrush toward the shore, Clyde right on his heels.

They burst out of the trees and ran right into the water. Aiden pulled himself into the first boat, stabilizing it by grabbing a low-hanging branch as Clyde's men burst out of the trees and leaped for the boats. The two seriously injured men were passed into the other boat, presumably with the team's medic.

The engines roared to life and both vessels raced like bats out of hell away from the coast and into the night. Gunfire erupted behind them and everyone ducked low as the boats flew over the water at close to seventy knots. A flurry of radio calls warned the *Nymph* to prepare for casualties, and the medic filled in Gemma on the condition of the patients they were bringing aboard and what medical equipment to have waiting for them.

Aiden, gazing toward the *Nymph,* momentarily thought he glimpsed something low and fast move across his field of vision close to the water. It could just be a dolphin or some big fish surfacing for a moment.

They drew close to the *Nymph* and there was a flurry of activity as the injured were passed aboard and whisked away for treatment. Aiden took the inhaler someone passed him and sucked greedily at it. The iron band around his chest eased a bit.

He offered to tie off the RIB while the less-injured team members boarded the *Nymph*. He slung a line around a chrome cleat, wrapping a mooring line around its T-shaped head. But as he did so, he noticed something odd. A scratch on the *Nymph*'s hull. And not just any scratch. He followed the gouge to where it ended and found a curved hole large enough to stick his finger in.

If he didn't know better, he'd say someone had sunk a grappling hook into the *Nymph*'s hull. He looked higher and spotted what looked like another one about three feet above the first one. If there were any more holes climbing the side of the yacht, they were hidden by the curve of the hull.

He glanced at his position, low and tucked in beneath the curve of the hull. And then it hit him. This was one of only two radar blind spots on the entire vessel.

He spoke urgently into his microphone. "Steig, did you get any proximity warnings tonight? Any intruder alerts?"

"*Intruder* alerts?" the Swede exclaimed.

"It looks like someone might have tried to climb the hull using grappling hooks. No one did any maintenance back here today, did they?"

"No one."

Aiden listened grimly as Steig put the vessel on full combat alert and ordered a stem-to-stern search of the *Nymph* by every available crew member. Dang, it seemed as if they'd been doing that a lot recently. Ever since they picked up Sunny and tangled with those pirates.

Frowning, he boarded the *Nymph* and headed for

the armory. His breathing still sucked, but if he moved slowly, he didn't go into horrible distress. And besides, it wasn't far to where he needed to go.

He stopped in front of Sunny's door and caught his breath for a moment before he knocked and let himself in. "Sunny, it's Aiden. I'm just checking to see if you're okay."

Nothing.

A chill shuddered through him. He'd been through this drill before, too. Where in the bloody hell was she *now?*

He spoke into his mouthpiece. "Sunny's not in her room, Steig."

It took nearly a half hour, but it was confirmed that Sunny was no longer aboard the *Sea Nymph*. Someone brought a nebulizer up to Aiden on the bridge and shoved it at him. He would have ignored it, but Steig snapped at him to use it or get carried forcibly down to the infirmary.

It didn't help. No matter how much medicine he sucked down, his panic overrode everything and kept him gasping ineffectually for air. Where was she? What had happened to her?

A quick investigation revealed that a diver had probably approached the *Nymph* undetected, climbed aboard using a pair of grappling hooks and made his way to Sunny's cabin.

After that, they could only guess, but given that there'd been no noise or evidence of a struggle, she must have been drugged or otherwise subdued and hauled off the boat.

And it was all his fault. He'd been the one hell-bent

to chase down the pirates, to barge full speed ahead into this trap, and Sunny had been the one to pay the price.

Where are you, baby?

But no matter how many times he asked the question, he got no answer.

Steig called a powwow on the bridge and was infuriatingly calm. "All right, gentlemen. We know this was a trap. I have this security footage of Sunny leaving her room at eleven-fifteen p.m. Any guesses as to where she headed?"

Aiden watched the grainy images, his heart in his throat. Please, God, let this not be his last sight of her alive. He spoke up, wincing mentally. "She sleeps in that T-shirt. If I had to guess, she headed for my room."

Thankfully, the situation was too tense for anyone to comment on that. Steig merely nodded. "That's a reasonable working assumption. Okay. She goes to your room. Sometime between eleven-fifteen and one-twenty, a diver boards the *Nymph,* drugs her and leaves the ship with her. Grisham, I need you to check every second of security film we've got."

"On it, boss."

Aiden knew as well as anyone else on board that the owner's suite was not covered by any security cameras. Leland Winston had liked his privacy over the years and insisted that no one be able to monitor him or his more private guests.

As the minutes ticked past with Grisham finding nothing, Aiden spoke the words they were all thinking. "If the intruder went out onto the master suite's deck, he could have lowered himself and Sunny into the water without detection."

Steig looked stymied, and the bridge fell silent. How were they supposed to figure out where Sunny had been taken and by whom? The ocean was a gigantic place. And, if she'd been taken ashore, Africa was an equally impossible size to search.

Time to call in the big dogs. Aiden picked up the satellite phone and dialed his boss, Jeff Winston.

"Hey, Aiden! How goes the pirate hunting? You didn't get the *Nymph* shot up again, did you?"

"No. The ship's fine. But a passenger was kidnapped tonight. We need you to buy one of those illegal satellite feeds you've been tracking down the source on. I need a real-time scan of our current location and the shoreline close to us."

"I'm sorry, Aiden. We shut down those satellite feeds a few weeks ago."

Aiden squeezed his eyes shut. Then Sunny was well and truly lost. The pain in his chest was almost more than he could bear. And it had nothing to do with asthma. He vaguely heard a female voice in the background at Jeff's end of the call.

"Hold on a sec, Aiden. I might be able to get you something. Jennifer may be able to pull some strings in the government and get you some video data."

Jennifer was Jeff's fiancée and a former CIA agent. "I'll kiss her if she can," he declared.

"There will be no kissing," Jeff growled.

Possessive, was he? Were he not so panicked over Sunny, Aiden might be amused.

"It'll take a while, Aiden, but we'll work it from this end. I'll call you back in a few minutes."

Aiden disconnected the call and looked around the

bridge. "How did someone get aboard this ship undetected, and how did they move around it without anyone spotting them? I'm not pointing fingers, here. But we need to figure it out. Maybe it'll give us a clue as to where Sunny went."

The men nodded and got to work rewinding security footage and replaying radar scans for the past few hours. No boats of any kind were picked up approaching the *Sea Nymph,* and they could only conclude that a diver or divers had made the incursion. Still, their scuba gear should have triggered various proximity alarms.

"Unless they were using nonmetal gear," Aiden surmised.

"That's expensive and high-tech stuff. Very few civilians can afford gear like that."

"Which leads to the obvious conclusion that a government was behind the kidnapping."

"Okay, so divers board the ship aft and make their way forward to my cabin. How'd they do it without being spotted?" Aiden asked.

Grisham spoke up grimly. "I think I know that one. If the intruder wore a sea-land suit like our guys use, he could've walked right down a passage without anyone thinking twice about it. Might even have passed crew members in the hall. As long as his face was covered, no one would have known he wasn't one of us."

Aiden groaned mentally. Grisham was right, dammit.

Someone else piped up. "I think I saw someone walking toward your stateroom on the security footage in a sea-land suit. Lemme back up the video… Yup, here it is."

Everyone leaned in close to stare at a man moving

quickly toward the front of the vessel. His face was not visible to the camera.

Aiden visualized the guy slipping into his cabin and scaring the hell out of Sunny. Why didn't she make a fuss? Scream and holler? "Sunny had to be asleep. She's a fighter. If someone jumped her, she'd have fought back."

Steig added, "The guy probably drugged her."

And then the obvious hit Aiden. "Why did our intruder proceed with the abduction once he realized he'd drugged the wrong person? There's no way that guy mistook Sunny for me once he picked her up. She's half my size and, well, a girl."

Everyone stared at the still image of the kidnapper in silence. It was Grisham who said slowly, "What if Sunny *was* the target?"

Chapter 10

Aiden sprinted for Sunny's cabin with Steig right on his heels. They burst into the tiny space and Aiden headed directly for her closet, where she stored the waterproof bag with her camera and memory cards. It was gone.

"Bastards took her camera and film, too."

"What the hell did she film that made them *kidnap* her to shut her up?" Steig demanded.

"I don't know. Have you still got a copy of the images that Grisham enhanced earlier?"

Steig nodded grimly.

"I think it's time to send those to Jeff and see what a supercomputer can do to analyze those images," Aiden declared.

"I think you're right."

The two men hurried back to the bridge, and after another brief, terse call to Jeff Winston, the images they'd been working on earlier were emailed to Winston Enterprises's Ops Center and its massive computer array.

Aiden paced impatiently until his asthma started to flare up and he was forced to sit. Divers had a limited range. Either a boat had been reasonably close and somehow not shown up on the *Nymph*'s radar, or the bastards had taken Sunny ashore. How in the hell were they supposed to track a diver?

He sat up abruptly. It was a long shot, but that was all they had at this point. "Grisham, can you pull up the marine radar images for the past several hours?"

"Yeah. Why?"

"There are a ton of dolphins in these waters. They tend to find human divers fascinating. What if the dolphins followed our intruder? We could use their movement on radar to track where our guy went."

"It's a flimsy theory," Steig commented.

"It's better than nothing," Aiden retorted.

In short order, he was poring over the underwater radar that painted fish movements in the water. Schools of small fish showed up as vague shadows on the screen, and larger species—tuna, sharks and dolphins—showed up as individual blips. Deep-sea fishermen used the fish radar to find their prey, but Aiden had always thought it took the sport out of fishing to find them this way.

He watched the radar images in real time but could make no sense of the random blips moving around the screen.

"Maybe if you speed it up," Grisham suggested, "you'll be able to see a pattern that way."

Aiden gave it a try. And sure enough, as soon as

the images sped up significantly, there was a definite flow of large fish along a line from the *Sea Nymph* directly toward a spot on the coastline a few miles south of where the pirate boat had been parked to lure them ashore.

"I'm going over there," Aiden announced.

"Whoa, there, big guy," Steig warned. "We've got no intel, no idea who's got her, how many men they've got or how they're armed. We'll send in a rescue team and do this right, after we've got the information we need."

"But who knows what they're doing to her!" he exclaimed.

"I know you're panicked and it is most difficult to have to sit here doing nothing. But patience is the key to success in operations like this. My men and I have tons of experience at this sort of thing."

Knowing that Steig was right and doing what the guy said were two entirely different things. Sitting around and waiting gave him far too much time to ask himself questions like how he would survive if he never saw her again. What could they have had between them if he hadn't been such an ass to her? What would he give to have a do-over with her, to court her and romance her the way she deserved? Nope, sitting and waiting didn't work at all.

Aiden slipped off the bridge with a muttered excuse about getting more meds from the infirmary, and no one challenged him. He did, indeed, head down to the infirmary to grab a spare inhaler and stuff it in his waist pouch. Gemma and the medic were still in surgery on the second badly injured man—the first had come through his surgery very well.

He'd never taken off his sea-land suit from earlier, and his face and hair were still mostly blacked. It was an easy matter to go the few steps from the infirmary to the swim deck. Hugging the shadows, he slipped into the water as quietly as he could and headed down into the sea.

He navigated underwater the way most people did on land, and he retraced the route of the dolphins toward the shore. A few of the sleek, ghostly forms actually flashed past him as he swam, as if urging him onward. He'd long believed dolphins were much more intelligent than most humans gave them credit for.

When one came close enough to brush up against him, Aiden grabbed the creature's dorsal fin and hitched a high-speed ride. As comfortable as he was in the water, these creatures could still swim ten times as fast as he could. The dolphin streaked toward shore as if it knew where Aiden was going. It was only when the water became shallow and turbulent that the creature veered off course.

In ten minutes, Aiden had covered a distance that would have taken him well over an hour to swim. He surfaced, looking for a likely landing spot. Where would a diver have come ashore with an unconscious woman in tow? This stretch of coast was too rugged and rocky for that. He paralleled the coast for a few minutes, searching, then spotted a tiny stretch of sand sandwiched between a stand of mangrove trees and a rock outcropping. He swam in cautiously.

Aiden crawled ashore on all fours, staying low and hugging the shadows close to the rocks. A path led away from the back of the tiny beach into the sparse brush.

Did he dare walk on it? Thing was, he'd be significantly slowed if he tried to be Mr. Sneaky through the brambles and weeds that lined the path. Not to mention Africa had a thriving population of dangerous snakes and insects that were not to be messed with. The path it was.

He eased upright and moved along the pale strip of dirt carefully, keeping a sharp eye out for trip wires or other hazards. Apparently, whoever was at the other end of this path was either confident in their ability to fend off anyone who followed them or believed they wouldn't be found anytime soon, for the path was trap free.

He walked for perhaps a half hour and was beginning to believe he'd come ashore at the wrong spot when he spied a structure ahead. It was dark and low and oddly shaped. He realized he was looking at a large canvas tent, except it was dug down into the ground partway. It was heavily camouflaged with branches and grass, and had a large camouflage net thrown over it. No way would this place show up on a satellite image.

And that told him a great deal about whoever was inside. They were aware of military satellites, aware that the people coming after Sunny might have access to them and these guys had the wherewithal to confound the satellites. They were probably military and definitely belonged to a government of some kind.

He'd found who he was looking for. Now, to find Sunny.

Sunny became aware of lying on her side on what felt like a canvas cot. Her shoulders ached. It took her a few minutes to deduce that her hands were tied—or more accurately, taped—behind her back, and that must be why her shoulders were so sore. Caution told her to fake continuing to be asleep. Or maybe she'd been unconscious. Her wits were clearing rapidly now, and the fuzzy feeling in her brain was retreating.

A man. She'd thought it was Aiden. He'd come close, except...

She struggled to remember, and then it came to her in a rush. It hadn't been Aiden at all. It had been a stranger, and he'd slapped something wet and cold over her face. She had a horrible nightmare about drowning that seemed too real to be a dream, and then she woke up here. She could only conclude she'd been kidnapped.

Thankfully, the drugs hadn't retreated enough for her to properly panic, yet. And besides, Aiden would come after her. No matter how conflicted he might be about having a relationship with her, he was a bornagain hero, through and through. He'd have to rescue the damsel in distress. It was part of his altered DNA. She only prayed he didn't do something stupidly heroic that got him killed in the process.

She slitted one eye open. A dirt floor came into view. She was in what looked like a large tent. A half-dozen soldiers lounged around a table in the middle, sitting in folding chairs and perched on top of big metal trunks painted olive-green. White Cyrillic characters were spray painted on the ends of the trunks.

Her mind raced. Russians had snatched her? That film footage of the strange ship must have been them, then. She had to find a way to get back to the *Nymph* and share that with Aiden. She tested her bonds. Her wrists and ankles were taped together, and a cloth was stuffed in her mouth and drying out terribly, but it didn't feel taped in. She could probably spit it out, but that would signal her captors that she was awake.

One of the soldiers glanced in her direction and she closed her eye. A male voice muttered something in what sounded like Russian, if the guttural syllables and weird consonant combinations were any indication.

Crud. One of the men was coming this way. She concentrated on going limp and lying perfectly still. The guy shook her shoulder and she let her upper body flop freely in his hand.

He said something short. Hopefully, he'd just announced that she was still out cold. If they were actively waiting for her to wake up, that must mean they were planning to question her. What information could they possibly need from her? They already knew she'd filmed them. And they already knew they needed to shut her up.

Ahh. They needed to know if anyone else had seen her film. She debated whether or not to tell them the truth. If she lied, she would protect Aiden and Steig and the others, but then the Russians could just kill her and be done with their security leak.

If she told the truth, the Russians would know someone was likely to attempt a rescue of her. It might distract them, and it might force them to keep her alive as a bargaining chip for a little while. However, giving up Aiden and the others would certainly get the *Sea Nymph* attacked or worse. The men in front of her looked fully capable of blowing up the yacht and everyone on it without a second thought.

She could hear Steig telling her not to underestimate his crew and to go ahead and put them in harm's way.

Actually, she didn't have any great qualms about doing that. He and his men were soldiers, after all.

But Aiden…the idea of putting him at risk made her ill. She couldn't do it. If she had to choose between her life and his, she would have to choose his. She couldn't imagine living with knowing she'd let him sacrifice himself for her. The very notion made her shudder.

The best option of all would be to escape from this place before the Russians could question her at all. But she didn't see how she was going to do that tied up and lying out here in plain sight of her very armed, very dangerous captors.

She was relieved when someone got the bright idea to pull out her camera and start watching her film footage. She supposed she should be surprised these guys had found her camera and snagged it, too, but they were too thorough to have missed it, she supposed. They must have searched the *Nymph* until they'd found her clothes and possessions.

The film of the spy ship had been on the third memory card. If these guys were impatient and fast-forwarded a lot, she had ten, maybe fifteen minutes to figure out a way out of here. She edged toward the back of her cot. By straining until her shoulders ached, she could brush her fingertips against the canvas. She scratched at it experimentally with her nails. No way was she going to be able to rip through it on her own.

Aiden studied the tent carefully. He could dig down to the bottom of one of the canvas panels and sneak inside easily enough. But without windows of any kind, he had no idea how many men were inside, how they were arrayed and where Sunny might be among them.

The good news was he didn't hear the sounds of any interrogation—or torture—ongoing inside. If they'd drugged Sunny, maybe she wasn't awake yet. But that respite would end soon enough. And then she'd have the undivided attention of whoever was in there, and his window for rescuing her would close.

There was no help for it. He was just going to have to choose a spot and start digging. He moved around to the back of the tent farthest from the tied-down flap that was the only entrance, and started to push sand and dirt away with his hands. It was hard work, and his asthma wasted no time complaining about it. He was forced to stop and rest, to catch his breath and risk a noisy puff on his inhaler.

Fury at his body for betraying him like this washed over him. What kind of man was he if he couldn't even do this small task to save the life of the woman he loved?

Whoa. The woman he—just whoa.

He had no choice. He had to press on. He resumed digging and did his damnedest to pace himself and control his breathing.

Aiden started as a quiet scratching noise came from his right. He froze, listening. There it was again. And that wasn't an animal. The noise was too rhythmic for that and, furthermore, sounded as if it came from the other side of the thin canvas wall. His heart pounding hopefully, he moved over to approximately where he thought the sound had come from.

He scratched once, carefully.

Immediately, the scratching resumed. He put his palm on the cloth and jolted when what felt like fingernails raked across his flesh through the canvas.

"Sunny?" he barely breathed.

Another scratch. Harder, this time.

He didn't risk speaking anymore but commenced digging with new vigor. It only lasted a minute or two, and then his lungs shut down hard. Frantic to keep going, he took a long pull on his inhaler. *C'mon, meds. Do your magic.* Silently begging his body not to fail him, not to fail Sunny, he dug down about three feet. It was murderous work. For every armful of loose sand he pulled aside, half of it slid back down into the hole.

But he persisted, and as he began to feel light-headed and dizzy, he spied the bottom edge of the tent. He lay down flat and lifted the canvas a few millimeters. He saw cot legs close by and a cluster of table legs, chair legs and combat boots in the middle of the large space.

He reached for the knife he always had strapped to his right calf and very, very carefully sawed at the canvas. It was hard to do it quietly, and the fabric's seams were tough and stubborn. He was barely able to breathe by the time he cut his way through the first quarter inch of the damned tent.

In danger of passing out, he lay back for a few seconds, closed his eyes and prayed for air. How could he be so strong in the water and so damned helpless on land? He wasn't even half a man.

Another scratch at the canvas made him sit up. He took a quick peek under the tent. The boots were still on the far side of the space. He commenced cutting the canvas again, but now that he was slicing through only a single layer of fabric, it went much more easily. His biggest problem was keeping it quiet and not letting the canvas make a big rip all at once.

He realized he was holding his breath and quickly let it out. Not a good idea in his current respiratory distress.

The rip in the tent should be covered by Sunny's cot, so he kept cutting upward until her hands came into sight. The bastards had duct taped her wrists together. He reached through the narrow opening and slipped his knife between her wrists. He took a second to give her hand a squeeze and then he cut through the tape. He tugged on her hands to signal her to move backward, but she didn't budge.

Confused, he peered through the opening and saw her pointing downward with a finger. He craned to see to her left and spotted her slowly pulling her feet backward and up toward her rear end. Ahh. Her ankles were taped, too.

He slipped his arm through the slit and reached toward her feet. A quick slash through that set of tape and she was free.

She eased very gradually onto her back. An arm came through the slit. A leg came through awkwardly. An exclamation came from inside from a few male voices, not as if someone was sending up an alarm, but more as if they'd seen something that surprised them.

Sunny rolled through the slit all in a rush, bowling him over. She drew breath as if to speak, and he pressed a finger across her lips. She nodded and scrambled off him. He stood up and immediately swayed violently.

Ever perceptive, Sunny slipped a shoulder under his armpit and guided him away from the tent. She turned toward the path that snaked away toward the water, and he shook his head. He pointed south into the brush.

She frowned but went along as he started moving in that direction. The Russians would assume he and Sunny would make a beeline for the shore. And if he could've run for squat, he would have. But no way could he run the mile or so back to the shore without passing out and stranding Sunny out here no closer to real rescue than before.

The good news about making their way through the tangle of weeds and thorns was they had to go slow. Really slow. Almost, but not quite, slow enough for him to breathe.

When they were perhaps a hundred feet away from the tent, a shout went up inside it. He and Sunny dropped flat on the ground by mutual, unspoken agreement. There was a lot of noise as a bunch of soldiers went barreling down the path toward the shore, shouting back and forth in Russian. As the voices grew distant, he and Sunny eased to crouches and continued on. Small problem, though. Proceeding like this took significantly more physical effort than walking, and in no time he was gasping like a dying fish.

Sunny tugged on his sleeve and signaled for him to stop. She made breathing motions with her hand in front of her chest. Right. If only it were that easy. He'd spent most of his life taking the simple act of inhaling and exhaling for granted. Who'd have guessed it was not an optional human activity?

When the overwhelming desire to lie down and pass out receded an inch or two, he nodded to her, and they continued. And so it was, a few minutes of careful sneaking cross-country followed by far too many minutes of resting and gasping. Lather, rinse and repeat, ad infinitum.

They weren't making nearly enough progress nearly fast enough. They had to get far enough away from their pursuers so they could angle toward the shore and the safety of the sea. Although how he was going to get Sunny to swim several miles of open ocean to the *Nymph,* he had no idea. One crisis at a time. He'd cross that bridge when he came to it.

Every nerve in Sunny's body screamed at her to run away from her captors as fast as she could. But maddeningly, Aiden couldn't. *They* couldn't. And no way on God's green earth was she leaving him behind. At one point he whispered to her to go on without him, and she cut him off midsentence with a sharp "Not happening."

She heard, very faint in the distance, a ruckus. It sounded as if it was coming from the direction of the tent. The Russians who'd raced down to the ocean must have figured out that she and her rescuers hadn't headed that way. Crud. Now the soldiers would come out into the bush looking for them.

How Aiden kept going, she had no idea. He staggered, and she wrapped her arm around his waist. "Put your arm across my shoulders." He leaned heavily on her, an indication of just how wiped out he really was. The man could barely support his own body weight.

"I think it's time we headed for the water," she whispered.

They'd been gradually angling southeast toward the water for a while now. Hopefully, the ocean and safety weren't far away. But she had no way of knowing. Aiden nodded wearily. The guy looked ready to drop where he stood. He'd been in bad shape when they'd fled their attackers in Djibouti City, but that had been nothing compared to this. With every step he tottered as if he might go down. But somehow, he was managing to stay upright. The man's courage was incredible. If she hadn't loved him a little before, she darned well did now.

Were it not for his dogged determination, she would probably be curled up in a ball under a bush somewhere with her eyes squeezed shut, praying for it all to go away. But for him, she had to be better than that. She couldn't give up. She drew strength from somewhere deep within her that she'd never known she had.

"Any idea how far it is to the shore?" she asked under her breath.

"Too far," he muttered.

"We'll make it. We have to."

He squeezed her hand but didn't waste breath answering.

She thought she smelled salt water and gave him an encouraging squeeze back. "Almost there." She was blatantly lying, but the man was clearly on his last legs. Encouragingly, she murmured, "Think how good it's going to feel to get into the water and breathe right again."

That got a snort out of him. She had no idea if that was how his gift worked. Would water cure one of his asthma attacks, or would it just drown him? She wouldn't think about that now. The first order of business was to get away from her kidnappers.

Sunny was lying to him about being close to the shore, but he loved her for it. Were it not for her, he'd have lain down and passed out about a mile back. He'd had a rough night before he'd even come ashore the second time. And he had no business running around like this even on a good day. He was a fish climbing a tree at the moment, and having about as much success as one.

By his estimation, they had nearly a half mile to go. Unless, by some lucky miracle, the coast took an inward dip down this way. For the life of him, he couldn't remember what it had looked like on the radar screen on the *Nymph*'s bridge. He'd been too panicked by her capture to register much of anything.

They stumbled around a nasty stand of scrub trees with long, eye-height thorns and stopped cold. A path ran left and right before them. Did they dare take it? God knew, it would make the going easier. And the only place a path going east-west could lead would be to the shore.

Sunny was looking at him beseechingly. He nodded to her and she sagged in relief.

"You set the pace," she breathed.

He moved off as fast as he dared, pushing each stride to be a little longer, a little faster. He still had to stop to huff and puff far too often. But they made significantly faster progress now that they weren't constantly having to detour around thickets and stop every few seconds to untangle their clothes from thorns. Of course, the minute the Russians found this path, they'd sprint down it to the water.

The two of them had been walking down the path for maybe five minutes, and he could definitely smell salt water close by when he heard the sound he'd dreaded. Shouts from behind them.

"Run," he ordered Sunny.

"Not without you," she snapped.

Dammit, she could live if she hit the water before the Russians caught up with them. But as sure as he was standing here, he knew she wouldn't go without him. Her loyalty, her willingness to put herself in mortal danger to stay with him, humbled him. He owed her a shot at surviving. If he was still conscious and could put one foot in front of another, he was going to keep going. He took as big a breath as his violently constricted bronchial tubes would allow and broke into a shambling run.

Gradually, as muscles completely unused to the motion adapted and his adrenal gland summoned one last burst of energy for his exhausted body, his strides lengthened. Evened out. Found a rhythm. It had been years since he'd actually run like this. He used to run all the time, play soccer and basketball and just jog for the hell of it. But once he'd started the stem-cell therapy, all that had stopped.

In a strange way, it felt good to stretch his legs out, to pump his arms. To race across the ground with ground-eating strides. But he knew the price he would pay for it in about two minutes. Hopefully, that would be enough time for him to get Sunny to safety before he turned and made what would no doubt be his last stand.

Chapter 11

Sunny was shocked when Aiden took off running. It had to be costing him unimaginable pain. She took off after him, marveling at his bravery. The ground underfoot became softer, whiter, sandier. The scrub gave way to sharp-edged grasses. And that was definitely the sound of waves ahead. They'd almost made it.

"Voht! Voht tak!" someone shouted behind them.

She swore mentally. They were out of time. The Russians had spotted them.

"Run!" she screamed at Aiden. Whether or not he had any more speed left in him, she had no idea. But she ran for her life. She pulled even with him. Pulled a step ahead of him. If she wasn't mistaken, he was slowing down. No. Oh, no. They'd almost made it. Just over the rise ahead was surely water.

"Come on," she spared enough breath to pant.

"You go on. I'll hold them off. Buy you time."

She grabbed his hand and pulled him forward by main force. "Don't need time. Won't leave without you. Both of us or nothing."

He threw her an exasperated look and sped up once more. Distrusting him, she hung on to his hand as they topped the rocky outcropping.

A sheer cliff dropped maybe thirty feet straight down into the sea. She screeched to a halt, yanking Aiden back with her. Gunfire erupted behind them, and she ducked as bullets flew over their heads.

"Jump!" Aiden shouted.

"I can't!" she shouted back.

"Both or nothing!"

Damn him. She raced forward the last few steps and, still holding his hand, leaped off into space. God, she hoped the water was more than a few feet deep, or this was going to really hurt.

They smashed into the surface of the water with a deafening ripping sound. Her entire body was jarred as the cold shocked her into a higher, heretofore unknown, state of panic.

Something crushed her right hand and gave a yank on her right arm that all but tore it out of the socket. Before she hardly knew what was happening, Aiden dragged her to the surface. Her face burst clear of the water and she took a gasping breath that was half scream.

"One more breath," Aiden grunted, "then back down. "I won't let you go. I swear. Keep your eyes closed."

It was a nightmare. For the next few minutes, which took an eternity, he dragged her along underwater, surfacing every thirty seconds or so for her to take a breath. It must be maddening to him to stop that often to breathe. Although, he was gasping nearly as loudly as she was. He'd been in pretty horrendous shape when they'd hit the water.

Finally, he surfaced and stayed afloat with her.

"Are we clear?" she spluttered.

"I think so. Can you tread water by yourself for a few minutes? I've got to make a deep dive or I'm going to pass out."

"Uhh, sure."

And he was gone. She was alone, bobbing in the wide-open expanse of the Pacific Ocean all by herself. The shore was a black hump in the distance, not that she had any desire to return to it and the armed men waiting for her there. Of course, with her luck, the jerks would be on their way out here any second in speedboats to run over her and Aiden.

Worry about him crowded forward. What if he was in too bad a shape to straighten out his breathing? She wasn't anywhere close to a strong enough swimmer to drag his inert form back to shore, let alone to swim around out here without him for any length of time.

What if he was drowning below? How would she know to rescue him? Should she go under and look for him now? Except the water was pitch-black even on the surface. How was she supposed to see him?

Her panic for him actually overrode her panic for herself, and she turned in circles, trying frantically to spot him. *Come on, Aiden. Surface already.* The minutes ticked by like hours, and she counted to sixty in her head over and over. Seven minutes. Eight. Nine. *Ten.*

Oh, God. She couldn't lose him. Not like this. Not to the sea where he was so at home. So at peace. It was his friend. It couldn't turn on him!

She needed him. How was she to go on without him? It dawned on her she wasn't asking that question in the context of getting out of the ocean in the next few hours. How was she to go on with her life without him? He had become an integral part of who she was. He already defined her future. Without him she was nothing. She had nothing.

As suddenly as he'd left, he surfaced beside her. "Miss me?"

She flung herself forward the few feet that separated them. "Don't you ever leave me like that again!" she cried. He caught her body against his, and she greedily hugged his warmth and vibrant energy. "How are you doing? I was terrified you were going to pass out and drown, and I'd have no way of finding you and saving you." She was babbling, but she couldn't help herself.

"I'm fine. I just had to go deep and sit while my body adapted to the pressure and reset itself."

"You can breathe now?"

"Wouldn't be here if I couldn't," he replied jauntily.

A little too jauntily. She stared at his shadowed face suspiciously. "You weren't sure going down there would work," she accused.

"In theory, it should. But I've never tried it before tonight."

"Remind me to kill you when we get back to the *Nymph*." She looked around at the endless water. "Speaking of which, how are we going to find her?"

He let go of her with one arm and fished around

down by his ankle. "No prob. GPS locator beacon. Steig makes me wear one when I go swimming by myself for a long time."

"God bless him," Sunny declared.

"If you don't object, I'm going to suggest we make our way farther out to sea. Our pursuers will stick close to the coast in their initial search for us."

"You mean they're out here somewhere?" she whispered, appalled.

"Of course. But two swimmers make for a very, very small target. They'll have a hard time spotting us unless they get practically on top of us."

"That's *not* encouraging, Aiden. And I don't think I can go underwater again."

"No problem. We'll just paddle along on the surface. You won't even have to put your face in the water."

That, she could handle. They took off swimming toward deeper water. It didn't feel as if they made any forward progress whatsoever, but Aiden insisted they were making great headway. The black hump of the coast retreated to a thin line in the distance behind them.

Across the water, she heard a faint noise. It grew louder fast, resolving from a distant buzz into the roar of a high-speed boat motor. She reached out and gripped Aiden's shoulder in panic.

"Relax. It's the good guys," he murmured.

"How can you be sure?"

"Because I recognize the vibration of that engine on my skin."

"Good Lord. You really are half fish, aren't you?"

"Nah. I just spend a ton of time in the water. Over time you start to notice things like that."

In another minute or so, one of the *Nymph*'s RIBs pulled up beside them and cut its engines. Steig himself was at the helm. He leaned over the side of the boat and asked casually, "You two enjoying your swim, or can I offer you a ride back to the *Nymph*?"

She tried not to sob as a pair of men lifted her aboard, but she failed. The night's events caught up with her all at once, and she shivered under the wool blanket someone tossed around her. Finally, as she completely broke down, Aiden collected her in his lap, where she curled up and let it all out.

As her crying jag wound down, it dawned on her how weird it was to cry like a baby in front of a half-dozen armed, grim-faced soldiers. To their credit, though, they were all looking out to sea with their backs to her and Aiden, and not one of them said a word about it.

The RIB's prow ran right up onto the swim platform, and she and Aiden stepped out onto the familiar teak deck. She wanted a hot shower and to collapse in bed with Aiden.

But Steig had other plans. He hustled the two of them up to the bridge and immediately passed a headset to Aiden, who donned it, looking puzzled.

The man on the other end of the line was broadcast over a speakerphone for everyone to hear. "Aiden, buddy, is that you?"

"Jeff. Yeah. It's me. Sunny and I are fine."

"You scared the bejesus out of us all tonight. Don't ever do anything like that again without letting someone know where you've gone!"

Sunny threw Aiden a dirty look to emphasize his boss's tirade.

"I hear you. But you know how it is when there's a woman involved."

Every pair of eyes in the place riveted on Sunny, and she squirmed as her face heated up.

Jeff Winston was speaking again. "I've been yelling at Uncle Sam for the past two hours, and Jennifer's been pulling strings like crazy. They finally caved in. If you guys look shoreward in about three minutes, you should get a nice show."

Sunny looked over at Aiden, confused. A grin lit his face and he pulled her over to the starboard window. She murmured, "What's up?"

"It's good to have friends in high places" was his cryptic reply.

She stared out at the blackness of the ocean and the night, just happy to be alive and holding on to Aiden. Gratitude at whatever fate had protected them both this night flooded her.

A flash of light abruptly disturbed the blackness outside. A distant orange glow lingered, a low smudge on the horizon. A second flash exploded to the right of the first. This one left a larger orange glow that lasted for longer.

"What's that?" she exclaimed.

"That's a predator drone taking out the Russian camp and the pirate vessel they used as bait to lure us in."

"A drone? I don't understand."

"Jeff and his fiancée convinced the U.S. government to deploy an unmanned aerial vehicle—a remote-controlled airplane, basically—to blow up the guys who kidnapped you."

"Why would the government do that?"

Aiden answered drily, "They have a mandate to combat piracy. An American citizen was kidnapped by pirates, and Uncle Sam was well within its rights to mount a rescue operation followed by a small cleanup operation."

Friends in high places, indeed. She couldn't even imagine the influence Winston Enterprises must have to be able to ask Uncle Sam to drop a few bombs as a favor. "Where does Jeff Winston get that much power from?" she asked.

"The government is *very* grateful that we're doing the stem-cell research for them and saving them the controversy of doing it themselves."

"Grateful enough to drop bombs?" she demanded, her journalist's instincts kicking in hard.

Aiden gestured at the fading glow on the horizon. "The thing speaks for itself, does it not?"

She just shook her head.

"And by the way," Aiden added gently, "you never saw anything tonight. For all you know, that could've been some local village shooting off fireworks."

Given the fact that Uncle Sam had just taken out the men who'd kidnapped her and tried to kill her and Aiden, and that she would sleep immeasurably better knowing those thugs were dead, she could work with the firework story.

"Got it," she replied briskly. "Too bad we weren't close enough to enjoy the fireworks more fully."

Everyone on the bridge grinned.

"Tired?" Aiden asked her.

"Beyond exhausted."

Steig commented, "I'll be posting armed guards outside your stateroom tonight, Aiden. I'd appreciate it if the two of you both stayed there so I can consolidate my shipboard security around a single location. I hear the sofa bed in your stateroom is quite comfortable."

"Mmm. Quite," Aiden retorted drily.

Sunny whacked him on the arm as he grinned at his friend.

"And I don't care what Leland Winston's privacy policy is," the Swede declared, "tomorrow I'm having cameras installed in the hall outside that room and on the private deck."

Aiden's grin faded. "I concur. Enough is enough. And while you're at it, shall we set sail for the coordinates of Sunny's film?"

"My film!" she wailed. "The Russians stole it and Uncle Sam just blew it up!"

Grisham piped up from across the bridge. "Begging your pardon, Miss Sunny, but I have digital copies of all your footage stored in my computer. I burned them onto my backup drive when I was digitally enhancing them."

She gave the guy a huge hug. "You're a lifesaver!"

Aiden cleared his throat behind her and everyone laughed. She turned the embarrassed sailor loose and gladly headed down to Aiden's stateroom to crash. True to his word, Steig already had a man stationed in the passage outside, toting a wicked-looking gun.

As she snuggled close to Aiden, her ear pressed against his chest. "I don't hear any wheezing in your lungs," she murmured sleepily.

"Gemma's going to be thrilled to find out that pressuring me up fixes my asthma so quickly. I have visions of spending the next year in a hyperbaric chamber while she tests the effect ad nauseam."

Sunny's eyes drifted closed as exhaustion dragged her under. "Can I go with you? I don't ever want to be apart from you again."

"Me, neither."

And those were the last words as she finally gave in to the urge to close her eyes and wish it all away. Except for Aiden. Never Aiden.

His last words to Sunny the night before still ringing in his ears, Aiden slipped out of bed late the next morning while she slept on. He gazed down at her in his bed, her hair spread out over the pillow and half-covering her face, one bare shoulder peeking out from under the sheets. There was nowhere else on Earth he'd rather have her than in his bed, looking totally at home.

But yesterday had been a grim reality check. She was more than a weakness for him. She was his own personal Achilles' heel. And in his line of work, he couldn't afford to give anyone the capacity to harm or manipulate him through her.

As much as he loved her—hell, *because* he loved her—he had to walk away from her. He didn't dare let her stay in his life. He couldn't ever put her in that kind of danger again. And as long as he was tangling with bad people for a living, his enemies would keep coming after her.

Although how he was going to explain all that to her, he hadn't a clue. How do you tell someone, "I love you, therefore, I have to leave you?"

As he'd expected, Gemma insisted on running every

test in her lab on him and a few new ones he was sure she thought up on the spot just to torture him. The good news was it tied him up for most of the afternoon. It was an easy enough matter to avoid private conversation with Sunny by lingering with the crew after dinner in the salon. Chef had prepared a celebration feast that everyone had gathered to enjoy, and the wine and laughter both flowed.

Sunny looked at him expectantly as the hour grew late, and he mentally cringed. If he'd thought forcing himself to keep running past exhaustion and nearly past the point of losing consciousness had been hard, it was nothing compared to forcing himself to face Sunny and break her heart.

But as the salon emptied and Sunny came over to stand beside him, the moment of truth was upon him. He stood and offered her his arm. He was most certainly not doing this in public in front of the security cameras that now bristled all over the yacht.

"Sunny, we need to talk."

Her face lit up. "Great! What's up?"

"In private, okay?"

Her eyes sparkled. Crap. Did she think he was going to propose? Oh, Lord. He was going to break her heart even worse than he'd realized.

They'd walked about halfway to his stateroom when Steig's voice came over the ship's intercom. "Aiden, if you could come to the bridge, we're approaching Sunny's coordinates."

Praise the Lord. Okay, so he was a coward. He admitted it. And he could live with that. Taking the escape Steig had given him with abject gratitude, he murmured, "Why don't you go on to bed? I don't know how long this will take."

"Like I'm not going up there with you?" she demanded belligerently.

He sighed. "Let's go."

Sunny took off running ahead of him and turned it into a race. Vixen. He took off running behind her. After all the bronchodilaters Gemma had pumped into him today, he could handle one lousy sprint to put one sassy female firmly in her place. He caught her just outside the bridge and grabbed her around the waist, pulling her back to him reflexively before he could stop and think about the message it sent her. The wrong message. No wonder she was so confused and accused him of giving her emotional whiplash. He had a bad case of it himself.

She turned in his arms, laughing, her golden-brown eyes glowing like the sun she was named after. It was like holding liquid light in his arms. She threw her arms around his neck and kissed him, bathing him in an all that warmth and joy. He couldn't help but bask in it until he was practically drunk on her.

God, he loved this woman.

And she was not for him.

Chapter 12

Sunny scanned the ocean beyond the *Nymph*. They were at the exact spot where she'd filmed the images that had apparently caused so much trouble. She wasn't sure what she'd expected to see, but this was decidedly anticlimactic. There was just water and more water glistening under a rising half-moon. "Where are the bad guys?" she demanded indignantly.

Everyone grinned and Aiden replied, "As if it would be that easy." To Steig, he asked, "Has Winston Ops gotten back to us yet with the enhanced images from Sunny's film?"

"I got a message saying they'd passed the images on to the NSA to have a look at."

"The NSA?" Sunny blurted. "As in National Security Agency?"

"The very same," Steig answered. "And to anticipate your next question, I don't know why. Probably because they specialize in high-caliber photo intelligence analysis."

Grisham started a detailed radar scan of the ocean below the *Nymph*. They sailed slowly in ever-expanding circles in search of whatever had caused the Russians to make three attempts to kidnap or kill her.

As time wore on and the painstakingly slow search became, quite frankly, as boring as watching grass grow, her mind drifted. How weird was it that her parents had died right in this area and that the Russians would try to kill her over something she'd seen here?

That rainy day of filming hadn't stood out as anything special in her mind. She'd known she was too far from the fishing ship and that the rain was too heavy to get any usable film. But she'd been bored to tears then, too, and had pulled out her camera simply to have something to do.

"You know," she said suddenly, "I think that Russian ship I filmed was sailing in circles, too."

"Searching for something?" Aiden asked quickly.

"I'm not aware of too many whales that swim in circles when being pursued by a whaling vessel," she replied drily.

Steig nodded. "Okay. So a surveillance ship was looking for something. Were its antennae and satellite dishes pointed up at the sky or down at the water?"

She and Grisham answered simultaneously. "Down."

"We're on the right track, then." Aiden nodded. "We're looking for something underwater. As soon as it gets light out, I'm going in. Maybe I can spot something the radar missed."

Like what, she couldn't imagine. But he was the big expert on the underwater world. Even though Aiden looked exhausted and would no doubt spend most of the next day swimming, he declined her offer to go to bed with him sometime in the wee hours of the night. A little warning bell tinkled in the back of her mind. Was he avoiding her?

She pshawed the notion. Nearly dying together was known for drawing people closer together, right? It had a name…the foxhole effect, or something like that.

She felt a little weird passing the armed guard as she stepped into Aiden's room, but hey, it wasn't any secret that the two of them were together at this point. She fell asleep before he joined her. But when she woke up in the morning, his pillow was smooth and undented, the blankets on his side of the bed still neatly tucked in. He hadn't come to bed last night? Did that mean they'd found something?

She leaped out of bed and hurried through getting dressed. She hustled up to the bridge and burst into the crowded space. A half-dozen men were up here, watching the water with binoculars.

"What's up?" she asked no one in particular.

"Aiden's diving," Steig answered absently.

"Of course he is. Why the big watching party?"

"We've got several unidentified ships on long-range radar."

"Incoming?" she asked tersely.

"Yup."

"You've got to get him out of the water! We've got to get away from here!" she cried.

Steig sent her a raised eyebrow. "If you know how to convince Aiden of that, by all means, give it a go."

"How long has he been down there?" she asked.

"Eight minutes so far this time," someone answered casually.

Grisham commented, "I've never seen him go twelve, and to have done it so many times already… he's having a heck of a good day."

"A good day?" she exclaimed. "Do you have any idea how dangerous it is to dive for that long? And I suppose he's alone and you guys and your binoculars are his only safety net. What if he passes out while he's underwater? Who's going to know to go rescue him? There should be a diver out there with him, particularly given that there are hostiles headed this way."

"Hostiles, huh? Listen to her, getting all military," Steig said indulgently. "Before long, you'll actually call the front of a boat a prow and the back a stern."

"This isn't a boat," she snapped. "It's a yacht." Chuckles sounded all round. "And quit trying to distract me. Someone should be out there with him."

Steig lifted his eyes away from his binoculars to stare at her. "I don't have anyone who can keep up with him. He can dive deeper and swim faster than anyone I've got. And believe me, my men are as good as they come at underwater operations."

"How deep is he going?" she asked, alarmed. When no one answered, she walked right up to Steig and asked him again, "How deep?"

Grisham answered reluctantly from behind him. "My radar painted him at a depth of nearly three hundred meters on his last dive."

"*What?* That's unsafe. It's more than unsafe. It's insane!"

"Sunny, Aiden is not a regular diver. He knows what he's doing."

"No, he doesn't. He's determined to be a hero. He's out there taking ridiculous risks in the name of finding whatever the Russians want to hide. You've got to stop him. Bring him in."

"I *can't.*"

She stormed off the bridge rather than scream—or worse, burst into tears—in front of Steig and his men. She stomped down to the infirmary to find Gemma. The scientist might not be exactly a social Einstein, but at least she was a woman. She'd understand how infuriating men could be sometimes. All women had that in common.

The doctor was just finishing up checking one of the two men who'd been shot in the big firefight two nights ago when Sunny barged into the infirmary.

"Hey, Pete." Sunny checked herself enough to ask pleasantly, "How're you doing?"

"Right as rain," he replied cheerfully.

"And Sykes?" Sunny asked Gemma.

"He's stable. As long as his gut doesn't infect, he should make a full recovery."

Grimacing, she asked the doctor, "Have you got a minute?"

"Sure. What's wrong?"

Nope, not a social Einstein. "In private?" she asked Gemma.

"Ahh. Of course."

Sunny followed the woman into a tiny office and

closed the door behind her. "Aiden's going to drive me crazy, and I need you to help me talk some sense into him!" Sunny burst out.

Gemma laughed. "Good luck with that. I've been trying for two years to no avail."

"But he's going to get himself killed!" Sunny exclaimed.

"Indeed, he will."

Wow. Not comforting. "What are we going to do?"

The doctor steepled her hands in front of her chin. "There's not much I can do. He's got it in his head that he has a sacred duty to use his enhanced abilities for the betterment of mankind, up to and including dying."

"He can better mankind all he wants. I just want him to have a little care for his safety. Did you know he's been diving three hundred meters down today and staying underwater for twelve minutes at a time?"

"Is he, now? That's very interesting." The doctor picked up a pen and scribbled on a pad of paper. It looked as if she was doing rapid mathematical calculations. "I wonder…" she muttered. "Supersaturating his body with bronchodilaters…twenty percent increase in maximum exposure. Another sixteen percent in tolerated pounds per square-inch pressure…very interesting, indeed…"

Sunny cleared her throat, and Gemma looked up, startled, as if she'd forgotten Sunny was there. The doctor nodded. "Thank you very much for this information. It's fascinating."

Sheesh. Problem focusing on the conversation much? "That's not why I came, Doctor. I'm worried about him. You've got to make him stop taking crazy risks."

"Oh, I think you're the only one who can do that," Gemma said vaguely.

"Excuse me? How's that?"

"He loves you. I figure that's about the only incentive strong enough to convince him to give up taking death-defying risks. Did you know that men's car-insurance rates go down by as much as fifty percent when they get married? Actuaries claim it has nothing to do with the wife nagging the husband to drive safer, but studies have shown that's the most likely statistical source of married men's abrupt improvement in driving safety—"

Sunny stood up, interrupting the doctor's tangent. "A) He's never said or done anything to indicate that his feelings rise to that level, and B) I'm not at all sure it matters to him. He's out there right now all but killing himself."

"He's fine. My research indicates he'll ultimately be able to tolerate depths approaching five hundred meters and stay underwater for up to twenty minutes. It's as much a psychological barrier as a physical one preventing him from already having done both—"

Sunny had heard enough. Gemma wasn't going to be the slightest bit helpful. The woman was too caught up in the science of it all to see the human beings behind her research. If she wasn't so frustrated at failing to gain an ally in her fight to stop Aiden from killing himself, Sunny might have been sorry for the woman.

She prowled the ship for the rest of the afternoon and into the evening before Aiden finally came aboard. She was waiting on the swim platform with Steig and several other men as he pulled himself wearily out of the water.

"What did you find?" Steig asked before she could open her mouth to rail at him.

"Interesting underwater rock formation," Aiden replied. "As our navigation charts and Grisham's radar scans showed, there is, indeed, an old volcano down there. Caldera's at least a mile across. The rim comes within about seventy feet of the surface. It's old. The various volcanic minerals are eroding at different rates. It's a maze of caves and crevices down there."

"Spot anything that would merit a Russian spy ship investigating?" Steig responded.

If she could've pushed through the line of big bodies between her and Aiden, she would have. And to go around them would bring her perilously close to the edge of the swim platform. After yesterday's fun with yet more swimming for her life, she *really* wasn't ever going into the water again. Next time, the Russians could just shoot her.

Aiden was speaking again. "...have only explored a tiny bit of the volcano's face. Is there any way we could have Winston Ops check to see if anything of interest to the Russians might have gone down in these waters recently? Then I might have some idea of what I'm looking for. It's a hell of a big haystack to search for a needle when you don't even know what the needle looks like."

The line of bodies parted, and without warning, she was face-to-face with Aiden. "Hi," she murmured.

"Hello."

She frowned. Wow. That sounded...formal.

"Everything okay?" she asked tentatively.

"Yes, thank you."

"What's up? Why the dinner-at-the-White-House formality?"

"I don't understand."

Oooh-kay. Stonewalling her, was he? What on earth was going on? "Aiden, stop acting like this and tell me what's wrong."

"Later," he bit out.

Her temper flared. "No. Not later. Here and now."

He looked uncomfortable, but ultimately faced her squarely. "All right, then. Here's the thing. I changed my ways when I agreed to take Gemma's shots. And now, my work has to come first. I care about you too much to risk your safety while I do it."

"How is *my* safety at risk because you do stupid things like dive three hundred meters deep and stay down too long?"

"Because I have enemies. And I'll make more of them. They may not be able to get to me, but they can get to you."

Panic erupted in her breast. He was breaking up with her! She said frantically, "They haven't gotten to me so far."

"Next time we might not be so lucky. I'm sorry. I won't take that risk."

And with that, he brushed past her and jogged up the steps to the companionway. His shoulders retreated down the hall while she stared. Shock and dismay combined in a toxic sludge in her stomach to make her ill.

If she wasn't mistaken, he'd just dumped her. And furthermore, he'd done it in front of a good chunk of the crew. Hot tears welled up in her eyes, stinging worse than salt water, and spilled over onto her cheeks. She would dissolve into a full-blown, snotty sob fest any second. Humiliation joined the roiling mess in her stomach. She ought to make a run for her room. Except her feet were rooted to the deck, her knees locked, her entire body, all the way to her soul, frozen in place.

Steig spoke quietly from beside her. "He's got to be exhausted. And he's not the kind of man to show weakness in front of anyone, especially the woman he loves."

That had been a moment of weakness? *That* had been a moment of no-holds-barred cruelty and no-question-about-it kicking her to the curb. Why was it everyone else on the ship was so convinced he was in love with her? Hadn't they just seen him slice her to ribbons without so much as batting an eyelash?

As hurt as she was, she couldn't just retreat to lick her wounds. She had to know why he'd really done it. This whole business of needing to keep her safe was just a smoke screen. But was it meant to blind her... or to blind him? It was probably an act of sheer self-mutilation to push him to give her the real reason he didn't want to be with her, but she was too panicked, too staggered, to do anything else.

If he was trying to avoid her, she'd just have to put herself in his path until he had no choice but to explain himself. Thankfully, the *Sea Nymph* was a finite space in which to hide. He couldn't avoid her forever. She headed for his stateroom and hunkered down to wait. She had to break through his walls. This had to work. Her entire life rode on it.

She waited. And waited. But he never came. She was almost desperate enough to go searching for him, except it was just a tiny bit more humiliating than her bruised pride could stand to admit to the crew that he didn't want to even speak to her. He might die for her, but he clearly didn't want her for a girlfriend...or anything more.

Oh, God. *More.* She'd been so certain they were going to have it all. But obviously, she'd misread his signals. Maybe she'd pushed too hard, too fast. Or maybe she'd been the only one sensing some kind of special connection between them. Maybe she'd been a casual roll in the hay for him, after all. Maybe in her loneliness and need for someone to love her, for an anchor in her life, she'd glommed on to him and freaked him out. Or maybe she just wasn't good enough for him.

She thought she'd lost just about everything when her boat had been sunk with her worldly goods on it. And when the United States had blown up her camera and film and last personal possessions in Africa, she'd been sure there was nothing left to lose. But oh, how wrong she'd been. She hadn't yet lost her heart. Or her pride. Or her soul. Heck, she didn't even have any tears left to shed.

Now she truly had nothing left.

Chapter 13

"What the hell are you doing, Aiden?" Steig demanded low and angry. "That girl is head-over-heels in love with you."

He glared at the Swede and snapped, "Stay out of it. It's complicated."

"No. It's not. You love her. She loves you. Go be with her. Tell her you're crazy about her and want to spend your life with her."

"But that's just the thing!" he burst out. "I can't! She's a weakness. I can't afford to have her in my life. She's a chink in my armor that can be exploited."

"That's rubbish. What's the real reason you won't let yourself have her? Do you feel so much guilt for how you've treated women in the past that you won't let yourself have her now?"

Aiden answered flatly, "Stay out of it."

The captain shook his head and stalked out of the salon, where Aiden had been trying to get some damned sleep on the damned couch before the Swede had tracked him down and barged in to give him some *damned* dating advice.

He tossed and turned on the sofa until he was so irritated he finally gave up and got up. His watch said it was nearly 4:00 a.m. His entire being yearned to head down to his stateroom. To slip under the covers and draw Sunny into his arms. To make love to her until there wasn't any question in her mind about how he felt about her. Stubbornly, he turned his steps to the bridge. Maybe Winston Ops or the NSA had something for them.

The bridge was surprisingly active for this time of night. Grisham was poring over what looked like the images Sunny had filmed. Steig was hunched in front of a computer terminal typing busily, and everyone jumped when he walked into the room.

"What's the news?" he asked tersely.

"NSA confirms that Sunny filmed a Russian spy ship. And they were definitely using downward-scanning sonar to search for something," Steig reported.

Grisham added, "They also said the equipment the Russians were using was so powerful it would kill the fish in the area. They wanted to find whatever they were looking for real bad."

"Any idea what it was?" he asked. "Did they find it?"

Steig looked up grimly. "Yes to the first, and Uncle Sam would like us to figure out if they found it or not."

Adrenaline surged through him, and interestingly, his body reacted as if he were deep underwater. His heart rate slowed, and his fingers and toes went cold and numb as the veins and arteries in his extremities constricted to hold blood in his vital organs. He really was turning into a fish.

Steig was talking. "...days before Sunny filmed that spy ship, a U.S. surveillance satellite came down in this neighborhood of the ocean."

He frowned. "Don't satellites break up into tiny pieces and mostly burn up on reentry?"

"They do if they're not hardened against laser and EMP attacks from the ground or from other satellites," Steig replied grimly.

"And I gather this one was hardened? How big a piece of the satellite are we talking, here?"

"NASA thinks it came down almost entirely intact. They've had submarines out here looking for it, but they didn't find it. If the Russians found it, the United States has a problem. The satellite had the latest in our surveillance technology on it."

Aiden frowned. "If the Russians were looking down from the ocean's surface, they wouldn't be able to paint caves and anomalies on the volcano face. A submarine could look into the big caves with its sonar, but it wouldn't be able to see into the smaller ones. How big was the satellite?"

"Twelve feet in diameter. About fourteen feet long. The antennae will have ripped off during reentry, of course. But the cameras and the power source are what the U.S. is worried about."

"How'd it come down?" Aiden asked.

"The guys at NSA got real quiet when I asked the

same thing. I got the impression it wasn't a planned obsolescence."

"It was attacked?" Aiden exclaimed. "That might explain why the Russians are so hot and bothered to find it. If there's evidence they shot it down, they may want to hide that."

"That's above my pay grade to know," Steig answered. "We're just tasked with finding it if we can."

"Any progress on identifying the ships in the area?" Aiden asked.

"I've still got three unidentified targets moving in this direction. The good news is the U.S. Navy has a high-speed vessel scheduled to pass through the neighborhood today. They've agreed to divert it this way to check in on us and provide any assistance we might need."

That was good news. A little backup from a heavily armed military ship was never a bad thing. Aiden nodded. "All right, then. As soon as it gets light, I go back down and find us a satellite."

Sunny groaned when she caught sight of herself in the bathroom mirror in the morning. Her eyes were red and swollen, her skin blotchy. She looked like hell. She felt worse. He'd never shown up last night. Someone must have warned him that she'd headed for his room, and he'd slept elsewhere rather than face her. She'd never taken him for a coward before.

A determination to tell him that, and that she was disappointed in him as a man, filled her. Great. She'd moved on to the second stage of grieving her dead hopes and dreams. First denial, then anger. What came next? Oh, yeah. Bargaining. Gee, that ought to be fun.

She could *so* picture herself begging him to take her back. It would be so easy to promise to be whoever or whatever he wanted if he'd just stop giving her the cold shoulder and love her. She silently vowed not to do it, but as surely as she made the promise to herself, she was going to break it. Love officially sucked.

She stepped onto the bridge where, if Aiden wasn't actually there, they would most certainly know where he was. She wasn't above guilting the crew into helping her corner him. And given the sympathetic looks everyone had been giving her last night when he dumped her, she thought they might be willing to help.

Steig got up out of his chair when he spotted her. He strode over and actually gave her a hug. It was big and warm and comforting, but he wasn't Aiden. "How are you doing this morning, Sunny?"

"I've been better. Where is he?"

"Where else? Diving."

She swore mentally. He was already off the ship? So she had another long day of waiting in store for her, then. "Is there anything I can do to be of help to you guys?" she asked Steig. "I'm going stir-crazy just sitting around."

"I can imagine" was the Swede's dry response. Gifted in the art of understatement, that man was. "How are you at reading sonar images?"

"Not half-bad, actually. I used sonar to find fish when I was filming."

In short order, the crew had her set up at one of the computer monitors, scanning gray blobs on a black screen. Some sort of automatic search pattern had been set up for the ship's sonar emitters, so all she had to do was watch the slowly scrolling images go past. It was boring work, but it kept her mind off topics she'd rather not dwell on for the next eight or ten hours.

Every now and then some large creature would move across her screen. It was probably just a good-size fish, but her heart always bumped hard with the possibility that it was Aiden.

She'd been sitting at her screen for maybe two hours when one of the sailors working the surface radar barked, "Sir, we've got flash traffic from Winston Ops."

Steig moved over to the computer monitor the guy was sitting at, and she couldn't see a thing past him. But the mood on the bridge went tense and alert. The Swede straightened and announced grimly, "Satellite imagery indicates that a Russian spy ship is inbound to our location at a high rate of speed. Estimated time of arrival eighteen minutes."

"Why aren't we painting the vessel on radar?" someone asked.

"Stealth technology, obviously," Steig replied absently.

Sunny asked urgently, "Do you have any means of signaling Aiden?"

"No," Steig answered. "And even if we did, if he's on a deep dive, he won't have time to surface and get aboard before we have to leave."

"Leave?" she exclaimed. "We can't leave him behind?"

"What would you have me do? Stay here to get us rammed or torpedoed and sunk? There are nearly forty people aboard this vessel, and I'm responsible for all of their lives."

"You're responsible for Aiden's life, too!"

"And his best chance of survival is for us to leave the area, wait for the Russians to have a look around and leave, and then for us to circle back later to pick him up."

"He has limits," she declared. "He can't swim forever, and he's been swimming a lot the past few days." She thought fast. "Can we ping him with the sonar? Send an audio tone through the water to get his attention?"

"Yes. But I need to leave in about five minutes. If he's not directly underneath us and already on his way to the surface, it won't do any good."

"Please, Steig. Do it. Give him at least a chance to get here."

"Three pings, please, Conn. A pause, and three more, and a second pause, and three more pings," Steig ordered. He glanced over at her and shrugged. "Maybe he'll figure out it's a modified SOS and get here in time."

She grabbed binoculars and ran out to the catwalk to search for Aiden. The water was choppy, and it would make spotting a human head breaking the surface nearly impossible, but she *had* to try.

All her anger at him evaporated in the face of a life-threatening crisis. Funny how when the chips were down, the truly important things in life emerged. She loved him. He might not love her back, but that didn't matter right now. She'd do whatever it took to keep him safe, the same way he'd gone on a mad rescue mission to save her.

And maybe that was the answer she'd been looking for out of him. Maybe at the end of the day, he loved her, too. But when they were safe, all the little stuff crowded in to cause him doubts. She would dearly love to latch onto the idea that he really did love her. But at the moment, finding him took precedence.

The *Nymph*'s motorized sea anchor commenced retracting into the ship. *C'mon, Aiden. Surface already. Where are you?* She willed him to hear her. To appear next to the swim platform and pop up onto the teak deck like he always did.

The first diesel engine revved up. No, no, no! Aiden wasn't back yet! Any second now, the propellers would bite into the water, and they would leave him behind.

She burst onto the bridge. "Steig, you can't do this! You can't just leave him!"

"I have no choice," he ground out. "If you want to jump overboard and go find him, be my guest."

That actually wasn't a horrible idea. Except for the whole jumping-into-the-water part. "How long until we leave?" she demanded.

"Three minutes."

She tore off the bridge and raced downstairs. She screeched to a halt just inside the companionway leading to the swim deck. *Where are you, Aiden?* She looked around frantically for someone to help her. But she was alone. She tore open the nearest locker in search of something to help her.

Neatly stowed scuba tanks, mask, fins and a wet suit

were packed into the space. Steig's words echoed in her ears. *If you want to jump overboard and go find him...*

She couldn't. She was terrified of the water. Although when push had come to shove, she'd been able to swim away from her would-be Russian killers a few nights ago. How was this so very different? This time the Russians were threatening Aiden and not her. It was her turn to come to his rescue, right?

Under her feet, the second diesel engine spun up. She was running out of time. Aiden was running out of time.

In quick decision, she grabbed the twin scuba tanks and checked the gauges quickly. They were high-pressure steel tanks, each filled with one-hundred-fifty cubic feet of air. In shallow water, she had air for nearly six hours. But if she had to go deep to find Aiden, she might have only an hour's worth of air. A small pony tank was clipped to one of the bottles. It would provide enough oxygen for an emergency ascent.

She didn't have time for the wet suit, and the water here was warm, anyway, so she yanked the fins onto her feet, buckled on the weight belt and threw the mask around her neck. She hoisted the heavy tanks, strapping them on like a backpack.

She felt, more than heard, the propellers start to turn beneath her feet. The metal blades bit into the water and the back end of the *Nymph* dipped ever so slightly. This was it. Now or never.

She clumped backward across the deck awkwardly, staggering under nearly ninety pounds of equipment. Clearly this rig was meant for a man. A big, strong one. This was insane. She couldn't think about it. Didn't dare. She just jammed in the mouthpiece and flung herself backward off the ship.

The first shock of the water caused her momentary panic. But then the necessity of donning and clearing her mask, checking her oxygen flow and going through the other routine safety checks of diving came back to her. She'd dived a thousand times and the familiarity of the routine calmed her slightly.

It helped that she could see. The water was bright and visibility was excellent. This was nothing like the night she'd nearly drowned, when everything had been black and so terribly cold. She backed away from the turbulence of the *Nymph*'s propellers as the white hull started to pull away. In a matter of moments, it had retreated entirely out of sight and the water calmed around her.

The ocean stretched away in every direction, blue and featureless. Below, she saw no hint of the underwater mountain she knew to be there, just more blue fading gradually to black. Where was Aiden? She'd had some vague notion of him materializing out of the depths by her side. But as the silence pressed in around her, the absurdity of that idea struck her forcefully.

In fact, the absurdity of this whole dive struck her forcefully. What on earth had she been thinking? Unlike Aiden, she couldn't swim all day long and just hang out underwater until the *Nymph* got around to reappearing. She was *alone.* In the middle of the freaking ocean. Okay, this had been a really stupid idea.

Her best bet was probably to find Aiden as soon as possible. There was a gigantic volcano underneath her that measured a mile across, and he was somewhere on its face, exploring the caves peppering its sides. Sure.

She'd just pop down a couple hundred feet and wave a cheery hello.

What in the *hell* had she been thinking? She hadn't been thinking at all; she'd panicked over the man she loved and had acted on impulse like she always did. And like always, she'd gotten herself into yet another awful pickle.

The first order of business was to manage her oxygen. She could be out here for hours. And that Russian ship might loiter for a while before it sailed on. Hopefully, it was just coming to check out a radar blip that had parked over a sensitive spot for a bit too long. When the Russians realized that whatever vessel had been anchored here had moved on, hopefully they would be on their way, as well.

Hopefully.

If not, she was screwed. The next order of business was to figure out where she was right now. If and when the *Nymph* came back to pick up her and Aiden, they would no doubt return to this spot. Before she drifted too far or got completely turned around, she needed to take a position fix.

But with what? She had no idea what equipment was stored in her combination utility and weight belt. She opened the various pouches, exploring their contents, and was mightily relieved to come across a GPS unit tethered to the belt. She wasn't familiar with the model, but fiddled with it for a minute or so and managed to get it to display a current position. She memorized the coordinates carefully. Her life no doubt depended on remembering those numbers. In addition to the GPS, she found an array of useful doodads. Compass, knife, nylon cord, flashlight, even a camera. Whoever maintained this rig was very good.

She had maybe ten minutes until the Russian spy ship arrived. She might as well surface until then and preserve her oxygen. And besides, she was curious to see if the ship was the same one that had sunk the *New Dawn*. She was, by God, taking pictures of it if it was, and suing the Russian government for damages when she got home. Assuming she *got* home.

She didn't have long to wait to spot a tall, sleek silhouette on the horizon. The Russian ship was much bigger than she'd expected. Or maybe it just looked that way from down here in the water without the illusory safety of a boat around her.

The prow was narrow and sharp, like she remembered. And the hull was black, too. She didn't remember the bristling array of antennae and satellite dishes from before, but maybe they hadn't been deployed, or maybe she'd been too busy jumping overboard to notice them. Scowling, she pulled out the digital camera and snapped a few pictures.

She dared not get too close to the massive ship lest she be spotted. As it was, she worried that her bulky steel dive tanks might set off some kind of alarm. Over the next few minutes, the ship executed a ponderous turn and came to a halt broadside to her, maybe a half mile away. Dang. No way would Aiden surface now, with them parked overhead. Assuming he thought to look up and spot the black hull. Maybe he could hear a ship that size. Sound traveled extraordinarily well and for long distances underwater, after all.

She pulled her mask back on and unstowed the snorkel from her belt. She paddled away from the spy ship, facedown in the water, searching for any sign of a blond merman rising up out of the depths. Aiden had to be here, somewhere. The act of floating on the light swells and letting the currents carry her along was actually kind of relaxing. She would probably never like deep water or dark water again, but she at least could handle it when she had to.

It was probably because she wasn't using her oxygen tanks and the water was silent around her that she heard the splashing. She lifted her head and looked toward the Russian ship. She was in time to see two black-and-yellow objects fall toward the water.

The Russians were putting divers into the water? Were they coming for her? Or worse, were they going after Aiden? He was down there free diving with no supplemental oxygen and no weapons to defend himself!

She looked down toward the beckoning abyss below. Aiden was down there somewhere. Alone. Unaware of the threat headed his way. Could she do it? Could she make a deep dive to find him and warn him?

She snorted mentally. Did she have any choice but to try?

Squeezing her eyes tightly shut, she put the mouthpiece in, turned on her oxygen tank and headed down.

Chapter 14

Sunny grimaced as her ears popped. That felt like about twenty feet deep. The belt probably had a depth gauge in it somewhere, but it didn't much matter how deep she was. She'd descend until she found the volcano.

She figured her best bet to find Aiden was to head pretty much straight down from the *Nymph*'s last position. The yacht had repositioned last night to the south face of the volcano, and although she hadn't been part of the discussions around that move, it was a good bet that was where Aiden was exploring today.

About thirty feet down, the water started to go dim. By fifty feet down, it was twilight dark, with no color and only shadowed shapes visible. A school of small fish flashed into sight, startling her horribly. She splashed backward violently as they flashed out of sight just as quickly.

Crud. She had to slow her heart rate. The faster she breathed, the less air she'd have to find Aiden. She could do this. She had plenty of oxygen. The pressure hadn't crushed her. She could swim back to the surface if she got too freaked out. She. Wasn't. Drowning.

Aiden rewound his rope as he backed out of the cave. He'd been hopeful that this cave with its heavy overhang and strong, inward current flow might have trapped the missing communications satellite. He had found a few planks of coral-encrusted wood that looked like part of a shipwreck, but that was it.

How ironic would it be if he found the wreck of Sunny's parents' boat down here? Although the idea of having to tell her he'd found the *Sunshine Girl,* or even their remains, made him shudder. That wound, although old for Sunny, wasn't the kind that ever healed.

He could only hope the new wounds he'd inflicted on her would heal with time. Steig was right. She did love him. She'd made no secret of it. But they hadn't known each other all that long. It would pass, right? Although he doubted his own feelings for her would pass anytime soon.

He'd had a lot of time alone down here to think over the past two days. He'd tried a hundred times to find a way to be with Sunny. He could even wrap his brain around the idea of her being a constant source of worry for him. It would stink, but he would work through his fear if it meant he could be with her.

But it all came back to her safety. If he loved her, he

would never expose her to the risks that came with his work. Russians had tried three times to kill her now, assuming those thugs in Djibouti hadn't been random thieves. Given how long and hard that bunch had followed him and Sunny, he didn't think they were.

But, he argued with himself, if she was already on the Russians' radar, maybe she'd be safer with him around to look out for her. His best bet to protect her was to find that damned satellite and render moot any film she might have shot of the Russians trying to find it.

But if not the Russians, the next enemy he made would find out about her and go after her, and he'd be right back in this position. And more important, she'd be right back in danger. It wasn't as if he could ask her to move onto the Winston compound in Colorado and never come out again.

The cave opening came into sight and he headed for the oxygen tank he'd dropped by the cave entrance. He took a long pull on the mouthpiece and checked the regulator. Plenty of air left. It saved him a ton of time not to have to surface several times per hour, and his body seemed to be adjusting more and more to these depths the longer he spent down here. He didn't want to think about the asthma attack he was going to suffer the first time he had to go running after Sunny again—

He swore to himself. Yet another reason to stay away from her.

Except no matter how logically his brain analyzed the problem, his heart was having none of it. He loved her. He wanted her. He felt as if he was cutting off his right arm to leave her. His heart shouted at him to give up this superhero stuff and live out a normal life with her. On land. Someplace anonymous. Far from any Russians or bad guys who might want to hurt either of them.

He swam to his right, scanning along the face of the volcano for the next likely cave to search. He particularly liked this face of the volcano because the prevailing currents pushed water into the caves, where jagged edges and crannies were waiting to snag any flotsam that drifted in.

His thoughts drifted back to Sunny as they always seemed to. Steig's damning accusation prodded at him. Was that it? Was the real reason he was being so pigheaded about Sunny nothing more than guilt? Lord knew, he had plenty of reason to feel guilty for the cavalier way he'd treated women over the years. Although it wasn't as if he'd made promises to any of them. And he wasn't getting hate mail and death threats from any of them. Was he being too hard on himself? Had two years' worth of self-imposed celibacy been punishment enough?

A school of fish flashed past him and he turned his head to watch them go by. Individually, the kingfish were mostly shorter than his forearm. But the entire school would have swallowed a bus. That wasn't a typical cruising speed for that species. They were fleeing from something in alarm. It was probably a barracuda or some other large predatory fish. While he'd never had any trouble from sharks or the like—they seemed to recognize him as a large predator fish to be given wide berth—he nonetheless didn't need to startle one. He scanned the water in the direction the kingfish had come from. The water was beautifully clear down here, but the darkness limited what he could see.

He thought he caught a glimpse of something large, but it was swimming nearly vertically downward. That was not at all typical of any fish. Alarm coursed through him. That wasn't…

Surely not. Why would Steig have sent another diver down here? He glided toward where he'd seen the shadow. Whoever it was, he was descending fast. But then the diver must have spotted the cliff face, for he stopped abruptly. Turned from side to side, no doubt examining the cave-pocked wall.

Aiden spotted the orange-and-yellow-striped dive tanks the *Sea Nymph* packed. Yup. One of Steig's guys. He swam toward the visitor. But as he neared, he spotted legs. Legs not wearing a wet suit. And a brightly colored T-shirt. What the heck? Alarmed anew, he kicked forward powerfully. The diver turned toward him and lurched hard.

He held his hands up in apology for startling the diver and drifted in close and saw…*Sunny?*

What on earth? And what was she doing down here? She hated even getting wet, let alone diving. And in deep, dark water? He was well and truly alarmed now. He flashed her the American Sign Language signal for a question mark and prayed she knew the language, which many divers used for underwater communication.

She spelled out a single word. *R-U-S-S-I-A-N-S.*

He pointed over his head and she nodded. He stared out of his mask in dismay. The Russians were up there? Was the *Nymph* all right? Was it under attack? Is that why she was down here? He signed rapidly and she shook her head, signaling him to go slower.

Is the Nymph *all right?*

Gone, she signed back.

Gone?

Left the area. Will come back later.

How much later? How much air do you have?

Maybe two hours at this depth. Do you need to go up to breathe?

I've got a tank, he signaled.

He should probably go fetch it and get her up to shallower water where her air would hold out longer. But then she reached out to touch his arm. He jolted at the contact of her fingers on his skin.

She was signing again. *Russian divers coming.*

Holy crap. *How many?* he signed urgently.

At least two.

He had to get her out of here. Now. *Follow me.*

She nodded as he turned and swam strongly for his air tanks. With her fins, she was able to keep up with him for the most part.

But then another wave of kingfish sped past them. And more alarmingly, a tuna that had to weigh five hundred pounds. Anything that fish would flee was bigger or badder than a shark. Like a human.

He kicked harder, burning more energy. Sunny looked as if she was going about as fast as she could.

And then he heard it. The rumble of an underwater propulsion device. They were like underwater Jet Skis for divers and could cruise at several times the speed even he could go.

Sunny looked over at him frantically and pointed at

her ear. He nodded grimly. They wouldn't be able to outrun the Russian divers. They would have to hide. They weren't even close to his tanks, yet. But they had no choice. He headed toward the volcano and picked out a likely cave. It was large enough to accommodate Sunny's gear, but otherwise unimposing.

He hadn't been inside this one and had no idea how deep it was or how fast it petered out. He took a moment to secure the end of his line to an outcropping just inside the entrance. He turned around to make sure Sunny's equipment didn't snag on anything, and spotted her outside the cave opening.

She was balking.

He swore violently to himself. He'd assumed because she'd made it down here that she'd somehow gotten over her fear of drowning. But apparently, her newfound courage didn't extend to dark, cramped caves.

He swam back out to her. Gestured for her to go in. She shook her head sharply in the negative. He pointed at his ear and then signed, *Have to.*

Even in the dark, and even through the thick glass of her mask, he could see the terror in her eyes.

I'll be with you, he tried. No dice. Crap. That UDV was getting really close now. He could feel the vibrations of it through his skin.

I love you, he signed. *I can't lose you. Not like this. Please.*

Shock registered in her eyes, followed loosely by doubt. He swore. She thought he was lying to her to coax her into the cave. He signed the universally recognized symbol for *cross my heart.*

She gave him a very small nod. He reached for her

and stretched out on his back. He pulled her down on top of him until they were body to body, mask to mask. The glass plates actually touched as he kicked them backward into the cave.

She stared down at him as the rocks swallowed them. And then it was too dark to see her face anymore. But she clung to him as if he was her only lifeline. As always, their bodies fit together perfectly. Lord, he would never get enough of this woman.

Her fingers tapped his mouth lightly. Then she fumbled behind her neck for something. Ahh. She must be looking for her pressure regulator. On most tanks, it had a valve that could be used as an alternate mouthpiece in case the main one failed. Smart girl. And if she was thinking about things like that, then she had her panic under control.

He reached around behind her and gently disengaged the regulator from its clip. He pulled the flexible metal tube around her and put it in his mouth. He drew in a long, badly needed breath of air. Her fingers touched his face beneath his mask, and he used his free hand to do the same to her. Even seventy feet under water, her skin felt smooth and warm, like sunshine made into flesh.

He was so proud of her. She'd pushed through true terror to come down here and warn him. And then it hit him. Only love could have made her do such a thing. *She loved him.* Really, truly loved him. His heart expanded with joy until it felt as if it would explode right out of his chest. Who was he trying to kid? He loved her, too.

He adjusted the buoyancy of her weight belt slightly so her body weight would hold him down, and they floated in equilibrium inside the cave together. It was spooky. He felt almost like an unborn child. The regulator was his umbilical cord, this cave and the ocean his mother.

Truth be told, Sunny was the one who'd given him life. She'd brought laughter and emotion and excitement into a world that now seemed dull and gray by comparison. She'd been his own personal sun and shined her love down upon him. How stupid had he been to think he could live without her?

They would simply have to find a way to make it work. She would have to agree to stay in the Winston compound when he was out on missions, or he'd have to hire a team of bodyguards to watch her. Assuming he hadn't already hurt her so badly she wanted nothing to do with a long-term relationship with him. If she'd have him, when they got out of here, he was taking her into his arms and into his life and never letting go.

A beam of light cut across his dreams, severing his thoughts as neatly as a sword. How had the Russians found them? Sunny exhaled hard beside him and a cascade of bubbles tickled his arm. He'd forgotten. Scuba divers left a trail of carbon dioxide in their wake. Unlike him; he held his breath when he was down here.

Taking one last, long pull on the regulator tube, he grabbed Sunny's tanks and shoved her over his head and behind him. He reached for his knife in its calf sheath and prepared to defend the woman he loved. A pair of divers hovered in the cave entrance. One of the silhouettes was fingering the safety line he'd anchored there. Dammit, no chance of hiding now.

He'd get one shot at surprising these guys. And he

had only two advantages going for him. He was in the dark and they were clearly visible to him. And he wasn't wearing air tanks. He would be more nimble than the Russians.

Bracing his feet on an outcropping of rock, he gathered his body and launched himself forward as hard as he could. If he were above water, he'd have shouted a war yell at the top of his lungs. As it was, he shot past the first diver, slashing at the guy's regulator hoses as he passed by. The guy immediately went into contortions trying to shed the tanks and access his emergency air bottle.

The second man, however, turned to face Aiden. The guy was wielding a knife every bit as big and deadly as his. The diver darted forward and Aiden backpeddled hard. He grabbed the Russian's wrist and managed to deflect the blade and shove off the guy, gaining a few feet of separation.

As long as he could stay out of the other diver's grasp, this guy would have a hard time delivering a fatal wound. But that would only last as long as the second diver was tied up trying to get his gear straightened out.

He and the first diver swam at each other, but each time the other was able to avoid the knife. Aiden steadily backed away from the cave entrance. If he could draw the divers off, give Sunny a chance to slip out and escape, she would at least live. And he was okay with that. He'd treated her terribly, and he owed her this. If he died for her today, that would be a fitting thing. His mind calmed. Focused.

When the object was not to win, or even survive, this fight became a relatively simple thing. Feint in, dart back. Draw the other guy a few feet forward. He did the same again and again until he couldn't make out the cave entrance in the gloom behind the Russian. Where was the second Russian diver? He should be about ready to—

As if on cue, another diver swam at him. The guy was coming in at a high rate of speed. This guy was going to be a problem. With that much momentum, the second diver would be able to grapple with him before he'd have a chance to avoid being caught.

He started to backpeddle, to turn away so he had some small chance of dodging. The move would open up his back to the first diver. But those were the breaks. He was going to lose this fight one way or another. Might as well be this way.

But then the second diver did a strange thing. As his buddy spotted his opening and pulled his knife back to plunge it into Aiden's kidney, the second diver changed direction slightly and angled right at his companion. Aiden glanced over his shoulder in time to see the first diver slam into the second diver from behind. A bloom of black erupted in the water between the two men.

And then it hit him. Those were striped air tanks. That wasn't the other Russian. *That was Sunny.*

What had she done to the other guy? But then he had no more time to ask himself rhetorical questions of strategy. For the diver who'd been attacking him turned and slashed at Sunny.

White-hot rage flashed through Aiden. That was *his* woman. He arrowed through the water, swimming with every ounce of speed and power he possessed. He shot forward and grabbed the Russian by the throat. To hell with the bastard's air hoses. He slit the guy's throat.

Sunny ripped out of the dying Russian's grasp. The guy struggled for a few more seconds, but bleeding out from the carotid artery was a quick thing. The body went limp and Aiden shoved it away in disgust.

He turned to Sunny and pointed urgently over her shoulder. *Where was the other diver?*

If he wasn't mistaken, she smiled a little around her mouthpiece and drew her index finger across her neck. He wasn't sure she meant she'd actually slit his throat, but it was clear the other Russian diver was no longer a problem.

He was stunned. He didn't mind at all that she'd killed a man who was attacking her, but he was shocked that she had overcome her fear to act with such decisiveness. He glided forward and wrapped her in his arms. Every time he turned around, she surprised him. He'd known she was a fighter, but he'd never guessed just how much of one.

He supposed he should have known from the very first time he'd seen her drifting down toward death. She'd fought back from that when most people wouldn't have made it. She'd fought past the death of her parents, fought past being alone in the world, past losing everything she owned, past her fear of drowning.

He'd been a fool to think he would ever win against her. That she would let him walk away from her without putting up the fight of her life for him.

He pushed her back far enough to look into her eyes. He pointed at his heart and then at hers. And then he drifted down until his head was at about the level of her waist while she stared down at him, perplexed. He took her left hand in his and pointed very deliberately at her ring finger and then at his. He looked up at her hopefully.

She stared in disbelief, and he touched her ring finger and then his again.

Tears spilled out of her eyes, pooling in the bottom of her mask. And then, belatedly, she nodded at him.

He surged up, wrapping his arms around her in an exuberant hug. They banged masks and both shook with laughter. A kiss was going to have to wait until they surfaced.

He signaled that they should swim up to shallower water, and she nodded her understanding. He detoured long enough to fetch his air tanks, and then they ascended slowly. While his body adapted rapidly enough to pressure changes to make him immune to the evolved gas disorders deadly to divers who surfaced too fast, he wasn't about to take any chances with her.

They paused at fifty feet for her to acclimate for a few minutes, and he spent the time running his hands over her face and arms, telling her without words how much he loved her and valued her. For her part, she seemed content to nestle in his arms with her ear pressed to his chest listening to his heartbeat.

They headed up to thirty feet, and then twenty. They probably could have skipped one of those stops, but she was more precious than life to him. It was during the pause at twenty feet that he heard something that made his head jerk up.

That was a ship. Incoming. Fast. Really fast. He'd never heard anything so big move so fast. He grabbed

Sunny and took her back down to thirty feet, well clear of the draft and propellers of most ships.

And that was when they saw it. A gray, triangular hull close to four hundred feet long. Twin jets of water roared out of the back of it, propelling it at what looked like close to fifty knots. It could only be one of the U.S. Navy's new fast ships. They were technically called Littoral Combat Ships and built for shallow-water combat along coasts, but they were also ideal for chasing down pirates and could move like bats out of hell.

The vessel passed, and Aiden signaled for the two of them to surface. Sunny nodded and they finished their ascent in a few seconds. They popped up to the surface, and he put an arm around her waist to support her as he treaded water easily.

"Watch this," he told her, nodding in the direction of the gray ship.

She turned in his arms and the two of them watched the U.S. vessel barrel toward the Russian ship, which was broadside to them at the moment. The Russian ship was clearly trying to gain a head of steam and turn away from the onrushing warship, but with its bulk, it didn't stand a chance.

"My God, the Americans are going to ram the Russians!" Sunny gasped.

He had a pretty good inkling of what the Americans intended. He'd heard a few rumors about it. "Just watch," he murmured.

At the last minute before the flying warship smashed into the Russian spy ship, the American vessel turned. The gray vessel tipped up on edge and pivoted like a ballerina. The speed and violence of the turn was shocking.

As 2,500 tons of steel turned on a dime, it threw up the mother of all wakes. A gigantic wave, easily seventy feet tall, slammed into the Russian ship, swamping its decks and rocking it nearly over on its side. The vessel righted itself, but antennae were hanging off it at weird angles, and two of the big satellite dishes had been completely ripped off. One was hanging by steel cables over the side of the badly damaged ship.

The U.S. ship sailed almost out of sight, maybe a mile off to their right, and turned around. It looked like a bull elephant about to charge.

"Here she comes again," Aiden announced. He and Sunny watched as the gray ship picked up speed for another pass at the Russian ship.

The Russian ship didn't bother trying to turn. It sailed straight ahead for all it was worth, clearly giving up and bugging out of the area. The U.S. ship slowed, settling lower in the water and coming to rest almost on top of the spot the Russians had vacated.

"Well, all right, then," Sunny declared. "I guess we don't have to wait for the *Nymph* to get around to coming back for us. We can hitch a ride with Uncle Sam."

"Have you got an Emergency Locator Beacon in your gear?" he asked her.

"I have no idea. I stole this from one of your divers."

"Then there's an ELT in there. He fished around and came up with the palm-size device. He activated it and let it float on the water beside them, safely tethered to her belt.

"Sunny, can you forgive me for how I've acted?"

"Of course I forgive you."

As relief rolled through him like a cool, soothing balm, he realized there was one small part of him the relief didn't touch. He asked slowly, "Can you forgive me for being such a womanizer before? I swear, I'll never be that guy again."

"Aiden, I'm not the one who needs to forgive you. You need to forgive yourself."

As soon as he heard the words, he knew them to be entirely true. And with that knowing—finally—came the peace he'd sought all these years. That part of his life truly was over. Past. It was high time to let it go and move on with his new life. With Sunny. He felt as if a massive weight had just lifted from his shoulders and he was lighter than air.

"By the way, future Mrs. McKay. I believe you owe me a kiss to seal the deal. Banging masks doesn't do it for me."

"Look, Aiden. I know you said you loved me to distract me. To get me to go into that cave. And I really appreciate it. But I'm not going to hold you to anything that got said—or signaled—down there when we thought we might die."

"Fair enough," he said evenly. "But I proposed to you well after all the immediate threats were taken care of."

Her mouth opened. Closed. Opened again.

"If you're accepting my proposal in fish-speak, I have to tell you I haven't morphed that far into a fish yet. I can't tell if that's a yes or a no."

"But why?" she spluttered.

"Why what?"

"Why on earth would you propose to me?"

"Well, in the first place, this isn't earth. In case you hadn't noticed, we're surrounded by nothing but water as far as the eye can see. I proposed to you because I realized I was never going to win against what you do to me. What you make me feel. I can't fight it—fight you—anymore. If you want me, I'm yours. You're going to have live someplace safe when I'm gone. But I swear, I'll make sure no harm comes to you. Ever."

"And I promise I won't ever let anyone hurt you," she declared stoutly.

He loved her spunk, and he might just believe her declaration. Lord knew, he wouldn't want to tangle with her in a dark alley when she was really riled up.

He cleared his throat. "Why you'd want less than a whole man, I have no idea. But I'm not going to talk you out of it."

"Less than— What are you talking about?" she demanded.

"I'm not...normal. I can't give you everything you deserve. I'm always going to need to live by water. I may or may not be able to have children safely, and I don't know if there will be health repercussions for me down the road. I'm not even entirely sure I'm all... human."

"Good grief, Aiden. You're more human, more of a man, than anyone I've ever met. What you do, the sacrifices you've made, are incredibly heroic. I admire you more than anyone I've ever known."

"Is it possible that you could even love me a little?" he asked cautiously.

"No."

His heart dropped out of his body like a block of lead.

"I love you more than a little, you wonderful idiot. I love you with all my heart. With every fiber of my being. In case you haven't figured it out yet, I don't tend to do things halfway in my life. And that goes for loving you, too."

There were no words for the joy that exploded in his chest then. He pulled her into his arms and kissed her for all he was worth. He kissed her for all the things she'd lost, for all the pain he'd caused her before she straightened out his head for him. And most of all he kissed her for the future that lay before them, a thing of joy and laughter and sunshine. Lots and lots of sunshine.

"Hey, there, buddy. You need help giving that lady mouth-to-mouth, or is she gonna live?"

He and Sunny looked up, startled, at the navy dinghy floating a few feet away.

"It looks like our ship has come in," she murmured, smiling against his lips.

She had no idea. He already knew what he was giving her as a wedding present…after he bought it he was changing its name from the *Sea Nymph* to the *Sunshine Girl.*

* * * * *

The Dark Side of Night

This book is for my real-life superhero friends
whose names I cannot print. You know who you are.
And may I just say, you ROCK!

For my mom and mother-in-law,
who in their courageous battles with cancer
have taught me that life's short, live hard.

Chapter 1

Smoking gun in hand, Mitch Perovski crouched over the crumpled form of the dead man and swore. One by one, droplets of blood plopped onto the boat's deck in the charged silence. Glancing furtively around him for watching eyes, he crouched even lower and pulled out his cell phone.

"Go ahead," a male voice said at the other end.

"Lancer here," he muttered. "I've got a problem. My Plan B is dead, I'm caught out in the open at a damned marina, and I've got two, possibly three, gunmen on my tail. I need you guys to pull a rabbit out of your hats and get me the hell out of here."

"We've got you on the satellite map in a marina near the south end of Tortola. The boss man says to stay put for a minute if you can. Meanwhile, say your status."

For a moment, Mitch allowed himself to register the

daggers of pain shooting from his left shoulder. Bad idea. He gritted his teeth, forced the agony back into a mental drawer and slammed it shut. No time for that, yet. "I'm shot," he ground out. "My left shoulder. I think the bullet passed through but I haven't had time to stop and take a look. I'm low on ammo and way exposed on this freaking dock."

"Are you bleeding?" the combat controller asked sharply.

"Hell, yes, I'm bleeding. I just took a bullet."

"Apply pressure to the entrance and exit wounds with a clean pad, and hold it until the bleeding stops."

"Gee, thanks, Doctor Kildaire. I had no idea what to do," Mitch retorted drily. All the guys in the H.O.T. Watch were qualified EMTs.

"Standard procedure to brief operatives on proper first aid when a wound is reported," the controller replied, equally as dry. "That way when you die, your family can't sue us over your sorry ass."

Mitch snorted. He hadn't spoken to any member of the Perovski clan in close to ten years and didn't plan on doing so for at least another ten. The seconds ticked by at half speed while he scanned the area for signs of his pursuers. They weren't showing themselves at the moment, but he didn't doubt for an instant that they were out there, waiting. Seconds turned into minutes, and he wondered how much longer his pursuers would sit tight. Eventually, they would run out of patience and come after him. He was dead meat if they caught him out here like this.

A new, deeper voice finally came on the line. "Lancer, this is White Horse." *His temporary boss. Navy Commander Brady Hathaway.* "I've got a Plan

C for you. About a half mile down the beach, Congressman Dick Hollingsworth has a vacation home. He has a fast boat, and I just got off the horn with him. He's given you permission to use it. The spare ignition key is taped to the back of a painting of a clipper ship in the below-deck cabin. You'll have to break into the cabin, though. I told him we'll repair any damage you do to the door."

A half mile? Damn, that sounded like a long way right now. "What does the boat look like?" Mitch bit out.

"It's a thirty-eight-foot cigarette. And—" Was that a wince he heard in Lancer's voice? His boss continued, "It's pink. Named *Baby Doll.* But it goes like a bat outta hell, apparently."

"It had better," Mitch growled. "If I die in a pink boat, I'm going to haunt you. And I won't be a nice ghost."

White Horse laughed shortly. "Call us when you're safe. And take care of that shoulder when you get a chance."

"Will do." Mitch tucked the cell phone in his pocket and briefly considered swimming for the pink boat. But his shoulder was throbbing like hell, and the idea of adding the burn of salt in the wound was more than even his pain tolerance would stand. He eased down the dock, staying low. If his luck held, he could sneak into that fringe of palmettos and bushes up the beach, and then make his way to the pink Plan C.

If his luck held.

Just another lousy day in paradise. Kinsey sighed and sat up. She'd spent the entire afternoon napping on the cigarette boat's sleek hull, which rocked gently beneath her as the waves rolled in. A strip of white-sand beach stretched away in both directions, fringed by rustling palm trees and kissed by turquoise seas so blue they almost hurt to look at.

As dull as it was down here, it was still better than being laughed at. Laughed at! Her. The darling of Newport society. She'd fled rather than face the cruel scorn of the country-club crowd and those who called themselves her friends. In a few months, when the scandal had been eclipsed by some new sensation, maybe she'd think about going home. But until then, she was hunkering down here at her father's beach house. Okay, she'd admit it—she was hiding.

The sun was beginning to dip toward the horizon. Not quite sunset, but the day's quality tanning time was over. She didn't feel like going inside yet, though. Maybe a spin in the *Baby Doll* would clear her head. She pulled a T-shirt on over her skimpy bikini and, jumping over to the pier, cast off the forward mooring line. She strolled down the dock to cast off the aft line.

A rapid slapping sound made Kinsey look over her shoulder sharply. Feet striking the dock. Urgent. Staccato. *Running full out.* Nobody ran around here. It was too hot and humid in this tropical climate—too damned languid—for anything so strenuous.

A tall man was charging down the long pier straight at her. Dark hair. Broad shoulders. Black clothes from head to foot. Bulky black duffel bag slung over his right shoulder. As mesmerizing—and lethal—as a panther charging on the attack. He never even slowed as he twisted to look behind him. She glanced in the direction of his gaze. Two more men were coming on the run…brandishing *guns*.

She leaped into the boat's open cockpit, searching frantically for the keys. Where in heck had she put them? There they were. In a cup holder. She dived for them, prayed she'd grabbed the right key and jabbed it at the ignition. *Missed!* She tried again.

Four thuds in quick succession made her duck instinctively. What was that noise? Whatever it was, it sounded bad.

The *Baby Doll*'s three Merc 700 horsepower motors turned over with a single smooth rumble. The man with the duffel bag was almost on her. She threw the engines into gear and yanked hard on the steering wheel. The boat pivoted around practically in place, the rear hull digging deep into the water.

As the *Baby Doll* exploded away from the dock, a dark shape went airborne, crashing onto the boat's deck behind her. Kinsey jerked violently. *The guy in black.* She started to throttle back.

"Go!" he shouted from where he sprawled. She hesitated, and he shouted, "Hit it, lady! You and I are both dead if they catch us!"

Wha—? She slammed the throttles forward while her brain hitched and stumbled, tripping over itself. *Dead? Both* of them? What had *she* done to merit getting killed? The boat shot forward like a Thoroughbred bursting out of the chute, slamming her back into the pilot's formfitting leather seat. In the time it took Kinsey to jerk in a startled breath and release it, the *Baby Doll* had accelerated to nearly seventy miles per hour.

Kinsey risked a glance at the man crawling into the

seat beside her. His hair was black-coffee brown, his skin bronze—by sun or genetics, she couldn't tell. He looked Italian in an elegant, lounge-around-a-Tuscan-villa way. He righted himself and commenced fishing in his duffel bag. His left sleeve was ripped at the shoulder seam and—holy cow—blood gleaned wetly over the tear.

"Who are you?" she shouted over the roar of the engines. She sincerely hoped this man was the good guy in that little chase scene back at the dock; otherwise, she could be in for a world of hurt, alone and on the open ocean with a potentially violent man. Heck, even if he *was* the good guy, she could very well be in deep trouble.

He looked over at her. Their gazes locked and time stopped for an instant, the power of that split second staggering. His eyes were amber. As gold as the sunset beginning to form in the west and positively hypnotic. *Was he the cop or the robber?* No telling by his dangerous good looks. A distant roar behind them sounded like an angry lion.

"Here they come." His voice was raspy from exertion and sent an involuntary shiver down her spine.

She glanced back toward shore. A boat was just pulling away from the next dock over, another long, sleek cigarette.

"Who are they?" she shouted.

He stared grimly over her shoulder at the cigarette roaring toward them. His reply was succinct. "Hired killers."

Terror rushed over her; cold certainty that death was very near. Her legs abruptly felt unbearably restless and she restrained an impulse to jump up and run away.

"Can we outrun them?" he asked.

She took a closer look at the boat pursuing them. A forty-three- or forty-four-foot SuperVee. "Nope. This boat tops out around eighty-five miles per hour. That one will push a hundred."

His metallic gaze swung back to her. It was cold. Utterly devoid of emotion. And that scared her worst of all. There wasn't any question of not doing exactly what he told her.

"Then we'll stand and fight."

The link between reality and the nightmare unfolding around her stretched. Broke. *Fight?* The synapses between her conscious thoughts and having any idea what to do next shut down. Completely.

"How good a driver are you?" he demanded, yanking her back from the void.

She answered without even thinking. She'd been around water and boats since she was born. "Very good."

"Can you get me close enough to that boat to shoot at it?"

"Get close? Intentionally?" she squeaked.

"Yes. So I can shoot them," he repeated impatiently.

Shoot? As in guns and bullets? *Was she about to die?* The thought gave a terrible clarity to every breath, every sound. Her hands gripped the contoured steering wheel until they ached.

"Damn," her passenger muttered. "He's got an angle on us."

If she could've forced words past the panic paralyzing her throat, she might have asked who "he" was and why having an angle sounded bad. But then her passenger reached into the duffel at his feet and pulled out a short, thick machine gun. *Oh. My. God.*

"Turn right!" he ordered tersely.

Kinsey yanked the wheel, and the nimble boat whipped around so hard it made her neck hurt. The *Baby Doll* slashed across the path of the black cigarette at nearly a right angle.

A flash of light exploded beside her. A burst of rattling, deafening sound. Her passenger had fired his gun at the other boat! As the other vessel passed behind them, he whirled and fired again.

"Bring us around for another pass!" he shouted. "Keep our nose or tail pointed at him and don't give him our broadside if you can help it."

Abjectly grateful for something to think about besides dying, her panicked brain kicked into overdrive. The sailor in her latched onto the problem his instructions posed. His orders were easier said than done. And frankly, she'd rather have the bastards shooting toward her pointed prow and the compact living quarters inside it than at her stern where the engines…and gas tanks…were housed.

The black boat slowed abruptly and turned hard to face them. Its engines roared a challenge. Coming in for a head-on pass, like a knight on a black charger. She dared not get into a contest of straight runs against the larger, faster boat. It would eat them alive. She had to keep them both going in circles. Use her more agile boat and tighter turn radius to her advantage. Keep speed out of the mix altogether.

The other boat accelerated. Coming straight at them. Her passenger grabbed the top of the short windshield to steady himself and his weapon.

"Don't get comfortable," she called. "I'm going to turn hard right just in front of him and you'll get a better shot to your left. We're going to send up a hell of a wake and it's going to rock him violently, so time your shots accordingly."

He spared her a startled glance. Then he grinned at her, a fleeting expression that passed across his face almost too fast to see. But she caught the flash of white, the sexy lift of the corner of his mouth. His eyes briefly glowed whiskey-warm—and then the smile was gone. He was gone. With a bunch and spring of powerful thighs, he'd leaped aft to crouch behind the seats.

The distance between the two boats closed shockingly fast. She made out the face of the other boat's driver, a swarthy man with death in his eyes. A second man stood up in the passenger's seat, brandishing some sort of machine gun over the windshield.

He wasn't looking at her, though. He was searching the deck of her vessel for her passenger. The black boat's engines roared even louder. Obviously the other driver expected to make a straight, high-speed pass and let the gunmen duke it out.

Wrongo, buckwheat. Just a few more seconds… almost…*there!* She yanked off the throttles and whipped the steering wheel over to the right, practically standing the *Baby Doll* up on her starboard side. As the port propeller came back down in the water, Kinsey jammed in the power. The boat leaped forward, up and over its own wake. Her prow slammed down and stabilized, giving her passenger a great look at the black boat.

Clearly stunned by her maneuver, the other driver slammed his throttles back and jerked right to avoid a collision. They'd have never hit; the *Baby Doll* had cut across his path too fast. But the guy's sharp turn combined with her wake hitting him full broadside rocked the big cigarette violently.

The other gunman staggered, grabbing for his windshield and hanging on desperately to avoid getting dumped out of the boat altogether.

"Now!" she screamed.

Her companion popped up, firing hard and fast. The crackling sound of bullets ripping into fiberglass peppered the air. The other gunman lurched left to face them...just in time to clutch at his chest and topple over into the water. Swear to God, it looked like a stunt straight out of a Hollywood movie. Except that rapidly spreading scarlet in the water was no movie prop.

And then the *Baby Doll* danced away, arcing away behind the black cigarette. The other driver craned his neck around, trying to keep her in visual range. His engines roared and the chase was on again. The guy tried to cut off the angle of her curve and come straight at her again, but she hadn't grown up on the water for nothing. She continued turning back and forth until the black cigarette was forced into following the same turning track behind her.

"Hang on," she warned her passenger. "We're about to zig right and hope he zags left!" She whipped her boat into a counterturn, arcing back into the path of the other boat. It was a maneuver an old Vietnam fighter pilot had shown her once. He called it a counterturn. Whatever it was called, it was highly effective. In a matter of seconds, her prow was pointed straight at the black boat's starboard side. Her client jumped up in the passenger seat and raked the black boat with automatic gunfire. Fist-size holes abruptly marred the sleek black hull.

"Lower!" she called. "Down by the waterline!"

He didn't acknowledge her instruction. But he must've changed his aim, for immediately a new line of fissures erupted along the black hull mere inches above the water. The fiberglass cracked and shattered under the relentless spray of lead. She peeled hard left, sending up a rooster tail of water that had to have drenched the other driver. If she was lucky, the other guy's hull should be badly compromised and starting to take on water.

"Get down!" her companion shouted.

She ducked as popping noises burst all around her. The *Baby Doll* shuddered as something—a whole bunch of somethings—hit her. *Not good.* The other gunman was firing back. Kinsey slammed the throttles forward. The *Baby Doll* bounded away from the spray of lead. The sound of the other boat diminished. She looked over her shoulder. The black boat wasn't giving chase. For that matter, it looked to be riding noticeably low in the water.

She guided the *Baby Doll* around a rocky point and the crippled black boat disappeared from view. They raced onward for another two minutes or so, flying down the coast of Tortola, the largest of the British Virgin Islands.

"I've got to slow down and check out my boat soon," she called. Although the *Baby Doll* didn't handle as if it was taking on water, it was a half-million-dollar piece of equipment, and it wasn't hers. Her father would kill her if she sank his favorite toy.

"Do it," her passenger replied.

She powered back to idle, and the sudden quiet was a shock. "Take the wheel while I have a look at the hull."

She stepped out of the cockpit and, balancing carefully, made her way out onto the forward hull. She stretched out on her stomach and leaned over the edge of the boat to have a look at the damage. A series of dents marred the cotton-candy-pink hull, but shockingly, it didn't look as if there were any holes. Stunned, she shifted over to the other side of the boat. No hull breaches there, either. *Thank God.*

"How's it looking?" the man asked.

"Fine," she replied in disbelief. She pressed to her feet and made her way back to the deck.

He offered her a hand as she stepped over the windshield. Their palms met, his large and callused and impossibly gentle. An actual tremor passed through her. And she wasn't a trembly kind of girl, thank you very much. *Wow.* She hopped down, still holding his hand. He waited a millisecond too long to release her fingers. But she noticed. And her stomach did a neat flip.

She cleared her throat nervously. "None of the bullets seem to have punctured the hull. Now that I think about it, I remember hearing something about this boat having a hybrid epoxy hull that uses layers of Kevlar instead of fiberglass or carbon cloth."

Her passenger's eyebrows shot straight up. "A bulletproof boat?"

"Sort of." Belatedly, caution speared through her. "Who are you? And who were those guys chasing you?"

"It doesn't matter. For what it's worth, my employer will pay for any damage to the boat incurred while you saved my a—" He amended, "My behind."

"Not to worry. Anyone who can afford a boat like this can afford repairs on it." She might have delivered that line in a supremely unconcerned manner, but she was shaking from head to foot. She'd actually been shot at! For that matter, this guy was still casually brandishing his machine gun. He'd slung it from a strap over his right shoulder, and it pointed down the length of his muscular thigh. She jerked her gaze away from his weapon nervously.

She ticked off on her fingers, "Boat chase, check. Gun battle, check. Narrow escape, check. What's next on the agenda, Mister—?" She broke off, leaving the obvious question of his name hanging.

He hesitated just an instant too long. "Perovski. Mitch Perovski."

"For today, at any rate?" she replied lightly.

"Something like that," he responded, as dry as the Gobi desert.

Not much of a talker. But then, she could relate. She'd come down here to the islands in search of silence herself. Relief from the vapid noise of humanity. "My name's Kinsey—" She hesitated. Rather than give him her well-known last name, she substituted her middle name. "Pierpont. Kinsey Pierpont."

She powered the boat up to a safe and inconspicuous cruising speed, closer to twenty knots than eighty. "Where can I take you?"

He snorted. "Anywhere that's not Tortola, or the British Virgin Islands for that matter."

The *Baby Doll* carried fuel for a few hours of cruising, which would reach several nearby islands outside the British chain—not that she'd decided to take him anywhere. "Did you kill that guy?" The words were out of her mouth before she could stop them.

He shrugged. "A gut shot like that is usually fatal,

but since we didn't stick around to check him out, I wouldn't call it a confirmed kill."

He sounded so bloody calm about it. Her heart practically pounded its way out of her chest at the mere thought of that guy toppling overboard.

"What islands can we reach on our current fuel load?" the man asked, abruptly serious again. He'd gone from relaxed to full predator mode in the blink of an eye. The shift was disconcerting.

She glanced down at the fuel gauges. "Where did you have in mind?"

Another shrug. *Cagey, he was.* "You were the Plan C I wasn't supposed to need. I didn't work out the details after the part where you saved my hide. Thanks, by the way."

"You're welcome, I think. You are one of the good guys, aren't you?"

"I am."

That was it? No explanation? No identification? No reason offered for carrying around that monstrous gun and using it on someone? "And the guy you shot?"

"Definite bad guy."

It would be far too easy to take this man at his word. She needed to believe him. Needed to believe he wouldn't turn that gun on her with the same casual ease he had those other guys. Heck, she *needed* to get on the radio and call the British Coast Guard. She reached for the radio mike and jumped violently when her passenger's hand whipped out to cover hers. His grip wasn't painful but was unmistakably powerful.

"What are you doing?" His voice was a low, dangerous rumble.

The sound vibrated deep in her belly, stirring part

fear and part something else altogether. She replied lightly, "I'm calling in the cavalry."

"Don't."

"But—"

"You don't know what you're involved in. Don't call the authorities, or the blood of a whole lot of good men could end up on your hands."

"But those guys were *shooting* at us—"

"And we shot back."

"*You* shot back."

"I shot back. I need you to leave the police out of this for now. I can't go into the details but you have to trust me."

Riiight. Trust him. Not.

"I need you to promise you won't contact the police. I don't want to have to restrain you."

"Restrain—"

He cut her off with a sharp slash of his hand through the air. "Promise."

Their gazes clashed, hers defiant and his…the sun turned his a molten gold that could consume her whole and melt her down to nothing. A girl could lose herself in those eyes if she wasn't careful. Very careful.

"Well?" he demanded. "Do we do this the easy way or the hard way?"

Chapter 2

Her gaze narrowed. Oh, how tempting it was to tell him to go to hell. But he was bigger than she was, stronger than she was and undoubtedly meaner. Then there was his machine gun to consider. Reining in her surliness, she retorted, "I won't call the police if you'll put that gun away."

He stared intently at her for a moment more, clearly weighing her honesty. Then he nodded. "Fair enough." He pivoted with that extreme, muscular grace of his and padded to the back of the deck where his duffel still lay. She caught the wince that passed across his features.

"Are you okay?" she asked in quick concern. If those guys in the black boat came back, Mitch was her only protection.

"Yeah. It's a flesh wound. I'll clean it up when I know we're safe."

"It looks bad."

He glanced down, surprised. "Nah, that's a little scratch. No organs hanging out or bones showing. I'm good."

He wasn't good—he was hurt.

She watched cautiously as he wiped down the machine gun and stowed it in the canvas bag.

Thank God. Being in the presence of that giant weapon made her too nervous to function rationally. Not to mention, he was gorgeous enough to send her pulse into the stratosphere. Her thoughts jumped around as disjointedly as caged monkeys.

"I know your name, but who are you?" she asked more sharply than she'd intended. Panic hovered too close, waiting for the slightest opening in which to pounce.

"I'm American."

"I can tell you're American from your accent. But who *are* you?"

Silence. A frown wrinkled his brow, but he ignored her question. *Or maybe chose not to answer.*

How rude was that? He'd dragged her into the middle of a shoot-out, for goodness' sake. A tiny voice in the back of her head said her anger was irrational, but the much louder voice of her fear-morphed-to-fury overruled it. "Who were those men chasing you?"

That got more reaction out of him. A full-blown shrug. *Wow. Some communicator.* A flinch flickered across his face, then his expression went smooth and impassive again. Except for those incredible eyes of his. They all but ate her alive.

Her insides quailing with some reaction she chose

not to examine closely, she tried again. "Why were they shooting at you?"

His gaze, now tinted orange by the blossoming sunset, snapped with irritation. What did he have to be irritated about? She was the injured party here. She announced, "I want you off the boat. Now."

"I'll bet you do," he purred.

He could stop sending shivers across her skin like that anytime now. "I'm serious."

He glanced around at the water on all sides with distaste. "You want me to jump overboard?"

"I was thinking more in terms of walking the plank. But I want you off the *Baby Doll.* I want no part of whatever it is you're mixed up in."

Dammit, the guy had a smile so hot it threatened to melt her righteous fury into a completely ineffectual puddle of lust. *Spine, woman. Spine!* Her gaze narrowed belatedly.

The humor drained from his expression, abruptly leaving it as cold as the arctic. Dread clawed her gut. Absolutely nothing radiated off him now. Not anger, not irritation, not even danger. He went absolutely, totally, completely still.

"There are sharks in these waters," he finally muttered.

Yeah, and she was looking at the most deadly one of all. Taking a deep breath and mustering up all her courage to stare him down, she replied, "There's no history in this area of shark attacks on humans. I don't want any trouble. Please go. The water's warm and it's only about a quarter mile to shore."

The southwestern tip of Tortola was sliding past their port side now.

He sighed and replied almost soothingly, "I'm sorry. I can't leave you."

"Can't you swim?" she challenged a bit tartly.

Aggravation flashed in his gaze, and matching satisfaction surged in her. He snapped, "I swim very well, thank you. Why, I've swum with—" He broke off. "Look. We have a little problem. The driver of that boat got a good look at you. Too good a look."

"And this is a problem why?"

"Because now he has to kill you."

She huffed in disbelieving laughter. "I've never seen that man in my life! Why in the world would he hurt me?"

Perovski's voice dropped into a careful, reasonable timbre. "I didn't say *hurt*. I said *kill*. And he'd do it because he thinks you got too good a look at him."

"I barely caught a glimpse of him what with all the bullets flying and wild driving I was doing."

In an even gentler tone, he replied, "But *he* doesn't know that. For all he knows, you could pick him out of a mug book or a lineup. He can't afford to let you live."

Her jaw dropped. A killer thought she could finger him? She felt a distinct urge to throw up. "Great. Why did I have to get dragged into this?"

Sounding downright apologetic now, he answered, "No one said anything about there being anyone aboard the *Baby Doll*. Congressman Hollingsworth said I could borrow his boat, but he didn't say anything about you being here."

"He doesn't know I'm here."

Perovski started. "Did you *steal* this boat?"

"Of course not! I just didn't tell my father I was coming down to the beach house."

"Your father?" His voice was deadly quiet.

She exhaled hard. "Yeah. My father. Richard Hollingsworth."

He pounced immediately. "I thought you said your name was Kinsey Pierpont."

"It is. Kinsey Pierpont Hollingsworth."

He absorbed that one in silence. So much for anonymity on this little retreat of hers. This guy would brag to someone in a bar about running into Kinsey Hollingsworth, and someone would overhear him. Before she knew it, the local paparazzi would mob her. And any chance at hiding in peace would be blown.

"Your middle name is really Pierpont?"

He didn't have to sound so bloody amused about it. "What's yours?" she challenged.

"Edgar," he admitted.

She suppressed a spurt of laughter. "And you're giving me grief about Pierpont?"

"I'm named after my grandfather," he said defensively.

"So am I," she retorted.

Laughter danced in his eyes, transforming their dangerous depths to a warm, inviting amber. Belatedly, she shook herself free of their spell.

She sighed. "Since you're the reason I've apparently run afoul of the guy in the boat, what do you suggest I do about it?"

He clammed up on her again. It figured. Honestly, the whole idea of some killer tracking her down and offing her was too preposterous. She faced her impromptu companion squarely and said resolutely, "Please leave."

His shoulders bunched up in annoyance, followed by a grimace of pain, but his voice was a low, steady rumble that made her want to curl up in it. "Ma'am, I'm not kidding. That bastard's gonna kill you."

"He doesn't even know who I am."

"And two minutes on the internet running the name of this boat or a couple quick phone calls wouldn't produce your identity and enough information to find you and kill you? With all due respect, you're not exactly a low-profile kind of girl."

"Low profile?" she repeated ominously.

He shrugged. "Yeah. Your dad's famous, and besides, you look…rich. With that lightbulb-blond hair and those legs—" He broke off.

She got the idea. Why the sour note in his voice when he described her, though? She studied him, and he glared back inscrutably. Something primitive deep inside her rose to the challenge of this man, relishing sparring with him.

What the heck was she supposed to do now? Pretend the shooting had never happened and take the *Baby Doll* back to Daddy's place? Run and hide? The pure insanity of such ruminations yanked her rudely back to reality. He was just trying to scare her. Perovski didn't want her to toss him off the boat and was probably making up the whole business of the other shooter coming after her.

He subsided into brooding silence, staring sphinx-like at the sunset's splendor. The moods of the sky were many, and at the moment the evening was quiet. Soft. Contemplative. Streaks of peach and lavender reached toward the east, where the distant horizon was darkening into a blue nearly as deep and unfathomable as the sea around them. Night would come soon. She got the distinct feeling the man beside her was a creature of the dark. An errant desire to walk in that world flashed through her. It might be a more interesting place than the gilded media microscope she lived under.

At least he hadn't threatened her. And his gun was put away. As armed-and-dangerous night stalkers went, he could've been worse.

St. John, one of the U.S. Virgin Islands, wasn't far away. She could duck into Cruz Bay—the U.S. Coast Guard guys there were on the ball. If she signaled them for help, they'd nab this man and his gun and get them off her boat. And after all, she'd only promised not to call the police. She hadn't said anything about not contacting the Coast Guard. She set course for St. John. Now all she had to do was keep this guy calm until she got there.

She glanced over at him. He slouched in the passenger seat, far too sexy for his own good. She almost missed having not been born in the good old days before AIDS and other nasty STDs, when a girl could casually jump a guy's bones without any thought to consequences. This guy just begged to be bedded.

He leaned his head back against the leather headrest. His eyes drifted closed. For an instant, he looked utterly exhausted. She shifted weight the slightest bit, and his eyes snapped open, alert and intelligent. His gaze traveled briefly up and down the length of her. "Are you done panicking yet?"

She blinked. Retorted with light sarcasm, "Why, yes, I'm perfectly fine. Thank you for asking. Lovely weather we're having, aren't we?"

A rusty sound escaped him. It took her a moment to identify it. That was a laugh—from a man who apparently didn't do it very often.

"Jeez, that was close," he mumbled.

Keep him talking. Make a human connection with him. So he wouldn't view her as an object to be kidnapped or killed at will. "And just what was *that*?"

"A hit. Or rather an attempted hit, since I'm still alive."

"Why were they trying to kill you?"

He shrugged. "The list of people who'd like to see me dead is long and distinguished."

"Were those old enemies or new ones?"

He shot her a speculative look. "A perceptive question. And one to which I don't know the answer."

Why would someone hire assassins to take this man out? What line of work *was* he in? "You're not a drug dealer, are you? Because I don't mess with drugs, regardless of what the tabloids say. And I certainly won't run them on this boat."

He made a wry face at her. "Trust me. My life would be a helluva lot simpler if I were a drug runner."

"So how do you know my father?"

"I don't."

"And he let you borrow his boat because…"

"Because my boss asked him for a favor. And no, I'm not going to tell you who my boss is."

"Did my father know you were running from hit men when he agreed to this favor?"

Mitch's lips twitched. "He probably surmised as much."

"Why?" She didn't waste her breath asking again what he did, but the question hung heavy in the air between them. Silence stretched out while she waited for an explanation, but none was forthcoming. She probed a little more. "Surely you're exaggerating the threat to me. I vaguely saw two men from a distance and one of them has a giant hole in his chest now. I certainly wasn't close enough to make out their faces."

"You saw more than you know."

"Like what?"

"You can accurately estimate their height and weight. Identify hair color. Skin color. Give a rough description of their clothing. Of how they ran. Their shooting stances. Tell that they used handguns and a shotgun. And if you know anything about firearms, you might be able to tell the police they used large-caliber, hollow-point slugs from the sounds of the shots."

She was tempted to swear under her breath. *He was right.* Darn it. She'd just wanted some peace and quiet. To be left alone. Was that too much to ask for? She fiddled with the GPS navigation system, checked the coordinates for St. John and made a course correction to point more directly at the island and its Coast Guard contingent. They'd remove this guy from her boat and her life, and then, if she was lucky, paradise would settle back down to its dull, safe and monotonous routine.

If she was lucky.

Mitch's cell phone vibrated insistently against his hip. *Again.* Yeah, he bet they wanted to talk to him. In a *big* way. They'd probably picked up a report of a dead man in the water from Coast Guard radio scanners in Tortola. Thank God Kinsey had already been on the *Baby Doll* and had the boat untied and engines running. Otherwise, he'd be shark bait now instead of the Cuban killer.

Interesting female, Kinsey Hollingsworth. Very East Coast upper crust. The whole package screamed *old money.* Her attractiveness went way beyond good grooming and expensive packaging. She was genuinely beautiful. Her blue eyes, long blond hair and aristocratic bones were very easy on the eye. She ran to the tall side, maybe five foot eight. In good shape. Just enough curves in the right places to give a man hot sweats. Which set his teeth thoroughly on edge. He probably shouldn't despise every leggy, gorgeous blonde he met, but damned if he could stop the reaction. Even after all these years, the gall of betrayal tasted bitter in his mouth.

At least the princess hadn't panicked when the chips were down.

Nobody should've known about tonight's meeting between him and Zaragosa. How in the hell had the Cubans found out about it? Worse, how had they found out about the meeting early enough to position assassins to disrupt it?

He didn't like it. Not one bit. This was the sort of wrinkle that got a mission scrubbed. But he wasn't so sure the boys upstairs would call this one off. Too much rode on it. And like it or not, he was the best man for the job. Hell, the only man for the job.

He pushed wearily to his feet. He probably ought to see to his shoulder now.

"I need somewhere dry to stow my bag," he announced.

Kinsey replied, "Inside the cabin. There's storage under the sofa cushions."

She turned away to have a look at the propellers, and he took the opportunity to surreptitiously unplug the microphone from the boat's radio. He pocketed it quickly, grabbed his bag and headed inside.

Sure enough, the bullet had grazed the meaty part of

his upper arm just below the shoulder joint. After awkwardly cleaning and bandaging the shallow wound, he fished out his cell phone. He needed to let the boys in the Bat Cave know he was alive and find out if the mission was still green-lighted after this fiasco.

The *Baby Doll*'s cabin was low and compact. A flat-screen TV, tufted leather upholstery and lots of brushed chrome oozed money. Nearly as sexy and expensive as the woman up top. A tiny porthole let in a wash of red light as he dialed. The phone barely finished a single ring before it was picked up.

"White Horse here. Go."

Usually, Mitch worked on the civilian side of the house for Jennifer Blackfoot, the civilian agent-in-charge of the Hunter Operation Team. Casually dubbed the H.O.T. Watch. But for this mission, he'd been put under the control of her equivalent on the military side of the operation, Commander Hathaway.

Mitch replied, "Lancer here. Thought you'd like an update."

"It's good to hear your voice."

Mitch snorted. "It's good to be alive. This afternoon was a little too close for me."

"Where are you now?"

"Sitting on the *Baby Doll* in the middle of the Caribbean watching the prettiest sunset you ever saw. Thanks for arranging the Plan C, by the way. Needless to say, I'm not gonna make the rendezvous at twenty hundred hours."

"What happened?"

He had to give Hathaway credit. The guy didn't waste time moaning and groaning when a plan went to hell. He got right to the point.

"I left the hotel early to sanitize my tail before the meeting with Zaragosa. A pair of men picked me up immediately. As soon as I made a move to shake them, they closed in and tried to off me. I ran for the emergency egress point. When I got there, the driver was dead and his boat's engine sabotaged. You know the next bit. I headed for Hollingsworth's boat."

"Did you get away clean?"

"Nope. The bastards followed me. Stole a boat and came after us."

"Us?" Hathaway asked sharply.

"Uhh, yeah. Small complication to Plan C. When I got to the *Baby Doll,* Hollingsworth's daughter was already aboard her. Which worked out pretty slick, by the way. She already had the boat untied and fired up when I got there. I jumped aboard and she took off. Probably saved my life."

"Then what?" Hathaway asked grimly.

"I exchanged fire with the hostiles while we fled."

"How's Hollingsworth's daughter?"

"Not a hair on her pretty little head out of place. She's a hell of a driver, by the way."

Hathaway replied wryly, "I'll be sure to pass your compliments on to the congressman. Status of the shooters?"

"One down. Probably dead but not confirmed. The other's still up."

"Any idea who they were?"

"I got a half-decent look at the one who's still alive. He's a Cuban player. Guy by the name of Camarillo."

Hathaway whistled between his teeth. "Camarillo's a heavy hitter. Rumor has it he used to work directly for Fidel himself."

Mitch retorted in mock shock, "Why, sir! Fidel was a peace-loving guy. He would never stoop to violence to gain an end."

Hathaway laughed. "Save the politically correct bull for the media. You and I have both operated in Cuba and know exactly what the Old Man was capable of."

"And to think, the new regime has exponentially less scruples than he had."

Silence fell between them for a moment. Then Hathaway said, "Any idea who sent Camarillo after you? He could be freelancing these days."

Mitch turned over the concept. Fidel Castro's personal assassin cut loose to sell his skills and knowledge to anyone willing to pay? Nah. The regime in Cuba was smarter than that. They'd keep the guy on retainer. "He's not freelancing. The Cuban government had to have sent Camarillo after me."

"How did *they* find out about your meeting?"

Mitch sighed. *Aye, and there was the rub.* "How well do you know Zaragosa, sir?"

Startled silence echoed in Mitch's ear. Finally, Hathaway answered, "I've never worked with him personally. Supposedly, he's one of the CIA's best sources in Cuba. And you've got to admit, we couldn't place a mole in a much higher position if we tried."

No kidding. Zaragosa was the deputy prime minister of Cuba and widely expected to be the next *presidente* of that tiny but pesky nation.

A shadow crossed the hatch, and Mitch's eyes narrowed. Was Kinsey eavesdropping or harmlessly moving around the deck?

He switched to rapid Spanish. Even if she spoke the

tongue, she probably wouldn't catch it at first. "Talk to me about the congressman's daughter, sir."

Hathaway didn't miss a beat. Mitch registered yet again how good it was to work with active field operators. It cut out so much red tape and bureaucratic hemming and hawing. The navy man answered evenly, "Miss Hollingsworth has had a tough year. She caught her fiancé humping her best friend a couple weeks back and dumped him. The tabloids have had a field day with it."

That was a switch. In his experience, it was the stunning blonde who screwed around.

Hathaway continued, "Apparently the ex wasn't appreciative of the negative media coverage. To divert attention from himself, he published a series of, uhh, explicit photos of Miss Hollingsworth on the internet."

Ouch. What a scumbag. Even spoiled little rich girls didn't deserve that.

"I expect she's looking to lie low. Blend in with the locals."

"On a hot-pink cigarette boat with her looks?" Mitch exclaimed.

Hathaway chuckled. "Any port in a storm, my friend."

Mitch thought fast. His job was to make contact with Zaragosa, infiltrate Cuba with identity papers the guy provided, then once in the country, spot any conspiracies against the guy and protect Zaragosa's back.

Of course, having now missed the meeting with Zaragosa, that plan was shot to hell. The Cuban politician was due to return to Havana later this evening and there would be no time to arrange for a second meeting. Mitch wasn't going to get his papers today.

Which meant his easy-as-pie, walk-through-the-front-door entry into Cuba was blown. Now he had to find his own way into that closed country. Illegally. Not that sneaking into Cuba posed any great challenge at the end of the day. He'd infiltrated a hell of a lot more difficult places to penetrate than Cuba in his career. But it was still a pain in the rear. Not to mention any change of plans represented a risk to the mission.

Mitch asked, "Can you guys contact Zaragosa and set up an alternate meeting with him in Cuba? Not Havana. Something on the south coast in a day or two. Maybe Cienfuegos. That's close to Zaragosa's old stomping grounds. He ought to be able to come up with an excuse to go there."

"What about you? Are *you* gonna be able to get there and blend in with the locals?"

"I've spent a fair bit of time operating in that neck of the woods. I'll be fine. Just tell Zaragosa to press on to Cuba without me and I'll hook up with him there."

Kinsey's shadow passed the porthole as she did some chore outside. Probably trying to keep busy to stave off the panic he'd seen lurking at the back of her baby blues. Odd how fate had thrust this woman into his path. Not being one to look gift horses in the mouth, however, an interesting thought struck him. He could just possibly use her looks to his advantage.

Mitch said thoughtfully, "I may have an idea of how to get into Cuba fast. Can you scrounge up a catamaran for me? Something berthed close to Cuba."

"I'll see what I can do. I show you sailing toward the U.S. Virgin Islands right now. Is that correct?"

He glanced out the porthole. "If that means we're

heading south by southwest in the middle of a whole bunch of water, that would be correct."

"I'll get the gang working on a catamaran for you."

"Not pink."

Hathaway laughed. "Roger that."

Mitch disconnected the call and pocketed the phone. He ducked through the hatch and squinted at the blazing wedge of red melting across the black water to their feet. It shrunk quickly to a narrow slash of red pulsing on the horizon.

Kinsey was already squinting at the fiery sunset. She commented over her shoulder, "Conditions are good to see the Green Flash tonight."

"The Green Flash?"

"When the sun dips below the horizon, there's an instant when its light refracts through the maximum thickness of the Earth's atmosphere and throws off the different colors of the spectrum. Sometimes you can see a flash of green. Legend says it's good luck to spot it."

Her enthusiasm was contagious. And hell, he'd take any luck he could get right about now. He squinted into the last vestiges of the setting sun. For just a second, its final rays turned a brilliant emerald-green. And then they winked out. "Hey! There it was!"

She smiled over at him. "I guess that means you're gonna have good luck on this trip."

Aww, hell. The princess had dimples. They added a little-girl charm to her bombshell looks that blew him clean away. Damn, damn, damn. He hated blondes. He didn't trust beautiful women. And he was not attracted to Kinsey Pierpont Hollingsworth!

Thankfully, his brain kicked back in before too many more seconds passed. Time to talk her into helping him.

He forcibly relaxed his shoulders and shrugged, packing as much casual friendliness into his expression as he could. "For what it's worth, I work in law enforcement. I can't go into a lot of details, though."

"Do you have a badge?"

He reached for his wallet. "Sort of." He pulled out his brand-spanking-new Alcohol, Tobacco and Firearms agent ID card in the name of one Mitch Perovski, and handed it to her.

She examined it carefully, looking from the picture to him a couple times. She held the ID card out to him. "Nice picture. You're a photogenic guy."

Unaccountably, the back of his neck heated up. Every now and then someone made a comment that pierced his current legend and went all the way to the real man. It never failed to catch him off guard.

Into the suddenly awkward silence, she asked, "What brings you to the sunny Caribbean? You're a long way from home, sailor."

"Cigars."

She blinked. Frowned.

He elaborated. "Cuban cigars." The papers Zaragosa was supposed to deliver declared him to be a tobacco importer looking for new sources of fine cigars.

"Ahh. I hear they can be lucrative."

He shrugged. "A good box of Cohibas runs six hundred bucks. If your father would like a box, I'll send him some when I get home."

"He doesn't smoke," she murmured.

The conversation lagged. He didn't know what to talk about with a socialite like her. Finally, he said, "Thanks again for saving my life."

"No problem."

"I'm serious. Thank you."

"Anytime," she mumbled, turning away to stare down at the navigation instruments.

The line of her neck arrested him. It was graceful. Slender. Sensuous. Wisps of hair curled at her nape underneath her short ponytail. What would happen if he breathed warmth across her skin just there? Would she cross her arms to rub away the goose bumps? Turn and melt into his arms? Kiss him into last week?

She'd kiss him right up to the part where she buried a knife in his back. He had places to go and things to do. A future president to protect. A few assassinations to commit along the way if he had to guess. Nothing out of the ordinary. He did *not* need a pampered princess like Kinsey Hollingsworth flitting around in his universe, fouling up the works and making him think thoughts he distinctly didn't want to think. First order of business: use the pretty lady to get into Cuba.

Next order of business: get rid of her.

Chapter 3

Kinsey was almost glad when darkness settled around the two of them. The rhythmic rumble of the two remaining engines soothed her—number three was running hot, and unable to find the source of the problem, she'd shut it down. The familiar salt-and-seaweed scent of the ocean was strong tonight. Everything about the night was magnified by the man's brooding presence beside her. Or maybe it was just her reaction to him heightening her senses to a near-painful pitch. She registered his slightest movement, even a change in the depth of his breathing, every blink of his eyes, every shift in his wary gaze.

The black sky and blacker sea merged into a single great expanse, a beast that had swallowed them whole. Normally, she loved this magnificent solitude. But tonight her soul was turbulent, disturbed by the leashed energy of the stranger beside her.

Reluctantly, she turned on the instrument backlighting. Its red glow intruded into the sensual mystery of the dark, breaking the spell.

"Head for the nearest inhabited island at our best forward speed."

He was back to orders and demands, this hard man. Nothing compromising or yielding about him.

She scanned the horizon and made out a faint black hump in the distance, a few lights twinkling along its spine. "There's the north coast of St. Thomas now," she replied.

"Find us somewhere to put ashore where we can hide this garish boat. Whatever possessed your father to paint it peppermint-pink, anyway?"

Kinsey rolled her eyes. "The trophy wife."

"I beg your pardon?"

"My father traded in my mother when she hit fifty for a new model. Giselle is twenty-eight now."

"Isn't that about how old you are?"

"Yeah. How creepy is that? But hey, she's gotten three *Vogue* covers and looks great on television."

Mitch sounded almost bitter when he commented, "I learned a long time ago not to put any stock in a woman's looks."

Wow. Definite raw nerve there. She changed the subject quickly. "If you want to hide this monster, we'll need to get her under a roof. There's a big marina near Frenchtown with some covered slips, but it's right by where the cruise ships come in. People crawl all over that area. Maybe something private..." She ran through the list of who she knew on the island. "I've got it. A sorority sister of mine and her husband have a place in Magen's Bay. And I think they have a boathouse."

A cynical look passed across his features. "Of course they do."

What was his problem? She shrugged and pointed the *Baby Doll* toward Magen's Bay. Only about half the estates lining its very exclusive, very private shores were lit tonight. Summer wasn't prime season for Caribbean vacation homes. She had a little trouble finding the right mansion, but eventually spotted it high above the water. Its windows were dark.

"Looks like nobody's home," she commented.

"Think they'll mind if we help ourselves to the boathouse?" Mitch murmured.

"No. We go way back. They'll understand."

"How do you know these people's boathouse will have an empty slip?"

She shrugged. "They always move their yacht up to Hyannis for the summer."

"Right. Hyannis."

She glanced over at him. "Look, I can't help it if I know some rich people. Mitzi and her husband are actually very nice."

"It's not the rich part I object to. It's the spoiled part."

She cut the engine and let the *Baby Doll* drift toward the boathouse. "Are you calling me spoiled?"

"If the shoe fits."

"The shoe does *not* fit. I can't help being born into a wealthy family." He was doing the same thing everyone else did. They took one look at her, labeled her a spoiled little rich girl and completely wrote her off as a waste of oxygen on the planet. What was it going to take for someone to take her seriously?

Gritting her teeth in frustration, she guided the *Baby Doll* to the dock and Mitch jumped ashore. He made his way to the locked boathouse doors and did something to them that didn't take more than a few seconds. And then they swung open. She eased the *Baby Doll* into the empty slip and tossed him a line. While he tied off the prow, she shut down the engines and tied off the aft line.

In the abrupt silence inside the barnlike structure, a thick blanket of darkness wrapped around them, as warm and sultry as the night without.

"What jobs have you ever held?" he challenged.

Still grinding that ax, was he? "I graduated with honors in English from Vassar and was an intern in my father's law firm. And I was a darned good one, too."

He shook his head, a sharp movement in the dark. "Not a paying job, and you were working for Daddy. Nobody was going to bust your chops or fire you from that place. Name me one real job you've ever had."

She huffed in irritation.

"I rest my case," he stated archly.

Annoyed, she replied, "How many charity balls for thousands of guests have you organized from scratch? How many millions of dollars have you raised for worthy causes and given away? How many scholarships have you interviewed a hundred people for and then granted? How many press conferences have you endured? How many political campaigns have you spent a year working on around the clock, road-tripping and stumping and getting by on two and three hours of sleep a night for months on end?"

He threw up his hands in mock surrender. "All right, all right. So you don't sit around on Daddy's fancy boat every day working on your perfect tan." But he still didn't sound convinced.

She wasn't quite sure why, but it was tremendously important to her that this supremely competent man perceive her as being able to do something worthwhile. Maybe she was sick of being compared to tabloid princesses. Or maybe it was because she'd felt so helpless in the face of being shot at. He, on the other hand, had taken action. He shot back. He took out his enemies. And she…she splashed some water at them with her cute pink boat.

Chad slept with her best friend and then posted those damned pictures of her on the internet when she dared to be mad about him sleeping with her maid of honor two weeks before their wedding. And all she'd managed to do was tuck her tail and run away. She wished she had a gun like Mitch's. She'd have blown off both their heads with it. Okay. Maybe not shot them. But she'd have scared them both to death. But no. She'd been as weak and spineless, as *useless,* as Mitch thought she was. Her face burned with the humiliation of it all.

She *was* useful, dammit! Just because her entire family and everyone she knew thought she was supposed to spend her life doing nothing more than being attractive fluff to decorate the arm of some powerful, successful man didn't mean it was true.

She finished buttoning up the *Baby Doll* for the night, her movements a little too jerky. Mitch prowled a circuit around both the outside and inside of the boat-house and finally came to a halt beside the boat. His gaze was black. Inscrutable in the near-total darkness.

"Now what?" she grumbled, still miffed.

"Now I make a phone call. And we sit tight until the cavalry comes for us."

She watched as he pulled out his cell phone.

"It's me," he muttered into it. "St. Thomas. In a boathouse at some private estate on Magen's Bay. Heh, *swanky* doesn't quite cover it. Any luck on a catamaran?"

A short pause while he listened to whomever he was talking with. She could swear his eyes glowed in the dark, gold and dangerous. It must be a trick of the faint moonlight creeping in through the boathouse windows, but the effect was eerie.

Without warning, his gaze speared into her, pinning her in place. "I'm telling you, she can do it. She's perfect for it." A short pause. "Yes, I know the risks. And yes, I'm sure."

He sounded as if he was trying to convince himself as much as the person on the other end of the line about whatever they were talking about.

"Okay. Call me back." He disconnected.

Not long on words, her pantherlike companion. When he didn't say anything to her after he pocketed the phone, she said, "And?"

"And we stay here while my people set up transportation for us."

"To where?"

He didn't answer right away. In fact, he almost looked hesitant to tell her. How bad could it be? He'd need to take her someplace secluded, far away from Cuba, where the killer wouldn't think to look for her. Maybe Europe. It was nice there at this time of year.

"How do you feel about big-game hunting?" he asked.

"Africa?" she blurted, surprised. "It's awfully hot there at this time of year. But I suppose I'm up for a safari. As long as we don't shoot anything. But I could go for some big-game photography." Now that she thought about it, she could see where he'd feel at home in Africa.

"Not Africa," he bit out.

"Then where?"

Finally, he said reluctantly, "Cuba."

"*What?*" she squawked. "But that's where your assassin is from."

"That's correct. It'll just be for a few days. Long enough for me to find our guy and neutralize him. His name's Camarillo, by the way."

"We need to stay away from him. He'll try to kill us again!"

"That's why we're going to hunt him down and eliminate him before he gets us. Ops thinks it would be safer to go on the offensive and not sit back and wait for him to come to us."

Shock rendered her speechless. They were going hunting for their would-be killer? She burst out, "That's the dumbest idea I've ever heard."

He snorted without humor. "Wait till you get a load of the next part, where you act as my cover to smuggle me into Cuba."

"How am I supposed to do that?"

"Can you handle a sailboat as well as you handle a motorboat?"

"Well, yes." She frowned. "How did you know that?"

He made a noise that might pass in some circles for a laugh. "Tortola? Hyannis? Magen's Bay? You grew up on water. And where there are rich people and water, there are sailboats."

"I happen to prefer motorboats," she replied a little stiffly. She hated fitting his stereotype of her, but she had, in fact, grown up around boats of all kinds.

Mitch's voice rasped across her skin like a cat's rough tongue, drawing her attention once more. "I need you to sail a wounded catamaran into port on the south side of Cuba and request repairs. They'll let you come ashore in an emergency. I'm going to hide in one of the pontoons. Once you've docked, I'll sneak out and we'll head inland from there."

"Sounds dangerous."

"Not especially. If the Cubans catch us, they'll only throw us into prison. In six months, a year tops, the U.S. government will negotiate our release. I figure with your father being who he is, the Cubans will spring us after a few weeks. At least, they'll spring *you* that fast."

"I do not want to be incarcerated in a Cuban jail, thank you very much."

"Me, neither. That's why you're going to pay attention and do what I tell you."

"I don't like it," she announced.

"Neither do I. But I've got no time to fool around with setting up another entry into Cuba. You're it, Miss Hollingsworth. We need to stick together, anyway, until I kill Camarillo. I may as well put you to some good use."

"Gee, thanks. I always love sounding like some sort of disposable power tool."

"You don't throw out power tools," he corrected gently.

She merely narrowed her eyes and glared at him. Fine. So she'd never seen a power tool in person in her life. He knew darn good and well what she had meant.

She sulked for several minutes, trying to figure out some better way to get into Cuba. But she was completely out of her league on this one. She turned her attention to something that had bothered her from the very beginning. "How did Camarillo find you? Wasn't your meeting with whoever you were supposed to meet with a secret?"

He looked roundly irritated that she dared to question his work and didn't bother to answer.

She wasn't about to let him go all strong and silent on her, as if she didn't matter enough to talk to. No, sirree. She got enough of that from her father. She poked again—something simple to get him talking. "How did you get those boathouse doors open?"

His teeth flashed white in the darkness. "Have you ever heard of a 'don't ask, don't tell' policy? If you won't ask, I won't tell."

She absorbed that one in silence. Eventually, she asked, "How long are we supposed to sit here, waiting for your phone call?"

He shrugged. "Could be all night."

Great. All night in a dark, secluded place with this macho male. Darned if that didn't make her heart beat a little faster. More in an attempt to distract herself than actually make conversation, she commented lightly, "I don't know about you, but I'm hungry."

"Gee, I'll just call the local French gourmet delivery joint and have them bring us a seven-course meal," he retorted.

She glared and replied loftily, "There's food in the *Baby Doll*'s galley."

He looked startled, as if he'd forgotten for a moment that the *Baby Doll* had a compact but completely stocked cabin.

She ducked below and turned on the halogen track lighting. It twinkled subtly overhead, lending the space a romantic glow. She opened the small cupboard above the microwave oven. "There's canned spaghetti or tuna fish," she called up.

"I'll take spaghetti." He joined her in the tiny cabin, filling its entire space with his dark presence. He sprawled on the leather couch, a feline predator at rest. She passed him a piping-hot container of spaghetti and zapped one for herself. When it was ready, she moved to the far end of the couch and perched cautiously on it. She promptly burned her tongue but did her best not to show it. Darn, that man flustered her! She shifted uncomfortably in her seat.

"We could always break into the main house and raid the pantry," he suggested.

"Let's not," Kinsey said drily. "We're already imposing. And these are my friends."

His only reply was a casual shrug.

They finished their meal, such as it was, in silence. Mitch arose and held out his hand for her cup and spoon. She handed them over and he tossed them in the galley's sink. He'd just turned to head for the steps when his cell phone shattered the deep silence. Kinsey jumped nearly as hard as he did. He fished it out of his pocket.

"Go," he bit out.

His eyebrows drew together in a frown as he listened, and his gaze flicked over to her. Whoever was on the other end of the conversation was talking about her, she was sure of it.

"I'll see what I can do," Mitch rumbled. He disconnected. Turned to face her. "Seems we've got a little problem. Your father doesn't want you to help us with this operation. He thinks it'll place you in too much danger. You're, and I quote, 'totally unprepared to deal with the pressures of the situation.'"

Heat flooded her face. This was exactly what she was talking about! People took one look at her and assumed she wasn't good for anything. "In other words, he thinks I can't hack it," she forced out.

"More or less."

"Give me your phone," she snapped. She held out her open palm expectantly. One eyebrow raised, he laid the device in her hand.

She stabbed out her father's private number and waited impatiently for the call to go through. Richard Hollingsworth's voice came on the line. "Hello?"

"Hi, Dad, it's your useless, spoiled daughter calling."

"Honey, are you all right? They told me some guy shot at you today."

"Oh, I'm fine. And that guy's shark bait," she replied breezily. "The man who saved my life today needs a favor from me, though, and I'm going to do it. I hear you're worried, so I'm calling to tell you I'll be fine. He says I need to stay with him and I believe him. I trust this man implicitly to keep me safe."

Mitch's gaze riveted on her at those words. Her embarrassed gaze skittered away from his.

"Kinsey, do you have any idea who this Perovski fellow is? I had my staff run a profile on him, and you can't believe some of the things he's done. Plainly put, he's a killer. He's a covert operator and runs around blowing things up and assassinating people for a living. You have no business being around someone like him."

The condescension in her father's voice set her teeth on edge. "Be that as it may, I'm going to help him with the next phase of his current mission."

"No."

"I wasn't calling to ask permission, Dad. I'm telling you how it's going to be."

Her father's voice rose to a bull roar. "Don't you take that tone with me, young lady. I control your trust fund. And I forbid you to do this."

"I'm sorry you feel that way. But I am going to do it."

"I'll cut you off. No money, no credit cards, no bank account. Nothing."

Twenty minutes ago, that threat might have given her pause. But after Mitch's scathing opinion of her utter uselessness as a human being, she'd be damned if her father would bully her out of this.

"Do what you have to, Dad, but my decision's made. Good night." She closed the phone and handed it back to Mitch in silence.

"What did he threaten to do to you?" Mitch asked quietly.

"He's cutting me off financially."

"Totally?" Mitch sounded surprised.

"Yup."

"Man, that sucks. I can look into having the boys put you on the payroll for the duration of this op if you'd like."

She grinned ruefully. "Thanks, but I'll muddle through until he gets over his snit. My mother is loaded, compliments of her divorce lawyer, and she'll slip me some cash if I empty my bank account before he gets over his snit. Besides, I can always threaten to go public with what my father's doing to me and he'll back off.

Negative publicity is very bad for a man in his position. He's up for reelection this November."

Mitch winced and grinned simultaneously. "Ouch. Blackmailing your old man? That's cold. I like it."

She grinned back, reassured she'd made the right decision. She wanted some of the competence that was Mitch Perovski for herself. If she spent a few days with him, maybe some of that cool confidence of his would rub off on her. Goodness knew, she needed it. If he could show her how to get people to take her even a little more seriously, it would be worth all the money in her trust fund and more. She was sick and tired of being walked all over.

In fact, the more she thought about it, the more she liked the idea. If she could shed her socialite image and become a strong, independent woman...oh, yes. The idea made her tingle from head to toe. Wild horses weren't going to keep her away from Mitch Perovski, no matter what risk that entailed.

Chapter 4

Mitch glanced around the tight confines of the *Baby Doll*'s cabin. The sofa no doubt folded out into a bed. One bed. Two people. He winced mentally. He could be a gentleman and offer to sleep up top, propped up in one of the chairs or stretched out on the hard deck. But this was likely to be the last decent night's sleep he got for the next several months, and dammit, they were both adults. They could sleep in the same bed without anything untoward happening between them.

Kinsey stifled a yawn.

He said lightly, "Let's get some shut-eye. No telling when the boys will be here to pick us up. Operations rule number one—sleep when you can."

She nodded without protest, unlocked the sofa and pulled it out into a bed. With her working at one end and him at the other, they made the bed with satin sheets—

what else for the *Baby Doll?*—cashmere blankets and fluffy eiderdown pillows.

"Where are you sleeping?" she asked, all innocence.

"Here. How about you?"

Her alarmed blue gaze snapped to his. She looked down at the inviting bed. Back up at him. "Oh."

He shrugged, but it didn't relieve the abrupt tension in his shoulders. "I don't know about you, but I'm beat. And tomorrow promises to be rougher than today." Why did he give a damn if she refused to sleep with him or not? She wasn't some princess—which she was taking great pains to convince him of. She was just a person. Just like him.

Dammit, not just like him. She lived in the lap of luxury, in a world of yachts and mansions and summers in Hyannis. They were as different as day and night. And he'd do well to remember that. He'd use her to get into Cuba, and he'd kill Camarillo before the bastard could kill her, thereby sending a powerful message to Camarillo's comrades that Kinsey Hollingsworth was off-limits. And then they'd each get on with their regularly scheduled lives. He'd go back to being a sewer rat, and she'd go back to doing whatever she did, hopefully unmolested. Tanning on sleek cigarette boats in a thousand-dollar bikini.

"You take the side by the hull," he directed. "I'll sleep closest to the hatch."

She lurched. "Do you think Camarillo might find us here?"

"Not a chance. He wouldn't look for me in a place like this in a thousand years." And that was why she was going to be such a great cover to get him into Cuba.

Nobody in their right mind would look at her and see a covert operative running a scam.

She crawled under the covers and scooted to the far side of the bed, plastered against the wall. He turned off the lights and, under cover of darkness, tucked his pistol under his pillow. He sat down on the edge of the bed and thought he heard her squirm even farther away from him

"I won't bite," he growled.

"I'm not so sure about that," she retorted.

He grinned into the dark. If she only knew. He'd bet he could bite her so he'd have her begging him for more in under five minutes. Hell, two minutes.

"Sweet dreams, Mitch."

Right. As if there was anything sweet about his dreams. Not after the life he'd lived. "You, too."

He stretched out on possibly the most comfortable mattress he'd ever experienced. One of those memory-foam things that contoured itself to fit his body to perfection. Some mission this was starting out to be. Here he was in the perfect bed—hell, the thing was even adorned with a blond bombshell—and all he could do was lie still, teeth gritted, and pray for the night to be over.

Kinsey's breathing lightened into the gentle rhythm of sleep more quickly than he expected. The gunfight earlier must've really taken the starch out of her. But then it occurred to him that her rapid sleep also meant she trusted him. How had she described it to her old man? She trusted him implicitly with her life? Ahh, if only she knew. If she had any idea of the thoughts of her dancing across his mind's eye right now, she'd run screaming from him.

Not that he meant anything by it. Stripping her naked in his mind was just an idle fancy to pass the time and distract him from his insomnia. He certainly wasn't about to act on it. She was a resource for a mission and emphatically not his sort of female. At least not anymore. As soon as she got him into Cuba, he'd send her home to Daddy and a raft of expensive, private bodyguards. And that was *not* a pang of regret stabbing his gut, dammit!

He must've drifted to sleep, because sometime later, he jerked awake abruptly. He froze, listening. What had wakened him? The night sounds of St. Thomas were mostly silent, a few crickets and frogs the only remaining chorus outside. The *Baby Doll* rocked ever so faintly beneath him, so soothing he was half-asleep again already.

Kinsey gave a faint start beside him and made a frightened sound. Aww, crap. She was having a nightmare. This was his cue to roll over and gather her into his arms and comfort her. Except he didn't want to put his hands on her, didn't want to press her against him. Women like her were poison. He'd just as soon hug a rattlesnake.

She jerked again, her breathing fast and hard. She half sat up, then collapsed back against her pillow.

"You all right?" he asked gruffly.

"I had a bad dream."

"Let me guess. It involved Cuban guys with giant guns chasing you."

"Something like that."

"Shrug it off. A nightmare is just your mind's way of blowing off some steam after a traumatic event. It doesn't mean anything."

"Right." A pause. Then her voice came out of the dark, faintly sarcastic. "Thanks for the comforting advice. I'll never fear another nightmare again as long as I live."

"Look. I don't do the whole touchy-feely thing. I'll stomp all over your emotions in the middle of an op and not think twice about it. I'm a bastard. The sooner you realize that, the better we'll get along."

Hurt silence was her only response to that salvo. Damn. He really was a bastard.

He thought she'd already gone back to sleep when her voice drifted out of the dark. "Then why are you insistent on protecting me until Camarillo's dead?"

"Because it's the right thing to do," he bit out.

"A real bastard wouldn't care enough about someone else to do the right thing. You're a grouch. But not a bastard."

"Thank you…I think," he retorted.

"You're welcome," she replied lightly.

"Go to sleep."

"Yes, sir, Mr. Grouch, sir."

A smile twitched at the corners of his mouth. How did she do that? She'd turned aside his irritation effortlessly. Alarm coursed through him. What had he done, saddling himself with this woman for days, or even weeks?

Kinsey went back to sleep with a smile on her lips and woke up with one on them in the morning…if the first hint of dawn could rightly be called morning. The sky in the east was pink, but the sun hadn't risen above the verdant mountains ringing Magen's Bay when Mitch touched her arm lightly. At the brush of his fingers against her skin, she popped wide-awake.

He looked even rougher and more dangerous this morning with a stubble of beard darkening his jaw. "It's time to go."

She sat up abruptly, the covers pooling around her waist. His gaze dropped to her chest for an instant but then jerked away as quickly. She was startled to find herself relieved at the brief verification that a red-blooded male actually did live inside the cold predator. She crawled on her hands and knees across the wide bed and swung her bare feet to the cold floor.

"I wish I had some real clothes," she remarked wistfully. "I'm going to get plenty sick of this bikini and T-shirt in the next week or two."

"I'm sure the folks at the Bat Cave can arrange for some real clothes. Maybe not the designer labels you're used to, but clothes."

"Would you get off your high horse about my financial background?"

"It's hard to forget with you looking the way you do."

She glared at him. "Whatever's left of yesterday's mascara is probably smeared all over my face by now. I undoubtedly have a bad case of bed head, and I haven't had a shower in twenty-four hours. I'm wearing a junky T-shirt and not a whole lot more. I look like hell, and I know it. So cut the crap about my looks."

He crossed his arms, his expression black. His molten gaze raked down her person, far too slowly and thoroughly, all the way to her pedicured toes and back up to her eyes. To say she felt stripped naked didn't quite cover it. She felt…invaded. And caressed. And, oh my, appreciated in a very, very female way.

"Honey, if that's as bad as it ever gets with you, I'd hate to see you gussied up. You look like a top-drawer princess just as you are."

She frowned. How did he manage to make such a lavish compliment sound like such an insult? A strange sound intruded upon her ruminations. A distant, heavy thumping. She lurched in surprise and bumped into Mitch.

"What's that?" she gasped.

Mitch turned quickly and took all three steps up onto deck in a single, athletic bound. "Stay here," he ordered as a pistol materialized in his hand.

She briefly considered hiding in the closet-size bathroom but decided any bad guy would search there right away.

"You can come out, Kinsey. It's the H.O.T. Watch."

The H.O.T. Watch? He'd mentioned that before. Sounded like a bunch of comic-book heroes. Cautiously, she went up onto deck. Three male silhouettes filled the boathouse doors. She recognized Mitch's sleek, powerful outline right away. He lifted a hand and gestured her to come over to him.

He was deep in conversation with another man in rapid Spanish she couldn't entirely follow. Strange, because she actually spoke the language reasonably well. They were using specialized vocabulary she only vaguely recognized as dealing with weapons of some kind. She moved to his side and was startled when he absently reached out and looped an arm about her shoulders, pulling her close to him.

Oh, yes. Entirely male. Powerful, protective alpha male. It was really quite nice to cuddle up to all that brawn.

Eventually there was a break in the discussion.

"This is Kinsey," Mitch said to the first man.

"I'm Brady. Nice to meet you, ma'am."

Was that his first name or last name? He didn't look like the kind of guy she could ask the question of readily. He had to be military with that short hair and ramrod-straight bearing. And then there was the whole ma'am thing. The other guy was introduced as Captain Scott Cash. His dancing green eyes were much more inviting than the first man's.

To him, she commented, "You get harassed about your name and rank a lot, don't you?"

He grinned back at her. "Wait until I become Major Cash."

Mitch interrupted sharply, "Ready to go?"

She looked up into his scowling visage. "Well, I've got a ton of stuff to pack. It'll take hours before I'm ready."

"Very funny. Let's move out, gentlemen."

His big hand wrapped around her elbow and he steered her out the door with easy strength. She felt like a panther cub with its mother's jaws around her neck, carrying her to safety. Mitch's touch was gentle but unmistakably powerful. The other men fell in behind her and Mitch as they stepped outside the boathouse. A chunky helicopter sat in the mansion's backyard, its rotors spinning and a pair of helmeted pilots sitting at the controls. The paint job was blue-gray on the bottom and green on the top.

Mitch hustled her up the stone steps from the beach to the wide lawn and urged her into a jog when they reached the manicured grass. She couldn't help crouching low as they moved under the rotor blades. A wide door swung open in front of them, and Mitch helped her inside.

She sat down on a hard seat and looked around for a seat belt. She started when Mitch crouched in front of her and plunged both hands behind her hips. His palms cupped her derriere and she'd have bolted out of the seat if that wouldn't have flung her straight into his arms.

Their gazes met, hers wide with shock, his narrow with irritation. He yanked his hands back roughly, bringing with them the halves of her seat belt. He guided a pair of shoulder straps over both of her breasts, the wide nylon blatantly rubbing the sensitive flesh they were smashing. His hands came together in her lap and she grew possibly more shocked. His nimble fingers fumbled embarrassingly close to the junction of her thighs, and then his hands lifted away. She looked down. Her seat belt was a five-point affair with a round buckle sitting low on her belly. Thankfully the shoulder straps hid the way her nipples had hardened under her thin T-shirt at his touch.

"Are you done?" she muttered.

His blazing gaze caught hers. "I haven't even gotten started yet," he growled back.

She gulped as he slid into the seat across from her and buckled his own safety harness. Scott Cash sat on her right, and the enigmatic Brady took a seat beside Mitch. Two crew members took the remaining seats. As soon as one of them slid the big door shut, the bird lifted off the ground, swooping forward fast and then banking into a steep, accelerating turn.

"Where are we going?" she shouted over the noise to Mitch.

"It'll take a couple hours to get there," he shouted

back. "If you want to take a nap, go ahead. I know you slept lousy last night."

And how did he know that? Other than the nightmare that had woken her up so abruptly, of course. She didn't want to ask in front of the other men, so she just glared at him for being rude enough to comment on it. He stared back at her implacably. Every now and then a jostle of the helicopter sent his knees banging into hers. At some point, he stretched his powerful legs out, his feet extending all the way under her seat. The pose forced her legs apart so his calves could slip between hers. It was intimate and aggressive. Like the man.

And yet, he'd declined to touch her last night, even when she'd needed and wanted a hug from him. Was he truly the bastard he claimed to be, or was there more to it than that? She studied him, his eyes closed, his arms crossed over his chest in an eye-catching display of bulging biceps. She'd been around plenty of men who were intimidated by her beauty and hesitated to touch her. Was that it? Was he actually attracted enough to her to be shy?

Mitch Perovski shy? The thought made her smile.

"What?" he bit out.

She started. How had he seen her smile? His eyes were closed. "I beg your pardon?"

"What are you grinning about like that?"

Her smile returned, wider than before. "Nothing. Nothing at all."

He humphed, recrossed his arms over his chest and closed his eyes once more. Whether or not he actually slept, she couldn't tell. But she eventually followed suit and let the rotor wash and jet noise coax her heavy eyelids closed. What was that thing he'd said last night about sleeping when she could? She took his advice and drifted off.

"Wake up, Kinsey."

She jolted to consciousness. The helicopter was still vibrating, thumping loudly around her. Mitch was leaning forward, his hand resting on her bare knee. Darned if heat wasn't shooting straight up the inside of her thigh to her nether regions. She drew in a quick breath of surprise. His all-too-perceptive eyes flashed in male satisfaction for the barest instant before he released her leg and leaned back, resuming his negligent, feline sprawl.

"Where are we?" she asked sleepily.

"Almost there."

She didn't even bother to ask where "there" was. If he'd wanted to tell her, he would have. She sighed. "How long was I asleep?"

"Three hours."

Wow. How fast could a helicopter go, anyway? Maybe two hundred miles per hour? That meant they could be anywhere up to six hundred miles away from St. Thomas. That encompassed a pretty big chunk of the eastern Caribbean.

The helicopter dropped alarmingly and she clutched at the nearest thing, which turned out to be Scott Cash's rock-hard forearm. "What was that?" she blurted.

Mitch scowled pointedly at her hand on the other man's arm. "We're coming in for a landing. Nothing to panic over."

She released the captain's arm with a smile of gratitude and apology. At least he was smiling back at her. Broadly. With dimples.

Mitch regained her attention abruptly by announcing, "Time to put the blindfold on you."

"What for?"

He shrugged. "Secret location. You're not allowed to see anything that might let you identify it later."

"You're kidding." Bat caves? Secret locations? This was definitely turning into a comic book.

He leaned forward with a black cloth blindfold like an airplane passenger might wear to sleep in flight. He placed it over her eyes, then slipped the elastic strap behind her head. He gathered her hair in a rough ponytail, his fingertips caressing the nape of her neck and sending shivers shooting all the way to her toes. He pulled her hair through the elastic strap and released it in a cascade of silken softness against her skin. Goose bumps erupted on her arms.

"Can you see anything?" he asked.

"Like I'd tell you if I could?" she retorted. Cash chuckled beside her. She felt Mitch's scowl without any need to see it. His fingers skimmed all the way around the edge of the mask, checking the seal and incidentally unleashing a horde of butterflies in her stomach. He was messing with her on purpose. Was he just trying to make her uncomfortable, or was he getting a kick out of her involuntary reactions to him? Or maybe he was testing her reactions to him for some other reason altogether. One that had to do with the way his eyes glowed whenever he looked at her.

The helicopter thudded gently to the ground. In a few moments the engines cut, and the thwocking of the rotor blades slowed rapidly.

"Okay, out we go," Mitch muttered. His hand fumbled at her lap belt and her breath hitched far too revealingly for her comfort. Just as well she couldn't see him. His strong hands guided her outside. A little light leaked around the edges of the mask, and the sun warmed her skin. She heard and smelled the ocean nearby and sand gave way underfoot. A beach, then.

"This way," Mitch murmured. His hand slid under her elbow, and his big body rubbed lightly against her side. She was surprised at how horribly disoriented she became in a matter of moments. She leaned closer to Mitch, intensely disliking this sudden vulnerability. And yet, of all the men she'd ever met, she had the most confidence in him to keep her safe. After his lethal display of skills yesterday, she had faith he was one of the deadliest people around. Although frankly, his buddies hadn't looked much less dangerous.

After maybe a hundred strides through more sand, she heard a door open in front of her.

"Steps downward," he murmured.

She felt with her foot, stumbling a bit on the first step. But Mitch's arm snaked around her waist, catching her and steadying her. Of course, it also plastered her against his side. Sensations of his body against hers slammed into her. Hard muscle. Lean waist. Hot. Vibrant. Powerful. Oh, so very male.

He cleared his throat and carefully set her away from him. She looped her left hand under his elbow once more. She stuck out her right hand for balance and encountered a cool, rough wall. *Stone.* The steps, while individually fairly shallow, went on forever. She lost count of them somewhere in the seventies.

And then, without warning, her foot reached out for another step and ran into level floor. It was hard and smooth like concrete. The air currents around her shifted, and the echo of their feet changed as if they'd stepped out into an open space.

Mitch stopped with her huddled close to him. She heard some metallic clanking and an odd hissing noise. Then he urged her forward with a solicitous hand on the small of her back. "Careful, now. This is a big step. You'll have to bend down. Grab that metal bar right there. Now swing your right leg out and down."

What in the world? It felt as if she was climbing down into something. As she put weight on her right foot, the surface beneath her gave slightly. Ahh. A boat. She frowned under the mask. A boat underground? What was this?

She stumbled forward a few more steps and then Mitch guided her down into a comfortable, cushioned seat. Her ears popped as if the space around her had pressurized and her frown deepened. "What is this?" she demanded. "Where am I?"

"You're aboard a submarine. Not too much longer, now, and you can take off your blindfold."

A *submarine*? Good grief. Sure enough, a low rumble started under her feet, and her seat began to sway gently. They must have motored forward and down for ten or fifteen minutes, and then the blindfold suddenly lifted away from her eyes.

She blinked around in the red-lit semidark. She was, indeed, on a minisub. A small, thick window at her left looked out on a mostly dark ocean. They were deep, then. From her experience with scuba diving, she'd estimate they were well over a hundred feet down. Momentary claustrophobia tightened her chest. So much water pressing down on top of them. The weight of it could crush them if this vessel failed.

"Where in the world are we going?" she asked Mitch, who sat across from her again.

"H.O.T. Watch headquarters. We've got to pick up some gear before we head into Cuba, and I need a last-minute intelligence briefing before we make our run." He glanced down at her unclad legs. "And we've got to get you some clothes. I'm not going to be able to concentrate if I have to keep looking at your legs all the time."

"What's wrong with my legs?" She'd just had them waxed, and she had a pretty good tan going if she said so herself. Her limbs were long and toned and sleek. She'd always thought of them as one of her best assets.

"Nothing's wrong with your legs," he grumbled. "That's the problem."

Captain Cash piped up from her right. "Hark. Is Lancer actually showing signs of being human after all?"

Lancer? Was that some sort of nickname of his? It was a good name for him. Sharp. Lethal. Something that drew blood.

Mitch scowled at his comrade. "Shut up, Scottie."

Brady laughed. "I think you're right, Scott. The guy's human after all. Thanks for answering that question for us, Miss Hollingsworth."

She crossed one slender leg over the other, dangling her flip-flop from her toes in Mitch's direction. "My pleasure," she drawled at Brady. For good measure, she crossed her arms, pushing up her chest under her T-shirt. Too bad she had the shirt over her bikini top. Nonetheless, Mitch's gaze dropped involuntarily to the sudden curves. When it lifted again to hers, as brilliant and turbulent as the surface of the sun, she smirked back at him.

He crossed his own arms and turned a shoulder to her, staring fixedly out the window.

Triumph surged in her breast. She glanced over at Brady. "How long is this little joyride going to take?"

He shrugged. "A while."

"Why all this secrecy?"

Brady replied, "The facility we're going to is highly classified. Only a handful of people know it exists, let alone where it is. The only reason you get to go there is because time is of the essence and your father is a congressman. It's as much for your protection as ours that we're concealing its location from you."

"Seems like you're going to an awful lot of trouble. You could always just ask me to promise not to tell where it is. I'd give you my word on it, you know."

Mitch interjected, saying harshly, "And when you're taken prisoner and tortured for the information, how long do you think you could hold out?"

She jerked back, stung. The rest of the ride, which lasted upward of an hour, finished in silence, stony from him and irritated from her. At one point, she caught Brady looking back and forth between the two of them in quiet amusement, as if he thought they were perfect for each other. Whatever. Mitch Perovski was a jerk. She would prove to him that she was no dimwit social-ite and smuggle his happy butt into Cuba, but then she was done with him.

Chapter 5

Mitch watched as the submarine ducked under a black overhang of rock, skimming close enough to it to make Kinsey gasp. He'd taken this ride a number of times and that spot never failed to make him hold his breath. There was a surface entrance to the Bat Cave, but because of its vulnerability to attack, *nobody* but H.O.T. Watch staff knew its location.

The sub slowed and came to a stop. Kinsey leaned forward to peer out the window, but Mitch knew she'd see nothing but blackness. The pilot was centering the vessel below a vertical tube formed aeons ago by up-welling magma. The sub would begin an elevator-like ascent up the tube momentarily. Sure enough, the vessel lurched gently beneath his feet and began to rise.

Kinsey glanced over at him for reassurance. He spared her a single nod to indicate that everything was okay. He kept trying to distance himself from her, to achieve cold, calm detachment from his temporary partner. But every time she succumbed to a moment of vulnerability, his protective instincts roared to the fore and there wasn't a damned thing he could do about it.

"Are you going to blindfold me when we get off this thing?" Kinsey asked, her musical voice wavering slightly.

Dammit, she was doing it again. He couldn't help the gentleness that crept into his voice. "No. We'll be underground. You won't be able to see any identifying features that might give away where we are."

She lapsed into apprehensive silence. Her blue eyes were big and dark, almost childlike, making her look like a girl-woman in a siren's body. Like it or not, she was beautiful. And he wanted her. Compared to Janine—the woman who'd put him off leggy blondes and their treacherous hearts in the first place—Kinsey was a diamond to Janine's lump of coal. Janine had been pretty, but Kinsey was gorgeous. Janine had been tall and leggy, as was Kinsey—but Kinsey also moved with the unconscious grace of a dancer. Janine knew she was hot and flaunted it. Kinsey didn't need to have everyone in a room looking at her. Which, of course, had exactly the opposite effect.

Regardless, he wasn't about to trust Kinsey's heart for a second. Women as beautiful as she was didn't wait around for men who disappeared for months at a time, mostly unable to communicate with their women while undercover. Janine sure as hell hadn't waited around for him. Who knew how long she'd fooled around on him before she came up pregnant, months after he could possibly have been the father. The hell of it was he still supported the boy. But dammit, he couldn't abandon a baby to Janine's erratic finances. Not even some other guy's kid.

The pilot's voice announcing that they were clear to open hatches startled Mitch out of his grim thoughts.

As he helped Kinsey climb out of the vessel, she murmured, "Are you all right?"

"Why do you ask?"

"You look like you're headed to your own execution."

He smiled reluctantly. "I was just ruminating on what a bastard I am."

She replied sympathetically, "No wonder you look so depressed."

A snort of laughter escaped him before he even felt it coming. He slipped a hand under her elbow, relishing the slide of tender flesh under the pad of his thumb, and helped her off the sub. She glanced up to smile her thanks at him, and their gazes met and held for a moment before hers slid away shyly.

Possessiveness roared through him, and he wrestled unsuccessfully with the sensation as Scott Cash led the way upstairs to the main facility. He actually had to bite back a protest when Jennifer Blackfoot took Kinsey in hand and whisked her away to the bowels of the Bat Cave to brief and, hopefully, scrounge up some clothes for her. Off balance, he headed for the infirmary with Hathaway in tow. The fastest way to the compact first-aid facility was through the ops center.

He stepped out onto the main floor and experienced the surreal sensation of having stepped into a science-fiction movie. The huge space, hollowed out of an extinct volcano, could easily hold a football field. The broad floor was crammed with the latest electronics and surveillance equipment on the planet today. At least two dozen technicians manned the consoles and banks of computers. His favorite feature of the room by far, though, was the twenty-foot-tall wall of digital screens currently displaying maps of the world and the Caribbean. Definite sci-fi-movie material. A few of the technicians looked up to greet him as he passed through, en route.

As a technician efficiently unwrapped his clumsy bandage and commenced cleaning the wound on his shoulder, Hathaway closed the door and moved around to stand in front of him.

"What's the status of Miss Hollingsworth? Is she in or out on this mission?"

"She's in."

Hathaway made a face. "Her old man's gonna have a fit."

"She has already discussed it with him."

"How'd that go?"

Mitch winced as disinfectant hit the raw wound. He let out a slow, hissing breath, then replied, "Let's just say it lacked in warm father-daughter bonding."

"Who won?"

"She hung up on him after announcing that she didn't care if he took away her trust fund, so I'd say it went to the lady."

Hathaway shook his head. "I'm worried about using her. She's a complete amateur."

Mitch looked down at his shoulder as one medic taped a bandage over the gauze and declared him patched up. Mitch reached for his shirt and shrugged it on. Must get a new one before they left. This one was torn and blood-stained. "But that's exactly the point.

You take one look at her and see a spoiled little rich girl who couldn't possibly be involved in any kind of covert ops. She's the perfect cover."

"It's not her ability to act as a cover I'm worried about. What if something goes wrong? She doesn't have the slightest idea how to handle herself in a tight spot."

"She did pretty damned good yesterday with bullets flying all over the place and dogfighting a cigarette boat at seventy miles per hour—like a pro, by the way. Kept her wits about her. She was a big help to me."

Hathaway didn't answer right away. He picked on some nonexistent lint on his slacks. Looked as if he was stalling. "Our background check on her shows she's a hell of a sailor. Been around boats her whole life. She and her brother won some New England championship a while back sailing Hobie Cats."

"So my catamaran idea is a go, then?" Mitch asked eagerly. Why was he so damned desperate to spend more time with Kinsey? She was bound to end up being a royal pain in the ass.

Hathaway sighed heavily. "Yeah. It's a go. But if she hurts a single hair on her pretty little head, you can expect to answer directly to Daddy dearest. Is that understood?"

Mitch nodded. A little voice at the back of his head hollered. *What was he getting himself into?*

Hathaway added direly, "I'm not kidding. Congressman Hollingsworth will have your head on a platter."

"I hear ya, Commander. Loud and clear."

Another sigh out of Hathaway. Poor guy wasn't happy about this development in the least. "All right, then. You've got your girl."

Mitch shot him a startled look. His girl? Yikes.

And yet, it did feel odd to Mitch to be separated from Kinsey for even this long. They'd been together less than a day, and he already felt some sort of link to her. Not good. Not good at all. He sat through his final briefing—no significant political developments to report in Cuba in the past couple of days. His mission was cleared to proceed.

Hathaway leaned against the wall. "If you're sure about this, go collect the lady and be on your way."

Mitch scowled. "I'm not sure about anything."

Hathaway shrugged. "Should be an interesting mission, at any rate."

Great. Just what he wanted. An *interesting* mission. He stepped out into a hallway that, like all the others in this facility, was low and rough, hewn directly out of the volcanic bedrock. Jennifer would no doubt take Kinsey to her office to finish prepping her for the mission. He strode down the long hallways toward Kinsey, all but running to her. The fastest way from the military side of the facility to the civilian area was back through the main ops center, so he cut across there, even though the staff didn't like through traffic. The floor supervisor threw him a dirty look before it occurred to Mitch what he was doing. He was not some lovesick kid who needed to chase around after Kinsey like an eager puppy, dammit. He screeched to a halt, glancing around more than a little abashed.

A red flash lit up the twenty-foot-tall global map on the far wall. A second look showed it to be in the Middle East. Most of the floor staff typed busily on their computers for a few moments. "Problem?" he asked one of them.

"Nah. Just a mundane explosion. Looks like a car bomb from the heat signature and seismic readings."

While Mitch had the guy's attention, he asked, "What's that yellow flashing light in the Bahamas?"

"Emergency locator transmitter. Probably a civilian boat in distress. They use equipment similar to the panic button you're equipped with. Whenever an ELT goes off, it shows up red on our screen. Once we've identified it and eliminated the signal as something we need to respond to, it's changed to yellow on the big board."

"Here's hoping I'm never a dot on your screen."

"Oh, you are. When you go into Cuba, you'll go up there as a green dot. We'll track your position indicator 24/7."

"You mean the one in my arm?"

"Yeah."

He'd always wondered who the little gizmo they'd surgically implanted under his biceps a few years back talked to. Now he knew. He was a green dot on somebody's radar. He continued across the floor and up the stairs to Agent-in-Charge Blackfoot's office, bounding up them three at a time. His stomach jumping, he knocked on the closed door.

"Come in," Jennifer's husky voice called.

He stepped in. Jennifer wore her issue jeans and T-shirt, Native American jewelry, her long hair glossy and black. He glanced around. No sign of Kinsey. Quick alarm flared in his gut. Jennifer was sitting on her sofa with another woman, a striking brunette. Maybe a subject-matter expert here to brief Kinsey. Except... her mouth was vaguely familiar... His brain locked up. No way.

He stared closely at the brunette. "Kinsey?" he asked incredulously.

She laughed gaily, her distinctive dimples flashing. Yup, that was Kinsey. He burst out, "What have you done to your hair?"

Jennifer replied. "We had to make sure she isn't recognized by paparazzi and pesky celebrity seekers when she takes you to Cuba, and you have to admit, she looks a great deal different as a brunette."

He examined her more closely. Her gentleness and unique spark still shone out of her eyes, and the refined bones and perfect smile were the same. Maybe at a glance she looked different, but when he looked closely, it was definitely her. He was still going to have to beat men off with sticks whenever she was around.

"Like my disguise?" Kinsey asked.

"You'll do," he said gruffly.

The two women exchanged smiling glances. Now, what was that all about?

Jennifer murmured, "See what I mean?"

Kinsey nodded. "Yup. Uncomfortable. I'll keep it in mind."

"Are you two accusing me of being uncomfortable around women?"

Kinsey looked him square in the eye and said blandly, "If the shoe fits."

"I do fine around women. I just don't like working with them."

"Oh, really?" Jennifer replied, a distinct edge in her voice.

He glared over at her. "You know perfectly well I don't have a problem with you. I meant in the field."

"You've never worked with a female operative before, so how can you be so sure you won't like it?"

"*Operative* being the key word," he shot back. "Kinsey's an amateur. She has no business playing spy. I'm happy to use her to get into Cuba, but she's not staying with me a minute longer than it takes me to track down Camarillo and kill him."

The laughter sparkling in Kinsey's eyes blinked out, leaving behind only hurt. Damn, he was a heel. He mentally kicked himself.

"Okay you two. Off you go," Jennifer said, standing up. "You've got a helicopter scheduled in a little under an hour, and by the time you collect the gear we've assembled for you, change into deck clothes and ride back to the surface, you'll have to hustle to make it." She glared over at him. "And you behave yourself. Be nice."

He'd have protested that his manners were just fine, but Kinsey stood up just then and Mitch gulped. She was wearing a thin wraparound dress made of a muted floral fabric, typical of what Cuban women might wear. It clung to her body in all the right places and plunged just enough between her breasts to make a guy's eyes want to dip downward constantly. He preferred the sloppy T-shirt and bikini to this. This made her look intensely feminine. Kissable. As if she needed to be swept up in his arms and danced with.

He didn't dance with his partner, dammit!

He led the way in silence back to the submarine loading dock. It was beneath him to sulk, but he couldn't help himself. Kinsey put a hand on his arm to steady herself as she climbed into the minisub, and his heart rate must've jumped twenty points. He had to pull himself together, and fast, if this mission wasn't going to fail colossally.

He faked sleeping for most of the ride to the surface. It was Kinsey who actually leaned forward to touch his knee, causing his eyes to fly open in alarm.

"I think it's time to put the blindfold back on."

He glanced outside. Dim turquoise light filtered down through the water outside, casting a flickering glow across the interior of the submarine. She was right. They were nearing the surface. He slipped the blindfold over her eyes, jerking his hands away clumsily when his fingertips brushed against the back of her neck. He was going to have to get over this phobia of touching her so they could— He broke off the thought sharply. No touching on this mission. Definitely no touching.

It wasn't five minutes later when the hatch opened, he climbed out and turned around to see Kinsey's hand held up to him for balance as she climbed out of the sub. So much for his no-touching rule. Her soft hand rested easily in his as she smiled her thanks up in his general direction. A growl of frustration built in the back of his throat. Exasperated, he tucked her hand under his elbow, closing his eyes in silent desperation as she leaned in against him for security. He couldn't blame her. He'd hate being deprived of his sight like this.

"Where to now?" she murmured.

"Your chariot awaits you," he grumbled.

"You mean the helicopter?"

"Yup." He led her carefully under the spinning rotors and guided her into the chopper. In no time they were skimming across the ocean, open water stretching away on all sides of them. He leaned forward and unmasked her. She blinked, squinting against the light, and smiled over at him.

"All this secrecy and mystery is fun."

"Fun? Are you kidding? This is a serious mission. Jennifer did brief you on what we're supposed to be doing, didn't she?"

"Yes. We're going to Cuba to gather intelligence on a possible plot to assassinate a high-ranking Cuban official who is…friendly…toward the United States."

"No, I am going to Cuba to do that. *We* are going to Cuba so *I* can find and kill Camarillo, and then *you* are going home."

The official who was the target of his mission, a man named Alejandro Zaragosa, had been passing information to the United States for nigh unto thirty years. He was an extremely valuable asset in need of protection. But in all honesty, Mitch was much more intent on finding and killing Camarillo. Kinsey wouldn't be safe until the guy was dead.

She shrugged, still far too animated for her own good. He growled, "Where in that equation do you come up with any fun whatsoever?"

"It's a beautiful day. The sun is shining, the sky is blue, and we're setting off on a grand adventure. What more could you ask for?"

He scowled. "This isn't a game, dammit."

"Oh, lighten up," she teased gently. "Don't take yourself so seriously."

A babe in the woods. She had *no* idea what they were headed into. His scowl deepened. He retreated into stony silence, crossing his arms over his chest. She did the same. He could swear she was mimicking him just to get his goat. Well, it wasn't going to work. He uncrossed his arms and shifted uncomfortably in his seat.

The fast chopper skimmed over the ocean for several exceedingly long hours. Mitch was abjectly grateful when the crew chief finally opened the back hatch and swung a pulley mechanism out the door.

"What's he doing?" Kinsey shouted over the noise.

"Rigging up the winch," he shouted back. "You and I will jump out of the copter, but the other captain will have to get hauled up into this bird."

"What are you talking about?"

"Didn't Jennifer tell you we were coming out here to pick up a boat?"

"She said we'd be dropped off at a catamaran, but she didn't say anything about jumping out of a helicopter into the Caribbean."

He rolled his eyes. "What did you think getting dropped off meant?"

"Certainly not that!"

He grinned. "Welcome to my world, princess."

He tried not to watch as she stripped off her dress and stuffed it into the waterproof duffel bag Jennifer had given her to hold all her stuff. The sight of Kinsey in a bikini ripped all the air out of his chest. Damn, that woman had curves in all the right places. His gut flared with desire, bright and hot. She was interested in him. If he played his cards right—

No card playing on this mission. None of that at all!

A movement out of the corner of his eye caused his head to snap around. The crew chief was taking a long, appreciative look at Kinsey. Mitch surged up out of his seat and all but shoved the guy out of the helicopter. He managed to control himself in time to merely place himself between Kinsey and the guy's line of sight, but a need to do violence made his palms itch.

The look of apprehension on Kinsey's face as she stepped into the doorway of the chopper and looked down reminded him of just how risky a job he had. But, to her credit, she climbed out onto the tread and gamely jumped off. He didn't think she had it in her. The seas were calm and the pilot was good, so the bird was no more than twelve feet or so above the water. Still, to an amateur, it must've looked as if they were a mile up. He stepped off the skid and endured the cold shock of slamming into the water. His eyes tightly closed, he made his way up to the surface and swam easily over to the catamaran. Kinsey was already aboard, shaking saltwater out of her eyes and having a look at the vessel's equipment.

While the outgoing captain briefed her up, Mitch hauled in their waterproof bags of equipment, both of which had been tethered to his waist and tossed out of the copter with him. In a few minutes, the captain bade them farewell and jumped overboard, swimming over to the padded loop that would lift him into the chopper. Mitch watched the crew chief efficiently haul up the guy. The chopper peeled away sharply and sped off into the distance.

And then they were alone. Relief at having her to himself once more filled him. Silence descended around them.

"Now what, Tonto?" Kinsey asked.

"Head for Cuba, Kemosabe."

"It's about fifty miles due north of us."

"How soon can we be there?"

She turned her face into the breeze. "If these winds hold up, sometime this evening."

"Let's do it."

She nodded and moved fore to weigh anchor and hoist the mainsail. He pitched in to help haul on the various lines she pointed out, and before long, they were skimming across the water at a decent clip. He stepped inside the low, flat cabin slung between the vessel's twin hulls. It was compact and he more or less had to crawl around on his knees inside, but it was well fitted out.

"Nice boat," Kinsey commented from behind him.

"Aren't you supposed to be on deck doing the captain thing?"

"The sails are trimmed, the wind is steady, and the autopilot's got the helm. I can spare a couple minutes to have a look around. Where did your people scare up this vessel on such short notice?"

"I have no idea. Maybe someone called in a favor, maybe a little cash got spread around. But that's how the H.O.T. Watch staff works. If an operator needs something, it's taken care of. That big room full of folks sitting at phones and computers is jammed with miracle workers."

Her hand strayed up toward her head. "I was impressed when they came up with hair dye and clothes that fit me on such short notice.

"What does *hot* in *Hot Watch* refer to?"

He grinned. "*H-O-T.* Hunter Operation Team."

Enlightenment dawned. "And the gang in the volcano watches you. Hence, H.O.T. Watch."

"You got it."

He examined her critically. "You make a good brunette."

A blush stained her cheeks. "Uhh, I'd better go find a cover-up. I don't need the entire Cuban navy ogling me."

No kidding. If one crew chief had driven him nuts, imagine how a whole boatload of sailors would affect him.

Kinsey stared down at the boat's controls, the dials an unfocused blob before her eyes. Every time Mitch turned that golden gaze of his on her, she melted into a puddle of nerves. She had to stop that! This was her chance to do something real, something important, and she wasn't going to blow it because she couldn't corral her runaway lust for a man who barely gave her the time of day.

The sunset tonight was even more spectacular than yesterday's and Mitch came out on deck to watch its magnificent display streak across the sky. He lounged on the broad sundeck, his hands clasped behind his head as he gazed up at the sky. He looked like a panther at rest, all sleek feline grace and explosive power waiting to spring into action.

Intense awareness of being alone with him in the middle of a vast ocean struck her. She'd made a giant leap of trust to place herself at his mercy like this. For she held no illusions about her ability to fend him off if he tried any funny business with her. Her mind wandered idly. What would she do if he made a pass at her? She was half-tempted to accept his offer. Okay, more than half-tempted. She seriously hoped he gave it a go. Unfortunately, he would never take her seriously if she initiated anything personal between them. But that didn't mean she couldn't wish for him to do it. She sighed. Fat chance of that happening with Mr. Mission-First.

When no more than a red glow remained on the far horizon, he made his way back to the helm. "Mother Nature did good today," he commented.

She glanced askance at the streaks of clouds fading from lavender to dark gray overhead. "Yeah, but those are rolled cirrus clouds. They indicate a front moving in." When he didn't show comprehension of the threat they posed, she elaborated, "And that means rain. Storms. We've got to get off the water, and soon. The wind is dying down, so I'm going to start up the engines and motor us in close to the Cuban coast."

He drawled, "How long till we arrive?"

"An hour, maybe a little more." She liked the lazy side of the predator. He was easier to be with when he was relaxed like this, not constantly eyeing everything around him as if he expected an attack at any second.

"I'll be back."

He disappeared below while she cranked up the twin diesels. She'd just finished retrimming the rudders when he emerged, carrying his black duffel bag. "Ever shoot a gun?" he bit out.

Drat. *Back in commando mode.* "I've handled a pistol or two, but I'm no great expert."

He stepped up behind her, invading her personal space with his broad shoulders and bristling male energy. His arm came around her right side to lay a big, scary revolver on the instrument panel beside the steering wheel.

"Colt .45," he murmured. "Not a lady's weapon, but it'll stop a Mack Truck."

Involuntarily, she stepped back from the gun...and

right into the wall that was Mitch Perovski. His strength and bulk were such that he didn't even budge when she banged into him. She about jumped out of her skin.

"Easy," he murmured. "It won't bite you."

No, but he might. Aggressive male potency engulfed her, and she edged forward to put a few inches between them. It didn't help. "Is it loaded?"

A rusty chuckle tickled her ear. "Wouldn't be good for much if it wasn't. Don't fire it until you're positive you'll hit your target. It only has six shots. Use them wisely."

Had the temperature just dropped ten degrees? She rubbed her arms to chase away the sudden goose bumps. *He was giving an untrained civilian a lethal weapon?* He must be scared spitless of this Camarillo guy to be teaching her to handle a gun like this.

"Pick it up," he murmured.

She lifted the pistol. It was heavy. Cold. Awkward in her hand. She lurched as his arms came around her from behind. His right hand closed over hers, wrapping her fingers more securely around the scored grip.

"Hold it nose high in front of you with your arms straight. Like this."

Damned if his mouth wasn't practically against her ear. Searing heat ripped through her, followed by embarrassment. Shyness. Intensely sexual awareness of him.

His cheek came to rest against her ear, slightly stubbly. Warm. *Intimate.* His arms slid up under hers. The silky hair on his forearms tickled the undersides of her arms, and his elbows gently squeezed the sides of her breasts. *Whoa, baby.*

"Look down the barrel." Was that amusement or

urgency—or something else altogether—pulling his voice tight like that? She couldn't tell. And didn't have the nerve to turn around and look.

"Don't worry about being accurate. At close range, a strike anywhere on the bad guy from a .45 will stop him cold. Rest the bottom of your right fist in the palm of your left hand. Push with the right, pull with the left. It'll steady the gun. Like this. Got it?"

She nodded fractionally. It was all the unbearable tension in her neck would allow for. But, wrapped around her like red on a rose, he apparently felt the microscopic movement.

"When you pull the trigger, this sucker will kick up in the air. Hard. Let it. Then bring it back down into firing position, aim and fire again."

"How do I aim?" Good grief. Was that *her* voice all husky and breathless like that?

"Look straight down the barrel. Whatever you see directly over the tip of the barrel is roughly what you'll hit. Fire at the bad guy's belly button. The torso is a big target and you're more likely to hit it than if you aim at something small like a head or a knee. Actual aiming of a weapon is more complicated than that, but we don't have time for more details right now. I'll show you the fine points some other time."

"It's a date." She froze. *Had she said that aloud?*

She'd swear his mouth turned up, smiling against the shell of her ear as he murmured, "Deal." Streaks of pure sex tore through her. Surely he felt her burning alive in his arms.

His lips definitely were moving against her ear now. "Don't fire toward me in a fight and I won't fire toward you. That way we won't hit each other by accident. Got it?"

Her knees all but buckled out from under her. Breathing fast and shallow, she nodded.

"One last thing. If I go down fighting it out with Camarillo and he's about to catch you, do yourself a favor. Save one bullet for yourself. Up into the brain through the back of the mouth is the most effective."

His words shocked her like ice water down her shirt. She pivoted to stare at him. *Big mistake.* She drew up short, chest to chest with him. His arms, still wrapped around her, gathered her close. *Kowabunga.* His eyes, blazing hollows in the shadowed planes of his face, incinerated her.

Was she insane? He'd just suggested the best way to *kill* herself. And she was lusting after him? "Are you serious?" she exclaimed.

He looked her dead in the eye. The last expression she would ever expect to see flashed into his gaze. *Compassion.* And that rattled her to the core.

"Promise me," he said with quiet urgency. "I need to know you won't let Camarillo capture you. I can't afford to make a stupid decision in the middle of a fight because I'm trying to protect the girl."

"The girl can take care of herself," Kinsey retorted drily. She wriggled to free herself from his suddenly suffocating embrace. His arms fell away immediately and night air replaced them, embracing her in dread's icy clasp.

"Without mincing words, Camarillo is one of the baddest SOBs on the planet. When we engage him, I need you to keep your wits about you. If bullets start flying, get down low, stay out of the line of fire and don't try to be a hero. I'll do the rest."

"You're sounding suspiciously like a macho jerk."

"I'm a macho *bastard* in a firefight. But I'll be *your* macho bastard. So stay out of my way and do what I tell you. All right?"

She nodded. With every passing second he was becoming more grim. More focused. Wiped clean of emotion. *Ready to kill.*

"How long till the Cuban coast?" he asked shortly.

She glanced at the radar, which was starting to paint the coastline. "At current speed, about twenty minutes."

"Can you limp in from here on sails only?"

She nodded.

"It's time to sabotage the engines, then."

She grabbed a wrench from the toolbox in the cabin and opened up the vessel's pontoon hatches. She went to work on the fuel system for it shared duty with both engines. If she truly wanted to be disabled and need believable emergency repairs, she had to take out both engines with whatever she broke. Her best bet was the fuel pump. If it failed, the fuel lines would lose pressure, air would enter the lines and both engines' fuel systems would have to be purged of air all the way down to the fuel injectors. Not an easy thing to do at sea. Particularly for a lone, hand-wringing female at sea with no clue how to do the job.

In point of fact, she'd seen the job done a couple of times and, in a real emergency, could probably muddle her way through it. But what the Cubans didn't know wouldn't hurt them. The boat would need to be towed into port, a new fuel pump ordered and installed, and both her fuel systems purged. All in all, it should take upward of a week.

She gave the fuel pump one last whack with her wrench for good measure. The engines made awful sucking sounds for a few moments, then sputtered and cut out. Silence. No more diesel power for them from here on out. She inched forward inside the pontoon to the escape hatch. The space in here was cramped and claustrophobic, but it certainly was big enough to conceal a man and all his gear.

They were ready. Now all she had to do was make her way into port. And pray. Pray they were allowed into Cuba, and that Mitch was better than Camarillo. Menace drew near. Its cool touch slid up her spine like a psychopathic lover. And they waited. She stood behind the wheel, terrified, minding the boat by rote, while Mitch crouched at the forward limit of the deck, peering at the sea through big, 30x binoculars.

For an about-to-be hunted man, he looked a lot like a predator in wait. Abject terror was going to shatter her into a million pieces any second, but he looked as steady as a rock. *Show-off.*

"Time to contact?" Mitch called.

She glanced down at the radar screen. "Fifteen minutes at this forward speed until we hit Cuban territorial waters. Their Coast Guard should come out to have a look at us pretty quickly after that."

Mitch nodded and made his way back to the pilothouse. "Ready?" he murmured.

She looked into his eyes. And then it hit. Panic. Paralyzing, brain-numbing panic.

Mitch swore under his breath. "There's nothing to worry about. Just be yourself. You're Kinsey Hollingsworth. Your boat has lost a couple vital systems—which it in fact has. You need repairs, which is the God's honest truth. You don't have to be clever or lie or try to keep your cool. Be upset. Be panicked. Be worried about being arrested for having to land in Cuba."

She nodded. That was exactly what Jennifer Blackfoot had told her to do. So why did she feel as if she was going to throw up any second?

Mitch stepped forward with that preternaturally quick grace of his, his powerful arms sweeping her up against him in an enveloping hug. He murmured into her hair, "Hey. I know you can do this."

"Yeah. Assuming I can keep my lunch down."

"Ahh. Pre-mission jitters. I get them all the time."

"Do you have them now?"

"No, I got mine on the chopper ride out here."

She mumbled into his chest, "Liar. You've got nerves of steel."

A low rumble of laughter shook his chest.

She lifted her head to glare up at him. Their gazes locked. Their wills tangled for a moment, hers skeptical, his certain. And the banked fire in the back of his eyes began to build, heating until it glowed like a lava flow, incinerating everything in its path. She stared into the mesmerizing depths of his gaze, fascinated, inevitably drawn into him.

His index finger touched her chin. Tipped her face up. And slowly, slowly, like a panther stalking its prey, he closed in on her. Except unlike the unwary antelope, she saw him coming. And merely watched and waited. For a moment, she contemplated fleeing for her life, but discarded the idea as ridiculous. In the last moment before their lips touched, when her common sense shouted its indignation at her foolishness, she realized she'd been waiting for this ever since the first moment she'd laid eyes on him. With a sigh of relief, she surrendered to the kiss.

His mouth was warm and firm against hers, exploring hers gently. And then, without warning, he groaned in the back of his throat and his arms swept her up against him, lifting her completely off the ground. Crushed in his embrace, she strained even closer, desperate for more of him.

"We shouldn't..." he mumbled against her mouth just before he devoured her whole, with tongue and lips and body.

"But I want it. I want you...." she mumbled back just before she returned the favor.

He cursed under his breath as he let her feet slide to the ground. Crying out in dismay, she flung her arms around his neck. He stumbled for a moment, then planted his powerful legs, absorbed her weight and plunged his hands into her hair, dragging her mouth up to his for more. He kissed her desperately, aggressively, like a starving man.

"This is madness," he bit out.

"Glorious madness," she agreed, dragging his head down to her.

Another groan, wrung from deep within him, made her heart leap with triumph. "If we don't stop now, I'm going to tear your clothes off, take you inside and make love to you until neither of us can walk."

She took a step toward the cabin, pulling him with her. He laughed, gathering her close. "We'll be in Cuban territorial waters in a few minutes, and their navy should arrive about two minutes after that. I've got to crawl into my coffin or else they'll see me."

The words only partially penetrated the haze of un-adulterated desire roaring through her brain. The taste of him, smoky and dark, swirled through her head until she could hardly think about anything else.

Gently, he peeled her arms from around his neck. She followed him to the starboard pontoon hatch and handed his duffel bag in after him. The thing was shockingly heavy. Must be chock-full of more giant guns like the one he'd shown her earlier.

As he stretched out on his back and nodded up at her, she couldn't resist. She leaned down into the opening and kissed him one last time. "Mmm. You taste amazing." She sighed.

"Close the hatch," he said grimly. Then he added, "But hold that thought."

Smiling dreamily, she brought the fiberglass down into place, locking the latch that held it in place. She made her way back to the pilothouse and absently checked their heading. If she stayed on this cource, she'd run smack-dab into the south coast of Cuba. She ought to be rehearsing a speech for the Cuban navy, but the only thought that kept running through her mind over and over was *That man could really, really kiss.*

She wanted more of that. Lots more.

She became aware of a faint sound carrying across the water from the north…the mechanical rumble of a boat motor incoming. Undoubtedly the Cuban navy.

Showtime.

Chapter 6

A male voice shouted through a bullhorn at her in heavily accented English, "You have entered Cuban territorial waters. Turn around and leave or prepare to be boarded!"

Kinsey squinted into the blinding glare of the floodlight they pointed at her. She called back, "My engines have conked out. I'm adrift. Can you tow me to someplace where I can make repairs?"

She thought she made out scowls behind the floodlight, but it was hard to see. The man shouted back, "How many souls on board?"

"Just me."

"Are you declaring a maritime emergency?"

Ahh. The officialese so they could legally tow her ashore. "Yes, I am."

After a long pause, the voice called back, "We will send a man over to secure a towline."

What? As if she couldn't tie a proper towline herself? She didn't argue, however. If they thought she was actually helpless, all the better. The catamaran rocked as the Cuban vessel pulled up alongside. A sailor leaped across the gap between the boats, hauling with him the end of a heavy line. He didn't tie the rope to the optimal tow point, but the one he chose wouldn't capsize her, so she let it go. The Cuban sailor manned her steering wheel in silence for the slow ride to port, while she stretched out and made herself comfortable on the sundeck. The Cuban navy crew made no secret of enjoying the view of her, lounging in her skimpy bikini and sloppy T-shirt. *Look all you want, boys.* The more distracted they were, the less likely they were to think about searching her vessel for contraband.

They pulled into port in Cienfuegos, a decent-size city on the south coast of Cuba. The navy cutter hauled her directly to a marina catering to pleasure craft. One of their men went ashore, and in a few minutes, they maneuvered her into a slip near the end of a long, wooden dock that had seen better days.

What looked like a Customs official and maybe a policeman accompanied the navy man back to her boat. No surprise, the Customs guy wanted her passport. He disappeared back down the dock with it, mumbling about needing to work up an emergency visa for her. It made her nervous to see that vitally important document being carried off like that, but she wasn't in any position to protest.

The policeman announced, "I will need to search

your boat. Any unauthorized vessel which comes ashore is required to be searched."

What else could she do? She shrugged and nodded her understanding, her mind racing. She had to stop him! But how? Anything she did to make the guy suspicious would make him doubly intent upon combing through the boat. Thankfully, he started in the cabin, which gave her a few minutes to think.

When he stepped outside once more, she stepped into his path, subtly herding him away from the foredeck and the hatches to the pontoons. "Here. Let me unlock the map cabinets for you. They're back here, at the pilot station."

She led the policeman to the rear of the vessel. As she'd hoped, he continued his exterior search of the boat from the aft end and worked his way forward. She even let him open the fore port pontoon hatch before she pulled out her cell phone.

"Do you mind if I make a phone call?" she asked politely.

"Who do you wish to call?"

"My father. He works in Washington, D.C."

The reference to Washington brought a faintly surprised look to the cop's face.

She continued chattily, "I think I can get cell-phone coverage here. And Daddy has a satellite phone. He has to, so when a bill comes up in Congress, he can be notified to go vote."

That shot the policeman's eyebrows straight up. In fact, it caused him to step away from her—toward the dock—and pull out his own cell phone. He held a quick, muttered conversation in Spanish. She edged closer to him twice, and both times, he moved away from her, closer to shore. The third time she edged closer as if to listen in, he actually stepped up onto the dock. Perfect.

The Customs man came into sight, carrying some paperwork. The policeman finished his call, and Kinsey cheerfully pocketed her cell phone. "Not working. Looks like I'll have to wait until I can get access to a landline. Any chance I can get a hotel room or something so I can clean up and make that call? Daddy will be terribly worried until I report in. Goodness knows who he'll send after me if I don't contact him soon."

The policeman answered nervously, "Uhh, certainly we can arrange a room for you, Señorita Hollingsworth."

"Thank you so much!" she gushed. "I could just hug you."

The guy seemed flustered at the prospect. He was saved from having to reply by the Customs official handing her back her passport. "The light blue paper inside is your temporary visa. It is good for two weeks. I assume your boat can be repaired and you can be on your way in that amount of time?"

She batted her eyes at him helplessly. "Well, I don't know. I'll need a mechanic to have a look at things and make an estimate. But I hope I can be out of your hair in a few days. You are all being so kind to me. I really appreciate this. I was starting to get worried out there. I only had food and water for a day or so more. It never occurred to me that I might need extra supplies. I was only going out for a short sail."

Both men threw her looks that damned her ignorance of basic boating safety, and she took the looks of rebuke without protest. "I know. I know. Boating 101.

I should've thrown a few emergency supplies on board just in case. I will from now on, I swear."

She put a hand on the policeman's arm. "Now, about that shower. What do I have to do to sweet-talk you into leading me to some hot water and soap?"

Both men reached out to help her ashore, and with a smile of apology at the Customs man, she took the policeman's hand. "Is there someplace nearby so I can keep an eye on my boat and monitor the repairs?"

"There is a nice place just up the beach. It's called La Bonita. I will help you check in and get settled if you wish."

She let them lead her up the dock and away from the catamaran…and Mitch. Mission accomplished. She'd distracted the cop before he could finish his search. If she wasn't mistaken, Mitch owed her one.

She wasn't clear on how Mitch was supposed to sneak ashore and hook up with her again. He'd told her they'd have to wing it once they got to Cuba.

La Bonita was an old building, shabby, but in reasonable repair. And it had a lingering attractiveness. Like a Hollywood glamour queen who'd seen her prime thirty or forty years ago. The policeman was helpful—too helpful—in getting her settled into a "nice" room. She began to wonder if it was bugged or something, the way he insisted on getting a specific room on a high floor with a view of the water, ostensibly so she could keep an eye on her boat.

Finally, the guy left. In case the place was bugged, she did exactly what they would expect of her. She didn't actually want to talk to her father, so she called his office and left a message on his answering machine.

Plus, the machine made it clear that she was, indeed, calling Congressman Hollingsworth.

Next, she jumped into the shower. The pressure of the water wasn't great and it smelled like sulphur, but it was hot and removed the feeling of salt crusted on her skin. Did she dare go back to the boat tonight to try to free Mitch? He'd said for her to sit tight, and knowing him, he'd get mad if she disobeyed his instructions. He struck her as that sort of guy.

She flipped through the television channels. Her Spanish wasn't up to the rapid-fire dialect of the programming, so she turned out the lights and went to bed. It took a while for her fraying nerves to settle down, but she eventually drifted off.

How long she was asleep, she had no idea. But one moment, she was peacefully resting, and the next, a powerful hand was pressed over her mouth. She all but jumped out of her skin as something heavy rolled on top of her, pressing her down into the mattress and immobilizing her.

"It's me," a voice breathed in her ear. *Mitch.* Warm relief flooded her. She relaxed, releasing the panic clenching her muscles. And then the sensation of lying beneath Mitch in a blatantly suggestive pose exploded in her brain. His knee pressed between her thighs, supporting his weight, but also pinning her so she couldn't possibly move out from under him. His eyes closed briefly. When they opened, the blazing sexual awareness in them all but lit the entire room.

"Don't say anything," he gritted out under his breath. "The room may be bugged. Understood?"

She nodded, and his hand lifted away from her

mouth. He pressed up and away from her with swift power, and her body ached with sudden loss.

She watched in silence as his dark silhouette prowled around her room, searching with ruthless efficiency. He stopped three times and pointed—once at a lamp, once at the clock radio and once at a hinge in the bathroom door. Great. So the two of them knew where the bugs were. Now what?

He came over to the bed and lifted the covers. She was on the verge of getting up when he crawled in beside her. Stunned, she scooted over to make room for him in the narrow double bed. His muscular bulk took up most of it, at least until he turned on his side and gathered her close against him. Yowza. She liked this even better than before. She couldn't help it. She snuggled up against him—in the name of giving him enough room, of course.

It was like cuddling up to a brick. Albeit a warm, vital, sexy one. He pulled the covers over their heads and pressed his mouth to her ear. "Three bugs. Audio only. You need to get dressed and pack your stuff without making any noise. Can you do that?"

She nodded, and his lips accidentally brushed against her neck. She all but groaned at the sensation. His arm tightened around her momentarily, but then he was gone, rolling away silently and disappearing into the shadows by the door. Her pulse raced, and parts of her throbbed that seriously didn't need to be doing any throbbing just now. Lord, that man was magnetic!

She tiptoed to her bag of gear and eased out a pair of black slacks and a dark shirt to match Mitch's dark clothing. She didn't want to risk closing the bathroom door, so she stepped into the shower to change and prayed Mitch didn't do a drive by in here to see how she was coming. Although the prospect of him seeing her undressed made that whole throbbing thing start back up again.

She tiptoed back out into the room and carefully repacked her overnight bag. Fortunately she hadn't gotten much out of it earlier. Mitch picked it up and gestured for her to follow him. He opened the hallway door a crack and peered outside cautiously. He slipped outside quickly and she followed him as he raced down the hallway on the balls of his feet, swift and silent. Man, she'd hate to be on the receiving end of this guy's predatory stealth.

Down a concrete-and-steel stairwell and out onto a loading dock, she did her best not to make too much of a racket behind him. Still not talking, he waved her into an alley, which he sprinted down. He turned into a side street and darted across it, then down another alley with her in tow. Good thing she hit the treadmill on a regular basis. He was moving fast and showing no signs of slowing down.

And then all of a sudden, he pulled up beside a vintage car that made her stare. It was big and black and sleek, all chrome and fenders and tiny windows. It looked like a gangster car out of the 1930s. She ventured to whisper, "What's this?"

"Our ride. Like it?" he murmured as he opened the driver's-side door and tossed her bag into the backseat. "Slide in. I'll drive," he directed under his breath.

The seat was cracked vinyl that scratched the back of her legs. The dials and needles looked original to the vehicle, yellowed with age and from another era.

Mitch closed the door and started the car. He pulled away from the curb.

"Where did you get this thing?"

"I bought it. Like it?"

"You bought it? How did you have time to get ashore and buy a car already?"

He laughed. "I was off the boat before you stepped off the dock. Nice misdirect of that cop, by the way. I didn't know you had it in you."

"What would you have done if I hadn't distracted him?"

"I'd scooted all the way to the back end of the pontoon and was behind the engine. He'd never have seen me unless he crawled into the pontoon, in which case…"

"In which case, what?"

Mitch sighed. "In which case, I'd have neutralized him and you'd have had to make some excuse to the Customs guy about where his cop friend disappeared to."

This man was a killer. Her mind knew the thought to be true, but her heart rejected the thought. She was attracted to him, darn it. Yet there was no denying what and who he was. Heck, she'd seen him kill with her own eyes. Although given that he had saved both her life and his, any murderous overtones were wiped away by the necessary self-defense of the act.

Her half of the deal was complete. She'd snuck Mitch into Cuba. Now all he had to do was uphold his end of the deal and eliminate Camarillo as a threat to her. Then they'd be even. She would walk away. And then she'd face the unenviable task of figuring out how to get over wanting to leap on him and kiss him senseless.

* * *

Mitch drove for nearly an hour. Long enough to be well away from Cienfuegos.

"Where are we going?" Kinsey asked from the passenger seat.

"Nowhere in particular at the moment. Just putting distance between you and any authorities who know you're on the island."

"What about your meeting with Zaragosa? Isn't it back in Cienfuegos?"

He shrugged. "It won't happen for another day or two. In the meantime, I'm going to work on tracking down Camarillo." The sooner he got Kinsey out of there, the better it would be for her. An unfamiliar twinge in his gut startled him, and he frowned. What was that about? Was he actually going to miss her when she left? The pampered princess? Nah. No way.

At 3:00 a.m., according to his watch, he turned into a closed gas station and pulled around back beside several other vintage cars waiting for service. He turned off the engine and the lights. In the sudden dark, he pulled out his cell phone and called the Bat Cave. Jennifer Blackfoot picked up. What was *she* doing manning the phones at this hour? She had enough seniority that she didn't have to pull shifts as the night supervisor.

"What are you doing up so late, boss?"

"Problem with another team," she replied shortly. "What's up?"

She clearly had no time to chat, so he got straight to the point. "As my little green dot on the big screen no doubt shows, I'm ashore and with Kinsey. We've got a car and are about a hundred kilometers from Cienfuegos. What have you got for me on when and where I'm hooking up with Zaragosa?"

"He says he can't do it. He's being watched too closely. Says for you to proceed to Havana on your own."

Mitch frowned, his mind racing. Why was the principal backing out of helping him? Was Zaragosa setting him up? Or was it exactly as the man said, a simple matter of it being too risky for them to make contact? He growled into the phone, "If I don't have identity papers, it fundamentally changes the nature of this op. I'll have to go underground and stay there."

"If the guy won't play ball, there's nothing we can do about it at this late date. If you were still here we could work up some fake credentials for you. But as it is, you're on your own."

"That's the problem," he retorted grimly. "I'm not on my own."

"Did the Cubans give Kinsey a visa?" Jennifer asked.

"Yeah. Two weeks. She's covered. I'm the only illegal alien in this outfit."

"Well, then, Lancer, I guess you'd better not get caught."

"Hah. I never get caught."

"Let's keep it that way," his boss snapped back.

"Yes, ma'am." He laughed at her.

He disconnected. Kinsey was looking over at him expectantly. "Change of plans. We're not going to meet Zaragosa after all."

"What does that mean?"

"Not much. We press on as briefed."

"Where's Camarillo?"

"No clue. I thought we'd head for Havana and poke

around a bit. If we hit the right nerve, he may show himself."

"Do you really think it'll be that easy?"

He snorted. "Not a chance. But sometimes you get lucky." He'd left out the part where Camarillo would come after them and try to kill them as soon as he got wind of them. But Kinsey didn't need to know that.

They drove across the island to the north shore, a short journey as the crow flies, but it took several hours. They wound along country roads through farming communities, up into the central highlands and back down the north slopes toward the Atlantic shore of Cuba. Stands of tropical jungle interspersed with fields in full summer growth, and the overall impression was of a lush, green country. By afternoon, it would be steamy and clothes would cling to damp flesh while beads of sweat rolled down foreheads and necks—and the valley between Kinsey's breasts, his errant imagination had to pipe up and add. Oh, yes. A sexy country, Cuba.

They came into the outskirts of Havana, a sprawling metropolis of several million people. The transition was abrupt. One moment they were cruising through rural acres, and the next, a high-rise city towered around them. Although aged and crumbling around the edges in this particular area, it was a vibrant place, full of noise and bright colors and bustling people.

All well and good, but this was not the side of Havana in which they would find their quarry. They needed the secret side of the city. The night side. The dark side. To that end, he found them a hotel room near the long strip of nightclubs along the shore, left over from the pre-Castro era. Using Kinsey's visa, they checked in.

The room looked as if it hadn't been redecorated

since Castro came to power in 1959, but it was clean. And dark. Like any good casino hotel room, it was set up for the occupant to sleep all day in anticipation of gambling all night. Thick, lined velvet curtains blocked out the bright Caribbean sunlight.

"You'd do well to take a nap, Kinsey. We'll be out late tonight."

"Doing what?" she asked curiously.

He grinned. "Partying the night away."

She frowned. "To what end?"

"We're going hunting. We're going to catch ourselves a killer."

Chapter 7

Kinsey frowned at the dress Mitch handed to her. Jennifer Blackfoot had predicted this would be the first dress he would want her to wear when the woman had pulled it off a rack of assorted clothing in the H.O.T. Watch complex. It had looked okay on a hanger, but right now it looked like hardly more than a dish towel. And it was red.

She shimmied into the slinky little sheath in the bathroom and looked at herself critically. It wasn't something she'd normally dream of choosing for herself, but she had to admit, she didn't look half-bad in it. The red complemented her newly dark hair, and the short hemline made her legs look a mile long. She plucked a scarlet silk hibiscus out of the flower arrangement on the bathroom counter and tucked it behind her left ear. A dab of perfume and she was ready to go hunting. As it were. She couldn't fathom what sort of hunting Mitch had in mind with her dressed like this.

She stepped out of the bathroom. Mitch glanced up from the gun he was cleaning. Froze. Looked all the way down to her toes and back up again to her eyes. Unaccountably, she was nervous. Usually, she didn't give a flip what other people thought of her looks, but she wanted to meet with Mitch's approval. Silence stretched out between them as he devoured the sight of her.

She finally said, "If you only tell me 'that'll do,' I'm putting my sloppy T-shirt over this thing before we go out."

He moved so fast she hardly had time to jump. But all of a sudden he loomed before her, his expression blacker than the night and more dangerous than sin. His hands were on her, cupping her derriere, climbing up her back, drawing her against him, then sliding up one vertebra at a time to the nape of her neck.

His gaze dropped to her mouth, then lifted back to her eyes. He murmured, his voice a low, tight rumble, "I'm going to spend the entire evening imagining ripping that dress off you, throwing you down and making love to you until you scream."

And now she was going to spend all evening imagining the very same thing.

She swayed, overcome by the images flashing through her head, igniting her body until it was hotter than her dress. "I can't believe what you do to me—" she murmured.

And then his mouth was on hers, his body hard and ready against her, vibrating with desire that set her on fire. Sex had always been a rather intellectual thing for her. You meet an intelligent, fascinating man, get to know him, become friends, contemplate enriching the relationship into something more intimate. And then, you allow attraction to build.

But this…

This was primal. Completely unthinking lust. It ripped away all veneer of civilized thought from her mind and left her wanting pure, raw sex. Muscle and bone pounding against her and into her, naked flesh on sweaty, naked flesh. Tongues and tangled legs and rasping breath. She wanted *him*.

"Mother of—" he groaned into her mouth. "Kinsey, you're killing me."

"I'm the one losing my mind here."

He pressed his forehead against hers and laughed painfully. "No, no. I'm the one going insane."

"Mmm. Kiss me again, you madman." She reached up, grabbed his head and tugged his mouth down to her. "I can't get enough of you."

"Don't say that to me," he growled harshly. "I'm having a hard enough time not picking you up and carrying you over to that bed as we speak."

"Do it," she whispered. "Whisk me off my feet and make love to me."

A fine shudder passed through him. She felt it from his mouth to his knees against her body. He swore under his breath. "You're officially killing me. We can't do this. Not now."

Piercing loss stabbed her. "Later?" she asked between featherlight kisses.

He lifted his head away to look down at her. She'd never seen him more grim. "I'm not good one-night-stand material," he warned. "Once I get in your head,

I'm not going to leave it. When I take you, I'll take all of you."

Was that a promise or a threat? He said it as if it was meant to be both. A chill of apprehension chattered through her. She didn't understand exactly what he was telling her, but she knew she ought to pay attention to it and heed the warning. Except the desire pounding through her from head to foot refused to give her any respite to think. Warning or no, she *wanted* him.

Regretfully, he stepped back from her, holding her at arm's length when she would have followed him. "I'm afraid you're going to have to fix your lipstick."

She grinned up at him impishly. "But it looks smashing on you."

He reached up to wipe his mouth, grinning in chagrin while she ducked back into the bathroom to right her hair and makeup. When she emerged, he stood on the far side of the room, over by the door, a study in black. Black slacks, black turtleneck, black hair, black expression. Afraid he couldn't keep his hands off her, huh? She smiled to herself. She could live with that.

They drove in silence, not toward the strip of casinos, but rather toward the center of Havana. They parked on a deserted street in a business district and Mitch held her door for her as she swung her bare legs out of the car and stood up. She caught the sizzling flash in his eyes as he held a hand out for her. Sheesh. Just touching his hand was sending up her temperature alarmingly.

Offering her his elbow, he turned and started down the uneven sidewalk. Her high heels clicked, but his steps made no sound at all.

"Where are we going?" she asked.

"A social club."

"What sort of club is that?"

"Think part restaurant, part nightclub, part disco. They don't officially exist, but everyone who's anyone is a member at one or more of these places."

"If they're members-only places, how are we going to get in?"

He grinned over at her. "I belong to several of the best ones."

She started. "How in the heck did you pull that off?"

"This isn't the first time I've been to Cuba. That's why the boys and girls in the bunker sent me to do this job."

"And which job are we working on this evening?"

His visage abruptly went grim in the shadows. "Both of them. But I *want* Camarillo."

"What's the plan?"

He shrugged. "Your job is to distract anyone who asks us too many questions. We'll eat a bit, drink a bit, dance a bit. Circulate."

"So we're going to work the room. What do I do if I spot Camarillo?"

"If he's actually in one of these clubs, duck. He'll start shooting the moment he lays eyes on us."

Shocked, she replied, "Won't he get arrested and go to jail if he shoots someone in downtown Havana?"

"Not him. As a boy, he fought beside Castro in the original revolution and then stepped into the job of being Castro's personal assassin. He's a hero of the revolution. Which means he's got a free ticket to do pretty much whatever he wants. The police would cover up for him."

"And what will you do if he starts shooting?"

He glanced over at her blandly. "What do you think? I'll shoot back."

"Won't you end up in jail then?"

"I'm good. I would probably stand about a fifty-fifty chance of escaping the shooting scene." He shrugged. "As long as Camarillo's dead and you're safe, I'll do the jail time if they catch me. Uncle Sam would get me out in a year or two."

She blinked, stunned. He'd go to jail for her? She didn't know whether to think that was the sweetest thing anyone had ever said to her or whether it crossed the line into psychopathic. The danger of the man beside her struck her anew. He lived by an entirely different code than anything she'd ever encountered before. It was intensely attractive and every bit as frightening at the same time. Being with him was playing with fire. All that remained to be seen was just how badly he could burn her.

Mitch took a quick look up and down the deserted sidewalk and swerved without warning into a narrow alley. They picked their way past puddles and overflowing trash cans toward a single lightbulb dangling far in the bowels of the alley.

"The best social clubs in town, eh?" she muttered.

He grinned. "Patience, princess."

She followed him doubtfully to an unmarked door that looked made of solid steel. A totally clichéd little window slid open at eye level, and part of a man's face stared out at them. *"¿Sí?"* the guy grunted.

Mitch replied in rapid, fluent Cuban. Wow. Apparently he wasn't kidding when he said he'd been here before.

The little window closed and the sound of bolts being

thrown came from behind the door. It swung open on a burst of color and music. Mitch's hand came to rest in the small of her back, sending lightning bolts shooting up and down her body. So distracted she could barely walk, she allowed him to guide her inside.

It was like stepping into a different world. The club's decor was tropical, full of greenery and vibrant colors. It was as unlike the city outside as a place could be. Live macaws perched on stands around the walls, lush palms and draped vines gave the place a jungle atmosphere, and the driving beat of a Latin band pulsed in the air.

Her Spanish was adequate to follow the conversation between Mitch and the maître d'. The Cuban was asking what their pleasure would be this evening.

"We'll be dining," Mitch replied. "Then maybe a little dancing."

The man nodded and led them through giant ferns and hanging bougainvilleas, past a dance floor full of bronze, gyrating flesh and to a separate dining room. Mitch indicated a table off to one side but still in plain view of the other guests.

She slid into her seat and was startled when Mitch ordered rapidly for them without bothering to see a menu. Apparently he not only belonged to this place, but was a regular. The waiter nodded efficiently and left them alone.

"If you're worried about Camarillo shooting us, you couldn't have put us out in plainer sight for him to target," she murmured.

Mitch leaned across the glow of the candle, his face beautiful, his eyes deadly. He grasped her fingers and murmured back, "He would never show himself at a place like this. Most of the customers have mob or drug

connections. If you take a casual look around, you'll
see big, beefy guys at regular intervals all around the
place. They're the house security staff. If anyone flashes
a weapon in here, you'd better believe those guys would
take them down before the first bullet flew."

"Then why are we here, if Camarillo wouldn't come
here?"

"Because his friends would come here. If we show
ourselves publicly enough, word will get back to him."
A pause, and then he added, "This way we let him know
we're here without direct danger to you."

She frowned. "Isn't going public with your presence
in Cuba going to interfere with your main job of protecting Za—"

He pressed a finger against her lips. Smiling seduc-
tively for anyone who might be watching, he murmured,
"Don't say it in here."

She nodded and smiled back her understanding.

He leaned back in his seat, playing with the stem
of his wineglass. "It's a trade-off. You or You-Know-
Who."

"But I'm not your job!" she exclaimed under her
breath.

His mouth curved up. "Ahh, but you are. You're—"
he glanced around quickly "—an important man's
daughter, and you're in danger. It's definitely my job
to protect you. Every last delicious inch of you."

Her breath caught at the sensual slide of his voice
across her skin. She struggled to form rational thought.
"But—" she frowned "—I'm supposed to be here to
help you, not get in your way."

His golden gaze clouded over. "You're here to act
as bait and leave as soon as we flush out our quarry.

You're not a trained operative and I'm not about to put you in harm's way by expecting you to act like one."

"But I want to go in harm's way."

His fingers tightened almost painfully on hers. "Why's that? You've mentioned something to that effect before. What are you looking to get out of this?"

She mulled that one over for a moment and was saved from answering by the arrival of spinach, mango and strawberry salads. But as soon as she pushed her plate aside, Mitch's penetrating gaze was upon her again, pressing, probing, demanding answers.

"Well?" he prompted.

Persistent guy, darn it. She sighed. "I guess I'm looking for a little self-respect. I'm sick of being useless arm fluff."

His eyebrows shot up. He toyed with his wineglass again, twirling its delicate stem deftly between his strong fingers. "Seems to me that self-respect's not the problem," he finally commented.

"What do you mean?" It was her turn to stare at him, silently demanding answers.

He spoke carefully. "You strike me as having plenty of self-esteem. I think your self-image is just fine. Which leads me to believe you're mainly interested in gaining someone else's respect. Who are you trying to impress?"

She squirmed beneath his all-too-seeing gaze. Who indeed?

"Your father?"

She scowled. "I gave up on impressing him a long time ago. He'll always see me as his helpless little girl and there's not a thing I can do about it."

Mitch nodded contemplatively. "The ex-fiancé, then?"

Kinsey gasped, stunned. He knew about that? She'd so hoped her humiliation would fade away, eclipsed by some other celebrity scandal. Mitch was an undercover agent for goodness' sake! How had he come across those damned pictures? Her face heated up. She was probably the same color as her dress.

Mitch frowned. "There's no need to be embarrassed. You're not the one who put the pictures on the web. Your ex should be ashamed of himself. And if I do say so myself, you're an incredibly beautiful woman. I suspect you photograph a whole lot better than most celebrities who get caught topless."

"Yeah, but it pretty much blows me ever being the kind of girl a nice guy wants to bring home to meet the parents. Nothing like doing a Google search of the girlfriend and having her pop up on the internet in all her glory."

"Is that what you're upset about? You think nice guys won't be interested in you anymore?"

She frowned. When he put it like that, it did sound kind of lame.

"Any decent guy would understand that you were taken advantage of. He wouldn't blame you."

"Would you want a girl who millions of men had seen topless?" she accused.

"As long as she was loyal to me, I wouldn't care. The human body is no big deal. But cheating on someone—" He broke off, his expression blacker than she'd ever seen it before.

Into his heavy silence, she murmured pleasantly, "Your casual attitude about nudity is refreshingly...

European." She wasn't entirely sure she believed him, though. What man didn't get possessive of his woman? Especially an aggressively alpha male like Mitch? She spied the murderous look in his eye and nodded to herself. Yup, his expression was at distinct odds with his words.

Or perhaps that murderous look in his eyes had something to do with his remark about cheating women? Had someone cheated on him? What woman in her right mind would step out on a man like Mitch Perovski if they'd actually landed him? The idea of Mitch giving her his unreserved affection took her breath away, as improbable as it was captivating to imagine.

As she turned over possible ways to probe him about his past love life without him growling her off the subject, Mitch seemed to shake off his grim thoughts and took a sip of his wine. He grinned over at her, back to his usual careless self. "Who wants a nice guy, anyway? We rogues are more fun."

She met his smiling gaze with a teasing one of her own. "I'm a spoiled jet-set baby, you know. I've partied with some pretty hard-core fun-seekers in my day. Are you sure you can cut it with me?"

He leaned forward, blatantly looking down her dress. "I'll do my best."

Her chest abruptly felt as if it was on fire, throbbing and swollen beneath his incendiary gaze. Her nipples puckered up hard and sensitive, her dress rubbing almost painfully against them.

His gaze lifted to hers, knowing. Satisfied. *Smug.* She laughed helplessly. "You're incorrigible."

Grinning, he lifted his glass to her in silent toast.

The meal was as spicy and colorful as the club, and

Kinsey savored every bite. Of course, part of the seasoning was the nonverbal exchange between her and Mitch as he watched her eat. She'd never thought of it as a particularly sexual experience to eat in front of a man, but she was abruptly aware of the smooth slide of the silverware against her lips, the texture and bite of the food on her tongue, the smoky heat of her prime rib and the tingly chill of the champagne. The chocolate mousse he ordered for their dessert was like sex on a spoon, smooth and rich and sensual. She'd eaten at some of the best restaurants on earth in her day, but never had she enjoyed a meal as much as this one.

They small-talked for a while after the meal, letting their food settle and establishing their cover as intimate acquaintances. Eventually, Mitch murmured, "Shall we dance?"

She glanced over at the dance floor. She'd spent plenty of time in jet-set discos and was a fair dancer, but the way the Cuban women were moving to the hot salsa rhythms was a little intimidating. Nonetheless, she smiled over at him and stood up. He took her hand and led her out onto the floor.

She needn't have worried. The music and the moment took hold of her and moved her body for her. Mitch's golden gaze dared her to let go, to meet him halfway. And safely surrounded by a wall of perspiring, gyrating bodies, she did just that. She threw her head back, closed her eyes and let the music roll through her.

Mitch took advantage of every gaze in the joint being riveted on Kinsey to scope out the patrons. She was obviously a trained dancer and moved with a lithe fluidity that made sweat pop out on his forehead. She seemed to be having that effect on a lot of men.

He recognized a number of the usual suspects— local criminal bosses, smugglers and a few midlevel drug traffickers. What he didn't see were the top-level government officials and high rollers Camarillo ran with. Damn.

He let the locals get an eyeful of Kinsey, then he gathered her close to his side, laying definite and aggressive claim to her as he escorted her, flushed and laughing, from the dance floor.

"That was fun," she proclaimed. "I want to dance some more."

He grinned. The princess was surprisingly uninhibited when she let her hair down. "How 'bout I take you to the hottest band in Cuba?"

"Lead on, good sir."

He looked down at her. She shone as brightly as the sun, joy bursting forth from deep within her to illuminate her whole being. Ahh, to dive into that light, to lose himself in it, to chase away the darkness in his soul…

She was not for him. Not her innocence, not her agenda to prove herself to her ex-fiancé or her father or whoever pushed her buttons. She was merely playing at being a spy and looked as if she thought this was all some elaborate James Bond game. She wouldn't be shining so brightly when she had to live in constant fear or run for her life. Or when she came face-to-face with death. He sure as hell didn't want to be the one to introduce her to the dark side of night.

But deep in his heart, he had a sinking feeling he would be the one to do just that. This mission had blood written all over it.

His pleasure sapped out of the moment, he took Kinsey's elbow and guided her out of the club. "C'mon. Time to throw our line into a bigger pond."

This time he drove them out to the island's north shore and its casino strip, Little Las Vegas. He pulled in at an exclusive hotel and handed over the cruiser's keys to a valet. He took possession of Kinsey from the bell captain, who'd solicitously helped her out of the car, and they strolled into the lobby. He made a point of ignoring the unobtrusive surveillance cameras sprinkled more thickly than any regular hotel warranted. With a nod to the concierge, he led Kinsey confidently through the lobby and back to the beachside casino.

She didn't act impressed by the assault of flashing lights, jumbled neon colors and noise as they stepped onto the gaming floor. But then, she'd probably been to the swankiest casinos in the world already. Being around a woman like her could seriously deflate a guy's ego. Good thing he had no ego. He was a sewer rat, a creature of the night, and he had no illusions to the contrary.

They approached an unmarked door near the back of the casino. It was remarkable only for the burly guard lounging casually on a bar stool beside it.

"Private gambling parlor?" Kinsey murmured.

"Nope. That band I promised you," he muttered back.

They stepped up to the guard, and Mitch nodded. In quiet Cuban, he dropped the right names and words into a few sentences. The guard looked Kinsey up and down appreciatively, and Mitch gritted his teeth. This was exactly what she was here for. No amount of money could pay for the legitimacy she gave his cover. No sewer rat could land a woman like her in a million years. Even in a sleazy little red dress, she radiated so much class it dripped from her. If the entry passwords happened to have changed since he was last here, Mitch would give it better than even money the guard would let them in, anyway, just because Kinsey looked so damn good.

For whatever reason, the guard reached out and keyed a rapid number sequence on a wall-mounted security pad. A green light came on over the number pad and the guy gave the door handle a tug. With a smarmy smile for Kinsey, the guy let them in. Mitch hung on tightly to his right fist, which seemed to have developed an alarming need to bury itself in the guard's leering face.

And then they were inside. While the last place had been as much restaurant as anything else, this place was primarily a dance club. The music was loud, the dance floor dominating the two-story space.

"Wow. Good-looking clientele," Kinsey commented.

He cast a glance at the row of unattached women artfully draped on bar stools around the margins of the room. "Hookers," he bit out.

Kinsey threw him a startled look. "Will the men in here think I'm one, too?"

Mitch grinned down at her. "Honey, there's not a man alive who could look at you and see a hooker. You're a princess from the top of your head to the tip of your toes."

"Thanks, I think."

His smile widened. "It's a compliment. Besides, I'm not leaving your side for a second in here. No other man's getting a shot at you. You're taken."

"Who all is here?"

Mitch didn't spare a glance for the male clientele.

He already knew who they were. "Government types. Management-tier guys in organized-crime rings. Businessmen looking to grease palms."

"Sounds like an unsavory lot."

"You hang on to that thought, princess. Don't mess with these guys. They'd chew you up and spit you out."

She pursed her lips. "I don't know about that. They can't be much worse than politicians and lobbyists. Or, heaven forbid, social climbers."

"Good point. Can I get you a drink?"

"Sure."

He guided her over to the bar and shouted in Cuban to the bartender to be heard over the blaring Latin-disco fusion music. Two condensation-covered glasses were forthcoming momentarily. He handed the red-orange one with the umbrella to Kinsey while he took the clear one.

She took a sip and nodded her approval. She leaned close to shout in his ear, "How did you know what I'd like?"

He turned his head, putting his mouth practically on her ear. "My Chicks 101 class, freshman year of college. Fastest way to get girls drunk and frisky is to feed 'em fruity rum drinks they can suck down like Kool-Aid."

"Frisky, eh?" Her eyes sparkled with laughter. God, he'd love to bottle all that brilliance, then guzzle it until he was completely drunk on it. "Since I seem to have missed How to Pick Up Guys 101 in college, what're you drinking?"

"Water."

"Water?" she echoed, surprised.

He leaned even closer, dropping a light kiss on her neck, just below her ear. She gasped as obvious sexual vibes rattled through her. He was all kinds of happy to share his suffering of that ilk with her. Belatedly, he murmured, "I never mix alcohol and firearms."

Watching her unfocused gaze, it clearly took a moment for his words to sink in. He smiled to himself. So responsive, his princess.

"You're armed?" she mumbled back, alarmed. "How'd you get through the metal detectors?"

He grinned and replied conversationally, "Did you know they make ceramics these days that are stronger than steel and more heat-resistant?"

She considered that for a moment. "So, I can pretty much forget feeling safe on an airplane ever again?"

He laughed. "Nah, you're okay most of the time."

"Maybe if you were there to handle anything that came up. After this is over, can I hire you to fly with me everywhere I go?"

Their gazes met. Blue melted into gold. He murmured, "I'll fly anywhere with you, princess."

"I'll hold you to that," she murmured back.

"You do that."

The music shifted into a slow, sexy ballad of love and loss, spurned lovers and heartbreak. But the melody spoke of smoky nights and unbearable passion. The ocean pounded outside and the muggy air made tendrils curl around Kinsey's face, accentuating her beauty even more. He shouldn't do it but had to get his hands on her.

"Dance with me," he murmured.

Without a word, she laid her hand in his and followed him out to the dance floor. The lights were turned down, the singer wailing for her lover to come back. He drew Kinsey to him, sighing in pleasure as her slender body gently pressed against his, absorbing his hard angles and power into her softness. It was like coming home. So right. So perfect. Her fingers played with the short hair at the back of his neck, her thigh rubbing gently between his. In heels, she was only a few inches shorter than him and her cheek rested against his neck. A single thought filled his brain, crowding out mission and duty until he could form only a single burning sentence. *He needed her.*

They swayed together like that until the singer's voice rose in an angry anthem to swearing off lovers forever and the song ended. He snorted mentally. How very dramatic.

Kinsey lifted her head off his shoulder but did not step away from him. She murmured into his ear, "We've attracted some attention."

"Honey, you've attracted all kinds of attention."

"I'm talking about the pair of men in black suits at the table by the window. East end of the room. They don't look any too happy to have spotted you."

Kinsey's words jolted him like a bucket of ice water to the face. Work. The mission. Both missions. Which sharks had taken the bait first? Camarillo's men or Zaragosa's?

Chapter 8

"Let's go for a walk."

The grim tone in Mitch's voice jolted Kinsey out of the magical haze enveloping her. Regret for the loss of his strong arms around her, his hard body cradling hers, stabbed her.

She sighed. "Is this walk for business or pleasure?"

"All business." He smiled down at her suggestively, his voice entirely grim under the sexy expression.

Taking her cue from him, she leaned into him, draping her arms around his neck wantonly and flashing him her best seductive smile. "Shall we, then?"

He reached up to untangle her arms, kissing her fingertips as he set her away from him. "C'mon. Let's make these guys earn their paychecks."

She was surprised when he led her toward the back of the dance club and not the door they'd come in by.

But then she spied another exit leading out to the beach. A bouncer/guard nodded to them as they stepped outside into the muggy night. Salt hung thick and warm in the air and she could all but feel her hair frizzing up.

"This way," Mitch bit out.

Drat. He was back in full-blown work mode. They moved quickly across a flagstone patio and toward the sand.

She stopped at the step-down onto the beach. "Just a second. I have to take my shoes off." He frowned, and she added, "I can move a lot faster this way. Besides, it helps maintain our cover of being lovers to walk barefoot in the sand."

"You learn fast. Let's go."

They stripped off their shoes and then slogged off through the sand, running toward the beach. She laughed brightly as if it was actually fun, while cursing Mitch for making her do this. Perspiration popped out on her forehead. Good thing she wore waterproof mascara and not much other makeup.

They stopped at the edge of the ocean, the waves just lapping over their toes. Mitch startled her by sweeping her up into his arms. "Look over my shoulder and tell me if you see any men who've just come outside."

"Yeah. A pair of them."

He swore under his breath. Against her lips he muttered, "Off to my right, there are a series of cliffs and sand dunes. We're going to head for those and see who follows. Stay just at the edge of the water. The sand is firmest there and gives the best footing."

"Two more men just stepped outside," she announced.

"Are they talking to the first pair?"

"Nope. If anything the two pairs look to be avoiding each other."

"Hmm. Interesting. Let's go."

Interesting? They had no less than four thugs commencing tailing them and he thought it was *interesting*? She'd hate to see what made him nervous. They took off at a jog, holding hands. He laughed at her, his gaze as grim and bleak as the black ocean behind him. She laughed back, worry no doubt shining back in her gaze.

Mitch led her along the beach until a series of rock outcroppings and undulating crests of sand rose on their right. The beach took a sharp turn, and the second they rounded the headland, Mitch swerved inland fast.

"Stay on the rocks," he hissed. "We can't leave footprints in the sand."

They leaped and skipped like mountain goats across the rocks. Her feet burned from the rough stone, but something in the urgent set of Mitch's shoulders kept her from complaining. They climbed for maybe a minute and then, without warning, Mitch grabbed her arm and yanked her down into a crouch beside him. She looked back toward the beach and their pursuers, and was startled to see how high up they were. It was probably thirty feet down to the water's edge.

"What are we doing?" she whispered.

"Seeing who's motivated enough to follow us."

In another minute, the first pair of men burst around the headland at a full run. They paused, obviously searching for her and Mitch. She started to duck, but Mitch grabbed her arm and muttered under the muted roar of the ocean, "Don't move."

The two men ran on.

After they'd gone and the crash of waves was all that

remained, Mitch murmured, "In conditions this dark, they'd have to be right on top of us to see our faces. But they can still pick out movement at a distance. When you're hiding, standing still is more important than being out of sight."

"Who were they?"

"Given the high-quality suits, the short hair and the general bearing, I'd say they're government."

"Why would they follow you?"

"They're likely part of the faction that wants Zaragosa eliminated, and they know the U.S. will send in someone like me to watch his back. I'm a known American operator in certain government circles. As soon as they spotted me, they would've followed me."

"With the intent to do what?" she asked in alarm.

"Get me out of the way so they can take out Zaragosa."

"As in kill you?" she squawked.

He shrugged. "It's all right. Now that I've seen their faces, I know who to go after myself. I'll capture one of those guys and find out who he works for. Or, if neither of them will cooperate, it won't be that hard to get names on them after they're eliminated and find out who they're aligned with. I'll have that faction cleaned up in a few weeks."

He sounded awfully confident of his ability to casually take out a whole group of well-connected and probably well-protected people. Her father had warned her. But still the question entered her mind: How dangerous *was* Mitch, anyway?

She glanced down at the beach. "We'd better be still again because here come two more guys."

Mitch froze beside her, predatory focus pouring off

him. It was like crouching beside a tiger, seconds before it sprang for the kill. The moment was dangerous. Thrilling. A second pair of men paused as they rounded the headland, searching the way the first pair had. Their faces turned up toward the cliffs, and Mitch hissed on an indrawn breath. He must recognize them. She studied the two men's faces as carefully as she could in the scant light, memorizing their features. Who knew if she'd recognize them in the light of day, but it was worth a try. This pair was more casually dressed than the first pair, both wearing white cotton shirts untucked over dark slacks. Their hair was longer, and their general demeanor less disciplined than the first men. She'd lay odds these guys were not Cuban government.

The men took off in a jog, moving on down the beach.

"Who were they?" she ventured to whisper. With the ocean below, she could probably have shouted safely, but Mitch's hunting alertness seemed to call for whispers.

"Camarillo's men. I've run into the taller one before."

And it didn't sound as if that had been a friendly meeting. Mitch's voice dripped with contained violence.

"Now what?" she asked.

"Now we wait."

"For what?"

They'll come back this way eventually. Their cars are back at the casino. Once they've given up the chase, we'll turn the tables and follow them."

"Which pair are you going to follow?"

He turned his gaze on her, frustration glinting in it. "That's a good question."

"Too bad we can't split up and each take one pair," she tossed out.

Mitch reacted violently. "No way. You're not leaving my side until we take out Camarillo and those two down on the beach." He paused and then added, "I guess that settles that. We go after Camarillo's flunkies and hope they lead us to him."

And then what? Her brain knew Mitch intended to kill Camarillo, but now that the reality of it was one step nearer, cold dread formed a knot in her stomach.

How long they waited up on that cliff, she wasn't sure. Long enough to relax a bit. Long enough to be aware of Mitch's contained power against her right side. Long enough to start fantasizing about turning to him and kissing him to distraction, stretching out on the sand beside him and making love in the shadow of the ocean's majesty. Long enough for Mitch's jaw, and then his whole body, to go tight and for him to glance over at her and mutter, "You can stop that now."

"Stop what?" she asked, startled.

"You think I can't feel what's going on in your head?"

Her eyebrows shot straight up. "You're psychic, too?"

"No, dammit, I'm a man." And with that, he leaned over, grabbed the back of her neck and dragged her forward to meet him—not that he had to force the issue all that hard. She leaned into him eagerly, seeking the fire within him, reveling in the leashed violence of the man.

He whispered, "And you're a woman with sex on her mind."

Their mouths collided, tongues tangling, hands seeking, bodies straining toward one another. He growled deep in the back of his throat, a call of need that reached right inside her. She turned on her knees to face him fully and flung herself against the wall of muscle and strength that was Mitch. His powerful arms caught her up against him, wrapping her in safety and desire. The combination enflamed her beyond all reason.

"Make love to me," she murmured against his mouth.

"Don't tempt me," he muttered back.

"I'm not tempting you," she declared. "I mean it. Right here. Right now."

He lifted his mouth away from hers, his eyes glittering, an eerie glow in the blackness of the night. "Not here. Not now. There are four armed-and-dangerous men down there, hunting us."

Disappointment speared into her. He must've seen it because he added, his lips moving against her neck, "Don't knock it. Sand and sex don't mix. If you want to make love, try me somewhere with no gunmen and no sand on the floor." As if to soften his rebuff, he nibbled his way along her shoulder until goose bumps popped out on her sensitized flesh.

She took his head in both her hands and lifted it until she could look into his eyes. "Do you mean that?"

His gaze flickered in hesitation. "You understand what I do, right?"

She nodded.

"And you understand that my job forces me to travel. A lot."

She nodded again.

"I'll leave for months on end and you'll never hear from me."

"Yes, yes, I know all that."

He shook his head. "You hear me, but you don't really get what I'm saying. I *will* walk out on you. Even if we make mind-blowing, passionate, addictive love, I'll still leave. Maybe I'll come back from the next mission and maybe I won't."

She frowned. He was talking as if they had to commit to one another forever if they made love. She wasn't at all sure she wanted forever with anyone. Not after the garbage her last boyfriend had pulled on her. "Mitch, I'm not looking for 2.5 kids and a white picket fence. I want you and you want me. Why does it have to be any more complicated than that?"

"Because women always want more. They start wanting something casual, and before you know it, they're looking for rings and I do's. I'm not opposed to making love with you, just as long as you understand that nothing between us is going to override my work. It comes first. It's nothing personal against you, mind you." He gestured down the cliff at the beach where they awaited four killers. "This is what I do. It's who I am."

She glanced down at the deserted surf. "I understand that."

"No. You don't. You have no idea what I really do and who I really am. You still think this is some expanded, live-action version of a James Bond movie."

"James Bond kills people."

"Yes, and it's all bloodless and clean and cut-and-dried in the movies. I assure you, real life isn't that way at all."

Okay, so maybe she didn't understand what he was trying to tell her. Maybe because he didn't have the words to convey it, or maybe because she had no frame of reference in which to comprehend his comments. And yet, she still wanted him. With every molecule in her body.

So, he only wanted a casual fling. Wasn't that exactly what she wanted, too? Was it a selfish thing with her? Was he a new toy she had to have for herself, or was there more to this attraction burning up the night between them? Would she be able to walk away from him? To let him walk away from her?

"Someone's coming," he murmured suddenly.

In an instant, the potential lover was gone, replaced by the panther, a great predatory cat stalking in the blackest night. His stillness was instant and complete, his intensity palpable in the air between them. Slowly, she turned her gaze to look down at the beach below. The government men. Kinsey frowned. How had they gotten in front of Camarillo's men? Had the pairs of men passed each other on the narrow beach? The way they'd avoided acknowledging each other back on the porch at the dance club, she found it hard to believe they'd walked past each other casually out here on a fifteen-foot-wide strip of sand.

Mitch must've had the same thought, for the second the government men passed out of sight below, he whirled around to look inland. She did the same, scanning the featureless undulations of the sand behind them. He thought Camarillo's thugs were out there. How would they ever spot the men?

"C'mon," Mitch whispered.

She followed him down the jagged outcropping. Crouching uncomfortably low, they made their way along the margin of the rocks and sand, gazing out into the undulating dunes for…something…some sign of their other two pursuers.

When her legs were screaming in so much pain she didn't think she could go another step, Mitch paused in the shadow of an overhang. Thankfully, he stood up straight. She nearly cried in relief as blood returned to her cramped thighs.

"Isn't it dangerous to stand up like this?" she breathed.

"With the rocks at our backs and overhead, our silhouettes won't be visible to anyone looking this way."

She nodded, too relieved to care if they were exposed or not.

But then he stepped near and her breath hitched in her throat. His left arm went around her waist, drawing her close. He put his mouth on her ear, and over the shiver that raced through her, he whispered, "Watch for movement. A head popping up over the line of a dune, a fall of sand, a shadow moving where it shouldn't. They're out there. I can feel it."

She nodded her understanding. Hidden under the overhang, they stood still, searching for their quarry. It didn't take long. Off to their left, she spotted something breaking the wavy line of a dune crest. It was round and dark. A human head.

She gripped Mitch's elbow tightly and pointed to where the man's head had been a moment before. She held up one finger. Mitch nodded. They studied the area just ahead of her sighting, waiting for the men to show themselves again.

Camarillo's men must realize how dangerous Mitch was, for they, too, were moving with extreme caution. They didn't show themselves again. It was only by an abrupt whoosh of sand as a dune crest collapsed that Mitch and Kinsey got an inkling of the men's position. Kinsey started. It was only two dunes over, maybe fifty feet away. No more.

Mitch yanked her down and took off crawling back

the way they'd come. It was murder moving on her hands and knees, scraping both on the rough rock and then grinding sand into the raw flesh. But *murder* was the operative word. She got the distinct impression that she and Mitch would be murdered if they didn't get out of there, and fast. After a few minutes of excruciating crawling, he stopped and eased back into a narrow cleft in the rock face.

They had to squeeze in tight together to fit, and it put them body to body in a way that left very little to the imagination.

"They're coming after us," Mitch breathed. "Take this."

Something cold and heavy pressed into her hand. She recognized the rough grip against her palm. A gun. From hunter back to hunted, were they? "You keep that," she whispered urgently. "You need it a whole lot more than I do. Besides, you know how to use it."

"I have another one. Two more, in fact. That has nine shots and the safety's off. Point and shoot. Got it?"

She nodded, alarmed. There was something very, very not James Bond about holding a loaded gun in her hand.

"You stay here. I'm going out there."

"But I thought we were going to follow them to Camarillo…."

"Change of plans. They're endangering you. I'm not playing games with your life. I'll be back in a while. Don't come out until I come back for you, or daylight."

Daylight? That was hours away! She started when he dropped a quick, hard kiss on her mouth. And then he was gone. She slid farther back into the crack and real- ized the back of it was not entirely vertical. By scrambling up a series of easy footholds, she was able to climb up high enough to see much of the field of sand below.

It didn't take her long to spot Camarillo's men. Their white shirts were easy to see against the gray sand. Mitch's black clothing ought to be equally easy to spot, but she had a hard time picking him out. Finally she realized she was looking right at him, but he'd taken off his shirt. His bronze skin blended in beautifully with the sand. She tried to keep him in sight, but he was just too good and she lost him. She took stock of the white-shirted men. Uh-oh. They'd split up. One was circling wide to their right while the other went left. What were they up to?

And then she stared in shock. Three more pale shapes were moving stealthily across the sand. Oh, no! Camarillo's men had called in reinforcements! Mitch was out there alone against five men! She had to warn him. But how?

She scrambled down the cleft and moved forward to the edge of the dunes. The last time she saw him, Mitch was off to her left at about a forty-five-degree angle. She headed that way, her ankles sinking deeply in the sand with every frantic step. She tried to run but only managed a clumsy shamble. She approached the first ridge. She lay down and rolled over it the way she'd seen Mitch do from her perch in the cleft. Then she tumbled to her feet, ignoring the sand sticking to her skin, and was off half running, half sliding down the lee face of the dune.

She could almost feel the three men closing in from her right and the fourth man from behind. The net grew tighter and tighter around her until she felt choked. Or maybe that was just panic squeezing her throat so tight.

Up another dune, roll across its peak and slide on her behind down its steep face. *Hang on, Mitch.*

And then she heard a noise that made her blood run cold. A metallic spit. If television had the sound effect right, that was the sound of a silenced pistol firing. Oh, God. Mitch!

She abandoned all attempt at stealth and sprinted for where she estimated he'd be. One, maybe two more ridges over. She scrambled up the next ridge. Threw herself flat on her belly. Flung herself into a roll over the crest.

And pulled up short with the round, deadly bore of a gun in her face.

Chapter 9

Kinsey jolted as Mitch jerked the weapon up and away from her.

"What in bloody hell are you doing out here?" he growled under his breath.

"There are five men now."

"What? Where?"

She gave him her best guess as to where the men were. Which was to say, they were surrounded.

Mitch talked low and fast. "I think I hit the guy on the far left already, but he's probably not out of action. Maybe I slowed him down, though. Let's move toward him before these bastards close in on us and shoot us like fish in a barrel. Stay right behind me. And if you can, keep an eye out behind us."

It was awkward going, scrambling on all fours be-hind Mitch and trying to look over her shoulder periodically. She was sweaty, covered in sand and scared to death. Her hands and knees hurt, her arms ached ferociously, and she was out of breath. But Mitch kept going in front of her, and she pushed on doggedly, her hair hanging in her face and generally getting in the way. So much for glamorous shoot-outs on yachts and the patios of casinos in evening gowns and tuxedos.

Mitch flopped onto his belly in front of her without warning. Two bright flashes of light came from his clenched fists. *Spit. Spit.*

He'd just shot at someone. Mitch took off crawling again. Did he hit the guy? She didn't dare stop long enough to ask.

She glanced back over her shoulder and gasped in alarm. Two men were just topping a tall ridge, two dunes back. Mitch must've heard her, for he ordered in a bare whisper, "Get down!"

She flattened herself instantly in the sand, getting it in her mouth and nose. Mitch's arm came across her back. "This way."

He reversed direction, crawling back up the steep, downwind ridge they'd just slid down. It was hard work. Her hands and feet slid almost as far back down as she reached up with every movement. But after scrambling madly for several harrowing seconds, she came up beside Mitch, who crouched just below the ridge.

He put his mouth directly on her ear. "When I say go, pop up beside me and shoot at the nearest guy to you. Understand?"

He wanted her to *shoot* at someone? She stared at him in shock.

"We're way outgunned here. I need you. Remember

what I showed you on the boat? Hold the gun in both hands, point at the guy's belly and pull the trigger."

Numbly, she nodded. She realized her knees—and hands—were shaking violently. She wasn't going to hit anything if she didn't get control of herself. But to *shoot* someone? What if she missed? Would she and Mitch both die? The thought dissolved the last of her control.

And then Mitch tensed beside her. By main force, she pushed her senses past her panic, past the roaring of blood in her ears, past the pounding of her pulse in her chest and temples. And heard what had made Mitch tighten up, preparing to spring. A noise. Just on the other side of the dune. Ohmigosh. Their pursuers couldn't be more than fifteen or twenty feet away. At least that solved the question of how she was possibly going to hit these guys. They were too close for her to miss.

And then, before she had any more time to fall apart, Mitch glanced over at her. Mouthed the word *Ready?*

For lack of anything else to do, she nodded. It was that or run screaming.

He waited one more heartbeat and then murmured, "Go."

She stood up by reflex, bringing the pistol up in front of her as Mitch did the same with two pistols, one in either hand. She jumped violently when she spotted a man no more than ten feet from her, coming up the dune face fast.

She didn't even take time to aim. She just pulled the trigger. A huge explosion of noise rocked her as the heavy weapon kicked up violently in her hand. The man in front of her staggered. Stopped.

She stared in utter horror at the red mass that had

been his face just a moment ago. He tottered. Fell backward like a tree. Rolled back down the slope. Came to a stop at the bottom of the dune.

"Get down!" Mitch yelled, spinning to their rear.

She dropped to her knees and swiveled around. Two round heads popped up over the ridge behind them.

"Jump!" Mitch shouted.

He didn't give her any more instruction than that, but she needed none. They leaped as one for the ridge at their backs and its scant protection from the gunmen in front of her.

She landed half on top of something warm and squishy. The sand was cool and wet under her hands. Black in the scant light. It smelled sharp. She turned her head. Protruding, glassy eyes stared at her, sand sticking to their unblinking surface. She jerked back with a scream.

More flashes from beside her and she realized Mitch was firing again.

Her stomach rumbling with nausea, she dragged her attention to the firefight blazing around her. There was practically no sound, just sand flying and the spit of silenced bullets in the pauses between waves breaking on the shore behind them.

She tried to peer over the ridge, tried to take aim on the men shooting at them, but she couldn't see anything in the dark, and there was no way she was hitting what tiny little target one of the shooters might give her in a careless moment. Helplessly, she watched on. And then Mitch flung one of the pistols away and shifted the remaining weapon to his right hand.

"I'm getting low on ammo. Bring me that guy's

gun." He jerked his head at the body below. The man she'd shot.

Obediently, she scrambled down the slope. She tugged on the dead man's shoulder. Lord, he was heavy. She moved around his other side to heave him onto his back. And stared, appalled, at the damage she'd wrought to another human being. His nose and upper jaw were mostly gone. Teeth perched in bloody gore that used to be his lower jaw, and one of his eye sockets had ruptured, leaving the eyeball hanging by several stringy nerves and veins beside his left ear. She dropped to her knees and retched in the sand.

"Hurry!" Mitch called from above.

Swiping at her mouth with the back of her hand, she jerked the gun out of the dead man's rubbery fingers. Nearly sick again, she turned away and headed back up to Mitch's position. He held his hand out the moment she arrived beside him, and she slapped the weapon into his palm. In one motion he drew the weapon forward, aimed and fired.

She flinched at the muzzle flash and crawled over to the dead man on their right to scavenge his gun, as well. Fortunately, this guy had fallen with his gun hand outstretched, and she left the body where it was. She snatched the gun and passed it to Mitch, as well. There was only one more dead guy and her weapon, and then they'd be out of ammo. Then what were they going to do?

Mitch apparently was thinking about that very same thing. As he reached for the third gun she passed him, he muttered, "We're getting the hell out of here. Start back toward the casino. Head for the beach, then run back to the club. I'll meet you at the car."

"What are you going to do?"

"I've had enough of these bastards. I'm going to kill them."

She didn't stop to ask how. She just started to retreat. She averted her gaze as she passed the man she'd shot, but it didn't matter. The sight of what she'd done to him was burned into her memory forever. As she topped the next ridge, she looked back. Mitch was just turning to follow her. He nodded reassuringly. And then it was a mad scramble, first over the dunes to the beach and then a dead sprint along the blessedly firm sand. She'd almost arrived back at the hotel when she heard footsteps behind her. Mitch. She stopped gratefully and turned to wait for him.

And jerked in shock as a beefy, dark-haired man closed in on her. Belatedly, she remembered the gun in her hand and raised it to shoot. He was almost upon her. She braced herself to pull the trigger, when another shape came hurtling out of the darkness from her right. In a flying tackle, the second man took out her attacker.

The two men rolled over and over in the sand, carrying them into the shallow surf. They struggled fiercely, and she couldn't make out anything but foam and sand and body parts. And then one of the men rose up over the other one, straddling his chest for a moment. A slash of dull metal, and the man on the bottom's throat exploded like a swollen sausage sliced open. The white, fibrous tube of an esophagus burst out, along with the dark, slimy strands of veins. Blood went everywhere.

She staggered back in terror, aiming her pistol at the dark form that rose away from the dead man and whirled to face her.

Mitch.

She leaped forward, flinging herself into his disheveled arms. "Are there any more of them?" she gasped.

"Nope. He was the last one. You're safe now."

And that was all it took for the shaking to set in. She'd seen more horror tonight than she needed in a lifetime. Somewhere in the aftermath she started to sob, and Mitch urged her face down to his chest to muffle the sound. But then he held her tight and let her cry it out.

How long they stood there like that, red waves washing up over their feet as the dead man bled out behind them, she had no idea. But finally, Mitch murmured into her hair, "We've got to get out of here, princess."

She nodded numbly against his chest and let him lead her around the casino and directly to the parking lot. He put her into the passenger seat of their car then went around and got in the driver's side.

She noticed his hands were steady and sure on the steering wheel as he guided the vehicle into the last vestiges of the night. Just another day at the office for him. Kill four men in cold blood and leave them for the vultures. Of course, her hands weren't clean, either. The destroyed visage of the man she'd shot haunted her, leering at her, a macabre reminder of her night's work.

Dawn was just breaking as they returned to their hotel. There was blood on her dress, but the red stain wasn't tremendously obvious against the scarlet background. Mitch hustled her past a sleepy clerk and up to their room.

"Why don't you take a shower, Kinsey?" he murmured quietly. "I've got to make a phone call."

To report his kills? Did they keep some sort of scoreboard back in the H.O.T. Watch ops center? Score four for Mitch Perovski, and one for the rookie, Kinsey Hollingsworth. She shuddered at the thought. "Am I a criminal now?"

She must have voiced the thought aloud, for Mitch responded gently, "No, you clearly acted in self-defense. No court would convict you, not in the United States or Cuba."

"But I killed a man."

"A man who would have killed you in another second or so. It was you or him. You did the right thing. Now go take that shower. A hot one. You'll feel better, I promise."

Mitch waited until the water was running in the bathroom to dial the ops center. "Lancer here."

Brady Hathaway picked up the line. "Looks like you had some excitement last night. We had you on satellite. Picked up quite a few muzzle flashes down there. You two okay?"

"Yeah. Five hostiles down, by the way. A mixed bag. Several of Camarillo's men, possibly a couple of *federales*."

"How's your girl?"

"Pretty shook up. She shot a guy in the face at point-blank range. Killed him."

Hathaway didn't comment. Both men knew what it was like to experience a first kill. Kinsey would have to work it out in her own way. No one could make it better for her. "Don't let her crash and burn too hard, eh?" Hathaway finally murmured.

"I'll do what I can."

"What are your plans now?"

"I got a knife to the throat of one of the guys before I killed him. He gave me an address where I can find

Camarillo. Thought I might go pay him a little visit this evening."

"Do you want to wait for backup? I can have a team in-country in twenty-four hours."

Mitch considered. Common sense said to wait for a half dozen of his colleagues and the extra gear they'd bring with them, but his gut said to take action immediately to keep Kinsey safe. "I'd better hit him before he has time to get ready for an assault. I'll take this one on my own."

"Don't make it personal, Lancer. This is business. Just business."

"I hear you." He might hear the words, but that didn't mean he agreed with them. This was personal. Camarillo's men had nearly succeeded at killing Kinsey. Payback was required. Now.

"Did you get pictures of your attackers?" Hathaway asked, jarring Mitch out of his grim thoughts.

"With my cell-phone camera. They're dead in the photos, but maybe you can make IDs, anyway. I'll send them to you as soon as we hang up."

"Roger. We'll get on it."

"Start with the database of Camarillo's henchmen."

"Will do. Get some rest. And take care of your girl."

Hathaway hung up. Mitch sent the pictures wirelessly to the ops center. And then, finally, he relaxed. He let the stark terror of the night flow over him and out of him. Damn, that had been close. Way, way too close. Thank God Kinsey had come out and warned him about the additional men. Without that, and the extra firepower she'd provided, it could've been dicey. Well, he'd wanted her to get over the James Bond fantasy. For better or worse, she'd seen the real deal now.

He swore under his breath. It had been fun while it lasted having a woman as beautiful and sexy as Kinsey chasing after him. He'd even let himself indulge in a fantasy of the two of them being together. But after tonight—

Now she knew him for the killer he was. It was one thing to shoot at some guys on a speedboat. But to order her to shoot a guy's face off…then to slit a guy's throat right in front of her…

She'd never look at him the same way again. James Bond was dead. Mitch got up heavily and went over to the small refrigerator. He pulled out two minibottles of whiskey and opened them. Grasping both bottles in his right hand, he tossed them back in one slug. The dark liquor burned a path through his gut but didn't do a thing to unwind the giant knot of tension at the base of his skull. He opened the refrigerator again. Stared at the rows of little bottles. Slammed the door shut without taking out any more booze.

Dammit, he'd really wanted her for himself.

Chapter 10

Kinsey hugged the hotel's thick complimentary bathrobe more tightly around her and headed for the window. She'd slept away most of the day. Her dreams had been bloody, and she felt intolerably soiled by them. When she awoke, she'd succumbed to a driving compulsion to take another shower. She'd scrubbed her skin until she was pink all over. It had helped a little. But not enough.

She lifted aside the drapes to gaze out at a sunset over Havana. Something seemed wrong with the daylight, all cheerful and normal out there. Didn't Mother Nature know she'd killed a man? It was still supposed to be dark outside, grim and black like her soul. As homeward-bound cars crowded the roads and pedestrians hurried to finish their daily business, none of them had any idea that last night she'd become a murderer.

The water cut off in the bathroom behind her. Mitch was in the shower now, although she highly doubted he was scrubbing his skin until it burned, trying to remove the indelible stains of death. The bathroom door opened on a rush of warm, humid air.

"Hungry?" Mitch murmured from close behind her.

"No. Thanks."

"You have to eat sometime. You need to keep your strength up."

"I don't think I could keep anything down right now."

She felt his sigh as much as heard it. "Getting over your first kill is always hard." He paused, as if searching for words. "I'm no expert at teaching anyone how to deal with it. You just sort of do."

She glanced over her shoulder at him, surprised. "Your first kill gave you trouble?"

He shrugged. "My first one was a buddy kill, so it wasn't nearly as…traumatic as yours."

"What's a buddy kill?"

"Two snipers shoot at the same target, a rookie and an experienced sniper. You both fire at the exact same instant, and that way you're not sure if your bullet or the other guy's killed the target. Makes it a little easier to wrap your brain around."

A fine shiver passed over her. "There's no doubt who blew that poor man's face off last night."

Mitch was beside her in an instant. "He wasn't a poor man, Kinsey. He was a hardened criminal. He worked for a cold-blooded killer and was no doubt a cold-blooded killer himself. You can be sure he was prepared to blow your face off without a second thought had he pulled the trigger just a little bit sooner than you."

Nausea roiled in her stomach. She hadn't even begun to deal with the fact that she'd nearly died herself, yet. One trauma at a time.

She watched the beach far below, while Mitch stared silently out the window beside her. Eventually, he muttered, "I want to make it better, but I don't know how to comfort you."

She looked over at him in surprise. Mitch Perovski was expressing uncertainty about anything? Wow. He must be really rattled. His troubled gaze met hers for a moment and then slid away.

She replied, "It's not that hard. You put your arms around me and tell me it's going to be all right. And then I cry a little and you wipe away my tears."

He lifted the heavy curtain out of her hand and let it fall closed. The room plunged into nightlike darkness. His voice came out of the gloom. "How did that go again?"

"Arms. Around me."

His big form loomed close. Mitch's familiar hands slid around her waist, his strong, impossibly gentle embrace drawing her close and wrapping her in warmth. "Arms, check."

She smiled against his chest. "Now tell me it'll be okay."

"It'll be okay." Then he ad-libbed, "I promise. It just takes a little time and distance." A pause. "How was that?"

Her smile widened. "That was fine."

"Now you're supposed to cry a little."

Her smile got even bigger. "Not happening right now."

He drew back to peer down at her. "Do you need me to make you cry?"

"No, that's okay. But thank you for offering."

They leaned into each other for several minutes in silence, resting in each other's company. Finally, she roused herself enough to murmur, "What's next for us?"

"Dunno. I'm not real experienced at this comforting stuff. I think I'm supposed to wipe away your tears once you have some for me to wipe."

"No, I mean what's next in the mission?"

"Oh." A pause. It stretched out until she wasn't entirely sure he was going to answer her. But then he said, "One of the men last night gave me an address before I...he...expired. Tonight, I'll go check it out."

"How do you know it's a real address and not a trap?"

A faint shrug beneath her cheek. "I don't. Only way to find out is to go see."

"I'm coming with you," she announced.

"Oh, no, you're not," he retorted instantly.

"Oh, yes, I am."

He leaned back a lot now, almost to the end of his reach. "This is not open to discussion. Last night was way too damned close a call. I'm not putting you in harm's way again like that."

"I put myself in harm's way, thank you very much. I'm the one who came after you out in the sand."

"And I'm not taking a chance on you pulling a foolish stunt like that again."

Indignation flared in her gut. She didn't stop to question whether or not it was the right reaction or too much reaction. "Hey. I saved your neck out there. Had I not warned you about those extra guys, who knows what would have happened?"

Mitch released her. Spun away. Paced the room once and came to a stop in front of her. "You were lucky. Plain and simple. It was sheer, dumb luck that you weren't killed out there."

She flared up. "Shooting that guy had nothing to do with luck! Who ran around and got those other guns and gave them to you? And who kept up with you up and down all those blasted sand dunes when I was so tired I wanted to sit down and die? None of that was luck."

"You don't know the first thing about field operations. You don't know how to do surveillance, how to tail someone, how to send or receive dead drops, how to work with a black-ops team—"

She interrupted. "You and I made a pretty good team last night."

"We shot like crazy and hoped to hit them before they shot us. That's not teamwork. That's desperation."

She paced in irritation. "Why are you being like this? All that stuff you just listed off can be learned. The main thing is I didn't panic under fire and I kept moving. I might not have saved the day, but I also wasn't dead weight." She stopped prowling to glare at him. "I think you don't want me out in the field at all."

"Damned straight I don't want you out there."

She inhaled sharply. Had she misjudged him? Was he that big a chauvinist? He did say to Jennifer Blackfoot that he didn't like working with women. Her eyes narrowed. "Well, like it or not, you're stuck with me, so you might as well get used to it."

"As soon as I get rid of Camarillo, I'm getting rid of you. I'm sending you back to that catamaran and you're sailing out of here."

"What if I don't want to go? What if I want to see

this operation through? I've already been seen around town. Won't it raise suspicion if suddenly you start hitting the dance clubs without me? Face it, Mitch. You need me. I'm your cover, and I'm a darned good one."

His gaze was dark and angry. He clearly did not like being maneuvered like this. But that was just tough. She was fighting for her future here. For her very identity as a useful, intelligent member of society. She was done hanging around the margins of life, pretty but useless, like…like…draperies!

She gritted her teeth and said as calmly as she could, "I killed a man for you. I've *earned* the right to be out there."

Their turbulent gazes locked, waging a silent struggle of wills. His was formidable, but she'd grown up with a dynamic and forceful politician for a father. She refused to back down. Finally, Mitch moved forward as fast as a striking snake and swept her up into his arms. His mouth swooped down upon hers, invading.

Like that wasn't a transparent tactic! But then his mouth moved against hers, mirroring the way his body moved sinuously, drawing her higher and closer into him, and her train of thought spun away like so much chaff on the wind. One of his big hands slid under her heavy, damp hair, cupping the back of her head.

"This isn't going to work," she grumbled against his lips. "You're not distracting me. I am staying with you."

She felt a tug at her waist and gasped as cool air wafted against her skin. And then his hands were on her body, sliding across her heated flesh and down to the small of her back. His fingertips stroked the sensitive spot at the base of her spine and she nearly sobbed with pleasure at the sensations ripping through her.

Then her right shoulder was bare. Cool air blew across it, but in a moment was replaced by the fire of his lips against her skin, kissing hot and wet, nipping at her just hard enough to make her wriggle.

"Mmm. You taste like candy."

"You taste like darkness."

He murmured against the column of her neck, "What does that taste like?"

"Wood smoke. And good vodka. Cool and biting with a hint of fire beneath."

"Honey, there isn't anything cool about me right now."

She laughed. "I don't know. The way you swagger around with those pistols is pretty cool."

He crushed her against him and all but inhaled her. A charge of energy built between them, crackling and snapping, biting everywhere they touched, sending need screaming all the way to her toes. "I don't swagger."

"Do, too."

"Do not."

She raked her fingernails lightly down the side of his neck to trail down the bulging muscles of his chest. Her fingers brushed one edge of the bandage on his shoulder, a reminder of the danger of his work. "Fine. You prowl, then."

"I can live with that."

"And they say women have egos." She started and gave a little cry of surprise when he bent down suddenly, whipping an arm behind her knees and sweeping her off her feet. He carried her easily across the room.

"You're not the kind of woman who likes a man with no ego. You want a strong man who knows exactly what and who he is."

Until two days ago, she'd have laughed at the very notion of being attracted to macho alpha males. In her experience, they were a royal pain to deal with. Give her some nice, quiet, thoughtful fellow with brains and good prospects for a secure future. Mitch wasn't particularly nice. He was...hard. Nor was he particularly quiet or reflective. He was decisive. A man of action. He was frighteningly intelligent, though. And exceedingly good at what he did. She wasn't sure about his future prospects. Spies must have a relatively short life span. No security in that.

But then he laid her down on the bed and commenced ably stripping her out of her bathrobe and underwear, and all thoughts of his prospects evaporated. The air-conditioned air sent a shiver across her skin. Or maybe Mitch's molten gaze, raking down her body and flaring with heat, was doing that to her. Hard to tell.

He started at her belly button, plunging his tongue into that incredibly sensitive spot, sending her straight up off the mattress and into his mouth again. Who'd have guessed her navel was connected to her female parts like that? Bolts of pure lust streaked through her. He kissed outward in ever-expanding circles, causing her to alternately contract her stomach muscles into knots of pleasure, then to stretch, catlike, under the ministrations of his talented mouth. If he was a panther, then she was his main course as he feasted upon her flesh. And she hadn't a bone left in her body to protest.

"I want you, Kinsey," he murmured.

She groaned in the back of her throat, shuddering in too much pleasure to form words just then.

"I need you," he whispered.

She arched up into him, crying out as his mouth

closed on the most sensitive parts of her, sending a jolt of pure sex all the way to her fingertips, so intense it robbed her of thought, let alone speech.

"And that's why you have to stay safe. For me."

And then he was looming over her, bracing on arms wreathed in bulging, corded muscle. She reached up, desperate for more of what he was doing to her, and looped her hands around his neck, pulling him down to her.

"I'm only going to say this one more time. Make love to me, Mitch. Now."

A smile of purely male satisfaction flitted across his features, and then his gaze locked with hers. Went dead serious. Pierced straight into her soul. "Are you sure? There's no going back."

"Yes, I'm sure!" She'd never been more sure of anything in her life. Wave after wave of pounding need throbbed through her, carrying her out to sea like so much flotsam on the riptide of Mitch's mouth and hands and body upon hers.

And then the darkness descended upon her. Mitch's big body was against her and on her and in her, a stretching fullness that set her on fire, writhing upon a sword of desire that cut all the way through her, leaving no part of her whole. She flung herself against the muscular darkness that was Mitch, reveling in the strength that pinned her easily, enforcing his will upon her. And that will was pleasure. Intense, searing pleasure that tore cries from her throat and made her limbs weak and left her wanting more, and yet more, of him.

"Sing for me, Kinsey," he growled.

And sing she did. Sound started at the back of her throat and shuddered all the way down her body, until it was a keening, wordless moan of release that said everything that needed to be said. White light exploded behind her eyelids and a curtain of blackness fell over her mind in which nothing remained but exquisite, perfect sensation. And then the moment exploded in a shower of sparks that zipped through her and over her and around her. Death and rebirth. All in a single, infinite moment out of time.

She felt the explosion envelop Mitch, too, as his body shuddered and bucked against hers. He gave a hoarse shout of pleasure, the triumphant mating roar of the panther, king of his domain, and yet consumed by it.

They collapsed together, the velvety darkness wrapping around them gently. Slowly, Kinsey regained awareness of her surroundings, of Mitch's world—this place of primal instinct, of survival, of sex, of man and woman. It was all very simple, really.

He rolled to his back, gathering her against his side. Her arm fell across the slabbed muscles of his stomach, and yet again, she registered his outstanding physical condition. This was a man who would always keep moving. He would never be satisfied to sit around thinking about what needed to be done. He was the kind of man who would go do it. The kind of man a girl could put her trust in. He'd take care of her. Keep her safe. Provide for her. Love her unswervingly for all his days. Give her his complete loyalty until his dying breath. Mitch was the kind of man she could very easily love back—with the same intensity he'd love her.

"I'm not leaving you, Mitch."

"You don't have any choice in the matter. I've already told you I'll walk away. I wasn't kidding."

She pushed up onto her forearm on his chest and stared down at him in shock. "After what we just shared, you can still say that?"

She'd never noticed before how cold a metal gold could be. But it glittered out of his gaze harder and colder than any steel. *This* was what he'd been talking about when he'd warned her off him. He'd been right. She'd had no idea what he'd been talking about when he said he'd get inside her head, but he would still leave her. Oh, God.

"But I felt… I thought…" She couldn't finish the sentence. Had she really been that wrong about what they'd just shared? Was she that big a fool? Or—aloud, she asked, "Are you really that big a bastard?"

He looked her dead in the eye. "I *will* walk away from you. I promise you that."

Chapter 11

Mitch stared up miserably at the ceiling, cursing himself in every language he knew, as Kinsey climbed out of bed in silence and went into the bathroom. He *hated* doing that to her. And yet, he had no choice. No choice at all. He had to protect her. He cared for her too much not to. Making love with her had been a revelation. A light in the darkness, a moment of such perfection that he almost didn't dare to breathe, lest it disappear, with the one woman he'd searched for his whole life.

And he'd just broken her heart. Irrevocably made her hate him. Irretrievably ruined any chance they had for a future together. He sat up, swung his feet to the floor and hung his head. He swore luridly. His job sucked. His life sucked. *He* sucked.

He should walk away from it all. Grab Kinsey, head for some deserted island on the other side of the world and chuck the whole shooting match. Except he knew darn good and well that wouldn't slow down Camarillo or a slew of other men like him. A guy didn't work in this business for decades and not amass a lifetime supply of enemies. There were certain very careful protocols an operator must adhere to if he wanted to walk away from the business and live. And grabbing the girl and splitting was not part of that protocol. He swore some more.

No light seeped around the edges of the heavy curtains. Night had fallen while they were making love. Time for him to go to work. To become the only kind of man he knew how to be.

He stood up, suddenly feeling old. Tired. Sore. Or maybe that was just heartsore. Either way, his gut felt full of lead. He rummaged in his luggage and threw on some clothes.

He strapped a knife to his left calf, an ankle holster to his right leg. He shrugged into his double shoulder holster. By rote, he checked each weapon. Safety on. Fully loaded. A round chambered. Safety off. A throwing knife in the pocket at the back of his neck. Brass knuckles in the slot behind his front pocket, ammo clips in the rows of narrow slots along the back of his slacks, underneath his belt with its custom-designed garrote inside. Methodically, he armed himself with the tools of his trade, cursing every radio, every high-tech gadget, every lethal reminder of why he could never have Kinsey Hollingsworth for himself.

No woman in her right mind would cuddle up to a guy loaded down like a one-man army. A killing machine. He had to keep Kinsey safe. No matter what the cost. At *all* costs.

Janine had taught him well. The only way for a guy in his line of work to stay sane was not to love anything or anyone. He made a practice of maintaining no personal possessions of any value to him. No pictures, no memorabilia, no keepsakes with sentimental value. Nothing he'd feel bad about losing. He didn't get attached to his car, his guns, not even his music collection or books. All were expendable and replaceable. But he'd finally found the one thing—the one person—who was not expendable. And if he couldn't have her, he was damn well going to see to it she was safe.

With that grim resolve firmly in mind, he hefted his duffel bag and took one last look around the hotel room. No signs left behind to hint to Kinsey where he'd gone. He would walk out of here and not look back. That was the rule. He always walked away.

Except, of course, Kinsey had already broken all his rules, showing them up for the sham they'd really been. He had no illusions about leaving her behind. It would be neither easy nor clean. He'd given her a piece of himself today—a big, fat slice of his heart. And he would never get it back. Ah well, he hoped she had fun stomping all over it. He deserved anything she thought or said of him in the days to come. Worse, probably.

The doorknob turned under his hand. He muttered, "Goodbye, Kinsey Hollingsworth. It was a pleasure knowing you."

Kinsey sat on the edge of the tub and listened to him go. She started when his quiet voice drifted through the flimsy bathroom door to her. *It was a pleasure...* He was leaving for good! She leaped up and ran out into the room.

All signs of him had disappeared. It was as if he'd never been here. His black duffel bag was gone, the clutter of weapons and wires and gadgets on the coffee table, all of it. Gone. She jumped to the door and tore it open. She poked her head out into the hallway. No sign of him. She started to dart toward the elevators, then remembered she was buck naked. She couldn't run after him.

She raced back into the room and threw on clothes, grabbed her purse and sprinted for the door. He wasn't getting away from her that easily. Whether she was going to kiss him or kill him when she caught up with him, she wasn't sure. She'd figure it out when the time came. But he wasn't getting away with this lame escape. She deserved better than that, and he was a better man than that—whether he was ready to admit it or not. He was going after Camarillo. And by golly, she wasn't letting him do that alone.

She ran to the front doors of the hotel and collected herself enough not to burst out into the street like a panicked amateur. She looked both ways and spotted the black cruiser just pulling out of the hotel's parking lot. She stepped outside and opened the back door of a taxi sitting at the curb. Thankfully, her Spanish was adequate to convey to the driver that she'd like to follow that black sedan, but not too close. The driver threw her a sympathetic look and did as she asked.

As Mitch wound his way into a frankly dangerous-looking part of town, the driver asked her if she wanted him to continue following the señor. She wasn't crazy about being out here by herself like this, and under normal circumstances, she'd tell the driver to take her back to the hotel. But these were not normal circumstances.

And as distasteful as the thought of using it might be, she still had one gun in her purse.

Mitch's car pulled over at a curb and parked. Ducking into the shadows in the backseat of the cab, she had the driver continue on past. "Turn right up ahead," she directed.

The cabbie complied. There was an awkward moment when she realized she only had American greenbacks in her wallet, but the cabbie was eager to take them. With a warm thanks for his help, she paid him and sent him on his way. Time to go find her man.

She eased forward and peered around the corner. No sign of Mitch. Damn. She hadn't lost him already, had she? She moved forward cautiously. The street was dark, and the few people loitering in sight could be described as unsavory at best. So. This was Mitch's world, was it? She took a deep breath and concentrated on blending in. On breathing normally. On spotting her quarry.

There was no sign of Mitch anywhere. He'd disappeared. And none of the establishments along the sidewalk looked like the kind she could safely pop into for a minute to see if he was there. In desperation, she stopped to ask a middle-aged man minus most of his teeth and in need of a shave if he'd seen the man get out of that black car over there. The guy peered at her as if she was a little green man from Mars gibbering some alien tongue. Hey. Her Spanish wasn't that bad. She pulled out a five-dollar bill and tried again.

Yup, cold, hard cash was the universal translator. The fellow pointed at what looked like a bar.

Kinsey winced. She knew full well if she went inside, she'd get hit on by every unattached guy in the place. No way would she be able to hide from Mitch if he were in there. She considered her options. On a hunch, she moved over to his sedan and tried the doors. Bingo. The driver's-side door was unlocked. He probably did that so he could make a quick getaway if need be.

She opened the door quickly. Not surprisingly, the overhead bulb didn't go on. Mitch had no doubt removed it. She crawled into the backseat and rummaged in Mitch's duffel bag, coming up with one of his black turtlenecks. She pulled it on over her light-colored shirt. She found a black T-shirt next and tore it into a rough head scarf. She wrapped it over her dark hair and left an end trailing down to pull over her face when the time came. It was the best she could do for camouflage. Then, she wriggled down onto the floor—thank goodness these old cars had tons of legroom—and pulled the duffel bag forward to hang off the edge of the seat so it mostly covered her hiding place.

And then she waited. It was hot and stuffy in the car, and before long, her cramped position became unbearably uncomfortable. She sat up twice, stretching out kinked muscles and cracking open one of the rear doors for a few seconds to let in some fresh air. What in the world was Mitch doing in there? He said he was going to pay Camarillo a visit tonight. And he never mixed booze and guns, so he wasn't likely drinking. Maybe working a contact? Finding out more about Camarillo's place before he barged in on the killer?

She passed the time thinking about making love with Mitch. And she arrived at several conclusions. First, she hadn't imagined the intense emotional connection between the two of them. Second, Mitch had felt it, too. Third, he might have walked away from her like he said he was going to, but he wasn't happy about it. And that meant there was still hope for them.

Maybe she was just being pitifully clingy or overly needy, but she wasn't ready to give up on him. If that made her a stalker, so be it. He was going to have to look her in the eye and tell her he wanted nothing more to do with her, that making love with her had meant nothing to him, before she was walking away from him—or letting him walk away from her.

Nearly two hours had passed when her senses abruptly went on full alert. Someone was coming. She covered her face with the dark cloth and lay perfectly still. The driver's door opened and someone got into the front seat. The engine started and the car pulled away from the curb. Assuming that was Mitch driving, she'd done it! He hadn't discovered her!

She had no idea that riding on the floor of a car was so bloody uncomfortable. She braced herself as best she could as the vehicle banged over the old roads of Cuba. Where was he going? The city noises outside faded, and the ride became even worse. Finally, it sounded like gravel began to spit out from under the tires. A dirt road, maybe?

The engine cut off. The car coasted to a stop. Silence enveloped the vehicle. Kinsey waited breathlessly. What was he waiting for? Finally, the front door opened and a cacophony of night sounds burst into the car. The door slammed shut. Kinsey gave him a few seconds, then sat up painfully and peered out over the rim of a window. His dark shape was just disappearing into the bushes. Quickly, she scrambled to her feet and slipped out the back door. Scared to death, she crept into the jungle after him.

Thankfully, his passing left a faint trail of crushed weeds and an absence of dew upon the dense foliage. She was able to move with relative ease along the pseudotrail he blazed through the jungle. How far ahead of her he was, she had no idea. She did know it would be a bad thing to surprise him from behind. She'd seen his reflexes in action, and he'd shoot her before he ever saw her face if she wasn't careful.

The ground began to rise and instinct made her slow down. She dropped to her knees and traveled the last few yards up the slope on her hands and knees. She sincerely hoped there were no poisonous snakes or scorpions or worse out here, because she couldn't see a blessed thing. A glow illuminated the other side of the hill. On her belly, she eased forward a few more feet. And stared at the compound sprawling before her. It was more than a villa. It was a whole collection of buildings behind a heavy fence and lit with spotlights.

The lights threw a series of dark shadows up the hillside toward her. Searching carefully from her vantage point, she picked out a dark form supine on the ground. Was that Mitch? She watched it for several minutes. And then, very slowly, the shadow moved. She'd know that sinuous grace anywhere. After all, she'd held all that sleek power in her arms. Oh, yes. That was Mitch.

He inched forward, moving from one shadow to the next, pausing frequently. If he'd had a tail, its tip would have twitched like a panther's. Mitch was hunting tonight.

She watched him for nearly a half hour, easing his way closer and closer to the buildings. At one point, she thought she saw him slowly lift a pair of binoculars to his eyes. What did he see? Had he spotted Camarillo?

She wouldn't have believed it possible two days ago, but she desperately hoped Mitch found the guy and killed him. She was ready to get on with her relationship with Mitch. Until the threat of Camarillo was removed, it would hang between them, a piece of unfinished business that would prevent either of them from moving on with their lives.

Mitch moved again, edging past the last of the boulders dotting the hillside. All that was left between him and the fence was a stretch of long grass, its seed heads nodding in a gentle whiff of night air. The mosquitoes were ferocious, and Kinsey couldn't stand them any longer. She slid back a few feet and dug in her purse for the tiny bottle of concentrated bug spray Jennifer Blackfoot had told her to put in her bag back at the ops center. God bless Jennifer.

Quickly, Kinsey rubbed the oily stuff on her skin. A faint musty odor rose from it. She pocketed the bottle and made her way back to the crest of the hill. Mitch had disappeared into the grass somewhere. She waited patiently, her gaze on the fence he would eventually have to get past. He would probably head for that shadowed area where a clump of palmettos butted up against the fence from the inside. She guessed it would take him fifteen minutes to make his way over there.

She studied the grass carefully, and although she spotted a number of suspicious waves of seed heads over the open stretch that didn't look like the breeze blowing, she couldn't spot Mitch.

His fifteen minutes was nearly up when an explosion of motion below caused her to jolt violently. What the—

No less than ten black-clad forms erupted out of the grass, shouting. They bore weapons, and all of them were pointed at roughly the patch of grass in front of the palmettos. A second violent movement made her jump, this time the familiar silhouette of Mitch springing up out of the grass and sprinting back toward her position. More shouting and the other men leaped forward.

Mitch never had a chance. The men tackled him and bodily subdued him. He put up a heck of a fight and, even with ten men on top of him, gave them a hard time. Finally, she saw the butt of a rifle rise up in the air and fall. She all but came over the hill in her horror. The heaving pile of men went still.

It was a trap! *And Mitch had walked right into it.* She felt hot all over. Sick to her stomach. She had to *do* something. But what? She couldn't take out that many men by herself even if she knew what to do! The group lifted Mitch's limp form and four men staggered forward under his weight. They moved along the fence but made no effort to go inside the compound, even by-passing a gate.

Frantic to do something, she followed along the ridge, paralleling the men, peeking over the top of it every few yards to check on the men's progress. Her ridge disappeared into trees, and she struggled to move through them quietly, skirting the edge of the jungle, in the foliage deeply enough to avoid being seen, but close enough to keep visual contact with Mitch. The men carried him around the perimeter of the compound and peeled off through the trees. The going got thicker here and she lost sight of them. In desperation, she battled her way closer to where she'd last seen them. A trail, no doubt trampled by the large group in front of her, unfolded. She raced along it as quietly as she could. She couldn't lose Mitch!

Startled, she heard an engine rev in front of her. She darted forward and emerged at the edge of a clearing in time to see two sets of taillights disappear down the road in front of her. Her stomach dropped sickly. She'd lost him. She raced in the opposite direction, praying this was the same road on which Mitch had parked his car.

Panic tightened her chest and made her so jittery she could hardly stay on her feet. Gasping for air she sprinted down the road, searching frantically for the car. It had been half hidden in a clump of bushes, and its black color would further camouflage it. She almost ran past it, but a glimmer of glass finally caught her attention.

She jumped in the front seat. No keys. She hunted furiously in the map pockets and under floor mats. *C'mon, Mitch. Where'd you hide the key?* There was no sign of it. Frustrated and close to tears, she slumped in the seat. Now what?

She twisted to reach into the backseat for Mitch's duffel bag. She lifted the heavy bag into the front seat beside her and commenced rifling through it. There had to be something useful in here. The seconds were ticking away and those cars were getting farther and farther away from her.

She dug past clothes and tools and ammunition desperately. Aha. A hybrid radio-telephone-looking thing. She yanked it out. She examined the switches and pressed what looked like a power button. The face glowed faintly. She pressed it to her ear. Static. It had a keypad that looked like telephone numbers. Who to call? There was no 911 in Cuba for illegal spies in need of rescue.

The Bat Cave. If she could get ahold of Mitch's head-quarters, maybe they could help. A phone number for them... She wracked her brains, but couldn't for the life of her remember the phone number on Jennifer Blackfoot's desk phone.

She examined the phone and started pressing random buttons. A menu popped up on the screen. She scrolled down through a bunch of unhelpful-sounding choices. How she ended up at a phone book of stored numbers, she wasn't quite sure. But she thanked her lucky star and thumbed through the entries. They were all seemingly random sequences of letters and numbers. Codes, probably.

Then one caught her attention. ICE11.

She'd heard a bit on the news not long ago about pro-gramming an emergency-contact phone number into your cell phone and labeling it *I-C-E*, which stood for In Case of Emergency. Apparently EMTs and police often found the cell phones of victims at accident and crime scenes but then had no idea who, out of a list of stored phone numbers, to call to notify a friend or family member. But ICE numbers solved that problem.

What the heck. The worst she could do was end up waking up some general or foreign spy. She hit the auto-dial button for ICE11.

It only rang once. A male voice bit out, "Go."

"Uhh, who is this?" she asked.

"Who the hell is this?" the male voice exclaimed.

"I can't tell you. This is an emergency, though. Who am I speaking to?"

"This is a government phone number...Kinsey? Is that you?"

She started. "Yes, it's me. Who is this?"

"Brady Hathaway. What are you doing on this line?"

Thank God. The Bat Cave. Relief nearly made her throw up. She spoke all in a rush. "Mitch has been kidnapped. I was following him, but he didn't know. And I saw him get jumped by about ten guys. They knocked him out and carried him to the road, but I lost sight of them. They threw him in a car and drove away. I'm in Mitch's car now but I can't find a key and it won't start and I don't know what to do—"

"Slow down, there, Kinsey. Take a deep breath. You did the right thing to call us. We've got all kinds of resources to help Mitch. There's no need to panic, okay?"

Hathaway's voice was calm and completely unruffled. He didn't seem the slightest bit concerned about Mitch's predicament. She did as he suggested and took several slow, deep breaths.

"I'm going to go off the horn for a couple minutes. I'm passing you to a guy named John Hollister. He's going to keep talking to you while I do a few things to help Mitch. Okay?"

"Okay."

Another man came on the line. He also had a soothing voice that conveyed that everything was under control. He gently questioned her, talking her through all the details of the evening up till this point. At the end of her recitation, he commented, "You've done very well, Kinsey. Your quick thinking may very well save Mitch's life."

She lurched. She'd almost forgotten in these guys' calmness that Mitch was in serious trouble.

Then Hollister surprised her by saying, "I'm going to talk you through how to hot-wire a car. Do you think you're up to it?"

She blinked, startled. "I guess so."

"You said you had Mitch's bag of tools, yes?"

"Yes."

"Reach inside and look for a pair of wire cutters and a pair of pliers. Do you know what both of those look like?"

She laughed. "Shockingly enough, I do know what those look like. And believe me, not too many of the women I know do."

She heard the smile in Hollister's voice. "You're going to do just fine, Kinsey. Now. You may need to open the car door and kneel on the ground to do this, but look on the bottom side of the steering column and find a screw. It'll be recessed in a little tube and may be hard to see in the dark...."

It took nearly a half hour, and there was a delay while someone was found who knew the wiring of a vintage 1950s automobile ignition system, but eventually, the sedan's engine roared to life.

Hollister congratulated her on hot-wiring her first car and passed her back to Brady Hathaway.

"Hi, Kinsey. It's me again, Brady."

"Hey."

"Okay. I've got a team of SEALs en route to your area. They'll be on the ground in six hours. It may take them a few more hours to join you. They'll be equipped and ready to rescue Mitch."

She let out a long breath of relief.

"We're going to give you directions, and you're going to drive to Havana and go to the American Embassy. We'll call them and they'll be waiting for you."

"No!"

"Kinsey—"

"Brady. I'm not arguing with you about this." She put the car in gear and eased it forward, accelerating when she reached the road. "I'm following Mitch."

"Kinsey, Camarillo is a big-time assassin, and you're an amateur. Your father's a congressman, for God's sake."

"And I'll raise heck through him if you don't help me find Mitch." She hesitated.

"Not a chance," Brady retorted flatly.

"Let's review. I'm in Cuba, I'm driving along a road and may stumble into Camarillo's men all by myself. I'm a hysterical female...oh, and I have a gun. I'm doing this whether you help me or not. Now, are you going to sit back and let the congressman's daughter get herself killed, or are you going to do your best to help her and keep her alive?"

A long, frustrated silence was her only reply.

Finally, Brady growled, "Fine. Have it your way. But let the record show I'm doing this under duress."

"So noted," Kinsey replied drily.

"If we let you help us find Mitch and give us eyes-on intelligence about where he is, will you *promise* not to do anything stupid and to wait for our SEAL team to extract him?"

"If it'll help Mitch, I promise."

A heavy sigh. "Pull out onto the road and proceed in the direction you're currently headed. I've got your car on the satellite."

"You mean you're looking at me right now?" she asked in surprise.

"If you stuck your arm out the window and waved at me, I'd see it," Hathaway replied grimly.

Wow. She'd heard the U.S. had some crazy-powerful

satellites, but knowing that cameras were peering down at her from space right now was kind of creepy.

Hathaway continued, "You'll go straight ahead for about ten miles. Take a look at your odometer, okay?"

"It says 599,221."

"Damn, they get a lot out of those cars," Hathaway muttered. "I gotta get me a Cuban mechanic."

"How old is this car, anyway?" she asked to distract herself as she drove.

"Probably pushing sixty years old. At the next intersection, you're going to turn right. It'll be a paved road. There may be a stop sign... I can't make it out in the dark."

Definitely creepy. She slowed down as what looked like a yield sign loomed in her headlights. For the next hour, she followed Hathaway's instructions and actually found herself unwinding a little from her earlier panic. It felt good to be doing something, not just sitting around worrying about Mitch.

Then Hathaway said, "Slow down. Turn off your headlights if you can."

"I can." She did as he asked, her pulse spiking hard.

"Stop wherever you can. If the ground looks solid, pull completely off the road and get behind some cover. Let me know when you've done that."

She crawled along in the dark, peering at the shadows until she found a thick clump of plants similar to the one Mitch had parked behind earlier. She maneuvered the cumbersome car behind the bushes. "Okay, done."

"Carefully pull apart the white wire and the blue wire without touching the exposed copper and bend them back so they won't touch. The engine should stop."

"Done."

"Now, in Mitch's bag, I need you to look for a few things."

Once Hathaway had armed her with a big pair of field glasses, night-vision goggles, an earbud for the satellite phone and a really big gun, he directed her to get out of the car. Leaving the door unlocked, she stepped out into the night. Once more, she was entering Mitch's dark shadow-world, and once more, she felt completely unequal to the task. But he was out here somewhere and in grave danger. She *had* to help him.

"How do you hear me?" Hathaway murmured into her earpiece.

"Fine," she murmured back.

"When you get close to the target location, you can respond to me by clicking that long black button on the side of the phone. One click means no and two clicks means yes. Got it?"

She double-clicked in response.

"Good girl. Okay, you're going on a little hike. I can't see you through the canopy of trees, but your phone has a GPS locator in it. You'll have to find your own way through the jungle and around any obstacles you run into. I'll give you course corrections to the left or right, but do what you have to in order to keep moving forward. Whatever you do, don't grab at any sticks or vines for balance. They could be a snake. And don't walk between any trees that seem to have a wide-open space between them without clearing the space first with a long stick. Spiders like to make webs between trees."

"You sure know how to give a girl warm fuzzies."

"You're doing great. Just hang in there with me."

"Here goes nothing," she mumbled and plunged into the wall of black-green before her.

The trek was a nightmare. Sharp leaves slashed at her arms like swords. Fallen trees tripped her, and vines and weeds clutched at her ankles. Were it not for Brady's constant course corrections, she'd have become hopelessly lost in the thick tangle of undergrowth. Sometimes the jungle pressed in on her so thickly she feared she couldn't move any of her limbs and was completely trapped. Only worry for what was happening to Mitch drove her to fight on, to wrestle against the living, breathing beast that had swallowed her whole.

When an impossibly thick vine slithered up into the trees right in front of her, she completely lost her composure. That snake had been as big around as her arm and easily ten feet long.

"Not to worry," Hathaway soothed as she hyperventilated in his ear. "That was a tree boa. They're more afraid of you than you are of them."

He allowed her a few minutes to rest and collect herself, and then he urged her onward again. "Not much farther to go. Mitch's signal is located under tree cover, so I can't tell you what you're walking into."

"Don't you guys have infrared cameras or something where you can see heat signatures through walls?"

"Been watching cable TV, huh?" he commented. "Yeah, we do. But for some reason we're not painting any signatures. They're probably inside some sort of metal structure that reflects the signal, or maybe underground. That's what we need you to tell us."

She gathered her remaining energy and slogged on. *I'm coming, Mitch. Just hang on.* As the minutes ticked past, she began to get a sick feeling in the pit of her stomach. It expanded into a cramplike feeling not centered in any one place. Something bad was happening to Mitch. She felt his pain as if it were her own. She tried to ignore the sensation, to reason with herself that it was just her frazzled nerves and overactive imagination, but the feeling kept getting stronger and stronger. The endless, throbbing ache would not be ignored.

"Something bad's happening to Mitch," she announced to Hathaway.

He replied sharply, "Can you hear him?"

"No. I can feel him." She added hastily, "I'm not just being a hysterical female here. I have this unshakable feeling in my gut that he's in pain."

"I believe you," Hathaway replied grimly. "I learned a long time ago to pay attention to gut feelings like yours. You've got about two hundred yards to go."

Two hundred steps. She counted them off in her head, thanking the stars when she reached open patches and could go ten or twelve steps unimpeded, and cursing the stars when she had to struggle forward a few inches at a time. And still the feeling in her gut grew. It was a sharp pain now.

"Twenty yards. Slow down and don't make any more verbal responses to me. Clicks only. Take a good look around, then retreat thirty yards or so into the jungle and give me a call to report what you see."

She double-clicked her understanding. Those last few yards were torture. An urge to bolt forward, to run screaming into the middle of whatever was going on, to find Mitch and rescue him, to stop the knifelike ghost pains shooting through her body, nearly overwhelmed her.

She eased forward, testing each step before she put her foot down. And then a small glade became visible through the trees. She eased forward, one foot at a time, sticking to the deepest shadows. A few minutes ago, they'd been frightening, but now those shadows were her friend, embracing her in their inky camouflage, bringing her closer to the man she craved.

A one-story, galvanized metal building with rust stains streaming down its sides stretched before her. Two men armed with rifles of some kind lounged at one end of it. The structure had no windows that she could see. She eased off to her left, circling the back of the building. The end opposite the guards had a small window up high, above a banged-up-looking air-conditioner unit. Some sort of vent opened up beside it at ground level, covered with a screen. It looked like a fan from inside the building blew through the lower opening. The far side of the building yielded no more windows.

She crouched on her heels and tried to figure out what else Hathaway and his SEALs would need to know to attack this place. She moved closer to the front and the guards. Two vans stood out front. Probably the same vehicles she'd seen pulling away from the site of Mitch's kidnapping. Which meant around eight more men must be inside the building. She noted electric lines running overhead into the structure, a glow of light coming from the closed front door. It looked as if the place had a concrete foundation that probably formed a floor. A few of the galvanized panels on this side of the building looked loose along the bottom.

And it was deathly quiet. All the jungle creatures, even the insects, were silent. A heavy, expectant hush blanketed the whole place.

And then a hoarse scream pierced the night. It tore through her like no sound she'd ever heard before. There was a loud crackle of noise, like lightning frying a bug, and the strip of light under the door flickered. Another hoarse shout of agony.

Oh. My. God.

Mitch.

Chapter 12

Mitch sagged against the wet ropes binding him to the metal chair. These boys hadn't missed a trick. The only reason he wasn't dead right now was because of the building's inferior wiring. An air conditioner labored behind him, stealing most of the electricity, and the current left over was barely sufficient to light a few bulbs overhead. While it was excruciatingly painful, it wasn't anywhere close to lethal. Thank God his torturers wanted to be comfortable and run the A/C while he suffered.

He studied his captors from beneath swollen lids. The bastards were military. He was sure of it. He thought he'd glimpsed a couple uniforms in the scrum when they jumped him back at Camarillo's estate. The men standing in front of him now, arguing over how much more to torture him before they went to get something to eat, were lean. Fit. Short-haired. All below the age of forty. Nope. Not Camarillo's men. The Cuban assassin was in his sixties and tended to hang out with his childhood friends, whom he trusted.

Who, then?

And then, he glimpsed a familiar insignia on the chest of the guy giving the orders. The Presidential Guard.

These were Zaragosa's men. The Cuban official had double-crossed him. Double-crossed the U.S. government. The Americans thought the guy was their loyal ally, but who knew what sort of misinformation he was feeding U.S. intelligence agencies? He *had* to get out of here and let someone know Zaragosa was unreliable!

If he was going to share what he knew, he was going to have to live long enough to get out of here. And at the moment, that prospect wasn't looking great.

He'd never dreamed Camarillo and Zaragosa might actually be in league. Hell, no one had. But now that he thought about it, he had to ask himself how Camarillo's men had known about the scheduled meeting with Zaragosa back in the Virgin Islands in time to show up early at the rendezvous point, lay an ambush and nearly kill him. Damn. It had been right there in front of him the whole time.

And he'd been so besotted with lust for Kinsey he hadn't stopped long enough to think about it. To see the connection. She'd tried to tell him. She'd asked how Camarillo had found him, and he'd ignored her because she was an amateur. God, he'd nearly gotten her killed because he hadn't been paying attention to her brains instead of her body. Stupid. Very, very stupid of him. And now he was paying the price for it.

He should've left her a note. At least told her what he was doing, if not where he was going tonight. But no. He'd been so focused on being noble, on walking away, on sacrificing his heart for her safety, that he'd neglected Spycraft 101—tell somebody where you're going, particularly when it involves engaging the bad guys.

Hell, he probably deserved this excruciating pain shooting through him like a thousand knives. He'd already gone through the mental exercise of separating himself from the agony, of compartmentalizing it in a walled-off corner of his mind. It took a certain amount of concentration to maintain the disconnect between himself and intense suffering, but he'd practiced the technique for years. It was manageable. And because his captors didn't know the technique, they projected themselves into his shoes and mistakenly assumed they were inflicting unbearable amounts of pain upon him. Throw in a few screams now and then to convince them they were right, and the situation was under control.

For the moment. Once they started trying to extract information from him, that would change. Then they'd steadily up the pain factor until they broke down both him and his walls and forced him to talk. Although, so far they'd shown no inclination to interrogate him. Which lent even further credibility to the evidence that these were Zaragosa's men. They weren't here to find out who he was. They already knew.

One of the men stepped over to the crude rheostat sitting on the table against the far wall. Playtime with electricity again. *Damn that Benjamin Franklin.* Mitch closed his eyes. Retreated down the long corridor of his mind, far, far away from the room in which he'd closeted all sensation from his twitching, jerking, spasming body.

Nearly crying aloud in pain, Kinsey backed away into the jungle far enough so the guards couldn't possibly hear her and keyed her microphone. "Are you there?" she whispered.

"Go ahead," Hathaway replied immediately.

"He's in a building. And I think they're torturing him." Her voice caught on the word.

"Why do you think that?"

She took a steadying breath. She couldn't very well tell this man she was having sympathy pains. He'd think she was nuts. Instead, she replied, "I heard him yelling. It's terrible." She added in a rush, "You have to do something. Get him out of there!"

"We're on our way, Kinsey."

"When? When will you get here?"

"Soon."

"How soon?"

"Four, maybe five hours."

"He won't make it that long!"

A sigh. "Here's the thing. Mitch is a trained operative. That means a couple things. First, he can take a hell of a lot of pain without cracking. Second, he may be shouting in hopes of someone hearing him. He could be using the excuse of getting roughed up a little to make a lot of noise."

Kinsey frowned. That wasn't what the sharp tingling in her limbs was telling her. "I dunno...he sounded pretty awful. Like the noise was being ripped out of him."

"Trust me. He'll be okay. Now, I need you to tell me everything you saw."

Hathaway spent the next ten minutes picking details out of her she hadn't even registered seeing—insignia on uniforms, exterior building lighting, terrain features. She was actually impressed at everything she had seen.

"Now what?" she asked.

"Now you sit tight. I'm not kidding. Don't mess with this situation. You've done what you could. When the SEALs get there, they'll handle the situation."

He was right. But the wrenching cramps clenching her body in a vise of pain said otherwise. How long could Mitch suffer like this and live? Heck, how long could she take it?

Hathaway was talking again. "Hang out in the fringe of the jungle and keep an eye on things. If anything changes—more men come or some men leave, or you hear any gunshots, that sort of thing—back into the underbrush and give us a call. Okay?"

"Okay."

"You're doing great. Just stay calm and try not to worry too much. This will all work out."

Easy for him to say. He didn't have to listen to Mitch's suffering. To *feel* it.

She did as Hathaway said and quietly made her way back to the edge of the little glade. She found a good spot to lie down and peer under some sort of fern-ish plant at the guards still lounging out front.

A jolt of agony shot through her, and another scream rent the night. Oh, God. Mitch. Tears streamed down her face unchecked. She couldn't do this. She couldn't lie here and listen to him dying by inches. And yet…she had to. He might not know it, but he wasn't alone. She was with him, if not physically, in spirit. She reached out with her mind and heart, begging him to feel her presence, to know she cared for him and was here for him.

How long the torture went on, she didn't know. She was afraid to look at her watch and find out how long Mitch had endured whatever they were doing to him in there. It felt like days. Weeks. Forever. She might not actually be suffering the same intensity of pain he was, but her ghost pains and her mental suffering, knowing what he was going through, were almost more than she could bear. With each renewed wave of agony that washed over her, a little more of her control slipped away, a little more of her soul was stripped bare.

The social niceties of her upbringing ceased to matter. Her family's wealth and position and power couldn't help her or Mitch now. Her need to prove herself didn't matter anymore. Mitch's stubborn refusal to acknowledge what they had between them revealed itself for the sham it was. The two of them had played all kinds of games with each other, danced all around their attraction—and ultimately, their feelings—for one another. Mitch had even obeyed his stupid rule about always walking away.

But when all of that was burned away by the fiery pain of their mutual torture, only two things remained that mattered.

She and Mitch both had to live.

And she loved him.

The only remaining question was whether or not she'd ever get a chance to tell him that.

Eventually, there came a lull. Maybe Mitch passed out, or maybe his captors took a break. But either way the pain stopped. She was almost more startled by its absence than its presence. Somewhere in the past few hours, she'd forgotten what not-pain felt like. It was a shock to her now.

And somehow she knew to dread the return of pain even more after having been granted this brief reprieve.

She was right.

A jolt of fury shot through her without warning, arching her entire body into a bow of agony so intense she couldn't even breathe. It went on and on and on until she thought she might pass out. And then it subsided, only to return a few seconds later. Panic washed over her. It was too much. They were breaking him. Breaking her.

Mitch! She mentally screamed out for him.

Silence was her only reply.

She couldn't stand it anymore. She had to do something. They were ripping Mitch's guts out, and they were tearing hers out at the same time. Like it or not, she and Mitch shared some sort of invisible but very real connection. His pain was hers, his panic hers. She knew without a shadow of a doubt that Mitch needed to get out of there, and soon. His urgency flowed through every pore of her being.

No way was Hathaway's SEAL team going to get here soon enough. Mitch's captors were all about causing him pain. This wasn't an interrogation he could draw out indefinitely while he eked out bits and pieces of information between rounds of torture. These men wanted to cause him suffering. And at some point they would tire of the game and put a gun to his head. How she knew all that, she couldn't say. But she knew it as certainly as she was lying here in the middle of the jungle.

She wriggled backward until she could safely stand up and backed away from the building. She keyed the microphone. "It's me again."

"Go ahead," Hathaway replied immediately.

"If I were going to go in there and rescue Mitch, how would you suggest I do it?"

"Don't even *think* about it," Hathaway growled. "You've got no training, no skills, no chance. If you go barging in there, you'll get Mitch killed. Do you understand me? Don't do anything."

She replied pleasantly, "If I hadn't grown up with a congressman who's used to getting his way for a father, that tone of voice might intimidate me, Commander."

Hathaway swore freely in her ear. He saw where this was going.

She continued, "But here's the deal. I'm standing here, a hundred feet from Mitch, and you're not. Neither he nor I can take any more of this. I am going in there to get him out, and you're not stopping me. Now, are you going to help me figure out a way to do it that *will* succeed, or am I on my own?"

"Stand by. Give us a minute to toss around some ideas."

"All right."

"Promise?" he demanded.

"I will if you will," she retorted.

"We're going to come up with a plan for you to execute. I swear. Just sit tight for a couple minutes, okay?"

"Okay."

Probably five minutes passed. Mitch wasn't shouting right now. Either the bad guys were taking a break, or he'd passed out. She wasn't getting any gut feelings at the moment that indicated which one was the case. But at least she wasn't experiencing any crippling pains spreading outward from her backbone to her fingertips and toes. For that, she was abjectly grateful.

Then Hathaway's voice startled her. Without preamble, he said, "Question. Are you willing to kill people or not?"

"Which one will give Mitch a better chance of walking out of there alive?"

He grunted. "The lethal option is by far the more effective way to go in this scenario."

She took a deep breath. She couldn't believe she was saying this, but faced with the alternative, it suddenly wasn't that awful a choice. "Then, I'm willing to kill. I've done it before. I'll do it again if I have to if that's what it takes to save Mitch."

"All right." In the background, she heard him say to someone, "She'll pull the trigger if it comes to it. Give me one more walk-through on Plan A." To her, he said, "Give me one more minute. And then we'll be ready to go."

Kinsey duly waited, and true to his word, Hathaway was back in a few moments. "Okay, Kinsey. Here's what we're going to do...."

Chapter 13

Time lost all meaning for Mitch. He measured it in minutes for a while, then in moments between waves of pain and then in individual breaths. Apparently, his captors had decided to finish him off before they took off to get a bite to eat. Bastards.

He nurtured the spark of anger, blew gently on it with a pep talk to himself that he'd outlast these yahoos, piled the dry tinder of Kinsey's smile and his desperate need to get back to her on the tiny flame, and gradually, it caught. A fire grew in his belly that he fanned into a roaring flame of determination to survive. He was going to see Kinsey again. He was going to lie beside her and feel her arms around him, kiss her sweet lips, lose himself in the infinite warmth of her eyes. These petty little twerps weren't going to stand in his way. He'd outlast them no matter what they threw at him.

Maybe they sensed the change in him, the renewed strength, for they broke off electrocuting him abruptly, cursing. One of them swore for a while and declared himself hungry and tired of this crap.

Mitch watched his captors carefully from the swollen slits of his eyes. Were they tired enough of messing with him to kill him now, or would they cook up some new-and-improved way to make him suffer? He thought fast. If they made a move to off him, he'd have to talk fast to prevent it. He rehearsed what he was going to say to give them pause.

A murmured argument ensued across the room. The jerk in charge's hand came to rest on the pistol holster at his waist. Crap. They were leaning toward just offing him now. He sat up straight, ignoring the agonizing protest from his abused kidneys. He shifted his weight so his chair scraped the floor loudly. All eyes turned toward him. His chin went up.

"Is that the best you can do?" he commented casually in Spanish. It hurt his loosened front teeth to talk, but he endured the shouting nerves in his mouth. Pain, no matter how bad, was preferable to death.

The men's eyebrows shot up in surprise, then slammed together in fury.

So much for a midnight snack, boys.

Snarling, they advanced on him, all thoughts of finishing this off fast gone from their minds.

I win.

The first heavy fist landed on his upraised jaw. His head snapped back and white shards of pain exploded behind his eyes.

Sort of.

* * *

Kinsey lay on the ground behind a fallen log only twenty-five feet or so from the front door of the metal building. She couldn't believe Hathaway and company had actually let her move in this close to the soldiers lounging on the fenders of their vans. She could smell the smoke from their inferior cigarettes. Mitch was seriously going to owe her one when this was all over. She refused to consider the idea of failure. She *would* rescue Mitch, and both of them would walk out of this in one piece.

Another groan issued from the building, this time genuine agony. Kinsey all but doubled over from the pain. Her face felt on fire, her ribs ached until she could hardly breathe and every bone in her body screamed its suffering.

Hathaway's voice was emotionless in her ear. "Final target locked in. Fire on my command in three…two… one…bombs away."

Somewhere high overhead, a Predator unmanned aerial vehicle was loitering, looking down on this nightmare. And it had just launched its pair of onboard Hellfire missiles at the two vans directly in front of her. Hathaway had warned her it would be dangerous to be this close to the targets, but she didn't trust her marksmanship any farther away from the door than this.

Hathaway spoke sharply. "Get down flat behind cover. Eyes closed, hands over your ears. Contact in five…four…three…"

His voice was drowned out by a faint but distinct whistling noise that quickly built to a scream too loud even for her hands clapped over her ears to block.

And then the explosions detonated. They were almost

simultaneous, and she barely distinguished the first from the second. The combined flash of light washed over her first, followed a millisecond later by a concussion of sound so loud it made her entire body hurt. The ground jumped beneath her, and dirt and twigs and leaves showered down upon her.

"Direct hit, gentlemen. You're on, Kinsey."

Still so stunned by the explosion that she felt numb all over, she nonetheless poked her head up from behind the log. Two blazing hulls were all that was left of the vans. The two guards lounging against them had been vaporized. The front wall of the building was dented in, the door hanging askew in its frame. On cue, someone from inside leaped into the doorway. She took careful aim with the MP-4 submachine gun from Mitch's black duffel bag and pulled the trigger. The weapon leaped in her hands and she fought to bring the muzzle back down into a firing position quickly.

She had no time to stop and think about having killed someone as the man lurched backward and fell, for another man appeared in the doorway. She pulled the trigger again. A secondary explosion rocked one of the burning van remains, and a third man staggered back into the building before she could get off a shot at him.

"Are they shooting back at you?" Hathaway bit out.

"No," she ventured to murmur into the radio. "Maybe they think the two guys I shot were hit by shrapnel. They're dragging them inside now."

"The explosions removed some of the canopy of tree cover. We have visual on part of the clearing now. Keep picking off guys in the doorway until they start shooting back. Then bug out."

"Got it," she replied grimly.

She felt nothing. So intensely focused was she on saving Mitch, she had no time for emotion. No time for horror. No time for moral self-recriminations. These guys were trying to kill Mitch; she was trying to kill them. The logic was simple. Clean. Straightforward.

Another man appeared in the doorway. She took aim and pulled the trigger. The side of his head exploded in a blossom of red. He spun, staggered outside against the wall, reached clumsily for the weapon at his hip. She pulled the trigger again, this time taking aim at the center of his chest.

He dropped to the ground.

She swung her sight back to the doorway. Two men came out this time, guns blazing. She dived behind her log. They were firing wildly, although a few shots winged by overhead. Time to go. She crawled backward on her belly, getting covered in muck and slime as she dragged herself through a puddle.

"You're clear," Hathaway announced. "Get up and run."

She sprinted through the jungle, tearing through branches and vines, heedless of them grabbing at her, uncaring if any of them were snakes or not. *Mitch needed her.*

Gunshots continued to ring out from the front of the building. The remaining soldiers were plenty panicked. They must think the entire American army had invaded.

"The second Predator will be on target in four minutes, Kinsey. As soon as it gets there, we'll give them something more to think about."

As she approached the back of the building, the gunshots out front subsided. Not good. The danger to this plan was that the bad guys would get a moment's pause and use it to blow away Mitch. She had to keep the pressure on these guys. She aimed at a small transformer box mounted high on a pole behind the building.

Darn it! She missed! She took another try at it. A shower of sparks erupted from the paint-can-size box. The lights inside the building flickered and went out. The air conditioner rumbled to a halt, and silence fell momentarily.

Then, to her vast relief, another fusillade of gunfire erupted from in front of the building. She fired as Hathaway had instructed her to at the roof of the metal building. The sound of her shots and the ping of metal would convince the bad guys that someone was firing back at them. In the chaos of their own shooting, they should have a hard time determining where the shots were coming from and what they were aimed at. Fortunately, the jungle was known to do weird things to sound.

Indeed, immediately after she squeezed off a couple rounds high—she surely didn't want to accidentally shoot Mitch through the flimsy walls of the building—a renewed frenzy of shooting erupted out front.

Her heart pounding so hard it hurt, she eased forward. Lord, she felt naked past the cover of the thick undergrowth. Who'd have thought she'd actually embrace the vines and brambles and threat of nasty critters the jungle represented? But here she was, wishing it went right up to the back of the building. She darted forward and crouched beside the air-conditioning unit and the low screen where its ducting entered the building.

Using the wire cutters she'd found in Mitch's bag of toys, she started snipping at the screen.

"Take a couple shots, Kinsey. They're getting bored out front."

She started. God bless the guys in the Bat Cave. She'd been so intent on getting to Mitch, she'd momentarily forgotten about distracting the Cubans at the front door. She fired a couple shots up at the roof.

As the rat-a-tat of gunfire duly started up again, she continued snipping. It was painfully slow work. Her hands ached dreadfully from the force of having to squeeze through the heavy wire, but she gritted her teeth and kept cutting. She remembered to pause to shoot again the next time herself. She held the weapon clumsily and accidentally held the trigger down longer than she intended. A barrage of fire spewed from her weapon, all but knocking it from her hands. *Whoa.* She dropped it, startled.

Must keep moving. Must free Mitch. She picked up the wire cutters and went back to work. Almost there. A few more inches and she'd be able to bend the wire back and slip between the fan inside and the wall. It would be a tight squeeze, but Mitch was in there. She'd make it work.

"Target lock-in on the clearing in front of the building," Hathaway announced in her ear. "Cease fire, Kinsey. Let's see if we can draw a couple of these guys outside."

She kept snipping frantically.

"Bingo," Hathaway bit out in grim satisfaction. "Two tangoes have exited the building. Fire when ready."

Perfect. The idea was for the folks in the Bat Cave to release another missile and cause a big diversion so she could slip into the building and find Mitch.

She wrestled the screen up and away from the opening, cutting her palms on its sharp edges, completely oblivious to the searing pain. On her hands and knees, she waited for Hathaway's command.

Kaboom!

"Go, Kinsey."

She slipped through the opening, careful not to snag her clothes on the screen. Dust choked her, and spiderwebs coated her face. She couldn't get a hand up to wipe it away, but that was the least of her worries. For a brief panicked moment, she got stuck between the ducting and the galvanized metal wall, but then the sheet metal flexed slightly and she was able to wriggle forward again. She had no idea how Mitch was going to get through this narrow gap. They'd cross that bridge when they got to it. The first order of business was to find him and free him.

The interior of the building was black. She couldn't see anything more than the barest of shapes. She pushed up to her hands and knees, hugging the wall. A brief flash of gunfire from outside faintly illuminated the doorway across the structure. It looked like a single open room. But in that brief moment, she didn't see Mitch. Had all of this been for nothing? Was he not here after all? Had she made a horrible mistake?

As her stomach sank, she heard a noise. An odd rasping sound. And a stab of agony so intense it stopped her breath shot through her lungs. *Mitch.*

She listened carefully. Another labored rasp. Off to her left. She darted that way, staying low. She kicked something hard and a grunt of pain sounded directly in front of her. She reached out in front of her with both hands. Cloth. The curve of a shoulder. A muscular one.

"Mitch?" she breathed. She thought his name as

much as said it, so terrified was she that they were not alone in here.

No answer. Either he was unconscious, or he had a reason not to make any noise. Pain coursed through her freely. She instinctively knew he was experiencing the same pain, which meant he had to be conscious. She moved around behind him, crouching with his chair between her and the door. Easing the knife out of her waistband, she began sawing at the cords holding his wrists. It was hard to do in the dark. She couldn't see what she was doing and was terrified she would slit his wrists with the wickedly sharp blade. The bonds were tight and swollen with moisture.

But, grimly, she continued to saw. A cord popped. Then another. It felt as if maybe there were two more strands wrapped around his wrists. But then his hands jerked and the bonds fell away.

The chair lurched gently. *His feet.* They must have bound his ankles to the chair.

She lay down, reaching forward under the chair to saw off the ropes around his legs. This was easier, for only the chair leg was behind the rope. Quickly, she released his right ankle and then his left. She was startled when he didn't stand up.

He still wasn't talking, so he must think they weren't alone in here. Crud. As hard as she listened and as intently as she stared around into the darkness, she couldn't make out anyone else. She felt Mitch moving just a little, then realized he was picking at his chest. They must have tied his torso to the chair, too. She reached up behind him and made quick work of those ropes, as well.

And still he didn't move. Flummoxed, she crouched

behind him, motionless. What was she supposed to do now? She'd assumed he'd take over from here, but he was just sitting there, not moving!

For lack of anything else to do, she eased the MP-4 upward very slowly, edging it forward along the side of the chair, up and under Mitch's right elbow. Its weight abruptly lifted out of her hands and she sagged with relief. Mitch continued to ease it forward by slow degrees. She marveled at his patience. She was on the verge of screaming in terror and frustration, her nerves stretched to the breaking point and beyond.

She started violently as a male voice mumbled in the dark...*in Spanish.*

A second voice answered.

Crap! They sounded as if they were near the front door.

She heard a faint shuffle of shoes on concrete. Mitch's captors were moving. Where, she had no idea. She couldn't see a thing back here behind this chair. And now that she'd passed the MP-4 to Mitch, she was unarmed, anyway, except for her knife. Fat lot of good that would do against these guys' guns.

A wave of helplessness washed over her. She hated this feeling! She was not giving in. They'd come this far, and they'd get out of here alive.

She jumped violently as Mitch fired his weapon without warning, a bright muzzle flash accompanying the deafening report of the weapon inside the building's metal walls.

Someone screamed, and the chair lurched violently to the side as Mitch flung himself off it. It occurred to her that she had better move, too, because the bad guys were bound to fire back at where Mitch's muzzle flash had just given away his position. She dived right, rolling fast for the nearest wall.

A hard hand closed over her mouth, and something heavy rolled on top of her. But then she recognized the muscular, familiar contours of Mitch's body against hers.

"Get out however you got in. Tell Hathaway these are Zaragosa's men. Zaragosa is in league with Camarillo and has turned on us. They've called for reinforcements. I'll hold them off as long as I can. Buy you time to run."

She froze in shock, absorbing all that in the blink of an eye.

A fusillade of gunfire lit up the front of the room.

"Move," Mitch grunted as he rolled off her and fired back. She scrambled toward the hole in the back wall, with Mitch close behind.

There was no cover in here. As soon as the Cubans just open fired and sprayed the heck out of the space, she and Mitch were both dead. She paused before the narrow slit. Mitch would never fit through here. From somewhere behind her, Mitch fired his weapon. She felt as much as heard his dive and roll across the floor as pain exploded in her body.

"We need a diversion. *Now,*" she muttered into her microphone.

"Coming up. Fire the second missile."

She tugged frantically at the metal duct, trying to widen the space so Mitch could escape.

The ground rocked and a blast of light and heat rocked the building. Mitch skidded to the floor beside her. He reached up, pushed her hands aside and ripped the entire air-conditioning duct free of the wall, greatly enlarging the hole as debris banged down on the building's roof.

"Go," Mitch ordered.

"Not without you."

He gave her a push and she stubbornly shook her head.

"Fine. We both go." He sounded plenty mad, but as if he also realized arguing with her would be futile. She paused, peering at him, trying to make out his expression.

"I swear," he bit out.

She dived through the now wide-open hole and rolled to her knees. A big burst of gunfire erupted inside, then Mitch's muscular body burst through the opening beside her. They took off running, diving to the ground in the first heavy tangle of jungle.

Grimly, Mitch took off crawling low on his belly. She followed, marveling that he could still move with such speed in the condition he—they—were in. She could really stop experiencing all his aches and pains anytime now.

He didn't go far, though, before he pulled up, leaning heavily against a tree trunk. She opened her mouth to ask him if he was okay, but he gestured her to silence and pointed at his ear. Ahh. He was listening for pursuit. She crouched stock-still, straining to hear any sound not of the jungle. She didn't know what the heck she was listening for, though.

He reached over and took the earbud and its attached mouthpiece out of her ear.

"I'm out. With Kinsey," he reported low.

He listened intently for a moment. "Roger."

Without speaking to her, he took off through the jungle. At least they were able to walk upright this time. As grueling as the next half hour was, she couldn't complain. She'd had enough wallowing around in the mud with the bugs for one night.

Finally, Mitch stopped, sliding to the ground, panting himself. Her pain was nearly unbearable, and she was only experiencing ghost pains of his. She couldn't imagine the agony he was suffering.

"Take the headset, Kinsey. The folks in the cave will vector you out of here."

"What are you going to be doing?"

He started to laugh, but it turned into a gasp of pain. "I'm going to sit here and rest awhile. Then I'm going to hook up with the SEAL team when it gets here. We've got an appointment with Camarillo and Zaragosa."

"I'm staying with you."

"Kinsey—"

"I'm not arguing with you about this. We're in this together."

He glared at her as balefully as he could from between the puffy slits of his eyes.

She squatted down in front of him and looked him square in the face. "You may think it's okay to walk away, Mitch, but I don't. Do you hear me? I'm *not* walking away. This time we're playing by *my* rules."

There, in the dark and the wet and fear, the jungle pressing in around them, their gazes met. Very slowly, his cracked and blackened lips curved up. She felt the pain of the smile in her own mouth. He leaned forward. Reached up with his right hand to grab a fistful of her shirt. He dragged her forward until their noses almost touched.

"Yeah. I hear you. Your rules from now on."

She stared. "Do you mean it?"

His other hand came up behind her head, pulling her the last few inches separating them and their two worlds. "I promise."

"Your word of honor?"

"My word of honor. I'm never walking away from you again."

On a sob, she gathered him in her arms, careful of his injuries. His arms wrapped painfully tight around her, but she didn't complain. She slid down to the ground beside him, still holding him. As she felt his consciousness slipping away, she said gently, "Give me the radio." She added, "And the gun."

With his last strength, he dragged the earpiece off his head and passed her the weapon.

"I'll take the watch," she murmured. "You rest now. I've got your back."

"I love the sound of that. I love you." He sighed. And then he passed out.

She stared down at his dark head. He loved her! Exultation exploded within her. She wanted to kiss him madly, to make passionate love with him, to sing and shout her joy, and the man had just passed out cold.

There'd be time enough later to share their love. A lifetime. Smiling, she donned the headset and laid the gun at the ready across her lap.

And all was right with the world. She sat there in the mud and filth, with rain streaming down her face, aching in every last muscle and so exhausted she could hardly see straight. Mitch's head was heavy on her shoulder, his battered body draped uncomfortably over hers. And none of it mattered. The trained predator and the pampered princess had found each other.

They'd become a team. A heck of a good one if she did say so herself. And neither of them would ever have to be alone again.

And as she sat there, the first birds of dawn began to sing and the sun rose on a new day. They'd found their way out of the darkness. Together.

Chapter 14

Not quite one week later, Mitch shifted uncomfortably in his chair, the bandage binding his broken ribs itching across his back. Kinsey reached up absently from the seat beside him and used her newly manicured nails to scratch the spot below his shoulder blades. How she did that, he couldn't begin to fathom, but she seemed to know exactly how he felt, to be aware of every ache or pain before he was barely aware of it himself.

After she'd eased the itch, he captured her fingers and carried them up to his mouth to kiss them briefly. She glanced away from the satellite imagery on the big screen in front of them and flashed him a smile of pure love.

Her beauty, both inside and out, made his breath catch in the back of his throat. What he'd ever done to deserve a woman like her he couldn't imagine, but he wasn't about to question his good luck. Hell, his great luck. He was the luckiest man alive. Not only had he cheated death in a major way in Cuba, but he'd fallen for Kinsey Hollingsworth, and miraculously, she'd fallen for him.

"What are they doing now?" she asked.

He glanced up at the screen where the SEAL team was preparing to launch a very quiet, very lethal assault on Camarillo's compound. Zaragosa had been confirmed entering the main house ten minutes earlier, and the SEALs, who'd been in place for the past several days, were closing in for the kill. "They're separating so they won't shoot each other if it comes to a firefight."

Kinsey grinned. "You can tell me they're managing their fields of fire. I know what that means now."

His eyebrows lifted. "Are you sure you want to become a field operative? When I talked to your father last night, he said he'd unfrozen all your bank accounts and has signed your entire trust fund over to you. You're a wealthy lady now."

"I'm sure. Good thing you proposed to me yesterday morning. I know you're not marrying me for my money."

He leaned over close and whispered, "If you came to me with nothing in the world but your name, I'd still want you. I don't know what your ex-fiancé was thinking, cheating on you. Damn goof. You sure you don't want me to kill him?"

She smiled gently. "Thanks for the offer, but no. If he needs killing, I'll do it myself. And speaking of exes, do you need me to take out Janine?"

He shrugged. "Nah. I owe her one. If she hadn't dumped me, I'd never have found you."

She reached behind his neck and drew him close enough to kiss. "God bless Janine for not knowing what she had."

He all but purred under her hand.

"What about Hunter?" she asked.

Mitch shrugged. "He'll be eighteen next year. He says he wants to join the army. I offered to help him out with college, but he seems to need more action than that."

Kinsey laughed. "Are you sure he's not yours?"

A shadow passed over Mitch's happiness. At least he was talking about his past now. Between the two of them they'd get beyond the ghosts lurking in his history. She reached out with her fingertips to smooth his eyebrow. "I love you," she murmured.

He gazed back at her solemnly. "I love you, too."

A throat cleared significantly nearby. Abruptly, Mitch recalled where they were and that they had an audience. A large one.

Kinsey blushed, and he caught Jennifer Blackfoot's knowing smile from across the table. He grinned back at her. She'd been hassling him for years to find a good woman and settle down. Looked as if the boss got her wish. As Jennifer opened her mouth, a mischievous glint in her eye, he cut off the poke he saw coming and said, "So when are you going to take the plunge?"

Jennifer drew back sharply. "Not me. I'm not the type. Wrong job. Wrong lifestyle. No time."

He nodded knowingly. "That's what I said. And look what happened to me."

He looped an arm around Kinsey's shoulder and reveled at how she snuggled close to his side.

"There he goes," Hathaway commented, drawing

Mitch's gaze back to the screen. One of the SEALs had broken away from the main group and was making his way with surprising speed toward the heating and cooling units behind the main house.

Camarillo's compound was about to suffer a most unfortunate natural-gas explosion that would vaporize all the occupants of the house. The last explosives were rigged, and then a quick double click came across the Bat Cave's loudspeaker system, which was broadcasting the SEALs' operational frequency at the moment.

The team withdrew as silently as it had come, retreating a safe distance back into the jungle.

Hathaway looked over at Kinsey from his place at the ops console. "Would you like to do the honors?" he asked.

She smiled over at Mitch, then leaned forward and pushed the button on the speakerphone on the table in front of her. "Fire at will, gentlemen."

An enormous explosion filled the screen, momentarily whiting out the satellite feed. Then a giant blaze came into focus. Smaller secondary explosions lit the night, and it became patently clear the SEALs had succeeded in their mission. No one was walking out of that conflagration alive.

"It's over," Kinsey breathed.

Mitch leaned over, drawing her close. "Oh, no. It's just begun. Now we can get on with our life—together."

And they kissed to seal the deal.

* * * * *

COMING NEXT MONTH from Harlequin®
Romantic Suspense
AVAILABLE AUGUST 21, 2012

#1719 THE COP'S MISSING CHILD
Karen Whiddon

Cop Mac Riordan thinks he's found the woman who might have stolen his baby. But will she also steal his heart?

#1720 COLTON DESTINY
The Coltons of Eden Falls
Justine Davis

When kidnappings of innocent young women bring FBI agent Emma Colton home, she never intends to end up longing for Caleb Troyer and his peaceful Amish life.

#1721 SURGEON SHEIK'S RESCUE
Sahara Kings
Loreth Anne White

A dark, scarred sheik hiding in a haunted monastery is brought to life by a feisty young reporter come to expose him.

#1722 HIDING HIS WITNESS
C.J. Miller

On the run from a dangerous criminal, Carey Smith witnesses an attempted murder. But she can't run from the handsome detective determined to keep her safe.

You can find more information on upcoming Harlequin® titles, free excerpts and more at www.Harlequin.com.

HRSCNM0812

REQUEST YOUR FREE BOOKS!
2 FREE NOVELS PLUS 2 FREE GIFTS!

ROMANTIC
SUSPENSE

Sparked by Danger, Fueled by Passion.

YES! Please send me 2 FREE Harlequin® Romantic Suspense novels and my 2 FREE gifts (gifts are worth about $10). After receiving them, if I don't wish to receive any more books, I can return the shipping statement marked "cancel." If I don't cancel, I will receive 4 brand-new novels every month and be billed just $4.49 per book in the U.S. or $5.24 per book in Canada. That's a saving of at least 14% off the cover price! It's quite a bargain! Shipping and handling is just 50¢ per book in the U.S. and 75¢ per book in Canada.* I understand that accepting the 2 free books and gifts places me under no obligation to buy anything. I can always return a shipment and cancel at any time. Even if I never buy another book, the two free books and gifts are mine to keep forever.

240/340 HDN FEFR

Name	(PLEASE PRINT)	

Address		Apt. #

City	State/Prov.	Zip/Postal Code

Signature (if under 18, a parent or guardian must sign)

Mail to the **Reader Service:**
IN U.S.A.: P.O. Box 1867, Buffalo, NY 14240-1867
IN CANADA: P.O. Box 609, Fort Erie, Ontario L2A 5X3

Not valid for current subscribers to Harlequin Romantic Suspense books.

Want to try two free books from another line?
Call 1-800-873-8635 or visit www.ReaderService.com.

* Terms and prices subject to change without notice. Prices do not include applicable taxes. Sales tax applicable in N.Y. Canadian residents will be charged applicable taxes. Offer not valid in Quebec. This offer is limited to one order per household. All orders subject to credit approval. Credit or debit balances in a customer's account(s) may be offset by any other outstanding balance owed by or to the customer. Please allow 4 to 6 weeks for delivery. Offer available while quantities last.

Your Privacy—The Reader Service is committed to protecting your privacy. Our Privacy Policy is available online at www.ReaderService.com or upon request from the Reader Service.

We make a portion of our mailing list available to reputable third parties that offer products we believe may interest you. If you prefer that we not exchange your name with third parties, or if you wish to clarify or modify your communication preferences, please visit us at www.ReaderService.com/consumerchoice or write to us at Reader Service Preference Service, P.O. Box 9062, Buffalo, NY 14269. Include your complete name and address.

HRS11B

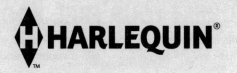

Harlequin and Mills & Boon are joining forces in a global search for new authors.

In September 2012 we're launching our biggest contest yet—with the prize of being published by the world's leader in romance fiction!

Look for more information on our website, **www.soyouthinkyoucanwrite.com**

So you think you can write? Show us!

SYTYCW0912

In the newest continuity series from Harlequin®
Romantic Suspense, the worlds of the Coltons and their
Amish neighbors collide—with dramatic results.

Take a sneak peek at the first book, COLTON DESTINY
by Justine Davis, available September 2012.

"**I**'m here to try and find your sister."

"I know this. But don't assume this will automatically ensure trust from all of us."

He was antagonizing her. Purposely.

Caleb realized it with a little jolt. While it was difficult for anyone in the community to turn to outsiders for help, they had all reluctantly agreed this was beyond their scope and that they would cooperate.

Including—in fact, especially—him.

"Then I will find these girls without your help," she said, sounding fierce.

Caleb appreciated her determination. He *wanted* that kind of determination in the search for Hannah. He attempted a fresh start.

"It is difficult for us—"

"What's difficult for me is to understand why anyone wouldn't pull out all the stops to save a child whose life could be in danger."

Caleb wasn't used to being interrupted. Annie would never have dreamed of it. But this woman was clearly nothing like his sweet, retiring Annie. She was sharp, forceful and very intense.

"I grew up just a couple of miles from here," she said. "And I always had the idea the Amish loved their kids just as we did."

"Of course we do."